D0176446

A GHOSTLY LIGHT

A Haunted Home Renovation Mystery

Juliet Blackwell

BERKLEY PRIME CRIME
New York

BERKLEY PRIME CRIME
Published by Berkley
An imprint of Penguin Random House LLC
375 Hudson Street, New York, New York 10014

ISBN: 9781101989357

First Edition: June 2017

Printed in the United States of America
1 3 5 7 9 10 8 6 4 2

Cover art by Brandon Dorman

To Sara and Dan

For loving my boy

Chapter One

The tower reached high into a gray sky. A faint glow—dare I say a ghostly light?—seemed to emanate from the lighthouse's narrow windows. Probably just a trick of light, the afternoon sun reflecting off curved stone walls.

Just looking up at the tower through the cracked bay window made me dizzy.

"I'm thinking of calling the inn 'Spirit of the Lighthouse.' Or maybe 'the Bay Light,'" said Alicia Withers as she checked an item off the list on her clipboard. Alicia was big on lists. And clipboards. "What do you think, Mel? Too simple?"

"I think you need to figure out your plumbing issues before you worry about the name," I replied. That's me, Mel Turner. General contractor and head of Turner Construction.

Also known as Killjoy.

Alicia and I stood in the central hallway of the former lighthouse keeper's home, a charming but dilapidated four-bedroom Victorian adjacent to the lighthouse tower. The structures had been built in 1871 on the small, rather un-imaginatively named Lighthouse Island, located in the strait connecting the San Francisco and San Pablo bays. Not far away, the Richmond–San Rafael Bridge loomed, and barely visible to the southwest was the elegant new span that linked Oakland to Treasure Island and on to San Francisco. The nearest shoreline was Richmond, with San Rafael—and San Quentin prison—situated across the nor-mally placid, though occasionally tempestuous, bay waters.

It was a view to die for.

Lighthouse Island's foghorn and lamp had been staffed by full-time keepers and their assistants and fam-ilies for decades, the flashing light and thunderous horn warning sea captains of the bay's surprisingly treacher-ous shallows and rocky shoals. But the humans had long since been replaced by less costly electronics, and the island's structures had fallen into disrepair.

The house itself had once been a beauty, and still boasted gingerbread trim and a cupola painted an ap-pealing (but now peeling) creamy white. Also in the compound were a supply shed, the original foghorn building, and a huge cistern that collected rainwater for the keeper and his family on this otherwise dry rock. The only other structures on the island were the docks and lavatory, located in a small natural harbor to the east, which were still used occasionally by pleasure boats seeking refuge from sudden squalls—and by those inter-ested in exploring Lighthouse Island, of course.

"I'm just saying," I continued. "There's a lot of dry rot to contend with before you start inviting guests to your Lighthouse Inn."

"Oh, *you*," Alicia said with a slight smile, which I answered with a big one.

I had known Alicia for quite a while before spying an

iota of good cheer in her. She was still a serious, hard-working person but had relaxed a lot since I first met her on a historic restoration in Marin. We had bonded late one night over a shared love of potato chips and home renovation television shows. And then we quite literally kicked the butt of a murderer, which had definitely improved her attitude.

"I'm sure you know I haven't lost sight of the all-important infrastructure," continued Alicia. "But I need to register my domain and business names, so no, it's *not* too early to think about such things."

She whipped out a thick sheaf of lists and flowcharts and handed them over. I flipped through the papers. There were preliminary schedules for demolition and foundation work, electrical and plumbing and Internet installation, Sheetrock and mudding, overhauls of baths and kitchen, and installations of moldings and flooring and painting and light fixtures.

I raised my eyebrows. "Thanks, Alicia, but I usually work up the schedules with Stan, my office manager."

"I know you do, but I was up late one night thinking about everything that had to be done, and figured I might as well get the paperwork started. I based these on your schedules for the job in Marin, you see? I can e-mail everything to Stan so you can rearrange it as you need, and plug in the actual dates and the like. I hope you don't think it was too presumptuous—I couldn't help myself. Ever since Ellis agreed to back me on this project, I can hardly *sleep* I'm so excited!"

Several months ago Alicia's boss, Ellis Elrich, had asked me to evaluate "a property" he was considering. It wasn't until he told me to meet him at the Point Moro Marina that I realized this would be no ordinary renovation: It was Lighthouse Island, and the Bay Light.

I—along with much of the population of the Bay Area—had watched over the years as the historic Victorian-era lighthouse descended into greater and greater decrepitude. Every time my family drove over the Richmond–San Rafael Bridge, my father would shake his head and grumble, "It's a damned shame." Mom would shush Dad for swearing in front of the children—"Little pitchers have big ears, Bill"—but, craning her neck to watch the sad little island as it receded from view, she would add, "You're right, though. Someone really ought to save that place."

Never did I imagine that, decades later, *I'd* be that person.

But historic renovation was my business, and Alicia's boss was filthy rich. Which was a very good thing, because this lighthouse was in need of a serious infusion of cash. I already had in hand the architect's detailed blueprints, as well as the necessary permits and variances from the city and county, which had also promised to fast-track the code inspections. The Bay Light's renovation would be a highly unusual public-private partnership that cash-strapped local officials had agreed to in the interest of saving the historical structures. I was impressed at the city's eager participation but didn't ask too many questions. Ellis Elrich had a way of making things happen.

"So, here's what we're thinking," Alicia said, making a sweeping gesture around the former front parlor. "We take down this wall, combine the space with the smaller drawing room next door, and make this whole area the bar and restaurant."

"It's not very large," I pointed out, comparing the blueprints in my hand to the existing floor plan.

"It doesn't have to be. There will be at most ten overnight guests, so only five small tables are required for their meals—or we might just do one big table and serve everything family-style, I haven't decided yet. And visitors won't be that frequent—there aren't that many people who stop in at the yacht harbor, and even with our boat ferrying people over from the mainland, it will still take some planning to come to the island. It's not as though we have to take into account foot traffic! So I'm thinking we'll be at capacity with about twenty guests for drinks and dinner. But for those that make it, we'll be a gorgeous little oasis in the bay."

Alicia sighed with happiness.

I was pleased for my friend, but experienced enough to be a wee bit jaded. At this point in a renovation, most clients couldn't see past the stars in their eyes and the longing in their hearts. Starting a historic renovation was a lot like falling in love: a blissful period of soaring romantic hope and infatuation that lasted until the grueling realities of sawdust and noise and confusion and delays—not to mention mounting cost overruns and unwelcome discoveries in the walls—brought a person back to earth with a resounding thud.

"We'll keep the bare bones of the kitchen, but include updated fixtures and some expansion, of course. But we'll make the study and part of the pantry into a first-floor suite for the live-in manager—"

"That would be you?"

"Oh, I dearly hope so, if I can find a replacement to serve as Ellis's assistant. I can't leave him high and dry."

"But he wants this for you, right? Isn't that why he's bankrolling the project?"

Alicia blushed. "Yes, he does. Ellis is very . . ."

"Sweet," I said when she trailed off.

She nodded but avoided my eyes. Now that she had

loosened up a little and was no longer the tight-lipped martinet I had first met, Alicia was charming. The scar on her upper lip and another by one eye—relics of difficult times at the hands of her abusive (now-ex) husband—only served to make her pretty face more interesting. The wounds on her psyche were another matter altogether, but through therapy and a whole lot of emotional hard work, Alicia had made great strides toward healing.

And now, unless I was mistaken, she had developed a serious crush on Ellis Elrich, her boss and savior. Ellis was a good guy, surprisingly down-to-earth for a billionaire. Still, the situation seemed . . . complicated.

Oh, what tangled webs we weave.

"Anyway, that will leave three guest suites upstairs, each with an attached bath. And one in the attic, awaiting renovation. Oh! Did I tell you? The attic is full of old furniture, and there's a trunk of old books. There are even the original keeper's logs!"

"Still? No one took them after all this time?"

"I suppose that's the advantage of being on an isolated island. Can you imagine? We can put some on display to add to the historic maritime ambiance!"

I smiled. "Of course we can. I can't wait to look through everything. You know me and old books." Me and old everything, actually.

"We might be able to create one more bedroom in the foghorn building, unless we decide to turn that into a separate office. The problem, though, is the noise."

"What noise?"

"The foghorn still sounds on foggy days. It's not the original horn; it's an electronic version. But still, it's loud."

"How loud?"

"*Really* loud."

"That could be a problem. So, what do you want to do with the tower itself? The architect hasn't specified anything here."

"That—"

She stopped midsentence and her face lost all color.

"Alicia?" I glanced behind me, but didn't notice anything out of place. "What's wrong?"

"I thought I saw . . ."

"What?"

"Nothing," she said with a shake of her auburn hair.

I turned back to scan the scene, paying careful attention to my peripheral vision. Fervently hoping not to see a ghost. Or a body. Or both.

Because I tend to see things. Things that would make many people scream, run, or faint dead away. Not all the time, but often enough for it to make an impression. Due to my profession I spend a lot of time in historic structures, so it probably isn't surprising—for the open-minded, anyway—that I've been exposed to more than a few wandering souls who aren't clear on the veil between our worlds.

The fact that I trip over dead bodies, on the other hand, is . . . disturbing.

For me most of all, I should add.

Happily, in this moment I saw only the debris-filled main parlor of the old Keeper's House. My mind's eye began to imagine the space filled with vivacious guests sharing meals and stories, children holding cold hands up to the fire in the raised stone hearth, perhaps a calico cat lounging on the windowsill. The visitors warm and happy, safe from the chill winds blowing off the bay, the occasional mournful blast of the foghorn or flash of the lamp atop the tower adding to the dreamy atmosphere, to the sense that they were a world away from a major metropolitan area, rather than minutes. Alicia was right; with Ellis's deep pockets and Turner Construction's building skills, the inn could be magical. *Would* be magical.

Who's the romantic now, Mel Turner?

"Let's . . . I think we should go, Mel," Alicia said, her voice tight.

"What's wrong, Alicia? Are you okay?"

"I'm fine, it's just . . ." She walked toward the front entry, its charming beadboard paneling buckling in the center, and led the way out to the deep wraparound porch. Thick wooden boards had been laid over rotten sections of the porch floor to allow safe passage to the steps. "I think I'm just spooked."

"Did you see something . . . ghostly?" I asked, surprised. Alicia had never mentioned being sensitive to the supernatural.

"No, it's nothing like that. It's—well, I'm a little jumpy. I received a letter not long ago."

"And?"

"It was from Thorn."

"Thorn?"

"Thorn Walker. He's . . . he was my husband. Thorn's my *ex*-husband."

"How did he find you? I thought you changed your name, covered your tracks."

"I did," Alicia said with a humorless laugh. "Ellis hired a lawyer and a skip tracer, and they helped me to create a new identity. But . . . it's all my fault. I haven't been as careful as I needed to be, and have let my guard down lately. When Ellis bought this island and announced plans to renovate the buildings and open an inn, I was photographed next to him. The photo appeared in several news outlets—it seems everyone loves stories about historic lighthouses! What was I thinking? Thorn's not stupid. I should know better than anyone that when he puts his mind to something, he can be quite determined."

"What did Ellis's security team suggest?"

She didn't answer.

"Alicia? Did you show Ellis the letter?"

She remained silent, heading down the shored-up porch steps, past an old NO TRESPASSING sign, and into a cement courtyard that had been built on a slight incline to funnel rainwater into the underground cistern. Back when these buildings were constructed, access to fresh water would have been a priority. Living on a virtually barren rock wasn't easy, and similar challenges had ultimately closed down Alcatraz, the famous federal penitentiary that still held pride of place on another island in the bay, much closer to San Francisco. When everything had to be brought in by supply boat, priorities shifted.

There would be no pizza delivery while on *this* job.

In fact, any and all construction supplies—lumber and concrete, nails and screws, equipment and tools—would have to be brought to the dock by boat and hoisted up with a winch.

The prospect was daunting, but exciting. I had been running Turner Construction for a few years now, and while I still enjoyed bringing historic San Francisco homes back from the brink, I had been itching for a new challenge. For something different.

And this was a *lighthouse*.

Still, one aspect of this renovation gave me pause: The lighthouse tower was several stories high, and ever since an altercation on the roof of a mansion high atop Pacific Heights, I had found myself dreading heights. Where once I wouldn't have given a second thought to scrambling up a tall ladder or hopping out an attic window to repair loose shingles, now the very idea made me quail. I told myself I was being silly, and that these feelings would dissipate as the memory of the attack faded. I would *not* let fear stop me.

If only my vertigo were subject to my stern general's voice.

Because this was a *lighthouse*. What was it about lighthouses that evoked such an aura of romance and mystery? Was it simply the idea of the keeper out here all alone, polishing the old lamps by day, keeping the fires burning at night, responsible for the lives of the equally lonely sailors passing by on the dark, vast waters?

"Alicia, I—"

My words were cut short when I realized she had frozen, a stricken look on her face.

A man stood in the greenery just past the edge of the courtyard. Smiling a smile that did not reach his eyes.

At least it isn't a ghost, was my first thought. My second: *Aw crap. Is this Alicia's ex? And he tracked her here, to a secluded island?*

A ghost would have been a better bet.

Chapter Two

The man was of average height and build, with light brown hair and a vaguely bookish air. He might have been attractive, if not for the threatening aura that enshrouded him like a malevolent fog.

Wait, was I seeing auras now?

"Who are you?" he demanded, looking at me.

"Funny, I was just about to ask you the same thing," I said. I tore my eyes away from the stranger to glance at Alicia. She remained stock-still, a deer in the headlights. "This is a closed construction site."

"Why don't you run along," he said to me, his eyes now locked on Alicia. "And let me talk to my wife in private."

So I had been right: this was Alicia's ex.

"*Thorn*," Alicia said, her voice breathless. "What in the world are you *doing* here?"

"You have no business here," I put in. "Get *off* this property."

The three of us stared at each other, no one moving. My mind cast about, assessing the situation and our options. All I had with me besides my cell phone—which was mostly useless since large swaths of the island were in a dead zone for cell service—was a mini-flashlight, a tape measure, a roll of blueprints, and a handy three-in-one screwdriver. It was for situations like these that my father had begun urging me to carry a firearm. I had some strong opinions about gun control, but given the life I led I was beginning to think Dad might have a point. Alicia's ex-husband wasn't a large man, but I wouldn't want to test my upper body strength against his in a fight over control of a screwdriver. Much less the mini-flashlight.

Still, we weren't alone on this island. Buzz, one of Ellis's big burly bodyguards, was somewhere nearby. My dad was also on the island, as well as my lead carpenter Jeremy, his new assistant Waquisha, and Dog. Last I saw they were heading for the foghorn building to assess the basement. If we could keep Thorn talking, one of them was bound to show up eventually.

"I need to talk to you, Amy," Thorn said. "Alone."

"I'm not *Amy* anymore, I'm Alicia." Alicia's voice shook, but her chin lifted in determination. "And I'm not your wife. I have nothing to say to you."

He laughed, a harsh sound. "The promises we made before our families, before *God*, mean nothing to you?"

Alicia's lips parted and she exhaled a quick puff of breath, as though he had punched her in the gut.

"Look, wait, *wait*. I'm sorry," said Thorn. He ran a hand through his hair, and his voice gentled. "I'm really sorry, Amy. Please let me start again. Could I talk to you in private?"

"*No*," I said.

"And who might you be?" he asked again. A muscle worked in his jaw, as though he was straining hard to rein in his temper.

"A cop."

"Sure you are," he said with a snort.

"I mean . . . actually, I'm married to a cop. Head of homicide, as a matter of fact. Inspector Crawford of the SFPD." I was lying through my teeth. Inspector Annette Crawford was a friend, but we weren't all that close. Still, it was worth a try. "If you have something to say to Alicia, say it now and stop wasting our time."

He glared at me. "You're being very controlling."

"I'm a general contractor," I said. "It's in the blood."

He scoffed and mumbled, "A lady general contractor? Sure ya are."

"I'm not going anywhere with you, Thorn." Alicia seemed to have gotten over the shock and drew herself up to her full height, her shoulders squared. "Anything you want to say, you can say in front of Mel—er, Mrs. Inspector Crawford here."

Thorn blew out a long breath. "All right, let me start again. Amy—"

"*Alicia*," she said.

"Okay, sorry, yes, Alicia. That will take a little getting used to." He smiled a chagrined little *aw shucks* smile and ducked his head slightly. It was charming. Had I not known his story, I might have fallen for it. "*Alicia*, I've changed."

Alicia and I snorted in concert.

"I know it's hard to believe—"

"Just a tad," I muttered.

"But I've been working on improving myself, on being the man you need me to be. The husband you need me to be. I completed the court-mandated anger management program, and I've been sober for almost a year now. But more importantly, I attended the Palm Project. Have you heard of it? Up the coast, past Green Gulch Farm?

It changed my life. It changed *me*. I understand things now, I have re-experienced my childhood, explored some root causes, and now own who I am, why I've done what I've done.

"That's where I found out where you were, Amy. When I was at the Palm Project center. You always used to say you'd never move to California, but then I saw your picture in the local paper. It was like fate. Like a sign."

A chilly, brine-scented wind wafted up from the water; overhead, the sky was a gray shroud. Alicia and I had our arms crossed, hugging ourselves, not so much due to the cold as the situation. I kept expecting Buzz to appear, or for Dad or Dog or *someone* to come around.

"I just . . . I don't expect you to believe me right away, I know that. I've broken your trust and I'll have to work to earn it back. But one thing we learn in the Palm Project is to bend like a palm tree, so as not to break. No matter how bad the storm, a palm tree bends, and every time it does, its roots grow stronger. It's a compelling image, if you think about it. I have weathered the storm, and grown stronger."

Again, Alicia and I seemed to have been struck by the mute stick. It was hard to know how to respond to these pseudo-therapeutic "bend like a palm" slogans coming from someone who used to beat his wife.

"You still haven't told us what you're doing here on Lighthouse Island," I said finally. "Just happened to be in the neighborhood?"

"Thorn's always been a gifted sailor," said Alicia quietly.

He smiled again, projecting warmth and charm. Aimed directly at her.

Suddenly, Alicia smiled, and my stomach clenched. Was she falling under his spell? I wasn't particularly schooled on the ins and outs of intimate partner violence, but this much I knew: It was extremely complicated, and abusers often relied on their charm and personality—as well as the threat of violence—to keep their victims in line.

But then, the smile never leaving her face, Alicia said, "Thorn, I'd like to introduce you to Buzz Simoni."

I had been so focused on Thorn I hadn't noticed the bodyguard had come up behind us. Back in the old days—before I started stumbling across bodies, for instance—I had thought it would be a drag to be followed around by a security detail, like a rock star or a head of state. I didn't think so anymore. Buzz, impeccably dressed as always in his double-breasted suit, shiny wing tips, and completely unnecessary sunglasses, was a welcome sight. All six feet, six inches of rippling muscle.

"What's up, Ms. Withers?" Buzz asked, his gaze focused on Thorn. "This a friend of yours?"

Alicia gave a barely discernible shake of her head.

"*Wait*," Thorn said, taking a step back and holding his hands up, as if in surrender. "I haven't done anything! I've got a boat at the yacht harbor. It's a public harbor—I'm not trespassing."

Buzz didn't say a word. He grabbed Thorn by one bicep, hitching him up slightly so Thorn was forced to awkwardly shuffle along in order not to fall, and hustled him off in the direction of the yacht harbor. We could hear Thorn arguing—calmly, I had to hand it to him—as they left. Buzz remained mute, as was his wont. In fact, those few words to Alicia were the most I'd ever heard him say.

"You okay?" I asked Alicia.

Alicia nodded but seemed to deflate, folding in on herself, holding her arms around her middle and crouching down until she was sitting on a large stone out-cropping.

I perched on the rock beside her and put my arm around her shoulders.

"It'll be okay, Alicia," I said. "Don't forget: You're not alone. You have friends to help you through this."

She closed her eyes, breathing deeply. I wondered what Thorn's sudden appearance meant for my friend. I had read enough about stalking to know that it could be difficult to keep someone away who hadn't broken any laws—at least not recently.

I tried to concentrate on the smell of the water, the tang of the brine, the bracing jolt of the wind, then shifted my gaze to a small copse of trees, their growth stunted by the bay breezes but stubborn enough to have survived on such an inhospitable piece of land. I noticed a few holes in the ground surrounded by low piles of dirt, as though something had been digging, and wondered what kinds of animals lived out here on the island, besides birds. Surely not prairie dogs. Moles?

And then the temperature plummeted.

There was a loud clanging, like footsteps running up the circular metal stairs of the lighthouse tower.

I glanced up to the top of the tower. A woman in a diaphanous white gown stood at the balcony railing, her long hair blown about by the wind.

I opened my mouth to yell a warning that the balcony wasn't safe. But before I could get the words out of my mouth, she climbed over the rail, then hurled herself off the lighthouse balcony.

Toward the rocky shore below.

Chapter Three

Correction: A *ghost* threw herself off, vanishing from sight as she approached the ground.

Vertigo closed in on me, its swirling depths drawing me down. I broke out in a sweat, squeezed my eyes shut, and ran through the bag of tricks that several experts had told me were supposed to help combat acrophobia: I attempted to regulate my breathing and the pounding of my heart. Tried counting, tried grounding myself.

Hoooo boy.

These days it wasn't the sight of a specter from another dimension that threw me, but the sight—or the *thought*—of anyone falling from up high.

Upon reflection, it wasn't surprising that a historic lighthouse island would host a ghost or two. I had been working in the home renovation business for several years now, and it was rare for historic structures *not* to house something. Most often what I encountered was not a ghost in the Hollywood style, but rather a suggestion of lives lived, loves won and lost, children grown and gone . . . It was precisely this sense of souls having passed through the doors and down the halls that had drawn me to historic homes long before I started encountering actual *ghost* ghosts.

Still, my admittedly short career as a ghost buster had taught me that suicidal ghosts were . . . problematic. The reasons for their agony were varied and complex. Although most guests at the proposed lighthouse inn would never see the specter—being tuned in to the supernatural world was a little like perfect pitch; one either had it or one didn't—but a few would, and that would not be good for business. And if I wanted to help the woman in the white dress to find eternal peace—or whatever it was she needed to be able to move on—I would have to figure out what had happened to make her forfeit her life.

And to do that meant that at some point I would probably have to climb that impossibly tall lighthouse tower.

But for the moment, I had other fish to fry. Abusive husband first; pesky ghosts—and terrifying tower—could wait.

"Alicia, I assume you have a restraining order against Thorn?" I asked.

She nodded. "But I don't have to tell you that too often those aren't worth the paper they're printed on. Mel, I . . . I'd rather not talk about this right now. Buzz will give him a scare, I'm sure, and I'll notify the authorities when we get back to shore. With luck that will be the end of it."

Yeah. Not so sure. If Thorn had tracked her to this island, he was one determined ex-husband. But at least Alicia had protection and could count on Ellis Elrich's not insignificant support.

"Okay, so what's the deal with the yacht harbor?" I asked, changing the subject. "It's considered public land, right?"

She nodded. "That portion of the island is in the public domain. The rest of the island, including all the structures—with the exception of the small boathouse and lavatories—is being held in a public-private partnership that was purchased by Ellis under a special agreement. The lighthouse is too expensive for the Coast Guard to maintain properly, obviously, so a percentage of the profits from the inn and restaurant will be dedicated to maintaining the historic structures as a public trust. As you know, we're also required to keep the light and foghorn functioning. Even with GPS and modern maritime technology, lighthouses still fulfill an important function."

I nodded. "I noticed a few boats in the harbor, but not many. There were a lot of empty slips."

"Well, at the moment there's really nothing much to do or see on the island. Officially, boaters are supposed to remain in the harbor area, away from the buildings and the old lighthouse—"

"But there's nothing to actually keep them out."

She shook her head. "No, no fence or anything like that. There's potable water and a lavatory at the harbor, but my sense is that it has been primarily used by boats that needed shelter during storms and couldn't make it back to proper harbors like Alameda or Jack London Square. Of course . . ." A troubled look came into her hazel eyes. "In calm weather someone could row over from Richmond in an inflatable dinghy and come ashore just about anywhere on Lighthouse Island. It's not that far; it would be easy enough, if you were determined."

"Do you think Thorn—" My words were cut off by the arrival of a giant cannonball of brown fluff. I petted the excited, squirming dog, and looked up to find my dad approaching.

"I see how it is," said Bill Turner, the founder and

former head of Turner Construction. I had asked Dad to come today to start working up materials estimates. I'd given Ellis Elrich ballpark figures several months ago when he'd first submitted his bid for the island, but now was the time to start ordering supplies. Accurate numbers were especially important on this job because all materials had to be brought in by boat or barge. This was no small thing, and we didn't have a lot of room for error. I was good at detailing proposals, but Dad was the best in the business. "I come here out of the goodness of my heart to work up estimates for you, and you two gals sit around, lollygagging in the sunshine, while there's work to be done."

"You caught us," I said with a smile as Dad and I exchanged significant glances. He had only to look at Alicia's face to know something had happened, and probably assumed I had seen a ghost. He wasn't all that comfortable with my supernatural abilities.

My father was an attractive man in his late sixties, with the physique of a former construction worker gradually yielding to the effects of time and a small potbelly. He was dressed, as usual, in worn jeans and scuffed leather work boots, but over his customary white T-shirt he wore an REI fleece jacket that I had given him for his birthday last December. When he opened the gift, he held the jacket up and said, *What the devil am I going to use something this fancy for? Probably cost an arm and a leg.*

He hadn't taken it off all winter.

Dad's loyal companion was Dog, a big brown mutt I had found abandoned at a jobsite and brought home "just for the night." Quite predictably, we had fallen in love and he had found his forever home. Recently we decided he should have a real name, so Dad proposed calling him "Doug" instead of the generic "Dog." Doug was happy to go along with the seemingly simple name change—he was happy to go along with just about anything—but his humans kept forgetting: We would start to say Dog, switch to Doug halfway through, and end up saying *Dawugh*. Dog/Doug/Daw-ugh wasn't the smartest canine of the litter, but he was brave and loyal and appeared to be the only member of the family, besides yours truly, who could sense ghosts.

"What's going on?" asked Dad. "Everything okay?"

Alicia looked at me and nodded, and I gave him an abbreviated version of our encounter with Thorn Walker.

"You think he has a boat in the harbor?" asked Dad.

"He said he did, and I'm not surprised," said Alicia. "He used to sail competitively."

"What's he after?" Dad asked with a frown.

"We don't know, exactly, but my guess is it's nothing good," I said.

"Does this have anything to do with the protestors? They were giving me an earful down at the harbor."

"What protestors?" I asked.

"Some of the boaters at the yacht harbor think the island should have been made into a public park," answered Alicia. "They weren't happy with the deal Ellis struck with the state."

I lifted my eyebrows. "I remember there were protestors at the last renovation project I did with you, as well. You deal a lot with this sort of thing?"

She shrugged. "I work for a high-profile billionaire. It's part of the cost of doing business."

She had me there.

"Why would a bunch of rich yacht owners care so much about this place?" I asked. "Can't they buy their own islands?"

"In this case, 'yacht owners' doesn't mean super rich,"

said Dad. "Most of them have little sailboats, that sort of thing. A 'yacht harbor' simply refers to a harbor that's not big enough for cargo ships."

"Ah. Okay, I guess I'm not up on my yacht harbor parlance."

"Anyway, they were asking about you, and the project. Jeremy and Waquisha are down there now. Let me introduce you around; you can explain to them what you're up to."

"Are you up to chatting with a group of unhappy sailors?" I asked Alicia.

She gave a game, determined nod. "Of course. Let's go."

We walked across the courtyard, passed by the foghorn building and supply shed, then headed down a rocky path toward the natural cove. The harbor's facilities were minimal: the docks and a shack with a water faucet on the outside, and a toilet within. Ellis's supply boat usually tied up closer to the lighthouse buildings, at a small wharf off a rock wall. A winch hoisted supplies to the property above the dock, and there was a ladder to the side.

I hadn't yet gathered my courage to climb that ladder, and always requested I be dropped off here at the harbor. But I was so focused on work when I arrived this morning that I hadn't paid much attention to the other boats, much less their occupants. Now I took note: There were half a dozen craft moored at the docks. One was a simple sailboat with no indoor area at all; the others appeared to have small cabins for storage or sleeping. As my father had noted, none of them looked particularly posh: There wasn't a true "yacht" in the bunch.

On the docks I spied two men and one woman standing with Jeremy and Waquisha. Waquisha was in her early twenties, tall and plump, with curly black hair and big, intense brown eyes. A six-foot Raphaelesque model in overalls. She was naturally reserved and had barely spoken word one to me, but I had been so excited to have another set of double-X chromosomes working the job-site that when Jeremy said he knew a young woman look-ing for work, I jumped at the chance to put her on the payroll. So far she seemed efficient and capable.

Still, I couldn't help but hope she'd start speaking up soon; I hated being the only snarky woman on the jobsite.

"Here they are now," said Jeremy. He wasn't a big talker, either, preferring to focus on getting his work done well, and in a timely fashion. Maybe it was a carpenter characteristic.

"Mel, this is Major Williston," Jeremy introduced me to one of the strangers, a good-looking man in his thirties with an athletic build and an unnaturally deep tan.

"You're in the service?" I asked.

"No, Major's my name."

"Ah," I said.

"I have a brother named Lieutenant, and another named Colonel," he said with a chuckle. "You'll have to take it up with my father."

"Let me guess, his name's General Williston?"

He smiled and shook his head. "Glenn, actually. But he has a passion for military history."

"And this is Paul . . ." Major gestured toward a large, hale blond man with a badly peeling nose; he looked like Bamm-Bamm, all grown up. His fair complexion didn't seem up to the rigors of sailing.

"Paul Halstrom, nice to meet you," he said politely, and we shook hands.

"And Terry," he said, gesturing to a thirtyish woman

with a deep tan. Her short hair was slightly spiky from the wind, or with gel, it was hard to tell. She wore designer sunglasses and had a yellow sweater tied around her shoulders. She put me in mind of a short-haired Katharine Hepburn: brash and sporty and capable.

All three sailors looked strong, as though they spent a lot of time in the gym or, I supposed, handling rigging and sails.

"Terry Re," the woman said, stepping forward and putting out her hand. We shook; her palm was warm and dry, her grip almost uncomfortably tight. "That's spelled R-E, as in 'do-re-mi.'"

"Nice to meet you," I said.

The lyrics *Doe, a deer, a female deer* . . . from *The Sound of Music* began running through my head. *Great*, I thought. Chances were *that* earworm would stick with me for the coming week.

"So," said Major Williston, presenting himself as the spokesperson of the group. "Are you the person we talk to about retaining free access to the island?"

"I'm really not, I'm sorry," I said. My eyes slewed over to Alicia, who was studying the horizon. She was the one they wanted, but she'd been through enough today. "I'm the general contractor on the project, so the most I can offer is to unstop your toilet."

No one said anything. I really had to find a more appreciative audience—or a better caliber of jokes.

"I just mean that you'll have to address any overarching concerns to Ellis Elrich. Or perhaps to the state, or the Coast Guard, or whoever made the deal with Elrich in the first place . . ."

Major continued smiling, his tanned skin crinkling fetchingly in the corners of his eyes. He had an easygoing manner, but something told me it could turn on a dime.

"It doesn't make sense, you building here," said Major with a slow shake of his head. "This island should be entirely open to the public, as it has been for decades."

"Actually, while part of the island has been open to boaters and hikers, and will continue to be, the rest of the island has been officially off-limits," I replied. "There are NO TRESPASSING signs posted all around the light-house buildings."

"My point is, our taxes pay for this place," Major continued, his tone growing testier.

"Given the current state of the buildings," I said. "I don't think *anyone's* taxes are paying for much of anything at the moment."

"You should think long and hard about this," Terry jumped in. "There are too many logistical issues to building here; the costs will be prohibitive."

"That's our concern, not yours," I said. "And really, any concerns you have should be addressed to El—"

"Aside from everything else," Paul interrupted. "There are some . . . special problems you should be aware of."

"What kinds of . . . special problems?"

Paul, Terry, and Major exchanged significant glances, and then Major announced, "Mostly at night, we've heard . . ." He paused and we all leaned in just a tad. "I don't want to feed our imaginations, but there's something seriously disturbing about that lighthouse tower. Something . . . *off*."

Chapter Four

"Such as?" I asked. I had my own misgivings about that tower, but was going to keep them to myself.

He hesitated, then wiped a hand over his chin and the back of his neck. He exchanged another glance with his fellow yachters. Finally, he said, "It's almost like . . . well, I know this sounds crazy, but it appears to be . . . *haunted*."

Dad rolled his eyes, threw up his hands, and strode away.

Dog looked longingly after him, then back at me, as though torn. He hated it when his people separated. Finally he trotted after Dad, no doubt hoping a snack of some kind would be involved. Other than his humans, food was a priority for Dog. Food, and squirrels.

"Your dad afraid of ghosts?" Terry asked in a loud whisper.

"Not particularly. But . . . he doesn't like to hear about them. He doesn't really believe."

"Neither did I," said Major. "Not until I saw it with my own eyes."

"What did you see, exactly?"

"There were lights in the tower."

"It *is* a lighthouse, after all," said Waquisha. I was so surprised to hear her speak that for a moment I lost the thread of the conversation.

"It wasn't the lamp," said Paul. "We're not talking about the lighthouse light. It was more as if . . . as if someone was climbing the stairs, maybe with a flashlight or a candle. You see it first in one narrow little window, and then the next. And you hear the clanging of the metal stairs."

Terry and Major nodded.

Waquisha piped up again, a decidedly cynical edge to her voice, "And you're saying no human could make such a noise, or carry a light up the stairs?"

"Look, lady, when you're the only person on this island, just you and your boat, who the hell's climbing the spire?"

I knew, better than most, that ghosts were real. I also knew how unsettling it could be to encounter one. Still, out on a secluded island, featuring a lighthouse no less, a person might be prone to misinterpreting simple sights and sounds: moonlight glinting off windowpanes, the wind moaning as it passed under loose doors, the lapping of the bay waters echoing in the night.

In this case, of course, I happened to have seen a spirit throw herself off the lighthouse balcony not twenty minutes earlier. But I wanted to deal with this tormented apparition on my own, not with an entourage of sailing enthusiasts who, I was going to assume, didn't know the first thing about being sensitive to a suicidal woman. Even if she was already dead.

A piece of paper skittered along the rocks, flapping up against the side of my boot. I leaned over to pick it up. The yellowing, slightly crumbly paper showed what appeared to be a hand-drawn map of the island. Scrawled behind the foghorn building was a large "X."

It looked like a . . . treasure map?

I looked up to find Major's eyes on me. He inclined his head and said, "We've found several of those scattered about."

"There's a *treasure* on this island?"

He scoffed. "*No.* It must be some sort of kid's prank, or a game, or something. Ignore it."

"It looks old."

"My kid did a project like that when he was in Boy Scouts; all you have to do to make paper look old is burn the edges a little and soak the whole thing in tea. So anyway, as we were saying: It's going to be tough to convert this place into a hotel and restaurant with ghosts running around. And we've all seen it; we're not crazy."

I nodded as I rolled up the map and stuck it in the pocket of my coveralls. "Okay, duly noted. Thanks. By the way, we ran into someone earlier, named Thorn Walker. Any of you know him?"

Nods all around.

"We've met. Seems like an okay guy," said Paul. "Came into harbor the other day, but left just a little while ago."

"What was he up to here, do you know?"

Paul shrugged. "Hiked around the island a little, but mostly just hung out. This is one of the few public harbors where a person can stop for a few days in the middle of the bay, enjoy the peace and quiet and spectacular views. And there's never a crowd. Doesn't get much better than this."

I nodded. "True."

"So, in the meantime can we use the island?" asked Terry. "We won't get in the way."

"I wouldn't advise it. It's going to be a construction site soon. Lots of comings and goings. So while you are of course free to use the harbor, for health and safety reasons the lighthouse site will be off-limits."

Paul's already red-hued face deepened with anger. "This is so totally bogus," he growled. "We've had the run of this place for years, and now you folks think you can just walk in here—"

"C'mon, Paul, calm down," said Major, putting a hand on Paul's shoulder. "I'll call Elrich directly, see if we can talk some sense into the boss."

I gave Major the phone number of Elrich's public relations person, a man who had grown up in West Oakland, was almost as broad as he was tall, and used to work security detail with Buzz. I thought it was no mistake that he was the new public relations face of Elrich Enterprises.

Paul glared at me some more, Terry nodded good-bye, and Major shook my hand and said he was sure he would be seeing me around. Then they headed back to their boats.

"Think they'll be trouble?" Jeremy asked.

"Maybe. But once they see we won't impede their access to the harbor, they should be fine, right? I think they're just annoyed that the island's not their own personal playground anymore."

"I've got all my notes and measurements and photos," said Dad as he and Dog rejoined us. "I'll work up the quotes at home. Time to head back; have to get supper started."

It was only three in the afternoon, but Dad didn't mess

around when it came to having supper on the table at six. Dog wagged his tail wildly and nosed Dad's thigh; though his vocabulary was limited, it was mostly food-related. "Supper" was one of his favorite words.

"Okay, Dad, and thanks," I said, kissing his cheek. Even though he claimed to have given up smoking, he smelled vaguely of tobacco, and I suspected he'd snuck a cigarette out behind the shed. "Tell Duncan I'll need another hour or so."

Duncan was the eternally patient skipper of the little motorboat Ellis Elrich had arranged to ferry passengers to and from Lighthouse Island from nearby Point Moro.

"Don't push it, babe," Dad warned. "This time of year you'll lose the light by four thirty, or thereabouts. And there's more rain expected soon, El Niño and all that."

After several years of drought, this winter the Bay Area had been drenched by storm after storm. Out on the island it was chilly and gray during the mornings, sometimes hot in the afternoon, and cold enough for a real jacket at night: winter, California-style. Not exactly perfect timing to tackle an island renovation, but construction timelines did not wait for weather.

Once Dad, Dog, Jeremy, and Waquisha left, I turned to Alicia, who was absorbed in yet another set of blueprints.

"I hate to say it," I said. "But I should check out this haunted tower."

"*Allegedly* haunted," she mumbled, still focused on the plans.

"Pretty sure we can go with 'haunted,'" I said.

That got her attention. "You saw something?"

"Yup."

"Do I want to know . . . ?"

"Probably not. Besides, I'm not really sure what I saw," I prevaricated. I didn't want to tell Alicia she had a suicidal ghost on her hands. Watching someone jump to her death, even if it was only happening in the spectral plane, was genuinely horrifying. "I'd rather not say more until I get a better sense of what's going on, okay? You wait here, and I'll be back before you can say 'abracadabra.'"

"No can do, Mel. Safety first, remember? That means the buddy system until we whip this place into shape. Besides, you won't be able to make it up that tower alone. I'm going with you." She pressed her lips together in a signature move, and marched off in the direction of the lighthouse.

Despite my desire to keep my new fear of heights to myself, I had been forced to fess up to Alicia when she noticed I was avoiding the lighthouse tower. My family and work crew had also caught on pretty quickly to my new phobia, and word had spread.

"Wait, Alicia—you had a bit of a shock earlier," I said, hurrying after her. "We can explore the tower another day."

"Absolutely not, Mel. I will *not* allow that . . . *person* to dictate my life *any*more," she said, her voice steely-edged and determined. "Nothing will spoil this project for me. Not ghosts. Not unhappy boat owners. And certainly not my loser of an ex-husband."

"Wow," I said, impressed. "You are Woman. I hear you roar."

"Damn straight."

As Alicia and I headed toward the tower, my phone rang. Frankly, I was relieved to hear it. Cell phone reception was sketchy out here on the island, which made me nervous. As a general contractor I *needed* my phone. I was typically juggling several projects at once; my foremen had to be able to contact me, suppliers had to check orders, and my office manager, Stan, had to consult me about paperwork issues. Without my phone, business ground to a snail's pace, which could not happen if I wanted to make payroll each week.

"Sorry, Alicia, give me one minute? I have to take this call."

"No problem," she said. "I'll meet you inside. And Mel? We'll go up those stairs together."

I smiled and nodded, but doubted it was that simple. If acrophobia could be cured by having a good friend at one's side, I would long ago have conquered my vertigo.

Still, I would give it a good old college try.

I lingered on the path outside the tower and answered the call from Stan, who had some questions about a workman's comp case. The reception kept cutting in and out, but I understood the gist of it and we got it straightened out. Stan also mentioned fielding calls from people who couldn't get through to me on my cell phone, which meant I would have a taller-than-usual stack of phone messages on my desk when I got home tonight. After hanging up, I checked the phone and saw that several people had tried calling but hadn't gotten through, so I sent text messages—for some reason those went through even when calls failed—answering questions and notifying people I would get back to them as soon as I could.

As I was texting, I caught a glimpse of someone down by the rocky shore but, absorbed by my phone business, it took a few moments for my brain to catch up to my eyes.

Wait.

It was a little boy. What was a child doing on the island? Major Williston had mentioned a son in Boy Scouts; could that be him? No, dressed in a cute pirate outfit—a red-and-white striped shirt, a little black pirate hat—this boy was too young.

When I looked directly at him, he vanished.

I blew out a long breath. *Another ghost.*

Child ghosts were the most wrenching apparitions, of course. What could have happened? What was he doing here?

I glanced back at my phone but continued to focus on my peripheral vision, which was no easy task. And there he was again, hopping from one rock to the next, a bucket in one hand and a shovel in the other. He seemed very young, probably no more than four or five. Too little to be out all alone, jumping along the rough, slippery rocks dangerously close to the water. As I concentrated, I could make out a very faint, piping voice chanting a singsong rhyme. *"Yo ho, yo ho . . . over the big blue sea!"*

I glanced over again, but though I could still hear the boy's voice, he had disappeared. *Should I try to talk to him?*

And then he materialized right in front of me.

A chill washed over me, and I forgot to breathe. He stared at me, a grave look on his little face. Wordlessly, he pointed toward the top of the tower, and my eyes followed to where he was pointing.

And then I heard the clanking of the metal steps, and saw a light passing by one of the narrow stairwell windows, visible even in the day.

Alicia screamed.

Chapter Five

"*Alicia?*" I yelled.

The door at the base of the light tower stood open. I ran through it, then stopped dead in my tracks at the bottom of the circular stairs as a man came tumbling down head over heels, arms and legs out of control, flailing, until at last landing on the hard stone floor with a sickening thud. The awful echoes of the body striking the metal steps filled the tower long after the man had come to rest.

He was covered in blood, a knife protruded from his chest, and his arm was folded under him at an unnatural angle. His eyes were wide open, gazing up at me in an uncomprehending stare.

Thorn Walker: ex-husband of Alicia, née Amy; wife beater; and self-proclaimed Palm Project success story. Gingerly, I stepped over his body to reach the spiral staircase.

"*Alicia?*" I yelled again, peering up into the center of the spiraling steps.

My words echoed: "*Alicia . . . ? 'licia . . . ? 'licia . . . ?*"

Fear seized my heart. Where could she be? Was she all right?

I started climbing. After only a few steps, my heart was pounding and I broke out in a sweat. Enclosed staircases didn't bother me, but anything with an open center that could potentially suck me in, or with a railing I could tumble over, caused a paralyzing fear. I pressed my back against the tower's stone wall and tried to keep my eyes level.

Don't look up, I told myself. *And don't look down. Look straight ahead and keep climbing. You can do this.*

I managed a few more steps before my vision started to swim. Dizziness washed over me, followed by nausea.

"Alicia!" I closed my eyes and yelled again. *"Are you all right?"*

With my hands on the curving stone wall to guide me, I forced myself to keep going, inch by inch, around and around. The stones were rough and damp under my palms; the old tower smelled of must and rust and brine. My legs trembled, and I could hear my own breath, loud and ragged, amplified by the acoustics of the tower.

Who are you kidding, Mel? said the damning little voice in my head. *Even if you manage to get all the way to the top, you're in no shape to help Alicia if she needs you. You're in no shape to help* anyone.

At last, I heard something.

"Mel?"

It was Alicia's voice, shaky and small.

I stopped, kept my hands on the wall, took a deep breath, and looked up.

Alicia was slowly descending the stairs, her hands at her sides. They were covered in blood, and her sweater and purse were dotted with deep red spots. Her clipboard was gone.

"What happened?" I asked quietly as she approached. "Alicia, are you hurt?"

She shook her head. "It's not my blood. It's Thorn's. Is he . . . ?"

I nodded.

Lord forgive me, but I was finding it tough to get too worked up over the death of a man who had so brutalized my friend. I hoped never to become so hardened by life that I would find pleasure in the death of another, but I wouldn't shed any tears over the demise of a wife beater, either. I was just glad Alicia wouldn't have to worry about him any longer, that she was free of the constant threat he posed. Nor would he be able to refocus his violent obsession on a new target.

Still, I wasn't sure the police would agree. Had Alicia . . . ?

Too dizzy to stand, I sank onto the tread. I had managed to climb only about fifteen steps.

Alicia sat beside me, sniffed loudly, and took a deep breath. "For years I dreamed Thorn would somehow disappear—drive off the road, fall off his sailboat, pick a fight with someone who could fight back—so I wouldn't have to look over my shoulder anymore, live in the shadows, be *afraid* all the time. Do you have any idea what that kind of constant fear does to a person?"

I shook my head.

"I wished him dead," she said quietly. "So many, many times."

"That's understandable, Alicia, given what he put you through." I paused, still concentrating on steadying my breathing and avoiding the view of the stone floor below. "So . . . is that what happened? You were arguing, he threatened you, and you pushed him down the stairs?"

She looked shocked. "Of course not! How could you think such a thing?"

"Um . . ." I trailed off. *Maybe because you were at the top of the stairs with blood on your hands, and your abu-*

sive ex-husband is dead at the bottom of said stairs with a bloody knife stuck in his chest?

"You think I would deliberately harm someone?" she asked, looking bewildered. "Even Thorn?"

"Well . . ." I remembered the rage with which she had responded to the murderer who terrorized us at the project in Marin, and thought, *yes, given sufficient motivation she was capable of harming someone.* So was I. "It would be natural, Alicia, even justifiable if he threatened you, made you fear for your life."

She shook her head vehemently.

"That's not what happened. *Please*, Mel, you have to believe me. I climbed up and found him in the watch room, covered in blood. He had been beaten, and there was a—" Her voice faltered for a moment. "There was a knife in his chest, but . . . he was still alive. He stumbled toward me, and I tried to catch him, tried to take the knife out, but he was . . . slippery with blood. I couldn't hold him and he . . . fell. Just tumbled over. Over and over and over."

Down seventy-four metal treads.

The image hung for a moment in my mind.

"Mel, do you believe me? I . . . part of me hated him, it's true, but I would never have . . ." She cleared her throat and shook her head. "No. That's not true. You're right; if he tried to harm me again, I would have done whatever was necessary to protect myself. But it wasn't like that."

"I believe you. But . . ." Suddenly it dawned on me that if Alicia hadn't murdered Thorn, then whoever had must still be up in the tower. Where else could he—or she?—be?

"Let's get out of here," I said in an urgent whisper.

As we got to our feet, Buzz burst in through the light-house door below. His gaze took in Thorn's bloody body, and then the two of us on the stairs, a silent question in his dark eyes.

"We're fine," Alicia told him.

"Ahhhh jeeeeez," Buzz breathed as he grabbed Thorn's wrists and started to pull.

"Buzz! Stop!" I said, standing. "You shouldn't move the bo—"

Before I could finish my sentence, Buzz had dragged Thorn's body outside, repeating all the while, *"Ah jeez, ah jeez, ah jeez . . ."*

I collapsed back onto the step. We weren't very far up the tower stairs, but even so I was overwhelmed with dizziness and nausea.

"Take my hand, Mel," Alicia said calmly. "Focus on my hand. Here we go." And together we made our slow way down the winding steps and out of the dim stone tower into the gray light of day.

Buzz had dragged Thorn over to a small patch of grass at the side of the lighthouse and was kneeling over him, performing CPR. Attempting to revive a dead man with a knife in his chest. It was a gruesome sight. Every time Buzz compressed Thorn's chest, more blood oozed out.

"Buzz . . . ," I said. "That's not going to work. He's gone. *Seriously*, Buzz," I continued as the bodyguard kept pumping Thorn's chest. "I'm no expert but he looks awfully dead."

Buzz shook his head and continued with his lifesaving procedure. "We can*not* have a man die out here, not officially. It would be terrible for business."

"Um, okay, but . . ." I glanced at Alicia, who was gazing at the bay as though unaware of what was happening. None of us was at our best. The shock of sudden violence—much less death—paralyzes some people and spurs others on to action, no matter how pointless.

"Have you called the police?" I asked.

He shook his head.

I tried my phone. No signal.

Dammit.

So I texted my buddy, my pal, my ersatz spouse, homicide inspector Annette Crawford. Annette worked for the city of San Francisco, so most likely she had no jurisdiction out here, but she was the only police officer for whom I had a private number.

On Lighthouse Island, I texted. *A man is dead. Phones not working out here. Please send help.*

I hesitated, then added, *And yes, I'm involved in another murder and no it's not my fault.*

"You didn't—did you see anybody up there, Alicia?" I gazed back at the lighthouse spire, tall against the gray sky. What was I looking for: a clue of some sort? A murderer hanging out one of the windows, gloating? I could easily imagine someone like Thorn having a lot of enemies. But whom did he know on Lighthouse Island who might have wanted him dead—other than Alicia?

Alicia kept staring at the water, not saying a word.

Buzz pressed two fingers against Thorn's neck, checking for a pulse, then sat back on his haunches and released a great sigh. Alicia collapsed onto a rock ledge and put her head between her knees.

"Mr. Elrich is not gonna like this," Buzz said, shaking his head. "He's not gonna like this one bit. I really wish she woulda asked me first. We coulda made it look like an accident, maybe."

"Buzz, Alicia didn't do it," I said in a quiet voice. "There must be someone else in the tower."

"What?" Buzz jumped up, grabbed a gun from his shoulder holster, and charged toward the tower.

"Buzz, wait!" I called out. "Let's just guard the door and wait for the police!"

Buzz ignored me and disappeared around the side of the tower. The murderer had probably slipped out while we were focused on Thorn. But what if he—or she— hadn't?

"Come on, Alicia. Let's go down to the harbor. We need people around us right now—safety in numbers. Maybe the phones will work down there, or we can borrow someone's marine radio."

I felt bad for leaving Buzz, but what was I going to do—offer myself as backup? He had a gun, after all, while I was plagued with vertigo. If I tried to help, he'd probably end up having to rescue me, too. And besides, Buzz was a trained security guy; he could take care of himself. I hoped.

What we really needed was the police. And soon.

There was no sign of life at the harbor. Only two boats remained.

"Hello?" I called out as we approached the docks. Unsure of boating etiquette—did sailboats have doorbells?—I called out, *"Ahoy there! Anybody home?"*

No one appeared.

Alicia trailed me wordlessly. In shock, probably. She kept staring at her blood-streaked hands.

She lingered on the dock while I climbed onto one small craft, hoping I might be able to use the radio to call the Coast Guard. I flicked buttons and got some static, but couldn't figure out the high-tech equipment. I peered through a window into the hatch, but saw nothing but a bright orange life vest, two dirt-caked shovels, some photography equipment, and a paper bag full of empty beer cans.

I tried the next boat, but its radio was just as bewildering. High tech, I wasn't.

And anyway, Inspector Crawford had no doubt already notified the local police. Best do what everyone always told me to do: wait and leave this to the professionals.

"Hey, Alicia, let's wash up," I said, leading her over to the outdoor sink that was attached to the shack near the docks.

As Alicia and I washed our hands, the water ran pink with Thorn's blood. It was pretty ghastly, but I'd been through this before. I wiped the blood off Alicia's leather purse, but her white sweater was a dead loss.

Using a rough brown paper towel from a rusted dispenser, I dried her hands as if she were a child. Then I put my arm around her and led her to a small bench. Alicia hadn't said a word since we'd left the tower, and her silence was beginning to worry me.

"Let's sit," I suggested. "I'll try the police again."

I checked my phone. Annette had sent a message:

Why am I not surprised? Richmond PD en route. A friend, Detective Santos. Be nice to him. Don't touch anything. I'll be in touch.

No point in calling again, Annette was on the case. Sort of. I wondered what her friend Detective Santos was like, and if he was aware of the whole ghost-talking thing.

Just as the thought crossed my mind, the temperature plummeted. Again.

Out of the corner of my eye I could see Thorn standing in a little wooded area to the side of the harbor, staring at us. Covered in blood, he had a knife in his chest.

I blew out a breath.

Great. A *third* ghost on this small island, and this one was a creepy wife-beating ghost. I shuddered at the thought of Thorn trailing me around, spouting Palm Project platitudes for the rest of my days.

I knew from experience that the dear departed—or not so "dear," but still departed—rarely know much about their own deaths. It's wildly frustrating for me, and I can only imagine how it is for them as homicide victims.

Still, I figured I had nothing to lose by asking Thorn what had happened. And while I wasn't sad he was gone, I thought at least I should give him the heads-up on his current situation. It was possible he didn't realize he was dead, much less know how to go about navigating the afterlife.

I have had to break this news to a ghost on more than one occasion. "I hate to be the one to have to tell you this, but you're dead" is a very weird thing to say. And the worse people were at handling life on earth, the harder it seemed to be for them to understand what was happening in the afterlife. It made sense, in an odd sort of way.

Just then, Buzz trotted over to us. He looked winded but, I noted with relief, there were no bullet holes or stab wounds on his person.

"Anything?"

"Nothin'. I don't understand it. I searched every inch of that tower. I mean, there aren't that many places to hide."

"We were outside with Thorn. Maybe the killer escaped while we were busy . . ."

"Busy tryin' to revive a dead man," Buzz said. "My bad. Sorry, I don't know what came over me. I just . . ." He swayed slightly on his feet, and I jumped up and led him over to the bench. Buzz was a large, square-jawed man built like a tank, but he was only human. "Ah *jeez*, I'm embarrassed. Truth is, I never seen a dead body before."

"Is that right?" I said, wondering what it meant that

little old me had more experience with corpses than big bad Buzz. Still, it came as something of a relief. Buzz's earlier suggestion that he could have taken care of Thorn more discreetly had made me wonder if he had experience as a hit man. I was happy to learn that was not the case.

Alicia shivered, and Buzz pulled his suit lapels tighter. Our breath made little clouds in the air; it was unnaturally cold for the Bay Area, even in January.

I glanced at the woods. Thorn still stood there, staring, watching us.

"Buzz, the Richmond police are on their way," I said. "A Detective Santos, who's a friend of a friend. I couldn't find anybody aboard their boats, but it's possible one of them might be involved in this. We should keep our guard up. I'll be right back—will you two be okay here for a minute?"

Buzz started to stand. "I should go with you."

"No, really, it's all right. I won't go far. I need to go alone, and you need to protect Alicia."

"We should stay together," he insisted.

"I'll be right over there." I pointed toward the little copse of trees. "You'll be able to see me the whole time."

Alicia put a hand on his arm. "It's all right, Buzz. Let her go."

He sat back down, a look of relief on his face.

"Alicia," I asked. "Do you have a mirror with you?"

She was the type to carry such a thing, just as I could usually be counted on to have a tape measure somewhere on or near my person. She reached into her purse, and handed me a compact.

Thus armed, I went to chat with a ghost in the woods.

Chapter Six

Thorn was leaning against a eucalyptus tree, his hands moving restlessly, toying with a long, fragrant leaf. Eucalyptus is an invasive, nonnative species that was brought to California from Australia, and a lot of conservationists were trying to eradicate it. But I loved the tall, soaring, pungent trees. Their strong astringent scent brought to mind memories of being a kid, running through the Presidio or making forts in Golden Gate Park.

And those memories, in turn, served as a reminder to ground myself, to do a calming body scan before speaking with Thorn, to assure myself that I was of this earth.

"Hi, Thorn," I said as I approached. I often—though not always—saw ghosts only in my peripheral vision, which made it hard to have a face-to-face conversation. To get around this, I had learned that I could see the ghost's reflection in a mirror. Sure enough, whenever I looked straight at Thorn he disappeared, so I brought out Alicia's compact to look him in the eye while we spoke.

"What is going *on*?" he whined.

"It's a little hard to explain."

"I want to talk to my wife."

"First off, she's not your wife. She's your *ex*-wife. Second, I have some news."

After a pause Thorn said, "*Bad* news?"

"Well, that depends." I leaned against the tree next to the ex-human ex-husband, and met Thorn's eyes in the mirror. "It's all in how you look at it. Do you remember what happened at the lighthouse?"

"I have a headache," he said.

"I'm not surprised. You fell down the lighthouse stairs."

"I did?"

I nodded. "But before that, someone beat you up. And stabbed you. Any idea who that was?"

Thorn looked blank.

I cleared my throat. I was going to have to get better at this sort of thing.

"The thing is, Thorn—and this is going to be tough to hear, much less believe—but the truth is, someone beat you up, stabbed you, and then you fell down the stairs of the tower. All the way down."

"Then how am I able to walk? That makes no sense."

He held up his hands, as if just now noticing the blood. Then he looked down at the knife in his chest. A look of horror came over his face. "What's happening to me?"

"I'm sorry to tell you this, Thorn, but you died. Maybe from the fall, maybe from the knife. But ultimately it doesn't really matter. You died."

"What are you talking about?"

"Your spirit is still here, but your body is dead."

"Dead."

"Yes."

"You want me to believe I'm *dead*?"

I nodded.

He sneered. "What the hell kind of game are you playing? I knew you were up to no good the minute I spotted you. The bossy type. Did you take my boat? I can't find it."

"No, Thorn, I—"

All of a sudden Thorn lunged at me. I dropped the mirror as I instinctively dodged him. He tumbled to the ground at my feet.

As disconcerting as it is to have a spirit try to tackle you, nothing actually happens. Spirits are immaterial; they're *spirits*. An older, more experienced ghost might be able to inflict some damage—where ghost abilities were concerned I was still learning—but Thorn was a newbie spirit. I had nothing to fear from him.

Being threatened by a ghost was still pretty strange, though.

I retrieved the compact to keep an eye on Thorn. He kept shaking his head.

"What is going *on*?" he repeated.

"It's like I said. This is a whole new phase in your life. Or your, *er*, existence. I'm not sure what happens now, but try to think of this as an opportunity to make a fresh start." Just call me Mel Turner, general contractor and motivational ghost whisperer. I wondered whether the Palm Project might have a position for me. "Or, if you see a bright light, you might want to walk toward it."

I watched his expression in the mirror. Realization seemed to dawn.

"You're saying . . . I *died*? As in *dead*, dead?"

I was getting impatient, acutely aware that Buzz and Alicia could hear me talking—seemingly to myself, like a crazy woman. Alicia knew about my spirit-communicating talents, but I wasn't sure about Buzz. Plus, I hadn't liked Thorn when he was alive, and while I tried to work up some compassion for his current situation, nothing about his attitude was changing my opinion. Another thing I had learned about ghosts: Those who were jerks in life tended to be jerks after death, too.

Then I reminded myself: How would I react to finding out that, in a split second, I was no longer part of this earthly realm? It had to be right up there on the list of difficult things to accept.

"Can you tell me anything about what happened, Thorn? What were you doing up in the tower? I thought Buzz had escorted you off the island."

"He tried," he said in a boastful tone. "He took me to my boat in the harbor, but I skirted the island, pulled up to the supply dock, and climbed the ladder. I just wanted to talk to Amy."

"Alicia."

"She'll always be Amy to me."

It was possible Thorn's spirit still lingered because he was confused and disoriented, and that he would soon depart of his own accord. But what if he didn't? I would not allow him to haunt Alicia—quite literally—for the rest of her life.

"So what were you doing in the tower?" I asked.

"I wish I could remember. It's all . . . a fog."

"And I suppose you don't remember who beat you up, or why?"

He shook his head. "I feel really strange."

"I'll bet you do," I said.

Death is so final, so irrevocable. And sudden death doesn't give a person a chance to wrap things up, to come to terms and put things in order. It must be wrenching to realize that this was it, no more do-overs. Unless, of course, death was the ultimate do-over.

"So, as I was saying . . . if you see a bright light, or something like that, you might just want to walk on toward it."

"What are you *talking* about? The lighthouse light?"

"No, I'm just . . ." What *was* I talking about? If Thorn wasn't still here out of confusion, then there was a reason he was trapped on Lighthouse Island. I just didn't know what that reason was. Was it simply his obsession with Alicia?

"Okay," I sighed. "Just hang out, try not to get in anyone's way, and let me try to figure out what's going on and why you can't leave."

"No one tells me when I can or can't leave. I'll go where I want."

"By all means, feel free."

"I can't find my boat. What did you do with it?"

"Why don't you hop a ride on someone's boat?" I was guessing Thorn's spirit wouldn't be able to leave the island, but it was just a guess. Since he was out in the woods, rather than restricted to the tower where he died, I would assume he was limited to the confines of the island. But I could be wrong about that—I was still a little fuzzy on the rulebook for Life as a Ghost.

Fear washed over Thorn's pale face.

"What are *they* doing here?"

I turned and saw a police boat approaching the dock, with uniformed officers on board.

Thorn turned and ran, vanishing altogether before he got past the first tree.

Talking with cops wasn't my favorite thing, either. But not only was I a good citizen, I also lacked Thorn's ability to simply disappear.

So I headed to the harbor to meet the police.

* * *

Detective Santos was good-looking in a rugged sort of way, his pockmarked skin only partially hidden by a scraggly beard. He smelled of cigarettes and didn't reveal a lot of personality, but I wasn't fooled. I'd spent enough time around police by now to recognize "cop face": the flat, almost emotionless affect many police officers assume while they size up the difficult situations they encounter.

The detective told Duncan, the boat captain waiting to ferry us back to the mainland, that it would be a little while before we could go. He spoke briefly with me, Buzz, and Alicia and then instructed a young uniformed officer to watch over us while he and his team checked out the crime scene and the victim. This took a very long time.

While we were waiting, Major Williston, Paul Halstrom, and Terry Re returned to the harbor—it seemed they had all been out on Terry's boat fishing and enjoying the day. They were told to be available for questioning as well.

I passed the time sending text messages. Most were work-related, but I also let my loved ones know I wouldn't be home in time for dinner. A person did not hold up dinner *chez* Turner, even in the case of murder.

After a spectacular sunset cast the lighthouse tower, the greenery, and our faces in gold and pink light, darkness fell and the fog for which San Francisco is justly famous rolled in off the Pacific Ocean and crept along the shores of the bay. The foghorn blared its mournful moan, and the tower light swept by us with a regular rhythm.

From our position at the harbor, the clutch of keeper's

buildings wasn't visible, but the top of the tower was. I watched it a long time, wondering if any of my new ghost friends—the suicidal woman, the little pirate, or Thorn—would appear, and who among the living would be able to see them if they did.

Finally, after what seemed like hours, Detective Santos returned to take our statements. As soon as he heard that Alicia had been alone in the tower with her abusive ex-husband shortly before his murder, he announced she would have to go to the station for further questioning and to undergo forensic testing.

"I'll call Ellis," I said to Alicia, who nodded numbly. "Don't say *anything* until the lawyer gets there."

"Anything else?" the detective asked me, rather pointedly. "Anything at all?"

The treasure map we had found was burning a hole in my pocket. As Major had said, it was probably nothing, some kind of joke or a child's game. But still.

I pulled it out and showed it to Detective Santos.

He eyed me suspiciously. "You're saying there's buried treasure on the island?"

"I'm not saying anything, actually. It's just that . . . well, my friend Annette Crawford, she's your friend, too, right? She's terrific, isn't she? I mean, a little intimidating, but really terrific." When I get nervous I talk too much. And cops make me nervous. "Anyway, Annette—I mean, Inspector Crawford—always says I should tell her everything, even if it doesn't seem to be directly related to the crime. So that's what I'm doing. I'm telling you everything, which includes this treasure map. It's probably nothing, but really, who knows? Not I, that's for sure. As Annette likes to point out, I'm not a cop, so really, how could I know what's pertinent and what's not? If you see what I mean."

Santos kept his expressionless eyes on me for another long moment before studying the map in his hands.

"All right," he said with a final nod, and tucked the map into his notepad. "Thank you for your help, Ms. Turner. You and Mr. Simoni are free to go. But we might have more questions in the future."

"Remember," I said to Alicia, who remained seated on the bench. "I'll call Ellis as soon as I get a signal. Wait for his lawyer."

"Ah, *jeez*," said Buzz, gazing at Alicia and looking as torn as Dog had been earlier in the day, when Dad and I separated. "Mr. Elrich won't like it if I leave without her."

"We don't have a choice, Buzz," I said, urging him toward the *Callisto*, the small passenger boat waiting to ferry us back to Point Moro. "The police won't allow us to go with her. It's better that you explain what happened to Ellis. She'll be okay."

I wasn't sure whom I was trying to comfort with these words, Buzz or myself.

"Everything okay, Mel?" asked Duncan as we climbed aboard. As usual he wore a navy blue Greek fishing cap and a smile. Duncan was always so upbeat it made me wonder whether the extra-large dose of vitamin D he got from his life on the water made for his sunny disposition. He kept a stack of dog-eared, rather waterlogged paperbacks by his station at the front of the boat to read while standing by to give us rides, which made up most of his job description.

"Does Alicia need me to come back for her?" Duncan continued.

"Ah, *jeez*," muttered Buzz.

"She'll be going with the police to the station," I said.

"I'll call Elrich as soon as I get reception. He'll send someone for her, I'm sure."

"I'm on it," said Buzz, puffing out his chest.

"What happened?" Duncan asked as we headed for shore.

I shook my head and shrugged, hoping I was pulling off the mien of a clueless contractor rather than a material witness to a crime. "A man was killed in the lighthouse. That's about all I know."

"That's . . . terrible. But you're okay?"

"No one else was hurt," I said.

Duncan nodded. There wasn't much else to say.

About halfway to Point Moro, my cell phone started working. I immediately dialed Ellis, who absorbed the stunning news in his usual calm manner.

"Where have they taken Alicia?" Ellis asked. "Is she under arrest?"

"She's still on the island, but they'll be taking her to the Richmond police station," I replied. "The detective didn't formally arrest her, at least not that I saw. But he's clearly suspicious. A Detective Santos is in charge of the case." I lowered my voice and spoke softly so as not to let Buzz or Duncan overhear. "It doesn't look good, Ellis."

"All right. Please ask Buzz to come see me as soon as he can. Thank you, Mel, for calling. I'll take care of it from here."

And with that, he hung up. Though still worried for Alicia, I felt some relief knowing Ellis Elrich was on the case. The man had resources. If anybody could help her, he could.

Next I called Landon.

My boyfriend.

Boyfriend. My mind stuck on that word, for many reasons. It sounded so high-schoolish, like we should be "playing kissy face"—as my father would say—and going steady. Why wasn't there a grown-up name for an adult's love interest? For another thing, I had gone through a doozy of a divorce a few years ago and for a while had sworn off men altogether. And for another, when I met Landon, I already had a boyfriend named Graham.

So that was awkward.

Graham was a wonderful man who had been part of my life, and my father's, for decades, and I genuinely hoped we could remain friends. Recently he had signed a yearlong contract to consult on green building techniques in Paris. He still wanted me to join him in France, and occasionally tried to tempt me with e-mails and photos of pastries and little wrought-iron balconies. But before he left I had come to believe we wanted different things in life . . . and then I met the quirky, absentminded mathematician named Landon.

My heart fluttered at the sound of Landon's voice on the phone, and a welcome warmth surged along my skin as I shivered from the bay's cold wind and spray. My light jacket had been fine for a temperate winter's day, but was wholly inadequate once the sun had gone down.

"*Mel.* Where are you?" Landon asked. "Are you all right? I was about to rent a boat to come after you myself."

"Yes, I'm sorry. I would have called earlier, but my cell phone doesn't work on the island."

"I figured as much. You're sure you're okay? According to your father, you must have found a body, or a ghost, or both."

"Dad knows me well."

"Which was it?" Landon's tone was grim.

"A bit of both, actually. I'll explain when I get there. How was dinner?"

"Excellent, as always—a culinary delight your father referred to as 'Turner Steak.'"

"I love Turner Steak," I said, a wistful note in my voice. My stomach growled. Turner Steak was one of my father's specialties: slow-cooked beef with onions and mushrooms in a rich brown gravy, served over rice. It was a classic comfort food, reminding me of my childhood, of home and safety. Just thinking about it brought the sting of tears to the backs of my eyes.

"Your dad saved you a plate. It was a nice dinner. Stan was as friendly as ever, and regaled us with stories from his childhood in Bull Hill, Oklahoma. Caleb still doesn't care for me, but I'm working on him. There's a postcard of Paris from your ex-boyfriend placed prominently on the refrigerator. And Stephen joined us, of course. He is now plagued by blisters, a complaint which appears to confuse your father."

This summed up my life lately. After a difficult divorce I had moved into my parents' house when my mother passed away suddenly and Dad needed my help. Stan Tomassi, an old family friend, lived with us and managed the Turner Construction home office. My teenage ex-stepson, Caleb, now also resided full-time with Dad and me; we were very close, though he hadn't forgiven me for ending my relationship with Graham, and blamed Landon for the breakup. My good friend Stephen had been evicted when his San Francisco apartment house converted to condos; he couldn't find an affordable apartment so was temporarily sleeping on our couch, and because his barista job in San Francisco was no longer worth the commute, I'd given him a menial job with Turner Construction. Stephen wasn't cut out for hard manual labor, but there wasn't a

lot of demand for his true talent, which was dress design-
ing, Vegas showgirl–style.

Landon had joined this already full household for a
short time while his Berkeley apartment was being fu-
migated for termites. My Dad couldn't hold a grudge
against anyone who loved his cooking, so even though
he was still very fond of Graham, he had warmed up to
Landon.

So that was my life: I worked all day, most days, almost
exclusively with men, and lived with a passel of them as
well. Even Dog was a boy. If it weren't for a few clients
and my best friend Luz—and now Waquisha—I would
have no women in my life at all. And that was not accept-
able. I'd grown up with a mother and two sisters, and
missed feminine company. I dreamed of a jobsite full of
hardworking women. Not to be sexist, but I was willing
to bet the porta potties would stay a darned sight cleaner.

"Well," I said to Landon, "I'll be at Point Moro in a
few minutes, home in another half an hour or so."

"Why don't I come pick you up?" suggested Landon.

"That's sweet, but how would I get my car in the
morning?"

"I'll bring you back before my class tomorrow. I want
to see you."

The warmth I had felt at the sound of his voice ratch-
eted up to full-on fire in my veins.

Still, it was a long drive from Oakland to Richmond, and
there was no need for him to waste the time and gas. Point
Moro wasn't exactly on the way to UC Berkeley, where
Landon was a math professor. Not to mention that I didn't
relish the idea of waiting for him on the dark, virtually
deserted Point Moro docks.

"I'll be home soon, I promise. I'll go directly, do not
pass go, do not collect two hundred dollars."

"I'm sorry?"

Although American by birth, Landon had an unusual upbringing, and by and large didn't get my oh-so-clever pop culture references. The fact that I found this cute instead of annoying was an indication of how enamored I was of him.

I translated, "I'll come straight home, and won't stop for ghosts, or murder, or anything of the sort."

"Or salvage yards?"

"Or salvage yards. I promise."

"*Good.* I'll be waiting with a plate of Turner Steak."

Chapter Seven

Morning came all too soon.

I sat at the pine table in the kitchen of a big old farmhouse in the Fruitvale section of Oakland. Hunched over a steaming cup of coffee, I was doing my best to avoid the gazes of several of the men in my life.

Caleb was glaring at me because Landon had spent the night. Stephen was glaring at me because I had told him he had to be ready to leave for work by six thirty. And my father was glaring at me because, as usual, I had (politely) refused breakfast, and because I had tripped over yet another body.

Dog was staring at me because he was hoping for some bacon.

"It's not my fault," I whined, feeling that covered just about everything but the bacon.

Landon was still upstairs, probably all ruffled-looking and adorable, spread-eagled under my soft down duvet. If I hadn't been juggling four different construction projects, I would have gone back upstairs to join him, hiding under the covers.

"What else?" demanded Dad.

"What do you mean, what else?"

"You found a body, and I presume there was a ghost or two hanging around. C'mon, fess up."

"Yeah," said Caleb. "It's a lighthouse, after all. Seems like a natural for a ghost."

Stan wheeled in and poured himself a cup of coffee. "Oooh, can't wait to hear this," he said with his Oklahoma drawl.

Stan had worked construction with my dad for decades, but several years ago a moment of carelessness had led to a bad fall off a roof, and he was now in a wheelchair. While Stan went through months of rehab in the hospital, my parents renovated a downstairs room to make it wheelchair accessible. Not long after Stan moved in, my mother passed away suddenly and Stan had supported my father in his grief—as well as roping me into taking over as head of Turner Construction. Now the two men were like an aging married couple who quarreled and finished each other's sentences and couldn't do without each other.

"At last, an ally," I said, getting up to give Stan a kiss on the cheek. "Good morning, Stan."

"Mornin', gorgeous. What's up? You find another body?"

"More like *it* found *me*. Landed right at my feet at the bottom of the lighthouse stairs, as a matter of fact."

Now four pairs of eyes looked at me with concern.

A fifth pair, belonging to Dog, was still focused on the plate of bacon.

"Are you saying there was a murderer *nearby*?" Stephen asked. "As in, up in the *tower*?"

I had gone through all of this with Landon when I got home last night, until I had begged him—for the sake of

A GHOSTLY LIGHT 59

my mental health—not to ask any more questions. I understood their concern, though. My loved ones were worried that I might be seriously hurt one of these days, and I couldn't blame them. There was no denying that I ran into more outright danger than the average general contractor. What I didn't know was how to change the situation. For the most part, I didn't seek out ghosts. Instead, they found *me*, and wouldn't go away until I was able to give them what they needed.

For the moment, anyway, this seemed to be my lot in life: trip over a body, see a ghost—or be seen *by* a ghost—then bumble around for a while, doing my best to keep my renovation projects on schedule while chasing after murderers and urging spirits to continue their journey to the great beyond.

It was all a little overwhelming when I laid it out like that.

"No one knows exactly where the murderer was," I hedged.

"Was there a *ghost* in the tower?" Dad asked.

I hesitated.

"Mel?" Dad urged.

"Some say there's a ghost in the tower, sure."

"Are you saying a *ghost* killed this guy? Because sorry to be the one to point it out, Mel, but even if that were true, it wouldn't look good for your friend Alicia," said Dad. "Can't imagine the police would be satisfied with that explanation."

"You're right about that. And no, I'm not suggesting a ghost killed Thorn. As far as I can tell, ghosts can't hurt anyone, much less kill them, even if they wanted to."

"I saw a show on TV where the people were accosted by ghosts, and they woke up with bruises and cuts and everything," said Caleb.

"That'd be demons, not ghosts," I said, sipping my coffee. "I'm pretty sure."

"You're suggesting a *demon* killed this guy?" demanded Stan.

"I don't—"

"*Wait.* You're dealing with demonic forces now?" Stephen asked, his voice scaling up as he tossed scoop after scoop of sugar in his coffee. As if he weren't naturally amped up. "I don't have to work on that place, do I? I already have blisters, and . . . maybe I'm more suited to office work."

"*No*," I said with a vehement shake of my head. "*No demons.* Everyone just calm down, please. A *human* killed Thorn, who, by the way, was a pretty despicable guy. Not that he deserved to be murdered, but just saying. I'm not losing a lot of sleep over it." At least I wouldn't be if he hadn't appeared to me in ghost form. I fervently hoped Thorn wasn't going to become a permanent feature at the "Spirit of the Lighthouse Inn."

Though, now that I thought about it, it sort of fit the name.

"Besides," I continued, "I'm sure soon the police will find the guilty party, and all will be well."

"Unless they think your friend Alicia did it," piped up Caleb. "'Cause then they won't bother looking for another suspect, right? And for all you know, you'll be working on an isolated island with a murderer lurking nearby."

We all fell silent for a moment.

Landon appeared in the kitchen doorway, dressed in his usual attire: an old-fashioned jacket, his longish hair and trim beard making him seem like a man from another era, like one of those romantic Civil War–era photographs of broad-shouldered, sloe-eyed soldiers.

He gave me a slow smile.

And said, "Mel, from now on I'm going to go to work with you."

I choked on my coffee. Caleb pounded me a tad too hard on the back, and Dog barked and danced around the kitchen at the commotion.

"I appreciate the offer, Landon, but I really don't need a bodyguard," I managed to say when I recovered. I had to raise my voice to be heard over the sound of Dad snorting. "And if I ever *do*, I'll borrow one of Ellis's. He's got plenty. They're licensed to carry and everything."

"Be that as it may," said Landon, accepting a cup of coffee from my dad with a warm smile of thanks. Landon has a strangely inflected speaking style, stemming from having been raised partly in the US, partly in England, and entirely oddly. He reminded me of a refugee from a Shakespearean acting troupe.

"Besides, you have class today, remember?" I said. "As do you, Caleb, so get your stuff together. Responsibilities, people! We're leaving in five. Did you finish the last of your college applications?"

Landon's eyes were still on me, and I could feel the heat of a blush in my cheeks, remembering last night. *Good heavens, no more sleepovers at Dad's house.* This was ridiculous.

"Hey, you two, get a room," said Stephen.

"Says the guy sleeping on my couch," grumbled Dad. "Anyway, Landon, good idea: You stick with Mel whenever she goes out to the island, there's a good man. Ignore her nonsense about feminism and what all."

"Says the man who insisted his daughters learn the trade on Turner Construction jobsites every summer," I grumbled. "Where, I might point out, we were the *only* females."

"Good habits begin early," Dad groused. "You know the old saying, 'train a child right . . .'"

"And she'll take over your business and support you in your old age?" Stan suggested.

"Nothing wrong with a little hard work," Dad and I said in unison, then looked at each other. I added, in my perkiest tone of voice, "As luck would have it, I'll be working in San Francisco today, not on Lighthouse Island, which happens to be a closed crime scene at the moment anyway. So no worries."

"You'll come up with something," grumbled Dad. "You're like the Calamity Jane of the ghostly set."

"Thanks, Dad," I said, giving his grizzled cheek a kiss, and slipping Dog a small piece of bacon. "Why don't I take Dog with me today?"

"I thought you just said you weren't messing with anything ghost-related," Dad said.

"I just want to give him some car time."

Actually, it was possible I'd see a ghost today since I promised a Realtor friend I'd check out a hundred-year-old house, and one never knew. But I wasn't going to open *that* can of worms.

Dog was the only member of my family who shared my ability to sense ghosts. I used to find it comforting, back when I worried I might be losing my mind because I saw things no one else did. Now having Dog at my side was like carrying a canary in a coal mine—he often sensed things before I did. But today I wanted to bring Dog along primarily to keep up with the desensitization process designed to curb his carsickness. He was getting a lot better about it, and I wanted to keep it that way.

"Will you and Stan pull together the revised estimates for Lighthouse Island today?" I asked my father. "I'll need to run those by Elrich, and then submit them to the vendors as soon as possible. Also, we have to be sure everything is ADA compliant."

Dad nodded. "Unless we put an elevator in the tower, that'll still be a problem, but otherwise the main floor of the main house, and the foghorn house and outbuildings will be accessible. I took measurements for the ramp up to the porch."

"Perfect. Thanks. We can go over the estimates tonight and put in the preliminary materials orders tomorrow."

"You really think this project is going to stay on track, given all that's happened?" Stan asked.

"Sure. The police usually release the scene within a few days." This wasn't my first rodeo, after all.

"But Mel, if Alicia's charged with murder . . . ," said Landon.

At the thought of Alicia under police suspicion, my stomach clenched again. I wouldn't have slept a wink last night if it hadn't been for Landon distracting me.

"She won't be. I'm sure of it. Ellis won't let that happen. And besides, she didn't do it."

He nodded. "If you say so."

"I *do* say so. I'm betting we'll be back on the job within the week."

I just hoped that bet was a sure one.

The morning air was crisp and cold; it was the middle of winter, Bay Area–style, which meant I wore a sweatshirt covered with a light windbreaker. My friends who moved from places like Canada assured me that I didn't know what true cold was. I believed them, and, not being overly fond of the cold, saw no reason to confirm this for myself. Landon carried the heavy cardboard box with my job files out to the car. I lugged the old toolbox that Caleb had decorated for me with Magic Markers, back when he was young and sweet and still thought I was cool.

"Promise me you won't go to the island without me," Landon said as he stowed the files in the back of my boxy Scion.

"Landon . . . here's the thing: I appreciate your concern for my well-being, I really do. But I'm not used to anyone telling me what to do, or what *not* to do."

"I believe, if you recall our conversation, that I have not once told you what to do, or what not to do. I simply exhorted you to inform me when you're going to the island, and allow me to accompany you."

I stared at him.

"Please, Mel. I'm not telling you, I'm *asking* you. Exhorting you."

I smiled. "And you 'exhort' so well."

We shared a kiss. His lips were soft and hard at the same time, and desire coursed through me, making me wonder if there was any way in the world to sneak back upstairs.

But Landon pulled away as Stephen approached, clearing his throat in an exaggerated way. My friend was wearing the new steel-toed boots I had bought him, and already had on his big leather gloves. Tall and thin, he looked like a gawky kid playing dress-up.

Stephen nodded toward the side of the house, where my sullen stepson emerged, heavy backpack slung over one shoulder. Caleb gave Landon a huge, totally fake smile, pushed past us without a word, climbed into the back of the car with Dog, and slammed the door.

Stephen winked and climbed into the front passenger's seat.

"Sorry," I whispered to Landon.

"I am undaunted."

"Good."

"And this Graham character was obviously quite a man."

"Yes, he was. He *is*."

"Hmmm." Landon raised one eyebrow. "This fellow's really starting to get on my nerves."

I smiled. "No need to worry."

"And Lighthouse Island?"

"Access will be restricted for at least a day or two anyway, plus I've got to check in with my San Francisco projects, as well as the one in Marin. Also, I promised a Realtor I'd go look at a house near the Grand Lake Theatre, in Oakland."

"A colleague of mine lives in that neighborhood; I've always liked it. It's a little urban oasis."

"Me too."

Our eyes held a little too long.

"You're headed to campus, then?" I said.

He nodded. "Just as soon as I have a good breakfast."

"You know the way to my father's heart, anyway."

"As luck would have it, I feel very privileged to be cooked a hearty breakfast before a long day of teaching."

We shared another quick kiss, and then I climbed in behind the wheel and took off, accompanied by my sullen ex-stepson, an underqualified construction worker, and a semi-carsick dog.

Just another day in the life of Mel Turner, general contractor.

Chapter Eight

I dropped Caleb off at his private school in an upscale section of San Francisco known as Pacific Heights, not far from his father's house.

Caleb's living arrangement was unusual, and it aroused a lot of questions in people accustomed to more traditional definitions of family. But it worked for us. I had been married to Caleb's dad for eight years, from the time Caleb was five to the age of thirteen. The only thing I missed from the marriage was being Caleb's stepmom. Happily, Caleb turned out to be as loath to give me up as I was to leave him behind, so even after the divorce we spent a lot of time together. My job was hectic but flexible, and although Caleb's mother loved him dearly, she was a busy financial power broker who had trouble setting—and sticking to—limits on her work schedule, and couldn't give him the time and attention an adolescent needed. Caleb's father, Daniel, had married for a third time, and his current wife not only didn't care much for teenagers but had recently given birth to a baby who was, according to reports, "practically perfect in every way."

So when Caleb had started getting into teenage-style trouble and needed more adult supervision, I intervened. Caleb now lived with us in Oakland most of the time, Dad had taken him on as a grandson—Dad had absolutely no problem setting boundaries—and so far we had made it work.

Caleb's attitude toward Landon was annoying, but I was hoping it would resolve itself with time. And he was looking forward to going to college in the fall, anyway, which would probably be a good transition for us all.

I adored my stepson with a love beyond all reason, and yet I was very happy to drop him off at school so he could work his sullen magic on his teachers and classmates instead of me.

"He'll find his way," said Stephen as we watched Caleb hitch his heavy backpack onto his shoulder, head down, and pass through the elaborately carved, arched entrance of his private high school.

"He'd best find it soon," I threatened.

Stephen chuckled. "Yeah, right, because otherwise you'll, what? Kick him out? Slap him upside his head? Go sell it somewhere else, Mel. You're a marshmallow, just like your dad."

"I thought you were scared of my dad."

"Only superficially. I'm sure I'll get to the squishy center soon."

I smiled as I pulled back into traffic. "Makes us sound like Easter Peeps."

"I was thinking the chocolate-covered marshmallow reindeer I get every year in my stocking at Christmas."

"You still get chocolate-covered marshmallow reindeer in your Christmas stocking?"

"Is that weird?" He blushed. "It's weird, isn't it? I'm unnaturally close to my mother."

"Nothing unnatural about it. At least I *hope* not—I really don't want to know that much about you." I laughed. Steven was the adored only child of a former Vegas showgirl. His dress designs were no doubt influenced by a childhood spent hanging out backstage, and featured lots of spangles and fringe. I loved his designs and wore them often, even to work. Dressing any darned way I pleased was one of the little perks of running a company and signing the checks. "But then you're talking to a grown woman who lives with her father, so you'll get no grief from me."

"Claire thinks it's bizarre." Claire was a whiskey-drinking, cigarette-smoking landscape designer with whom Stephen had a love-hate relationship. Lately I'd had the sneaking suspicion there was more love there than either would admit, but since they weren't asking for my opinion I kept those thoughts to myself.

"I love Claire, but I'm not sure I would take relationship advice from her. Especially when it comes to family. She had a pretty rough upbringing."

He nodded, staring out the window, absorbed in thought. Or maybe he was sleeping. Either way, I was free to drive in silence, and to ponder what had happened yesterday.

I had tried Alicia's number last night and again this morning, but the calls went straight to voice mail. Then I called Ellis, who told me he had gotten her a good lawyer, and that Alicia had been released from questioning very early this morning. He had no further information, but at least she hadn't been arrested.

Yet.

I drove to a project on Russian Hill, escorted Stephen onto the jobsite, told him to apply sunscreen even though it was a cold January day, and asked a young worker named Enrique to keep an eye on him. Then I met with my foreman, answered a question about the sensor on the automatic lights, and checked the lumber supplies. This was a relatively small job: We were building a deck in the rear garden, putting in a new set of French doors leading out from the kitchen, and installing a kitchenette to turn a downstairs bedroom suite into an in-law unit with a separate entrance. These days Turner Construction focused mostly on larger projects, but my dad had renovated this home a decade ago, when he was still running things and my mom was alive, and it was company policy to take care of good clients. Which was why, from time to time, I found myself crawling out of my bed at three in the morning to tend to sewer mishaps or electrical failures.

With Stephen gone, Dog claimed shotgun and jumped into the copilot's seat.

Next, we checked in with my foreman at a "Painted Lady" Victorian renovation in the Haight, then fielded a call from a custom door manufacturer trying to explain where the hell my already-two-months-late special order was.

I checked the time on my phone. I was meeting Brittany Humm, my Realtor friend, in Oakland at eleven, which meant I had forty-five minutes to kill.

"Let's look through the lighthouse file," I said to Dog, who was dozing but was always happy to be included. "What do you say?"

He thumped his tail.

"I'll take that as a yes."

I dug the dossier on Lighthouse Island out of the file box.

Months ago, when Ellis Elrich first asked me to check out the buildings on the island, Stan helped me research the basic history of the island on the Internet. The Coast Guard was in charge of lighthouses in California; they maintained a website devoted to lighthouses and the keepers who had tended them over the years until modernization had rendered them obsolete.

I had read this all before, of course, but now thumbed through the downloaded pages looking for something that might cast light on the origins of the lighthouse's ghosts: the woman at the top of the tower, or the young boy on the shore. Or maybe even something that might offer a clue to yesterday's murder.

The lighthouse had been proposed in the late 1860s, when ships were crowding the strait, carrying goods and gold from inland areas to San Francisco and back again. The construction of the Mare Island military facility further increased the ship traffic, so in 1870 the lighthouse authority allocated funds and decided upon building designs. Construction began in 1871, and was completed the following year. The island posed two special challenges: the need to provide sufficient water for the residents and the steam whistle foghorn—hence the rainwater shed and cistern—and the difficulty in maintaining the docks, which were vulnerable during bad storms.

That was . . . worrying. I hadn't imagined the bay—which was typically serene—could host storms violent enough to tear apart the docks on the island. I hoped we wouldn't witness such ravages this winter while we were under construction.

Once built, the lighthouse was tended by keepers and their assistants until 1953, when technological advances rendered their service unnecessary. I glanced at the list of names and dates: R. B. Mathews, 1872–1886; D. P. Page, 1886–1899; G. H. Vigilance, 1899–1905; I. P. Vigilance, 1905–1915; O. C. Shell, 1915-1927; J. R. Wright, 1927–1947; R. P. Andrews, 1947–1953.

There were grainy black-and-white photos of the buildings, as well as a few portraits of stern-looking, bewhiskered men standing on the porch steps of the Keeper's House or posed in the doorway to the tower, proudly accepting their official commissions as keepers of the lighthouse. But there were no photographs of children, or of a woman who might have hurled herself off the lighthouse tower. And no clues as to what might still be worth killing for on the island.

Which reminded me . . . surely that treasure map had been of no significance, right? Maps to buried treasure were a staple of fiction, not reality. As Major Williston had suggested, it was probably part of a game of some sort. I wondered: Did the Scouts ever camp out on Lighthouse Island?

My phone beeped. I answered a text about an earthquake retrofit, then glanced at the Oakland address of the old home Brittany had asked me to check out. Just in case there were any resident ghosts.

The thing was, Brittany was actually *hoping* I would detect a house spirit or two. It surprised the heck out of me, but apparently some folks liked the idea of living with souls from beyond the veil. I supposed as long as everyone—alive and dead—had the right attitude, it could be an interesting arrangement.

I didn't usually oblige Realtors this way, but Brittany was one of my first ghost-related friends, who had lent a sympathetic ear—and some valuable insights—when I first became aware of my ability to communicate with spirits. Besides, I wouldn't mind landing a job in my hometown for a change.

So Dog and I headed back over the Bay Bridge toward Oakland. Just a contractor and her pup, on the hunt for spirits. The way we do.

I met Brittany outside a house in the Grand Lake neighborhood, which was clear across town from my father's house. Twenty years ago this area had been considered "transitional," by which folks meant run-down and a little on the trashy side. But in the last couple of decades Oakland had been rising like a phoenix, stepping out of the shadow of its much more famous sister to the west, San Francisco.

Before the original Bay Bridge was completed in the fall of 1936, Oakland had been the major city in Northern California, and a crucial stop on the train line, to which a gorgeous downtown full of Art Deco architecture still gave testament. After World War II, the city underwent a sharp decline, but recently that had been changing. San Francisco had become too expensive for artists and immigrants and pretty much anyone who wasn't stinking rich, and Oakland was the beneficiary. Rising house prices and a hot real estate market reflected Oakland's new desirability.

So it was unusual to find a big old home that had sat empty and essentially abandoned for two years. The house I was looking at had been built in the Bay Area Arts and Crafts style, which was characterized by simple but elegant wood construction, numerous built-ins, and, in this case at least, a lot of grand windows.

"The home was built in 1911, and the last owners lived here for more than fifty years," said Brittany after we'd traded hellos and got caught up on the latest goings-on in our lives. Brittany was exceedingly blond and perky, and always well put-together, which would have made me dislike her if she weren't so nice. "Their names were Victoria and Ziggy Wittowski. Ziggy passed away in 2015, and Victoria moved into a skilled nursing facility until she passed away a few months ago. They had no children, so a niece inherited the place. But she's up in Alaska and hasn't been very interested in it."

"She doesn't want to relocate?" I asked, scanning the facade of the house, which, for some reason, seemed awfully familiar. I wondered why; I wasn't well acquainted with this neighborhood and hadn't done much work in the area. "I thought everyone wanted to move to California."

"I guess she prefers Alaska. If she put a little money into fixing it up, she could sell it for a lot more than she's asking, but she just wants to be rid of it."

This surprised me. I loved my city, and the home's location was especially nice. The beautiful old place on a hill was within easy walking distance of Lake Merritt and the newly invigorated Lakeshore-Grand shopping area, which was chock-full of cafés and boutiques and restaurants, as well as the huge old 1920s Grand Lake Theatre.

"Okay if I bring Dog in?" I asked. "He's a good ghost dog."

"Sure! I love Dog, and the house is empty anyway."

Brittany and Dog shared a happy reunion, and then we climbed the front steps to a side porch and unlocked the front door. A sunroom opened onto a grand paneled entry, with wooden Moroccan-arched doorways leading off in several directions and a large landing on the stairwell that looked big enough to be a stage.

The house had the distinctive, musty scent of a vacant home that was meant to be filled with life and energy and furniture. Still, for a place that hadn't been lived in for a long time, it was in great shape. Phenomenal shape, actually. Not only had it been well built to begin with, but miraculously the wood finishes hadn't been painted over, and most windows still had their original wavy glass. The stained glass light fixtures appeared original as well, and the electrical switches featured mother-of-pearl buttons.

Sometimes a little neglect is good for a house. Brittany had warned me about ugly 1970s-era bathrooms and kitchen, but otherwise this home appeared to have avoided any major wretched remodels.

But something was wrong.

As we stood in the entryway, I had a vision of a set of curtains made of bed sheets, hanging on a piece of clothesline, strung across the landing at the bottom of the stairs. Children were putting on some sort of performance, and chairs were set out in the main hallway for the grown-ups.

A vision, or a memory? Surely this wasn't an actual memory. I'd never set foot in this house before. Maybe it reminded me of something out of a movie, or a photo I'd seen.

But I couldn't shake the feeling that I had been here before. I knew the home's layout: To the right was the dining room with a built-in hutch and bar on one wall, a swinging door to the butler's pantry on another wall, and a bowed wall of windows overlooking the garden. The swinging door was propped open ever since the accident that broke a favorite platter one Thanksgiving. Off the hallway to the left, a massive set of French doors opened onto a living room with a beautifully beamed cathedral ceiling and huge windows on two sides. The Christmas tree would sit in front of the east-facing window. To one side was a fireplace with an inglenook made of wooden benches that doubled as storage. Puzzles were kept in one bench, blankets in the other. How could I possibly know—much less *remember*—such things?

I started feeling dizzy. Oh, *great*. Was I going to start experiencing vertigo while standing on flat land?

"Mel? Everything all right?" asked Brittany.

Her voice brought me back to the here and now. "Yes, I . . . sure."

"Did you see something?"

"No. I mean yes. I mean, no, not a ghost, anyway. But . . . it's the oddest thing. I feel like I've been here before."

"You mean like déjà vu?"

"Sort of." I glanced down at Dog, who was sniffing around but seemed entirely unperturbed. Clearly he was not sensing anything. So what was this feeling? "Maybe . . . could my parents have done work on this place when I was a kid, do you think?"

"I suppose it's possible," Brittany said. "Though I don't think the former owners did much of anything, other than the bathrooms and the kitchen, which look home-remodeled to me. But you're the expert."

"Who was the architect, again?"

"His name was John Hudson Thomas. In his day he was ranked up there with the likes of Bernard Maybeck and Julia Morgan, but he isn't nearly as well-known to-day, possibly because he didn't design many public build-ings. He focused on residential projects in the East Bay; you'll find his houses all through Berkeley and Oakland and Piedmont."

"Have you been in any of his other houses?" Maybe I'd visited another place he had built, which reminded me of this one.

"Sure, I've seen several. His style is very distinctive; a lot of the design elements are repeated, such as the pattern of the windowpanes and the foursquare pattern of raised tiles." She gestured toward four wooden tiles arranged to form a simple square.

"What about the homes' layouts? Are they similar as well?"

She shook her head. "Not that I've seen. As far as I know his houses were all custom built to each client's specifications. This house was, for sure. I can't imagine there's another quite like it. Isn't it special?"

"Yes, it's beautiful. So, let me guess: The doorway over there leads to a small study, and beyond that is a bedroom and bathroom, right?"

Brittany's eyebrows rose. "Right. That's some pretty powerful déjà vu."

"If Thomas was a well-known architect, maybe I've seen photos of this house in a book, or on a website. Or maybe . . . maybe I saw the blueprints and conjured the house in my imagination?"

Brittany smiled. "I suppose it's possible. Do you look at old sets of archived blueprints in your spare time, then?"

"Not really," I said. "But I swear I know this house. Off the kitchen is a door that opens onto a small hallway. It leads to the rear door, as well as a small room with a sink, and a WC. It's the maid's room; a servant used to live there."

Brittany blinked. "Um, yes, pretty much."

"This is so weird." I glanced down at my canine companion. He tended to do a strange mewling, barky thing when he sensed spirits. But at the moment he seemed fine; a little bothered, perhaps, by the lack of interesting morsels of food anywhere, but otherwise completely mellow. Making me doubt myself. "What am I sensing?"

"You got me," Brittany said, concerned. "I thought I was open-minded with all the ghost stuff. But this seems like something else, doesn't it? Do you want to keep going? We can leave if it's bothering you."

"I'm okay," I said, shaking my head. "Let's keep going."

The wide central stairway with shallow steps led to an upstairs landing. There was a small storage closet with a wooden laundry chute, as well as three bedrooms, one with a small enclosed porch. A large bathroom had a claw-foot tub and a separate shower; it had been redone in ugly seventies colors and styles, yet I could see how it used to be: seafoam green walls, white subway tiles, a pedestal sink. And Brittany had been right: This looked nothing like a Turner Construction remodel, even from the early days. The peeling linoleum tiles and pitted grout job were signs of a do-it-yourselfer.

Still, I anticipated every view, knew where every closet was. I could hear my mother's voice: *The old closets had windows in them so the clothes didn't get stuffy.*

"I'm . . . I'm sorry, Brittany, I can't go any further."

"Of course. Whatever you say, Mel; I apologize if this has upset you. I just hoped you'd be able to tell me about any possible lingering spirits . . ."

"Have you had any reports of ghosts here?"

"No, not at all. I only thought there might be something because of the age of the place. Hoped, I suppose."

"I'm not sensing any spirits," I said. "But I can't shake this feeling of familiarity. It's too . . . weird. I feel spooked."

"I'm really sorry! I got nothing but good vibes from this place. I thought you'd like it."

"I do, I mean, I sort of love it, actually. But . . ."

"But you sense something bad?"

"Not bad, no. Just . . . weird."

"Let's call it a day, then, shall we?"

As Brittany locked the door, I stood on the front lawn and gazed at the house, wondering how a place I had never seen before could feel so darned familiar.

Clearly I had a lot more to learn about the exciting, multilayered world of ghost busting.

Chapter Nine

I told Brittany I'd be in touch, and she waved as she drove off in her shiny new Prius. Dog jumped into the passenger's seat of my battered little Scion, and I climbed behind the wheel, but paused before starting the engine.

"Is it just me, or was there something really strange going on in there?"

Dog's head lolled over to me. Not that I expected him to answer. Dog was the hairy, silent type. Except for an occasional fit of maniacal barking, but that was usually squirrel-related.

"I mean, it wasn't a ghost, right? I mean, not a *ghost* ghost. You didn't do that weird mewling thing you do around spirits."

He thumped his tail. I smiled and petted his head. Just the feel of his silky hair under my fingers made me feel calmer, more centered.

Dog shed a lot, but he was a great copilot.

Back in San Francisco I parked in a lot whose attendant was an animal lover and always made a big fuss over Dog.

He agreed to watch Dog for me while I went to the city's permit office, where I politely harassed the new guy at the counter until he called his manager, Jordan, over. Jordan and I go way back. He knew I was a pain in his neck, but also that I was a stickler for adhering to the city's building codes. After some good-natured ribbing, he agreed to expedite my permits for a job in Cow Hollow.

On the street I passed a cart selling Belgian waffles sprinkled with powdered sugar. They smelled like heaven, and put me in mind of Luz Cabrera. I checked the time; if I remembered correctly, she had office hours around now.

Luz and I had been friends for years, and she was my touchstone whenever my life started to feel unmanageable. Such occasions weren't as rare as one would hope, even *before* I started seeing spirits. And she had a sweet tooth.

I bought two waffles, gave one to the parking attendant along with my thanks and a healthy tip for dogsitting, shared a very small taste of waffle with Dog, and drove over to the urban campus of San Francisco State University, where Luz was a professor in the School of Social Work.

Dog and I waited outside her open office door, unintentionally eavesdropping as a tearful student tried to explain that, although she had managed to show up for only two classes that semester and hadn't completed the final paper, she felt a failing grade was unfair because "I tried really hard but this class is a lot of work and I have other classes, too, you know." I imagined the expression on Luz's face. Luz had clawed her way out of a difficult neighborhood in East LA, won a scholarship to an Ivy League school, and is smarter than almost anyone I know. She doesn't do excuses.

The student finally gave up and stormed out, threatening to report Luz to the department chair.

I poked my head through the open door. Luz was sipping a mug of coffee and perusing something on her computer screen. She looked singularly unfazed.

"Everything okay?" I asked.

"Mel! C'mon in. And Daw-ugh, too." She came around the desk to give me a quick hug and Dog a proper hello, rubbing his neck and accepting a kiss. "He's not strictly legal in here, you know."

"I'm calling him my therapy dog."

"Good. I could use some therapy of the four-legged variety."

"I brought you a snack," I said, handing her the waffle bag.

"Mmmmm, waffles! Awesome." She returned to her seat behind the desk and extracted her treat, while I collapsed into the chair opposite.

"Everything okay with your student?" I asked.

"What student?"

"The young woman who just left . . . threatening to report you to your department chair."

"She should go, with my blessing." Luz bit into the waffle and let out a little moan of pleasure. Then she shrugged. "My chair knows the score. Some students— not all of them, thank goodness—think paying tuition guarantees them a passing grade. I keep trying to explain that what they're paying for is the *opportunity* to learn, and they have to put in the time and effort necessary to produce results. I design my courses, do plenty of research, write lectures and plans, put extra resources up on my Web page, link to writing tutors and life coaches and—heaven forbid—the library. But if a student's not willing to help herself, no one else can help her. She'll figure it out eventually—either that, or crash and burn."

"Or the crashing and burning will help her figure it out."

She nodded but seemed far more interested in the waffle than her student's failing grade.

"Speaking of crashing and burning . . . ," I said.

"Uh-oh," Luz said, using a napkin to brush powdered sugar from her lips. "More ghosts? Or bodies? Or both?"

"I see I'm gaining a disturbing reputation."

"Which is it?" Alarm lit her eyes and she cast a glance around the small office. "Nothing followed you here, did it? I would *really* like for this to be a safe space."

Luz wasn't fond of ghosts. At all. A few months ago she'd had what I thought was something of a break-through with the spirit world when she came to the aid of a lost ghost looking for a way home. Apparently I was overly optimistic: While Luz didn't seem quite as freaked out as she used to be, she was still wary.

"No worries. I left him, or *them*, on the island."

"Lighthouse Island? That's sort of cool though, right? Seems only natural a lighthouse would have a ghost or two hanging around. Sailors lost at sea, shipwreck victims who wash ashore, lighthouse keepers who can't bear to leave their posts . . ."

"There might be some historic spirits there, true. But the guy I'm most worried about is Alicia Withers's ex, a man named Thorn Walker. Her abusive ex. He fell down the stairs of the tower yesterday. And died."

Luz raised an eyebrow. "An accident?"

I shook my head. "He had a knife in his chest, so that seems a little suspicious. The police suspect Alicia."

Luz snorted. "Alicia? That's ridiculous. Unless . . . was he trying to hurt her? Was it self-defense?"

"That was the first question I asked her. She said no, he wasn't trying to hurt her."

"Still, it could be more complicated," Luz mused. "There are cases of abused women going after their abusers years later, in what's seen as a kind of delayed PTSD. I could put you in touch with some specialists in domestic abuse and its long-term effects if Alicia's defense lawyer needs an expert witness."

"Thank you, Luz, I'll let you know if it gets to that point. At the moment, the police are just talking to her. I'm hoping the evidence will point to her innocence."

"Let's hope so. Please give her my best."

"I'll do that. But that wasn't actually what I wanted to talk to you about."

"You okay? Now that you mention it, you seem a little worried."

"I'm spooked, to tell you the truth. I just checked out a house in Oakland, for my Realtor friend, Brittany, who wanted to know if it might be haunted. It's a really great old place, and I didn't see any ghosts—and neither did Dog. But when I went inside, it was like a case of déjà vu—only ten times stronger. I *knew* the house. I knew the layout, the floor plan, everything, like I know the back of my hand. Every inch of that house was familiar. It was downright spooky."

"Was it a place your parents worked on, at some point?"

I shook my head. "I'll check with my dad to make sure, but I don't think so. The former owners had lived there for fifty years, and it didn't look like they'd had any professional renovations done."

"You see a lot of houses. Could you have just guessed the floor plan?"

"There was more to it than that, Luz. There was an old laundry chute; I knew exactly where to find it and had a memory of climbing into it, and sliding down. Outside there was a garden shed that used to be a playhouse, and my mother—"

My voice caught. Though I'm an adult and my mother passed several years ago, losing her was such a great loss that, from time to time, the grief slammed into me like a body blow, out of the blue.

"—I remember my mother being there. Somehow. It was as if I could see her sitting on the window seat in front of the fire. And her hands . . . I looked down at my hands, and it was as though *my* hands were *her* hands."

Luz nodded, almost imperceptibly. She wasn't a therapist, though she taught in the School of Social Work. Luz was more comfortable with psychological theory than with practice, and always said she didn't enjoy hearing about other people's problems because she had enough of her own, thank you very much. Luckily, she made an exception for me.

"So what do you think? Am I nuts?" I asked.

She gave me a small smile. "A little, but not because of this. Two possibilities come to mind. You ready to hear them?"

No.

"Sure," I said. "Fire away."

"Maybe your sensitivity to the supernatural has developed over time, and you have graduated from ghost seer to full-blown psychic."

"I don't like the sound of that. Seeing ghosts is plenty bizarre as it is," I replied. "I don't want to know what other people are thinking all the time."

"A psychic isn't the same as a mind reader, Mel. It doesn't work that way."

"Maybe not, but I still don't like it. What's the second possibility?"

"Something in that house triggered a shadow memory."

"Shadow memory?"

"Memory is a very difficult and complicated field of research. The more we research the brain and how it works, the more complex and less reliable memory appears to be. I don't know that much about it, to tell you the truth, but one of my colleagues has built her career researching how humans create and store memories."

"And what is a 'shadow memory'?"

"Sometimes our brain creates false memories to explain something we want an answer to; at other times, a memory is stored in a different area in the brain for some reason. But . . . you know, in dream interpretation the house represents the self: If you discover new rooms you didn't know were there, for instance, or a new attic or something like that, it means you are opening up your mind and your world to new possibilities, discovering new aspects of the psyche."

"That's all fascinating, but why this house, as opposed to every other house I've ever been in?"

"Good question. Does it remind you of your childhood home?"

"I didn't have a childhood home. Dad bought the Fruitvale house when I was in my early teens; until then, we moved every couple of years. Mom and Dad bought homes to fix up and flip, and at the time they didn't have the money to live elsewhere while that happened."

"So when you say you grew up on a construction site, you aren't exaggerating."

"Exactly."

She shook her head slowly. "I really don't know what to tell you, Mel. I could do some research if you want, talk to my colleague about it."

"Really? That would be great, thank you."

"You're welcome. But just for the record: No, you're not crazy. I'm a professional. I know from crazy."

I wasn't entirely sure I believed her, but was relieved to hear her say it.

"Now, let's talk about the acrophobia." Luz had been trying to help me find a way to deal with my newfound fear of heights. It wasn't going well. "Dr. Peters says you didn't keep your second appointment."

"I hate to cast aspersions on your colleague, Luz, but the man's certifiable."

"He is certified in therapy, that's true."

"You know what I mean. I think he might be a sociopath."

"His suggesting that you cut down on your caffeine consumption—which, by the way, is excessive by any standard—doesn't mean he's a sociopath, Mel. Acrophobia is often connected to general anxiety, which caffeine can worsen."

"I am *not* giving up coffee." I stroked Dog's velvet-soft head.

She blew out a breath. "And meds are still off the table?"

"I can't do my job if I'm using drugs."

"Meds, not drugs. But I won't argue if you're dead set against it. Still, may I point out that you can't do your job if you can't get off the ground? Isn't that why you came to me in the first place?"

"I came to you because you're my friend and I thought you'd fix me. Not suggest I stop drinking coffee, for the love of all that is holy."

She smiled and started counting off using her fingers. "Let's see . . . So far you've tried and rejected cognitive behavioral therapy, biofeedback, situational condition-ing, and hypnotherapy. Sorry, my friend. Next up are needles."

"I said no drugs."

"I'm not suggesting drugs, I'm suggesting acupuncture. And stop shaking your head. San Francisco is home to some of the finest doctors of acupuncture in the world. It's a medical system much older—and some say wiser—than our western approach. Dr. Victor Weng is very good. I wouldn't refer you to him unless I thought he could help. Shall I give him a call?"

I hesitated, and she gave me the stink-eye.

"You have a problem, Mel," Luz said bluntly. "You can try wishing it away, but that hasn't worked, has it?"

I shook my head.

"You asked for my help, O Stubborn One, but have rejected everything I suggested. Ultimatum time: Either do what I say or stop complaining—your choice. Which is it?"

Chastened, I reached out and took the scrap of paper on which she had written a name and address: *Dr. Victor Weng, 142B Hang Ah Alley.*

"Hang Ah Alley?"

"Off Sacramento. Right next to Willie 'Woo Woo' Wong Playground."

"You can't be serious."

"That's the man's name. Willie 'Woo Woo' Wong. Why would I make up something like that?"

"I meant about the acupuncture."

"Perfectly serious. And as luck would have it, there's a great dim sum restaurant right on the corner. Why don't I take you to your appointment, and afterward you can buy me lunch?"

This was classic Luz: identify the problem, offer friendship and support, and toss in a little kick-assedness to make sure I followed through.

"All right, sure," I said, sitting back and giving up. "I love needles. The more, the better. Give Dr. Weng a call."

She picked up the phone and finagled an appointment for me the day after tomorrow.

"Thank you, Luz."

"I'm in it for the dim sum. Lunch is on you."

Chapter Ten

I took Dog for a brief walk around campus to stretch his legs, then headed to Olivier's Ghost Supply Shoppe, in Jackson Square. This was one of the oldest sections of San Francisco. In the Barbary Coast days—before the city was made larger by way of a massive landfill—it had been waterfront property, and crews continued to dig up the remains of old ships when excavating basements and the like. Because of the age of the neighborhood, there were a number of brick buildings, which were rare in San Francisco. Ever since the devastation caused by unreinforced masonry during the 1906 earthquake, brick was not a popular choice for building materials in the city.

"Ready?" I asked Dog, whose tail beat an enthusiastic rhythm on the car seat. One nice thing about being friends with the shop owner was that I knew Dog was welcome to come inside while I asked Olivier Galopin, the French ghost hunter, for a little free advice.

I found Olivier dusting some crystal pyramids on a display shelf near the front counter, where his assistant Dingo staffed the cash register. Olivier had been traveling abroad recently so I hadn't seen him for several weeks. He greeted Dog and me with warm hugs, but I sensed something was wrong when the normally voluble Olivier returned to his task without engaging in conversation.

"How was your trip?" I asked.

Olivier shrugged.

"Don't mind him," said Dingo in a stage whisper that no one in the shop failed to hear. "He's been a little down ever since the incident in Hungary."

Olivier shot him a glare.

"What happened?" I asked.

"Didn't go well," said Dingo unnecessarily.

I looked at Olivier. He let out a sigh and finally came over to join us at the counter. "It was a disaster. I don't want to talk about this."

"I'm sorry to hear that. Are you okay?"

"I'm alive," he said.

"Well, that's . . ." *rather ominous*, I thought to myself. "Good. I'm glad you're alive."

"Did you have a question?" Olivier asked. "Not that I have any answers."

"I *would* like to ask you something, if you don't mind." I gave him the rundown of what had happened with Thorn—and Alicia—on Lighthouse Island last night. While I spoke, Dingo surreptitiously pushed a big coffee-table book across the counter toward me. It was entitled *Lighthouses and Their Ghosts.*

"Does this book deal with the Bay Light, on Lighthouse Island?" I asked, turning the volume around to thumb through it.

"Nah," said Dingo.

"Oh, thanks anyway, Dingo, it looks interesting, but I really don't have time for it at the moment," I said, turning back to Olivier. "Let me just be clear on one thing: Thorn couldn't have been pushed down the stairs by a ghost, could he?"

"I don't think so," he said with a shake of his head. What could have happened to Olivier in Hungary? I wondered. He was usually so sure of himself, and of the rules—such as they were—of the ghost world. But now there was a decided wariness in his blue eyes. Then he shrugged again. "Or . . . maybe."

"But you've always told me ghosts can't *hurt* people," I protested, perhaps slightly more stridently than I'd intended. A couple of customers looked up from the shelves they'd been perusing.

"I think it's . . . unusual," said Olivier. "But I've come to believe . . . perhaps if there is enough anger or anguish there . . . perhaps they can build enough strength to make this happen."

I glared at him. I didn't like him changing the rules on me. But the truth was, there weren't any hard-and-fast laws in this ghost-busting business. I'd best get used to doing what I'd done in the past: working the ghost problems by the seat of my pants.

Dingo nudged the lighthouse book toward me again.

"I thought you said it didn't deal with the Bay Light," I said.

"It doesn't, not specifically. But it sure is a beautiful book, ain't it?"

"It is."

"And I think a lot of those lighthouse spirits have something in common. If you think about it, it makes sense. The sense of isolation, the commitment to tending the light, night after night—a lot of them can't bring themselves to stop, even after they pass. I love lighthouses. Visit 'em every chance I get. Know all about 'em."

"Have you ever been to Lighthouse Island?" I asked.

He shook his head. "I'd love to go, though. Anytime. Just say the word."

"You don't happen to know of any ghost stories from there, do you? Rumors, maybe? Something that didn't make it into the book or on the Internet?"

"Let me see if we can shed some light on the subject," said Dingo, bringing out the huge journal where he kept notes. "Get it? Shed some light on a lighthouse?"

Dingo was a great fan of bad puns.

Olivier rolled his eyes and went back to organizing shelves.

"Let's see, now . . . ," said Dingo as he riffled through the pages. The process took a while. He didn't have an index or any other apparent system of organization for his handwritten notes, but I knew he kept some juicy tidbits in this well-thumbed tome.

"Uh-huh, uh-huh . . . Hmmm. All's I see is the usual: A few folks take a boat over there, sneak around the old buildings. Supposed to be off-limits but you know how that goes."

"And what did they see?" I was trying to read upside down, but Dingo's chicken-scratch handwriting didn't lend itself to legibility, even right side up.

"Ghost in the tower. The usual."

"Nothing more than that? Just a ghost in the tower?"

"Oh, here's something: A few years back a man was hired to repair a broken window in the attic, but he got scared nearly off his ladder. Almost fell off. He claims another one of the panes cracked and then full broke, right in front of him. Refused to go back, and when the folks went into the attic to assess the damage, the pane was whole again, but inside the attic, glass shards had been swept up into a nice little pile."

"A housekeeping ghost?" Not long ago I'd had experience with a ghost who cleaned her kitchen incessantly. A big part of me thought this wouldn't be such a terrible arrangement if one could broker a deal, like a sort of housekeeping service from the afterlife. Housework wasn't my strong suit.

"Something like that. They say there are never any cobwebs up in that attic, nothing like that."

"Is there any kind of description of what she looks like?" I asked.

He shook his head.

Because of the typical gender roles of yesteryear, housekeeping ghosts were most often women. But there was no way to know whether this spirit was the same woman I had seen at the top of the light tower.

I remembered Alicia mentioning there were furniture and books and even old keeper's logs in the attic. Amazing that vandals hadn't broken in over the years and stolen or ruined everything. Unless . . . could the ghost have been keeping them out?

My phone rang. Though it seemed rude to answer the phone while in the middle of a conversation, I made an exception for SFPD homicide inspector Annette Crawford.

"Where are you?" she asked without preamble.

"Jackson Square."

"I'm not far away. Meet you in ten. Where exactly?"

I considered lying, but finally told the truth, "The Ghost Supply Shoppe, on Gold Street."

There was a short pause. "You've got to be kidding me."

"I'm really not."

I heard what sounded like a sigh. "I'll meet you in ten minutes. *Outside.*"

"Roger that."

I hung up and slipped the phone back into my bag.

"All righty, then, Dingo, I've got ten minutes. Talk to me about lighthouses."

"The lantern room is at the top of a lighthouse tower, of course; that's where the lens is. Most times it's a metal and glass room on top of a masonry or wood tower. The dome is made of metal and topped by a lightning rod."

While he spoke, he pointed to a detailed illustration from his lighthouse book.

"Below that is the lower watch room. That's where the clockworks for the rotating optics—"

"Clockworks?"

"Oh, sure. How d'ya think they get the light to go round and round before electricity?"

"I guess I never thought about it."

"The Bay Light still has its original mechanism, right?"

I was loath to admit that I hadn't yet been up the light tower. "Um, yeah, sure it does," I mumbled.

A structural engineer—and my father—had carefully inspected the integrity of the lighthouse tower and the winding metal stairs. Since the light was still in use, it had been kept in much better condition than the residence and outbuildings. Lighthouse towers were built to endure inclement weather and to survive the ages. My crew had replaced a few rusty bolts, but other than that the structure was remarkably sound. The only unsafe part was the exterior catwalk, which would have to be replaced. At the moment it was off-limits.

To all but the suicidal specter in a white gown, that is.

Soon, I hoped, I would be able to climb that tower myself, take in the views, and allow myself to be buffeted by the bay winds. But for now I was going to take the structural engineer's word for it.

Dingo kept speaking. "Also in the watch room are the fuel tanks, and that's where the keeper cleaned the lamp chimneys and prepared the lantern for the coming night. The optic section is surrounded by storm panes; there are handholds on the exterior to grip while standing on a ladder cleaning the exterior sides of the windows."

"There's a lot of cleaning, it sounds like."

"Oh, sure. Gotta keep the light as bright as possible. Can't have dirty windowpanes, or a smudged lamp face. The keeper had to wear a linen smock, no rough wool that might scratch the optic or lens. He had to clean the interior and exterior of the lantern panes, clean the optics with vinegar, and once a year polish the lens with rouge. The clock weight was wound and the clockworks cleaned and oiled. And get this: All these preparations were to be completed by ten in the morning."

"Why so early?"

"Rest of the day they dealt with supplies or making other repairs. And if something went wrong, they had all day to see to it—to go ashore if need be, that sort of thing. At night, the keeper would climb to the lantern room and check the direction of the wind so he could adjust the vents to allow just enough draft into the lantern to keep the temperature down, and to suck out the fumes from the burning oil. During the evening the keeper had to wind the weights and trim the wicks of the lamp, as necessary.

"You know, lighthouses are ancient—ever hear of the lighthouse of Alexandria? Built a couple of hundred years BC. Back in the day, they used parabolic reflectors. But it was with the invention of the Fresnel lens in 1820 that they got really good—"

"*Putain!*" Olivier swore in French and threw up his hands. "She does not want to hear all of this. Is it that you know anything specifically about the haunting of Lighthouse Island light, Dingo?"

Dingo pushed out his bottom lip, then shook his head. "Not really. But like I say, I think it's likely they're all haunted by one keeper or another, who just keeps climbing that tower, tending to his light. Hey, Mel," Dingo said in a loud whisper, gesturing toward Olivier with his head. "You should take him out to the island with you. Let him meet the ghosts. You know, boost his confidence."

"This isn't a game, Dingo," I said. "A man was killed there yesterday."

"Not much of a loss, sounds like. Don't take to wife beaters."

"You're not going to get much of an argument from me on that point. But a human life was taken. That's a big deal, and besides, the island's still a crime scene."

"Yeah," said Dingo, dropping his voice. "But it would be neighborly of you to let Olivier tag along."

I watched for a long moment as the French ghost buster rearranged some spirit photography books. Dingo was right; there was a decidedly defeated slant to Olivier's shoulders.

"All right," I said. "I don't know when I'll be allowed back on the island, but when I am I'll give Olivier a call and see if he wants to come along."

"Hot damn!" Dingo slammed his hand on the counter so loudly everyone in the shop looked around to see the ruckus. "That's the ticket."

"Hey, Olivier, let me ask you something else: Have you ever had a sense of déjà vu when you go into a house? What would that mean?"

"Déjà vu doesn't usually mean anything much," he said. "But in this case it continued as I walked throughout the whole house. That's what was so weird. I felt like I knew what was around every corner."

"You could be channeling someone, perhaps."

"Excuse me?"

"Channeling. A ghost could be using you as a capsule, to experience things."

"*Whoa*, Nellie," I said, aghast. "Seeing ghosts is one thing, communicating with them I can deal with. But I am *not* up for being their capsule. That's like . . . like the *Invasion of the Body Snatchers* or something."

"Good movie," said Dingo with a nod. "Course, I like the original best."

"I'm not sure it's up to you, Mel," Olivier said. "You've always been hesitant to embrace your abilities to communicate with the beyond, but spirits have reached out to you anyway. Perhaps this is simply a different kind of communication. Did you do the body scan and prepare yourself before entering the building?"

"No," I admitted. "I wasn't really expecting . . ." What *had* I been expecting? A standard, run-of-the-mill ghost, I supposed. I realized that now that I was an old hand, I was getting a little jaded about the ghostly experience. Maybe even a little cocky.

"You mustn't skip that part, Mel," Olivier said, taking my hands in his. "I'm very serious, don't underestimate the spirit world. We never know—" He cut himself off, squeezed my hands, dropped them, and turned away. "I just want to urge you to be careful, at all times. Don't be careless with yourself. It's the only self you have."

Chapter Eleven

Outside, a cop was standing by my car.

I wasn't getting a ticket. It was homicide inspector Annette Crawford. Annette was in her fifties, curvy and strong-looking, with a regal posture and a definite no-nonsense manner about her.

She held two cardboard cups in her hands, and handed me one.

"Uh-oh," I said, wary.

"What?"

"You've never bought me coffee before. Is there bad news?"

"Not a lot of news at all, actually," she said, leaning down to greet Dog. "You see? That's what I get for trying to be nice."

"Thank you for the coffee."

"Anytime."

"So . . . you haven't heard anything about the case? About Alicia Withers?"

"Detective Santos is checking out known associates, talking to anyone and everyone on or near the island, seeing if somebody might have followed the victim to the island to settle a score. I hate to say it, Mel, though you've probably already figured it out: There's a real issue of opportunity here. As in, who was on the island, and who knew and hated the victim enough to kill him? He's not even from this area, is he?"

"He was from Tacoma," I said. "But surely a man like that would have a lot of enemies, wouldn't he?"

As Inspector Crawford had pointed out to me before, people with a criminal bent did not tend to be law-abiding in their daily interactions. They weren't only bank robbers or murderers or rapists, they also littered, broke the speed limit, parked in handicapped zones, cut in and out of traffic, and refused to pay their tickets. By and large they believed the rules the rest of us followed were for chumps, and ignored them. Which was a boon for law enforcement because violent criminals were often caught doing something stupid, like jaywalking or speeding, totally unrelated to their greater crime.

"True," said Annette. "But not local enemies."

"I suppose I should look into Thorn's life recently. He mentioned he'd been at the Palm Project, up the coast, near Green Gulch Farm. Seems as good a place to start as any, especially since I don't feel like hopping a plane for Tacoma."

"No, you *don't* need to go talk to the Palm Project people, Mel. Must I remind you yet again that you are not in law enforcement? Leave it to Detective Santos. He knows what he's doing."

"But you once told me yourself that if the police have a suspect they're pretty sure they can nail, they stop looking."

There was a pause. We both knew Alicia was the ob-vious suspect. Who else could have been up in that lighthouse? Not to mention she had grabbed the knife, and was covered in Thorn's blood. She couldn't have set herself up worse if she'd tried.

"I'm serious, Mel," Annette said. "I don't want to hear you were sticking your nose into this investigation by going up to the Palm Project. Promise me."

"Mphhh," I mumbled, but nodded.

"And you're sure you didn't see anyone else leaving the tower?"

"No one. I wish—*oh*, how I wish—I had been paying more attention." I thought back on that nightmarish scene. "One of the bodyguards, Buzz, was freaked out and thought he could revive the extremely dead Thorn. Alicia was practically catatonic. It was all so . . . fraught, and we were focused on Thorn. Frankly, it didn't occur to me to guard the entrance until afterward."

"You'd think by your fifth murder you'd be a little savvier."

I gave a mirthless chuckle. "I'm better with the *ghosts* than I used to be. At least I'm making progress, in that regard." As I said this, I recalled Olivier's words and my own earlier thoughts: Perhaps I'd become *too* casual with the ghostly realm.

After all, if ghosts were simply humans on a different spiritual plane, then some would be real jerks—or even homicidal.

A few of the ghosts I'd encountered had been unpleasant but not truly malevolent. But suppose I ran across one that was? Not that I was prepared to blame Thorn's murder on a ghost; I still believed the perpetrator was a living human. But perhaps a malevolent ghost could cause other kinds of havoc.

What about the woman I saw at the top of the tower? She had made me feel truly awful, sick to my core. At the time I thought it was because of the vertigo. But could it be something else? Something worse? Still . . . since Thorn wasn't able to tell me what happened, perhaps I should try to make contact with the woman in the tower. If she was forever vigilant, as Dingo had suggested, maybe she could tell me something. Often, I had found, the ghosts that appeared to me were connected with the current crime. Or, at the very least, their past somehow mirrored the present.

In any case, I needed to get back on that island. Annette would be no help in that regard. She was a cop first, my friend second.

"Anyway, there are a lot of other suspects," I said. "Really, given the island setting, there are a surprising number of suspects. Some of the people in Point Moro are pretty sketchy. And if you ask me, the guys moored in the harbor were a little fishy."

"That wasn't a pun, was it? I hate puns."

"Sorry. Unintentional."

"So in what way are the boaters suspicious?"

"Just for starters, one of them is named Major. That's not his title, it's his name. Doesn't that seem sort of disrespectful to our men and women in uniform?"

"Mel, my friend, I think you're reaching."

"Okay, I'll admit there's nothing overtly suspicious about any of them. But the other one, named Halstrom, was not happy when he was told to stay away from the lighthouse buildings due to construction. He glared at me, more than once. Also, immediately after the murder, we went down to the harbor, and no one was there. They didn't show up until quite a while later. Claimed they had been out fishing."

"What makes you think they hadn't been? Besides, you seem to be suggesting they were in it together. Stabbing a man and pushing him down the stairs is rarely a group activity."

"I only met Thorn once, but he was pretty annoying."

"I'm certain Detective Santos is checking them out, but if you think you have anything to add to his assessment, you should call him."

"Um . . . okay."

"What is it?"

"Detective Santos is sort of . . . scary."

"So am I."

"Not in the same way."

She chuckled. "That's only because you've taken the time to get to know me. Find a few more ghosts and bodies in Richmond, and let Santos be your man."

"All right," I said, kicking my tire.

"Mel?" Annette said, her voice taking on a serious tone. "I was just kidding about the bodies and ghosts. Stick to San Francisco from now on, so I can keep an eye on you."

"I guess you're right. I gotta say, so far this lighthouse isn't nearly as much fun as I thought it would be."

"Hang in there. So, how's it going with the fear of heights?"

"How did you— What, is there a billboard someplace with my face on it?" I sketched a big poster with my hands. *"'Mel Turner has acrophobia!'"*

"Almost." She smiled. "Ran into your father the other day at the youth center. He may have mentioned it."

I blew out a frustrated breath.

"Hang in there, Mel," Annette said quietly. "What happened to you up on the roof of Crosswinds was no walk in the park. It's not surprising you'd be traumatized by it. But you're strong; you'll conquer this. I have faith. And as for Lighthouse Island, I'm sure it'll all work out for you."

But would it work out for Alicia?

*   *   *

As Dog jumped into the car, I told myself that Annette was
right: I should call Detective Santos. But I hesitated—was
I flat-out too cowardly?

No, I thought as I settled in behind the wheel. That
wasn't the problem. I didn't want to phone Detective
Santos because I knew from the look in his eye that he
was convinced Alicia had murdered Thorn and believed
I knew it, too, and probably assumed I was supporting
Alicia in some kind of gender solidarity. And that meant
that I had to tread carefully, because if I wasn't absolutely
sure of what I was saying, and didn't express myself well,
I would make everything worse and probably wind up
incriminating Alicia.

In short, Detective Santos made me nervous.

Annette's words made me smile. She was right; she
used to make me very nervous, too. Still did, in some
ways. But I now knew how smart she was, and how dedicated to finding justice for the victims with whom she
dealt, from the humblest junkie to the wealthiest debu-
tante. She was a great cop. So I should take her word for
it that Santos, too, would impress me.

For now, I needed to get back to work. My phone had
been beeping while I was with Annette. I answered several texts—including one from Landon, *Just checking in;
stay away from ghosts!*—made a couple of phone calls,
and then drove to my friend Matt's house in Pacific
Heights, where two of my crew were putting the finishing
touches on a new Murphy bed in his state-of-the-art,
entirely paneled library.

Matt's house was also, coincidentally, the first place
I'd ever seen a ghost. At least, that I knew of. Turns out,

I'd probably seen one or two as a kid, but had assumed they were figments of my imagination.

They weren't.

Turner Construction had been working on Matt's house for several years at this point. Not constantly, but consistently. As with most big projects, we had finished the bulk of the work—foundation repair and upgrade, replumbing and rewiring, knocking down walls, putting up others, reimagining space, renovating the kitchen and bathrooms, re-doing HVAC, applying new stucco, and installing new moldings—in the first few months. It was the other stuff that dragged on: the surprise water issues that developed with the first rain; the wildly expensive dishwasher that didn't work properly; the garden water feature that looked great on paper but in reality became a slimy mosquito breeding ground due to lack of water flow. There were always a thousand small, miscellaneous items that drove contractors crazy.

And that's not including the problems caused by the whims of the wealthy client. Matt was a lovely person and a good friend, but prone to changing his mind, as when he realized that the east-facing bedroom window he had insisted upon meant the sun would awaken him at dawn each morning. "Sorry, love, keep forgetting I'm on the West Coast," had been his nonsensical explanation. "Be a sport and relocate it, yes?"

I found Ramon and Emerson upstairs and hard at work, fitting together joinery, covering up unsightly hinges and nails and screws. The room smelled of freshly milled, hand-polished wood and boasted a breathtaking view of the Palace of Fine Arts and the Golden Gate Bridge. I always felt like I was sitting on a movie set when I was in this third-floor library.

I checked the overall progress and we discussed the solution for fitting a straight molding into a crooked frame. Then Ramon, Emerson, Matt, and I had a nice visit over lunch on the terrace. One thing I loved about Matt was that even though he had made a fortune years ago as the lead singer of a wildly popular rock band, he was simple and straightforward, unaffected by fame. Everyone on the job came together at lunchtime to break bread, whether architect, project manager, gardener, or day laborer. Today Matt had arranged for lunch to be catered by an Italian deli: prosciutto and salami sandwiches and caprese salad.

Matt had once been falsely accused of killing a man, so he listened with interest to my tale of what had happened on Lighthouse Island.

"This is probably out of left field, as you Yanks say," he said in his charming British accent. "But this wouldn't have anything to do with the alleged treasure, would it?"

"Treasure?" I asked around a mouthful of Italian cold cuts. "*What* alleged treasure?"

"There's buried treasure on some of the islands in San Francisco Bay, haven't you heard?"

"You're probably thinking of Treasure Island," suggested Emerson, slipping Dog a bite of his sandwich.

"Which is a way cool name for a fairly boring place," I said. "That's the 'island' the military built and attached to the natural Yerba Buena Island."

"I went there once," said Matt. "I kept seeing the Treasure Island exit signs on the Bay Bridge, and got curious. Drove around the island to check it out, and was sorely disappointed. I think I'd been imagining a scene reminiscent of Disneyland. Took me forever to get back on the bridge."

I nodded, having done the same thing once. Treasure

Island was a former military base that now had a spooky ghost-town feel. There was a lot of cheap military housing, some larger abandoned buildings, a few attempts at renovating some of the structures, and incredible views. But Treasure Island was most famous locally for being difficult to merge back into traffic on the Bay Bridge.

"Still and all," Matt said with a shake of his head. "I thought there was something more to a treasure . . . Wish I could remember. Probably the drugs."

During his years as a rock musician, Matt had partied hard and abused all kinds of substances. He'd since retired, and had been clean and sober for a while now. His new wife seemed intent on his staying that way.

"Something about a ship from Peru," Matt mused. "It was down there during the Peruvian revolution, or something like that, and a bunch of rich people asked the captain to keep their gold for them offshore so it would be safe. But they never came to get it and the ship's captain finally left with the treasure on board, and sailed to San Francisco."

"And buried it on an island in the bay?" I asked.

"Something like that," Matt said. "Not ringing any bells?"

I looked at Emerson and Ramon. They both shook their heads.

"I hate to admit it, but I have absolutely no idea when the Peruvian revolution took place," I said. "Not even which century. Anybody?"

Ramon shook his head. "Ours started in 1910 in Mexico, but it lasted another ten years."

"We had one in 1944 in Guatemala," offered Emerson, handing me the salad. "But then the US unseated our democratically elected president in 1954."

"Oh, um, sorry about that," I mumbled around a

mouthful of food. I never knew quite what to say in these situations.

Emerson shrugged. "United Fruit Company had a lot of clout, back then."

"I'm impressed with both of you," said Matt. "Personally, I can barely remember our own revolution."

"You guys didn't have one, remember?" I said. "We colonials did, though: kicked you out in 1776."

"Hey, we had the 'glorious revolution,'" Matt said. "Not terribly exciting, all things considered. Still stuck with the queen and all that rot." I smiled. I knew he was secretly enthralled with Prince William, his wife Kate, and their roly-poly royal babies.

"So, that's all you got?" I said. "Maybe some captain sailed in with treasure from Peru and buried it on an island in the bay?"

"It's possible. Remember what happened here in this house? How those guys were looking for jewels from back in the Gold Rush days? It was a wild place back then, the Barbary Coast and all that."

True. Maybe I should run the idea by my friend Trish, who worked at the California Historical Society. Still, I recalled that the treasure map I found had shown the keeper's buildings on the island, so unless the Peruvian revolution took place after 1871, it couldn't have applied.

"Matt, I have an unrelated question for you," I said after Ramon and Emerson excused themselves and went back to work. Matt was fixing me an espresso with a huge brass contraption he'd had shipped over from Milan. "Have you ever heard of the Palm Project?"

"Sure."

"You have?"

"It's up the coast, isn't it? Past Green Gulch Farm?"

"That's what I hear, yes. Can you tell me anything about it?"

The espresso machine belched steam and made a racket, while dark brown goodness streamed into a delicate little cup.

"I don't know much, except that it was offered to me as an option when I needed rehab. I went to the New Leaf Clinic instead, but to tell you the truth, I can't remember exactly what factored into my decision. Why?"

"The fellow who died on Lighthouse Island, Thorn Walker, had graduated from the program recently. He was very proud of himself."

Matt nodded. "It's a pretty big deal to make it through one of those programs. You have to face some hard realities, and commit to changing your life, to changing your*self*."

"You believe people can fundamentally change, then?"

"With the proper motivation," he said with a quick nod. "If I didn't, I'd be dead by now, wouldn't I?"

I nodded, sipped my espresso, and pondered that for a moment. "One more thing: You got pretty close to other people in the program, right?"

"Sure. You can't bare your soul to people without feeling a certain closeness, can you? No secrets, everything out in the open, totally vulnerable."

Thorn didn't know a lot of local people, but he'd been at the Palm Project long enough to claim to have made some fundamental changes. Might he have shared some secrets that were worth killing over?

I thanked Matt for lunch, the conversation, and the espresso, and drove north over the Golden Gate Bridge to Marin to Wakefield, Ellis Elrich's Scottish castle retreat center. My crew had long since finished reconstructing the old stone walls that had been shipped over from Scotland, but as always there were thousands of details: interiors, baseboards, painting, and everything it took to transform an ancient Scottish monastery into beautiful guest quarters and conference facilities. In order to meet an insane deadline for a grand opening, we had divided the project into several phases, and were now on the third phase. This included creating extra accommodations in several outbuildings, as well as installing decorative landscaping not included in the organic garden and composting stations.

Today I needed to help my guys rejigger the bathroom layouts. We had managed to carve lavatories out of the former monk's cells—needless to say, back in the day the monks didn't have plumbing, much less en suite bathrooms—but the way the architect had drawn them up wasn't meshing with reality.

There was a lot of grumbling on this job, partly because of the commute. Most of my crew lived in the East Bay— in Oakland or further out, in Concord and beyond—and would be glad when the job moved to Lighthouse Island, which would be much closer. Then, of course, they would grumble about having to park their trucks at Point Moro and taking the boat over instead of being able to drive to the jobsite. It was always something. Luckily, most of my crew were easily cheered up with donuts.

I was not above bribery.

In addition to helping with the bathrooms, I was anxious to see Ellis Elrich and get an update on Alicia. But when I knocked on the door of his house, it was opened by my wannabe innkeeper friend, in the flesh.

"Alicia."

We hugged. And held on for a long moment.

Why is it that some people seem to live charmed lives, while others take a pounding at every turn? Alicia had grown up with an abusive alcoholic father, married a charming fellow who turned out to be an abuser himself, was forced to go in hiding to escape him, and now stood accused of his murder. Why had she pulled such a short stick?

Other than getting divorced, and my mother dying too early, I had lived a remarkably charmed life.

"Ellis hired the *best* lawyer," said Alicia as she poured us cups of coffee. I thought about my earlier discussion with Luz; maybe she was right, I should consider cutting down on my caffeine consumption. But not today. "Her name's Marla Chu. And I haven't actually been charged with anything." The "yet" hung in the air, unspoken. "And anyway, I didn't do anything wrong, so I'm sure it will all be worked out. Of course I had *motive* to harm Thorn, but as I explained to Detective Santos, that doesn't mean that I *did* harm him."

"And what did Detective Santos say?"

There was a long pause.

"Alicia?"

"He didn't seem convinced. But then, I suppose he's just doing his job. Why should he believe me? Marla says they're probably doing forensic testing and that sort of thing. If someone else's prints are on the knife, I should be off the hook."

I hated to be the one to point out the obvious, but . . . "Didn't you say you grabbed the knife as he fell?"

"Yes, but we're hoping someone else's prints are on the knife as well. Or there might be evidence that someone else was there at the top of the tower. There were only a handful of people on the island when this occurred; how difficult could it be to figure out the killer?"

Faces flashed through my mind: Terry Re, Paul Halstrom, Major Williston. Happily, my people had left the island before the murder. But did that mean much? There were no controlled borders; Thorn had pulled his boat to shore elsewhere on the island than the yacht harbor, and, as Alicia had pointed out, in calm weather a person in an inflatable dinghy could make it across to the island from the Richmond shore easily enough. So who was to say there wasn't someone *else* on the island yesterday? Someone who landed on the island unseen, climbed the wide-open tower, and had done the dirty deed.

But who? And almost as important, why?

Some random person who held a grudge against Thorn? Another ex-wife, perhaps? Or a girlfriend? Or even more likely: the loved one of someone with whom he'd been violent, or had stalked?

Or . . . could this all be about buried treasure? Could Thorn have known the location of something, and refused to tell? Or maybe he just happened to be in the wrong place at the wrong time? But how coincidental that Alicia would be working on that same island? And if the incident wasn't directly tied to Thorn at all—if he was just in the wrong place at the wrong time—then was there still danger surrounding my lighthouse project?

It was all very complicated.

I spent the rest of the day trying to gracefully shoehorn modern bathrooms into medieval-era stone chambers. Though it was frustrating, it was a lot more straightforward—and a darned sight more fun—than figuring out what had happened to Thorn.

By a long shot.

Chapter Twelve

I honked the car horn lightly at the pack of students hanging out in front of the Pacific Heights high school. Caleb looked up, said something to his friends, and ambled over to the car.

"Hey, Dog!" he said, tossing his backpack in the rear seat and encouraging Dog to yield the shotgun position. As he strapped on his seat belt Caleb asked, "So, is this Landon person going to be at dinner?"

"Hello, sweetie pie," I said. "What, no kiss?"

He snorted. "So is he?"

"Just like last night," I nodded. "And the night before."

"That was sort of my point."

"I know you love Graham, Caleb. So do I. But . . . none of this is Landon's fault. It's no one's fault. It's just the way it is. Life is . . . complicated."

He shrugged and stared out the window.

Then we stopped by the Russian Hill project to pick up Stephen.

"How was your day?" I asked, my tone forced cheeriness.

"I have three new blisters," he whined, inspecting the palms of his pale hands.

"Well, girls like blisters. Right, Caleb?"

Caleb shrugged and put his earphones in. I turned up NPR and headed into the thick traffic on the Bay Bridge inching toward Oakland, glad to be headed home.

The old farmhouse was redolent of spices and ground beef. As we walked in the kitchen door, we found Dad at the old Wedgewood stove, making enchiladas. It was one of several dishes he had learned how to make from some Latino college students who stayed with us for a few days while I busted the ghost in their apartment. The students preferred cheese in their enchiladas, but Dad was a big believer in beef.

"Hey, babe," said Dad as I kissed his cheek. "Enchiladas and guacamole for dinner. Landon just got in."

"He did indeed," Landon said, stepping into the doorway from the living room. Caleb rolled his eyes and went upstairs to his room.

"He'll come around," said Dad.

"That's what *I* said," said Stephen.

"Before he goes off to college, you think?" I asked.

"Give him time," Landon said, and gave me a kiss before opening a hearty Bordeaux and pouring each of us a glass. We sat at the kitchen table watching Dad cook while Stephen regaled us with a funny story about getting a piece of sawdust in his eye and sending a plank flying. Stephen was a lovely person but a truly wretched construction worker.

"You think *that's* bad," said Dad as he shredded a mix of Monterey Jack and cheddar cheese to melt on top of the enchiladas. "I remember one time . . ."

He continued, making us laugh with his own funny story of the worst worker he'd ever had, on a job in the Mission, who forgot to turn off the water before opening a pipe, resulting in a waterfall from the fourth floor; and the time a bathtub fell from the second floor, clear through the ceiling of the first.

A home owner prone to anxiety should never listen to construction workers swap stories after hours. One would think working on a home was nothing but plumbing snafus and falling bathtubs.

As we chatted, I realized Landon was staring at me. I was trying hard to pretend I didn't notice, but couldn't keep the smile from my face.

"What?" I finally whispered.

"Do you have any gowns?"

"Gowns? Like . . . nightgowns?"

"Evening gowns."

"You mean, dressier than this?" I looked down at the bright green sparkly shift I was wearing under my sweatshirt. It was one of Stephen's Vegas-inspired designs. "This is one of my favorites."

Stephen beamed. Dad's story had wound down, and at the mention of my wardrobe, he rolled his eyes. I was beginning to see where Caleb got it from. Dad wasn't exactly a fan of my sartorial style.

"The San Francisco Ballet is celebrating the opening of its eighty-fourth season with a gala on Saturday with a theme of 'Old San Francisco,'" Landon continued. "They'll be honoring a few fourth- and fifth-generation families. I'm embarrassed to say I only now heard about it."

"The what, now?"

"The eighty-fourth season—" began Stephen.

"Actually, sorry," I interrupted him. "I really did hear that. I just wasn't sure how it applied."

"You're not a ballet fan?" Landon asked.

"Of course I am," I lied. "Who doesn't like the ballet?"

"I took you to see *The Nutcracker* one year, remember?" said Dad. "It was your mom's idea. Had to drag you there kicking and screaming. You insisted on wearing your overalls, and slept through the whole thing."

Everyone stared at me. One interesting aspect of living with one's father as an adult woman: Every stupid, childish thing I'd ever done as a youngster was liable to be thrown in my face. And there were plenty of stupid things because, after all, I had been a child.

It was very humbling.

"Yes, in fact, I do remember going to *The Nutcracker*, thanks, Dad. As I recall, I was also ten years old."

"A very tired ten-year-old, it seems," Stephen muttered.

"Don't worry, Mel, our seats are on the main floor. I knew you wouldn't want the balcony," Landon said. Speaking of humbling. Landon had been up on that Pacific Heights roof with me, rolling around only inches from death—how come *he* hadn't developed acrophobia? "I can't wait to see you all dressed up."

"Again, just to clarify, my current spangles will not suffice?"

"I don't particularly care what you wear—though overalls might not be the thing. But I always see a gala as a chance to bring out that evening gown you hardly ever have the occasion to use."

"But I have so *many* formal gowns," I teased. "How will I possibly choose?"

"Mel, I am already seeing you in a sort of lemon chiffon, maybe off the shoulder . . . you will be lovely!" Stephen exclaimed, gazing at me and clapping his hands under his chin.

My father gaped at him.

"That's very sweet of you, Stephen," I said. "But you don't have time to make me a dress before Saturday, do you?"

"You just watch, my friend," he said with a wink, a determined gleam in his eye. "You just *watch*."

"But . . ." I made a last stab at avoiding the ballet. "We were supposed to go see the outdoor movie on First Friday."

"The gala's on Saturday," Landon pointed out.

"But that's two nights out in a row out on the town."

For a normal person that might not be an issue. But as a contractor I got up at five in the morning, which meant I was usually down for the count each night around nine. For very special occasions I could force myself to stay up later, but two late nights in a row might do me in. It occurred to me that it was very possible that in dating me, Landon had won the booby prize in the Love Lottery.

"If you don't want to go, Mel, we won't go," said Landon. "But I adore the ballet. It's a chance to contribute to the fund-raising effort, show you off, and expose you to another side of the city besides drywall and sewer systems."

Our gaze met and held. Landon wanted to "show me off." What could I say?

Stephen elbowed me and whispered, "I accept with pleasure . . ."

"I accept with pleasure your kind invitation, good sir," I uttered. "I would love to attend the gala with you. Draped in lemon chiffon, no less." I pushed away from the table and headed toward the short hallway that led to Turner Construction's home office. "But for now, I'm going to go talk to Stan about drywall and sewer systems—and the supply estimates—before dinner."

As Stan and I were discussing the estimates he had worked up, based on the numbers and measurements Dad had given him, the office phone rang.

"Turner Construction, this is Stan." Stan listened briefly and handed me the phone.

"Mel Turner," I said, feeling Very Professional.

"Mel? It's Ellis. Alicia said you came by Wakefield today; I'm sorry I missed you. The Richmond police just notified me that the crime scene has been released, and we're okayed to get back to work on the island tomorrow."

"That was fast," I said.

I wondered, but didn't ask aloud, how Ellis had managed this one. The billionaire got things done.

The only complication was that I had made a promise to spend time with Landon, who had the day free. So the next morning I headed back to Lighthouse Island with both Landon and Stephen at my sides.

We drove to Point Moro, a small "village" made up of a few dozen people, not far from the historic town of Point Richmond. The winding road was hilly and bumpy, not well maintained; there were sections where the pavement was gone completely, leaving massive potholes in the dirt and gravel. The hills surrounding the town were undeveloped chaparral featuring blue agave, palms, and eucalyptus trees; we passed three deer grazing, undisturbed, in a meadow. It would have been bucolic if not for the huge tanks of the nearby Chevron Richmond Refinery perched on the top of the hills.

Point Moro itself was located in a ravine alongside a small cove, where the docks were mostly protected from waves. A long time ago, before the Richmond–San Rafael Bridge was built, a ferry ran across the strait between Point Moro and Marin County. In 1939 a ferry captain tried to make a marina, but creating a proper breakwater was too expensive, so in the spirit of the wild frontier, he sank a bunch of old ships here instead.

The flag of the "Point Moro Yacht Club" was a skull and crossbones, and the inhabitants of the small settlement liked to refer to themselves as pirates.

Point Moro wasn't typical for the Bay Area, at least not anymore. A few boats in the harbor were nice, but others were downright rickety and appeared on the verge of sinking. The handful of tiny houses onshore appeared to have been built by hand; a few had been fashioned out of rusting shipping containers. There were several still-inhabited but ancient RVs, and the backwater harbor was dotted with broken-down lawnmowers, green plastic garbage cans, an Army jeep, a stolen road sign. Wildflowers mingled with weeds along a set of long-abandoned railroad tracks.

"This is . . . different," said Landon.

"That would be the word for it," murmured Stephen.

"I like it," I said as I parked the car next to an old fifty-gallon drum. "It reminds me of places I remember from when I was a kid: like the stinky old cannery we used to crawl around."

"You used to crawl around an old cannery?" Landon asked.

"I don't mean when it was still working; it was abandoned."

"That makes me feel so much better."

We walked toward the dock. The morning was cold and hazy. Out on Lighthouse Island, the mournful foghorn blew, and the light flashed, its powerful beam cutting through the mist.

"Now that so much of the Bay Area is covered in beige tract houses in neighborhoods with all the personality of a bar code," I continued, "I find holdouts like Point Moro sort of . . . quaint. Anyway, Duncan—the skipper who ferries us across—is usually up in the café. Wait here for the rest of the crew; I'll go get him."

The Gentleman's Café was the only business establishment in Point Moro, and its biggest selling point—according to the posters in the window—appeared to be two-dollar beer. It was like a diner out of a time warp, but not in a kicky retro way. More like in a "has the window been washed in the last fifty years? And I don't even want to inquire as to the cooking facilities" way. It sold truly wretched coffee and stale pastries, and I hadn't been able to bring myself to try the actual cooked food.

The thin young woman behind the counter had a name tag that said, HI! I'M FERNANDA! But that was the friendliest thing about her. She would have made a good cop—her face was as emotionless and hard to read as Detective Santos's had been. I nodded at her before heading over to sit with Duncan at his usual linoleum table by the window. He was finishing up a dubious plate of watery scrambled eggs and burned hash browns.

"Good morning, Duncan, how are you?" I asked.

"I'm wonderful! Just wonderful." He smiled his typical smile, his Greek fisherman cap perched on his balding head. "Life is good, my friend. Life is very, very good."

Duncan was clearly one of those people who worked on maintaining a positive attitude. Normally I appreciated his cheery approach to life, though on the early morning runs it could be a bit much. In contrast, the pilot of the supply barge—a large, bald man named Lyle who sported multiple painful-looking piercings and a huge grizzly bear tattoo on one brawny arm—was taciturn and quiet.

"I was so happy to get your call," Duncan said. "I feared we might have a few days off, what with all that happened."

"The police released the scene early. So I suppose the project must go on."

Even though the coffee was wretched, I ordered a large cup to go, hoping to ingratiate myself with the surly Fernanda. No luck. She pushed it across the counter laconically, putting out a small carton of cream that looked like it had been out of the cooler too long. Luckily, I take it black.

By the time Duncan and I returned to the dock, half a dozen of my workers were waiting. Waquisha was one of them; she seemed more out of place than ever without Jeremy, who had been needed on Matt's library project in Pacific Heights. Yet another group consisted of several large young men, my friend Nico's nephews, whom I could never keep straight, so I referred to them collectively as "the demo guys." Luckily, construction workers were slow to take offense at such things.

Duncan greeted everyone effusively, invited us all aboard, handed out life vests, and skillfully guided the boat out of the harbor.

The vessel lurched and I grabbed for the side. Personally, I didn't quite have my sea legs. I liked boats well enough, I supposed—I mean, they were a darned sight better than swimming these frigid waters—but I was more the "I'll just sit here quietly and smile while secretly praying we don't sink" type.

Landon, in contrast, wore a blue wool pea coat, had a worn leather backpack slung over one brawny shoulder, and stood at the helm with his arms crossed over his chest and the wind blowing through his hair. The Old Spice jingle started running through my head.

"You know," Duncan said, "Richmond has a bad reputation, sure, but I've never had a problem. But then out on an isolated island, someone pushes a guy down the lighthouse stairs? How does that even happen? It's a real shame."

I nodded. I didn't particularly want to talk about what happened to Thorn in front of the demo guys; no sense in stirring up their imaginations. Besides, I didn't want to think about Thorn any more than I had to. My mind was already focused on the job ahead: getting enough supplies out here, orienting the crew, and getting the demo started.

"I tell you what, though," Duncan continued. "Point Moro's not real pretty, but they're good folks. And sometimes you look at a real nice house, but the things that go on inside are downright ugly. So I guess you just never know. Anything can happen, anywhere."

"So true," I murmured. And it was. A "pretty" life didn't necessarily equate with a happy one. Turner Construction dealt with a lot of wealthy people and worked in some of the best neighborhoods in one of the most expensive cities in the nation. But a lot of people raised in luxury seemed unable to enjoy life, or were somehow compelled to destroy everything they had. My family life was decidedly messy—in more ways than one—but it was happy. We weren't rich, but we did all right and I wouldn't trade my situation for the world.

And yet. . . I glanced up at Landon, who still looked like he was filming an Old Spice commercial. I needed to find new digs. Seriously. It was mortifying to have sex under my father's roof.

I was going to move "find an apartment" up on my to-do list. Right after I 1) rid Lighthouse Island of ghosts and 2) found Thorn's murderer(s).

"You really don't have to do what my dad says and stick with me all day, you know," I said to Landon when he finally joined me at the back of the boat. "After all, it's not as though the killer is still lurking on the island. I've got the demo team with me, and Buzz brought yet another bodyguard, Krauss. He texted me already; they've been on the island for the last hour, checking out all the buildings. And if that weren't enough for Calamity Mel, I have Stephen."

Stephen was holding on to the side of the boat with a white-knuckle grip, and looked a little green around the gills. Still, he nodded gamely.

"Yep, I've got her back, no worries there," he managed in a weak voice.

"You just keep breathing deeply, Stephen. We'll be there soon," Landon said in a kind tone, and then turned back to me. "I like and respect your father, Mel, but I'm here for my own reasons. If you think I'm going to let you wander around alone on an island with even the possibility of a murderer lurking, I guess we need to talk about our relationship."

"It's sort of scary, isn't it?"

"Yes, I'd say a murderer on an island is certainly scary."

"I meant the word."

"What word?"

"*Relationship.*" I shivered from a spray of cold bay water.

"It depends on your perspective. It's not scary to me." Landon lowered his voice. "Anyway, you just focus on talking to ghosts. Let me watch for potential threats. Me and Buzz and Krauss—and Stephen, of course."

Chapter Thirteen

Also on the boat were a couple of small water tanks, a pallet of snacks—energy bars, nuts, chips—that Alicia had arranged for the workers, several coolers containing sandwiches, and basic equipment such as sledgehammers, crowbars, and power tools. The larger supply barge would start bringing over lumber, cement, and other heavier items as soon as we were set up to receive them.

The ride from Point Moro would last another five minutes or so. It seemed as good a time as any to study a little physics. Landon had tried to explain it to me before, but I'd had a hard time following along.

Ever since Landon had seen me in action with ghosts, he had been searching for a logical explanation. Like many men of science, if he couldn't prove it, he didn't quite believe it. And yet he kept his mind open to possibilities since, as he said, science was forever finding or proving things heretofore unsuspected.

"So, Landon, run this ghostly physics stuff by me one more time."

"There are several theories," he said, always happy to talk shop. "The one that first comes to mind, of course, is the multiverse or meta-universe, a hypothetical set of finite and infinite possible universes that comprise everything that exists, and would suggest the existence of parallel universes. And because the possibilities are infinite, then of course there could be multiple personalities, essentially an infinite number of you, leading an infinite number of different lives."

"A multitude of *me* and *you* out in the universe."

He gave me a secret smile. "Just imagine."

I punched him lightly in the stomach.

"What was that for?" he asked.

"Because if there are an infinite number of you, there are at least some universes in which you aren't with me."

"I'm going to leave aside the possibility of jealousy over infinite universes, for the moment," he said. "Especially since you're the one with the Parisian postcard from the barely ex-boyfriend on the refrigerator."

"I took it down this morning."

"Be that as it may. Shall I go on?"

"Of course you shall."

"Many scientists believe that this is more a philosophical debate than scientific, because finding the precise value of quark masses and other constants is impossible, since of course their values would be dependent upon the particular circumstances of the universe in which we live."

"Sometimes I lie awake half the night worrying about quark masses."

Landon continued as though he hadn't heard me. "There are really four levels of the multiverse discussion, and I think what you call 'ghosts' are most likely to be a part of the many-worlds interpretation of quantum mechanics. In these, one's doppelgängers live on a different quantum branch in infinitely dimensional space."

I stared at him for a long moment. "Just to clarify, when you say doppelgänger, you don't mean the spooky kind in the movies, right? Or . . . this isn't like an *Invasion of the Body Snatchers* situation, is it?"

"Good movie," said Duncan. "I liked the original."

"Me too," said Landon. "But no, I don't mean it in a spooky way. In an infinite number of parallel universes, there would be any number of you, or of me, at all ages, in all circumstances."

This, I told myself, *is what happens when you have a smarty-pants for a boyfriend. And then you ask him a question.* "My brain hurts."

He chuckled. "For me, deciding how I want my coffee hurts my brain, but thinking about quarks and string theory is restful, somehow. Speaking of which, I do think M-theory might shed some light on the situation."

"I'm afraid to ask." The boat slowed and bobbed, the water splashed, and Lighthouse Island loomed up in front of us.

"It's not as strange as it sounds. M-theory is basically a higher-dimensional extension of the string-theory vision of multiverses."

"Oh, sure."

"These theories require the presence of ten or eleven space-time dimensions, respectively."

"Uh-huh."

"This presents the possibility that there are other branes, of course, which could support other universes."

"Hold on—brains?"

"Not 'brains,' 'branes.' B-R-A-N-E-S. It's a type of bulk that particles are bound to. And it goes without saying that while these are unlike the universes in the quantum universe theory, both can operate at the same time."

"I'm going to stop you right there, Landon," I said. "You lost me at 'branes.' Actually, you lost me at 'infinite universes.' Or perhaps when you uttered the phrase 'several theories.'"

"I guess the easiest way to put it is that if there are multiple universes, with different kinds of physical laws and dimensions than those we're familiar with, it opens the possibility of spirits existing on other planes, essentially."

"You mean life after death?"

He tilted his head with an expression of uncertainty. "I wouldn't say that exactly, at least not in the way I think you, or most people, mean it. But in the sense that there is energy, even *souls* or whatever you want to call them, existing on wavelengths other than the ones we're familiar with."

"Brain hurting again. And that's B-R-A-I-N, not B-R-A-N-E."

"And yet your brain doesn't hurt when it's making sense of ghosts?"

"Oh, it hurts, all right. But . . . the whole ghost thing involves the heart more than the mind. In fact, if I think too much about it, I go a little crazy. But if I open my heart to the possibilities, then sometimes the spirits can talk to me, and I can help them."

Landon held my gaze.

"Hey," said Duncan. "Speaking of brains, I heard a good zombie joke."

"I can hardly wait," I said.

"What do zombies say during a protest rally?"

"What?"

"'What do we want? *Brains!* When do we want them? *Brains.*'"

Duncan laughed so hard he had tears in his eyes, but still managed to ease the *Callisto* up to the island's rock wall. The tide was high, so the ladder was only about four feet high. Sort of like climbing up the side of a very deep swimming pool.

The demo guys, then Waquisha, and then even Stephen climbed the ladder. It was no big deal.

Surely if I could climb this ladder, I would be well on my way to conquering my phobia. I grabbed for the cold metal rung, tried to regulate my breathing and ignore the bobbing of the boat . . . but no. I made the mistake of looking up, and started to sway. Dizziness washed over me.

"Could you take us around to the yacht harbor, please?" Landon asked Duncan, so I wouldn't have to. "And then come back and we'll winch the supplies up."

"Sure thing," Duncan said, a sympathetic look in his eyes.

I silently berated myself, angry at this weakness.

Landon rubbed my shoulders gently. "Hey, ease up. Give yourself a little more time."

"Back to the ghosts." I changed the subject as the boat headed to the little yacht harbor on the east side of the island. "Do you really think this multiple-universe theory might explain different planes of existence?"

He shrugged. "It might well be a load of rubbish. 'Ghosts' might be nothing more than the result of infrasound waves."

"How so?"

"The human eyeball has a resonant frequency of eighteen cycles per second; normal waking brain is between seven and fourteen cycles per second in a beta state. Above or below that are states of drug-induced euphoria or meditation or sleep or near sleep. So if you have a situation where low-level waves are caught inside a building, such as with certain pipes or machinery, they might help mold human perception so you think you see a ghost."

"I really don't think low-level sound waves are making me stand in the woods talking to Alicia's dead ex-husband. Anyway . . . what do you *believe*?"

Landon gave me his patented slow smile, the one that carried a million thoughts and ideas and drove me crazy.

"I believe that my girlfriend has introduced me to a whole world I never knew existed, and against which I would have argued in the past. But now, knowing she's awfully smart and not completely nuts, I have to figure this thing out."

"And therefore figure *me* out? I thought men liked women of mystery."

"Not me." He shook his head and smiled. "Figuring things out is what I do."

Duncan pulled the boat up to the harbor dock. The usual boats were in their slips, plus a new one. I waved to Paul Halstrom, who sat on the deck of a boat named *Flora*, and appeared to be whittling something.

I dropped my hand when Halstrom glared at me. So much for trying to be neighborly. I was guessing he was still angry about no longer having the run of the island.

I climbed off the boat, searching my peripheral vision for Thorn. I doubted he'd be able to answer my questions any more satisfactorily than two days ago, but I didn't want him popping up at an inopportune time and scaring the you-know-what out of me.

No sign of Thorn. Not lurking in the woods, not peeking out one of the lighthouse's narrow windows. At least for now.

Fingers crossed that he had been lingering the other

day out of sheer confusion, and that by now he would have gone wherever it is we go. I hoped so. Maybe he'd be able to work out some of his disastrous personal issues in the afterlife. Or some parallel universe.

I wasn't sure I bought Landon's attempt to explain the existence of ghosts through physics, but I did wonder, not for the first time, whether we moved on to another plane after death, or got a do-over in a new life as a new person. It was intriguing, but so far none of my other-worldly sources had been able to give me the slightest clue. All I knew for sure was that our spirits existed long after our deaths, which was comforting. I liked knowing, for instance, that my mother was still extant, in some form or another. At times, when I was half asleep, I could feel the soft weight of her hand on my head, stroking my hair. Perhaps it was simply my imagination, but it was nice to think she would come back to visit, from time to time.

Landon and I walked the five minutes from the harbor to the lighthouse buildings. The frosty day had brightened, the gray haze slowly thinning as the sun burned through it. Birds sang and fluttered through the trees. The air carried the scent of brine and eucalyptus. I tried to imagine what it must have been like, back in the day, to live here day in, day out, watching the bay and tending to the lamp.

I doubted Landon noticed any of it, intent as he was on trying to get a signal on his phone. He kept holding it at different angles, high and low, to the left then the right, as though searching out stray radio waves.

"I told you, cell phones rarely work out here on the island," I said. "But you can send texts, for some reason. Makes no sense, but that's how it is."

"Texts require much less bandwidth than voice calls,"

Landon explained, "and they terminate after sending, so even if a connection is intermittent, a text might slip through, whereas a call won't be able to establish connectivity."

"Oh. I guess it *does* make sense, when you put it like that."

By the time we got to the courtyard, the crew had already unloaded Duncan's boat, winching the pallet up the rock wall. I had everyone gather around while Buzz and Krauss—another hulking man with close-cropped hair who wore expensive sunglasses even on the foggiest days—checked out the Keeper's House, calling out "Clear!" as they moved from room to room. They had already been on the island for an hour this morning, and had checked out the buildings, but now that we were here they did it again. I got the sense neither of them would be able to face Ellis Elrich were they to find another body on this isle.

Their efforts were reassuring, but I couldn't imagine that whoever had killed Thorn was still hiding in a closet somewhere. The island had been crawling with police officers for the past two days, after all.

While we waited, I gazed up at the tower. I knew from my earlier inspection that these buildings had good foundations, built into the bedrock. They had been constructed with pride and care, based on designs sturdy enough to withstand the brutal weather of New England or the Great Lakes. And though we saw some rough seas—the Pacific Ocean is not nearly as tranquil as its name would suggest—in general California was a sight more temperate than Maine.

The house, too, was built to last. I walked the perimeter of the exterior, taking notes. Once we rid it of dry rot and mold, we would be able to reconfigure the layout to Alicia's specifications without losing too much of the original charm. Many, if not most, of the built-ins and hardware were salvageable. The walls stood straight, the doorframes plumb. And with the exception of the windowsills, the exterior walls appeared to be intact.

I paused as my boots trod on broken glass. I looked up. Overhead, several of the attic windowpanes were broken. No surprise; the windows of abandoned houses seemed irresistible to kids throwing rocks. But . . . if that were the case, the glass shards should be on the inside of the house, rather than the outside, wouldn't they?

A woman's face appeared at the window.

Pale, haunting. Fleeting. She vanished as quickly as she had appeared.

Dingo had mentioned a worker trying to repair a pane in the attic window, and getting scared away. I had inspected the attic months ago, when I first toured the island, but at the time I had been looking for dry rot and roof problems, not spirits.

"How do you plan to resolve the Internet issue?" Landon asked as we waited.

"Alicia said she might just do without Internet. Make it a selling point instead of a drawback: 'Come to the island for a real getaway.' I think she's onto something."

Landon looked as if I had suggested we kick some puppies. "What an insane notion."

"It's relaxing to unplug," I said. "You should try it."

"I'll take that under advisement," Landon said.

Once Buzz and Krauss gave us the all clear, I led my crew on a walk-through of the main rooms of the house, explaining what I did—and most decidedly did *not*—want them to salvage. More than once I thought I was seeing a ghost out of the corner of my eye, and then it turned out to be the silent Waquisha, lagging behind.

The blast of a horn signaled the arrival of the big supply barge, and the crew got to work unloading, under Lyle's grumpy direction. As soon as the supplies were secured, I designated an area for the junk pile, and the general cleanup began. We'd start a more careful demo next—stripping out wood ruined by dry rot, plaster spotted with mold, floorboards warped and brittle from exposure to the elements. Too often demo teams treated this step as a demolition derby, and I had to admit that method was kind of fun: Getting one's frustrations out by ripping a place apart, hearing the crack and splinter and crash, was decidedly therapeutic. But Turner Construction didn't do it that way.

"Stay out of the attic, for now," I told the crew. "Start down in the main rooms, that's where most of the damage is. We'll assess the second floor and the attic afterward."

I put Waquisha and Stephen in charge of gathering the salvage in piles, cleaning and sorting items as the crew brought them over.

"With historical structures it's essential to save everything we can," I explained to Waquisha. Stephen, along with everyone else who knew me, was used to my spiel. But if she was going to work for me, she was going to have to get on the historic salvage bandwagon.

"I don't usually like to take a building back to its studs, but it's necessary in this case because of the mold damage to the plaster and the need to redo electrical and plumbing throughout the building. Still, we always keep as much as we can, of everything, even the wood." I held up a splintery piece of molding as an example. "The tiny nicks and dents, the very wood itself, holds the spirit of the building as it once was; and even when materials are beyond repair, we retain samples in order to get knives cut to re-mill moldings in the original design. We also need sample swatches to match historical paint colors and wallpapers."

"So," Waquisha said, "essentially you're saying: Don't throw anything away."

"You should see her bedroom," Stephen muttered.

"Yes, in a nutshell, don't throw anything away," I said, ignoring my friend's snide comment. He was right, in any case. Note to self: When looking for a new apartment, make sure it has plenty of shelf space for my salvaged treasures. And books.

"Even old newspaper?" Waquisha asked, holding up a few shreds attached to a baseboard one of the demo guys had just placed on the already-growing pile.

I checked it out: part of an article on an election, and an ad for a long-closed San Francisco butchery.

"Even old newspapers—how cool is this?" I asked, excited, trying to show them the wonder of ancient newsprint. Waquisha and Stephen exchanged a glance, appearing underwhelmed. "Anyway, yes, please keep the old newspapers. In the old days builders often stuffed walls with newspapers as a form of insulation. They can provide hints about the date the work was carried out, and what was going on locally at the time. And they're just plain cool. Anyway, you two can sort things out and clean things up, so we can start to get an idea of what we have, what we can reuse, what we'll need to replace. And Waquisha, Jeremy says you know wood."

She nodded. "My dad has a woodworking shop."

"Good. Show Stephen how to determine if a piece of wood is worth salvaging or not—and it's probably no surprise by now, but I'm fine with the liberal use of wood fillers and reconstruction if that's what it takes to keep an original window frame, for example."

She nodded again, and she and Stephen got to work.

The biggest, most obvious problem in the Keeper's House was that many of the wooden horizontal surfaces—parts of the floors, the outdoor steps, a few counters and lintels—had rotted through, victim of the wear and tear of the bay breezes, salt, and storms—and the general lack of upkeep. Fortunately, the interior stairs were still solid, and we had already placed plywood over the spongy areas of floor where a person might be in danger of putting a foot through the rotting wood.

Once the demo was in full swing, Landon turned to me.

"Ghost time?"

I nodded. "Ghost time."

Chapter Fourteen

"Somehow I don't think I'm going to make it up the light tower," I said.

"Do you think there's another way to touch base with the spirits?"

I nodded. "I want to check out the attic."

Inside the Keeper's House, we were enveloped by the racket of demolition—the screech of nails being pulled from wood, the crack of splintering wood, the very loud music on the radio—as we climbed up to the second floor and proceeded down a small hallway to another set of enclosed stairs. These were steep and narrow, but the wood was still intact. A tight switchback led to a short door with several locks on it.

"Looks like someone was trying to keep something safe," Landon commented.

"Alicia gave me all the old keys to try," I said, unlocking one of several antique-looking locksets. "Though it looks like someone's jimmied a couple of them already. I sure hope no one got in here."

After several minutes of trying multiple keys, I finally got the door open. "Let me go in alone first."

Landon nodded and stood back. "Shout if you need me. I'll be right here."

Heeding Olivier's warning not to take my spirit encounters lightly, I took the time to prepare myself. I did a full-body scan, breathing deeply. I closed my eyes and reminded myself that the soles of my feet were connected to my boots, which were connected to the wood floor beneath them, which was connected to beams and walls and studs clear to the foundation, itself built into bedrock. *I am of this earthly plane.* Finally, I rubbed the gold ring I kept on a small chain around my neck; it was my grandmother's, and had been given to me by my mother. It reminded me that I was connected, across the generations, to a line of strong women.

Only then did I enter the attic. In classic haunted house fashion, the door creaked a loud protest when I swung it open.

The room was dim. The sun hadn't quite burned off the mist this morning, so only a soft gray light sifted in through dormer windows on either side.

On the opposite wall seemed to be some kind of mural. I tried to make it out—was it the face of a woman? Had vandals entered after all, but simply graffitied the wall?

I noted a light switch to the left and flicked it on.

A bare bulb overhead flared to life.

The mural—or whatever it was I thought I saw— disappeared. The wall was made of lath and plaster and bare wooden studs. Nothing more.

I tried turning off the light again, but this time saw nothing. It was possible I was talking myself into things. I switched the light back on and started to investigate.

The chamber was jammed with miscellaneous items: an old baby crib with intricate turned posts; two wooden chairs, one broken; an old storm window; a couple of small side tables; several old neatly stacked wooden crates; half a dozen rotting cardboard boxes. Christmas decorations, a few small paintings, and framed photographs had been stashed together in an open box. A nice old pendulum clock sat on an oak filing cabinet next to a dressmaker's form, which, I was certain, I was bound to mistake for a human figure and scare myself with in dim light one of these days soon. Mannequins gave me the creeps.

It took me a moment to realize what was amiss. While the rest of the building carried the distinct musty scent of a long-abandoned home, the attic smelled of lemon polish and furniture wax. Nary a cobweb in the corners, not a visible dust mote on the floor. The windowpanes—made of slightly wavy glass, several of which were cracked or broken—were clean and sparkling, despite their condition.

I looked out the window where I thought I had seen a face from the outside. There were six panes in each window, and three of each were broken. On the floor at the base of the window was a neat pile of broken glass, and immediately above it, a piece of plywood had been nailed over one broken pane.

Dingo had been right.

Another housecleaning ghost. This was my second; the last one and I had engaged in a gnarly food fight when I suggested she stop baking pies and instead leave this earthly plane. But so far, in my experience, each spirit is distinct. Just like living, breathing people. And fortunately, there were no pies or other groceries in the attic, so I was probably safe from that particular form of ignominious treatment.

I peered down to the ground below. Broken glass sparkled at the footing of the house. There were far more shards outside than within. So . . . what did that mean? Had someone thrown rocks from the *in*side? That wasn't very likely, was it?

I walked around the attic slowly, palms out, trying to make myself available to anyone—the woman in white, the little boy collecting seashells, even Thorn?—who might want to talk to me.

"Hello?" I said. "Anyone here?"

Nothing.

"I'd like to talk to you," I continued. "I'd like to help you, if I can."

A noise.

I stopped in my tracks.

I heard it again. A faint scratching sound. Perhaps a mouse or a squirrel. Again I wondered what kind of animals might live out here on the island.

Then one of the framed photos in the box fell on its face.

Not an animal, then.

"Hello?" I said again. If this ghost was trying to communicate by making noises, it was likely it—she?—couldn't speak to me directly. But perhaps she could understand me.

The foghorn blew, making me jump. The noise was deafening. I clapped my hands over my ears and squeezed my eyes shut, waiting for it to stop.

Alicia was right to worry about guests trying to sleep while in the foghorn building, but folks in the Keeper's House were going to find the horn challenging as well. I couldn't imagine sleeping through *that*. How had the denizens done so, over the years?

When the horn stopped blowing, I opened my eyes. The overhead light had gone out.

Whispers. Barely there, tantalizingly out of reach of my hearing. The back of my neck tingled and goose bumps rose along my arms, but I forced myself to steady my breathing and said, "Hello? I know you're there, but it's hard to understand you."

A face appeared, the face I had mistaken for a mural on the far wall. A woman. I froze.

The spirit wavered, a hazy mist more than anything. I couldn't tell whether or not she was the same woman I had seen throw herself from the tower. That vision had been very clear and lifelike, whereas this one seemed more like a dream. She was speaking, her tone pleading. I tried to make out the words, but the only one I could make out was something that sounded like "vigilance." Was she worried about not being vigilant enough? Could she be concerned that the light wasn't being tended?

"I can't understand you," I said. "I know you're there. I want to help you. Let's—"

The barely-there image dissipated.

"Come back, please!" I waited for a long time, searching my peripheral vision just in case. Finally, I flicked the lights back on, then crossed over to the box to pick up the photo that had fallen.

It was a sepia-toned image of young child, about three or four. He was in formal attire: a coat and tie and short pants, black shiny shoes and bulky socks at the ends of skinny legs. He stared straight at the camera, looking solemn.

Could this be the boy I had seen down by the water?

I flipped through the other photos. There were several cranky-looking, bewhiskered men, whom I assumed had been the keepers and assistant keepers, and a couple of group shots of men and women in Victorian dress gathered on the large porch and front steps. I lugged the crate to the top of the stairs to take back with us. If nothing else these would be perfect to frame and use to decorate the hallways of the inn. Maybe my librarian friend Trish at the California Historical Society could help me identify the individuals in the photos. We could mount biographies on plaques next to the photos so visitors could learn about the people who used to live here.

Keeping my eyes and ears open to another appearance of my mysterious hostess, I opened a wooden crate. Inside were some very old books, several of which seemed particularly apt for a lighthouse: *Moby Dick*, *Treasure Island*, *The Swiss Family Robinson*, Jules Verne's *The Mysterious Island*. The pages of these old tomes were foxed and crumbling slightly at the edges; a few had marbled endpapers and leather bindings; their title pages featured that elongated, classical printing common to books of certain age. Beautiful. They would look great on a shelf in the main room, or perhaps kept in a glass display cabinet.

I flipped open *Treasure Island*. Inside was an inscription in faded ink, in a dramatically slanted, feminine script:

To Franklin, my little pirate,
on your fifth birthday.
Love you forever and ever,
Mama

I glanced back at the photograph of the little boy. Could that be Franklin? And if this was the child whose ghost I had seen by the water—what had happened to him?

I set aside the books and turned to the old wooden filing cabinet. In the second drawer I hit paydirt—the keeper's logs. I flipped through the first few. The old, faded brown ink and slanted cursive writing was hard to read. A few passages described the grand opening of the Bay Light; then I skipped from one month to the next, skimming over page after page of entries describing days of endless tedium:

> *August 27 Wind SW. Mist but good visibility.*
> *October 13 Wind S. The* Specklin *and the* Invincible *passed.*
> *December 14 Wind SW. Storm. All is well.*
> *January 2 Wind S, strong. Cleaned engine room.*
> *February 5 Wind so bad, I think it should blow the tower over.*

I passed toward some newer ones, and my eye fell on the word "Vigilance." Was this what the ghost had been referring to? It was the name of someone, not a characteristic. A name particularly well suited to this profession, I thought.

> *December 10 Wind SW. Wind still bad, but clouds have lifted—Mrs. Vigilance keeping the lighthouse in my husband's stead for the evening.*
> *December 25 Wind S. Not a vessel for two days, and nothing to light for and this is such a dreary place.*
> *January 16 So dull. Wind blowing violently.*
> *May 19 Nothing but gloom without and WITH IN.*
> *June 27 Wind SW. Summer never arrives in such a place.* Tender Manzanita *pilot uncooperative, talked to wife.*
> *September 2 Wind N. Hazy but calm. The* Manzanita *passed. Two Other vessels.*

September 5 Wind NNE. Commenced blowing at two o'clock a.m. Noon, blowing a gale and a heavy sea running over the wharf at three p.m.; washed away lower portion of steps.

October 8 Wind NW. La Belle France spotted, apparently in distress. Docked, repairs made. Set sail for San Francisco before nightfall.

October 9 Wind NE, cold, light, foggy. Sustained an injured ankle. My search is fruitless. My heart is broken. Several vessels have passed. Mr. Vigilance has fallen.

October 10 Wind NE squally. Still I search.

October 11 Wind SW. Search is fruitless. I shall not relinquish hope.

October 12 Wind S. Light haze. Since Mr. Vigilance has departed this earth, keeping the lamp has fallen to me. The search continues.

Search? What had she been she searching for?

"Mel?"

I jumped.

"Sorry," said Landon. "I didn't mean to scare you."

"No problem. I was just a little absorbed in these books."

"So I see," said Landon, his eyes casting about the attic. "You've been up here awhile, and the silence was beginning to make me nervous. Have you seen or heard anything?"

"I saw something at first, but nothing now," I said, standing and gathering the later journals—there were eight volumes—and heading toward the stairs. "But look what I found: some photos, and these keeper's logs. They're fascinating."

"Here, pass them to me," Landon said.

Landon packed the logs and photos into cardboard boxes; we would take them home to read at our leisure.

"Here," I said, handing him a few of the old books, as well. If they belonged to the boy I'd seen by the shore, they might well be significant. If not, they were still cool old books.

As I stepped out of the attic onto the little stair landing, I had the strongest sensation I was being watched. I turned back.

Find . . .

I felt, rather than heard the word.

"Find what?" I asked.

"What did you say?" asked Landon, waiting with the boxes on the landing below.

"Sorry," I said with a shake of my head, then nodded toward the attic. And repeated, "Find *what*?"

I heard, or rather felt, nothing more. After several long moments, I continued down the stairs. When I stepped into the hallway, my work boot trod on a yellowed, crumbly old piece of paper. It had a drawing on it, marked with an "X." I picked it up.

Another map? This was getting ridiculous.

"Is that a treasure map?" asked Landon, peering over my shoulder.

"It looks like it, doesn't it? I found a similar one the other day, and handed it over to the police."

"You're thinking there's a treasure buried on this island? And that it might be connected to the murder?"

"No, I think it's some sort of children's game, probably," I said while I studied the map. This one was similar to the other one in style, but the clutch of keeper's buildings was positioned lower on the page, and the "X" was near the rocks behind the lighthouse tower, rather than behind the foghorn building.

"It looks old," Landon said.

"True, but . . . surely it's not real. Even if there were such thing as real pirate treasure maps, just how many treasures could have been buried on an island this size? If there was rampant piracy—and buried treasure—in the San Francisco Bay, why don't I know about it?"

"Why would you know about it?"

"I'm a native. I know stuff like this. Pirates frequenting the San Francisco Bay and burying treasure is not something the local history buffs would have overlooked. At least, I'm pretty sure they wouldn't."

Landon smiled. "You're not a tour guide. Often locals are the last to know. Why don't you run it by your friend Trish at the historical society before dismissing it out of hand?"

"I guess you're right. I wanted to enlist her help anyway, to see if she can identify some of the people in those old photographs. But . . . *especially* if these maps are real, why would they just be wafting around the island like some sort of leftover party favor?"

"That's an excellent question. I can think of one straightforward way to test if the map's real."

"Go to where 'X' marks the spot, and dig?"

Landon smiled. "Great minds think alike."

Inside the Keeper's House demolition was progressing nicely, the men laughing and occasionally bursting into raucous Samoan folk songs as they wielded sledgehammers and crowbars to tear the place apart. My fingers itched to join them. There was something very satisfying about smashing things. Maybe I should suggest Luz start a therapy program in which wealthy people paid a lot of money to destroy old buildings in order to relieve stress.

On second thought . . . frustrated CEOs probably wouldn't be careful about saving the dentil moldings.

Landon and I carried the boxes of attic goodies down to leave with Stephen and Waquisha.

Already a small pile of valuables to be saved and re-stored had formed: carved balusters, newel posts, a leaded window; porcelain sinks and lavatory taps; a pair of sconces and a small crystal chandelier; several locksets and back plates and crystal and brass doorknobs. And wood of all sorts, since I insisted the crew salvage even baseboards and dentil moldings, as well as all doorframes and doors that were taken off their hinges. And the hinges, for that matter.

Waquisha was cleaning wood pieces with a small stiff brush, while Stephen buffed brass door hardware with a wad of cotton balls and a few drops of solvent.

"This is a great start, guys, thank you. Landon and I are going to check out something behind the lighthouse tower. Shout if you need me."

"Oh sure," said Stephen, waggling his eyebrows. "You two lovebirds go 'check out something' behind the light-house tower. Have fun."

I glared at him, but wasn't about to explain what we were up to in front of the always-serious Waquisha. What was her deal? Not everyone had to be cheerful all the time, after all; I lived in the Bay Area, I was well schooled in the need to respect different cultures and personalities and approaches to everything from sexuality to how one spiced one's tacos.

Still, I hoped she would loosen up soon.

Landon and I grabbed shovels from the toolshed. One was caked with dirt, which reminded me of something.

"The day of the murder," I said, "when I was trying to borrow a boat radio, I saw a dirty shovel in the hutch of one of the boats."

"Why would someone on a boat need a shovel?"

"That's what I was wondering."

"Whose boat was it?"

"I'm not sure." The sailing trio had been on Terry's boat when they returned to harbor, and Paul Halstrom was aboard one named *Flora* when he glared at me earlier. "But . . . it could have been Major's. Possibly."

"You might want to mention that to the police at some point."

I nodded and took the treasure map out of my pocket. "You're probably right. But my phone doesn't work out here, and for now we have a treasure to uncover."

Following the map, we skirted the cluster of buildings and headed for the rocky shoal on the other side of the light tower. The map showed a small thumb of land sticking out into the bay. A few trees and plants were sketched on the plan, as well.

"Obviously the trees and bushes would have changed over the years," Landon said, studying the yellowed paper. He pointed. "But this cove looks about the same, doesn't it?"

"Yes—and look, that's the little cave, right there!" I said, feeling like a child on a quest for Easter eggs.

We made our way down a sandy slope and over jagged boulders to the cove. Near an outcropping a large crevice in the rock wall formed a small cave.

"So, now what?" I asked, brushing dirt and moss from the seat of my dress. I'd had to slide down the slope's last few feet. "It should be right around here, right?"

We studied the map. Landon nodded. "Looks like it's located between the cave and this rock formation. Right about . . . ." He marked an "X" in the sand with the heel of his boot. "Here."

We started digging.

Chapter Fifteen

Forty-five minutes later we were still at it. We had unearthed a number of seashells, a little bottle, a couple of smooth stones, a marble, half a crab carcass, and two coins: a nickel from 1903 and a penny from 1900.

No treasure chest, no mounds of gleaming jewels. No Spanish bullion or Peruvian treasure of any type.

"Well, this is a bust," I said, disappointed, perched on a rough brown rock and kicking aside the crab shells.

I had forgotten to apply sunscreen, and the morning's fog had ceded to a brilliant January afternoon, the sun burning my cheeks; I had sand under my fingernails and a blister between thumb and forefinger. I felt whiny.

I was turning into Stephen.

"That nickel might be worth something," said Landon. "Old coins can be very valuable."

"Maybe. But it's certainly not a treasure worth killing for."

"It was worth a try," said Landon, surprisingly upbeat for someone who had given up his free day to chase island ghosts and dig in the sand with yours truly. I studied his cable-knit sweater and longish brown hair, handsome face aglow from the exercise, and felt a surge of affection and desire.

He tilted his head. "What?"

"Nothing," I said, feigning a sudden interest in the barnacles clinging to the rock I was sitting on. I could feel the telltale heat of a blush in my cheeks, though that might have been the sunburn. I cleared my throat. "So, I suppose it's possible the treasure was already discovered. Either that, or we misread the map."

"Or, most likely, there was never any treasure in the first place," said Landon. He came to stand right in front of me. His voice dropped. "Hey, Mel, are you okay?"

I nodded.

"You sure?"

I nodded again.

"Perhaps being back at this crime scene has shaken you up more than you'd like to admit?"

I laughed at that. "The truth is . . . my reaction to you shakes me up more than the crime scene. How twisted is *that*?"

He gave me a questioning smile. "What reaction to me?"

"Look at you: You're gorgeous, and smart, and . . . I dunno, sexy."

Now he laughed out loud. "And this is a bad thing?"

"Not bad. Just . . . a little scary."

His mouth came down on mine in a brief but intimate kiss. Then he wrapped me in his arms. "Murder and ghosts don't faze you, but a man in love is scary?"

I went still. This was the first time the "L" word had been said between us. I was at a loss with how to respond.

"Mel, I've been thinking," Landon began. "We—"

"Mel?" A shout came from up above—one of the demo guys was calling for me.

"Be right there!" I yelled back. "Sorry, Landon, I'd better get back to work."

He gave me a small, slightly sad smile, and nodded. "Of course."

"I'm sorry," I hesitated. "You were about to say something?"

"No worries, as you Californians say. It can wait. This isn't the right moment, anyway."

I slipped the grimy coins into my jacket pocket. I didn't hold out a lot of hope that they were worth enough to qualify as a treasure, but what did I know?

The lath and plaster had been peeled away inside the Keeper's House, revealing ancient plumbing and almost-as-ancient wiring. All of it would have to be ripped out and replaced. As much as I love most old stuff in historic homes, plumbing and wiring weren't among them. Old pipes corroded and often were made of lead, and old joints were prone to bursting. Ragged wires were easily overloaded, and the old and knob-and-tube system was a fire hazard.

"Check this out," said the head demo guy, pointing to an exterior wall. The space between the wooden studs was filled in with mortared brick.

"I've never seen anything like that," I said.

"Do you suppose that was done to make the walls sturdier?" asked Stephen.

"I would expect so," I said. "I've seen the original blueprints, but there were no building specs with it, so it's hard to know exactly why they did what they did. But yes, I would imagine they wanted the house to last as long as the lighthouse tower itself. This would explain why all the walls are still so straight."

"Unless there's an earthquake, then it's just unreinforced masonry," said a new voice. I turned to see Terry Re.

"Hi, Terry," I said. "Something I can help you with?"

She gave me a slightly mocking smile. "Am I not supposed to be on the lighthouse grounds? Sorry, Turner. We've had the run of the place for so long it's habit, I suppose."

"It's not a problem today, but when this becomes an active construction site things will get messy—and dangerous. I wouldn't want anyone to get hurt."

She gazed up at the tower. I wondered whether she was thinking of the last man who had been hurt here, Thorn. When she didn't say anything further, I asked again, "Is there something I can help you with?"

That same old song started running through my head: *Doe, a deer, a female deer, ray, a drop of golden suuuuuun . . .* I tried to counter it with a country tune that I had just heard on the radio with the demo guys, but I doubted I'd be successful at getting the song out of my head for days.

"Yeah, uh," she began. "I was wondering if you had come across any antiques, or collectibles or anything? In the house?"

"We found a few things in the attic, but—"

"You did?" Her eyes flickered up to the attic dormer windows. "You went up into the attic?"

"Yes . . . ," I said, wondering what she was really asking.

"*This* attic?"

"Why? Have *you* tried going into the attic?"

"No. Of course not. That would be trespassing," she said. "It's clearly marked, No Trespassing."

"Yes, it is."

"Anyway, the thing is . . . I love antiques. Nothing I

like more than antiquing. So . . . if you came across some collectibles, I'd be happy to take them off your hands."

I didn't say anything.

"For a good price, of course."

"It's not mine to sell. Everything here belongs to Ellis Elrich. As far as I know, he intends to incorporate everything into the inn."

"There *is* no inn."

"The *future* inn," I clarified. "Was there something in particular that interested you?"

Her gaze shifted back to the attic's dormer windows. "If there's anything of historical value, it should belong to the people of California, not to the man who happened to have enough money and clout to buy this place."

"In my experience Mr. Elrich is very sensitive to items of historical importance. Perhaps he'll donate them to a local museum. But again, anything of this sort should be taken up with him, not me. I just rip out walls and put in flooring, that sort of thing."

"So I see." She shrugged. "Just thought I'd ask."

Terry turned on her heel and strode out of the court-yard, toward the woods.

"Friend of yours?" Landon asked.

"Not exactly. Let me ask you something: Does she look like a person who does a lot of antiquing?"

"What does a person who does a lot of antiquing look like?"

"Good question. Like me, I guess, but with money." I was more the "junk" type. By the time something was referred to as an antique, I usually couldn't afford it.

"I honestly can't say," said Landon. "If you asked me to make an assessment based solely on her looks, I would probably guess she was 'sporty.' Why?"

"I think she's been snooping around, but wasn't able

to get into the attic. Maybe the ghost kept her out. And if so, why didn't the spirit keep *me* out?"

"Maybe she sensed she could communicate with you."

"I suppose that's possible," I said. "Anyway, the spirit let us take those items from the attic. We should go through them at home tonight, see if they can tell us anything."

He nodded. "In the meantime, presuming you are safe here for the time being . . ." He glanced around the busy scene. "I'd like to take the equipment up to the top of the tower and down to the cove, see if I can detect anything."

"Good idea."

Landon was no ghost buster, but he'd bought some of the high-tech accoutrements: an infrared camera, an EMF detector, and an electronic voice phenomena recorder. And his phone, of course, on which he had installed a number of interesting ghost-related apps. As I watched him hurry across the courtyard like an eager little boy conducting an experiment, I wondered if the phone—and the apps—would work on Lighthouse Island.

Since the demolition was moving along at such a good clip, I assigned two men to start excavating an area for the state-of-the-art system to filter the rainwater from the cistern. It would be used primarily as "gray water"— for the toilets, sinks, and showers—but nonetheless needed to be filtered. The drinking water would be brought in by boat. We weren't more than a ten-minute ride from Point Moro, but still it seemed like an expensive proposition to keep a boat, and a skipper, permanently employed for the relatively few guests the island could accommodate.

Did Ellis Elrich really think this inn and restaurant would be a moneymaking enterprise, considering the major investment it was taking just to get things up and running? Or was he doing it for the sake of saving the old buildings? Or was it simply to please Alicia?

But as a general, none of that was my problem. I was just here to renovate the place.

I sent a few texts to make sure Stan had put in the rest of the orders for lumber, cement, and other supplies, and to confirm that the plumber and electrician were set to come out tomorrow for an overview, and that their crews were still slated to start work in earnest as early as next week.

And then I started building a temporary ramp to the porch. So far the guys had just been tossing items into the sorting pile, but soon they would need to shovel dust and debris into wheelbarrows. That's where a ramp came in.

I could have delegated this aspect of the job. But this was the fun part of construction, which I rarely got to do anymore, busy as I was with management. I like getting my hands dirty. So I carried some lumber over to the table saw that had been set up in one of the outbuildings, grabbed my tape measure and pencil, and started measuring out the beams.

Then Thorn showed up.

"You're doing it wrong," he said.

"Says you," I said.

"Sorry, what?" Waquisha asked, suddenly standing in the doorway. "Did you say something?"

I jumped. "Nothing. Talking to myself. What's up?"

"Do you want to save this sort of thing, too?" she asked, holding out a few bits of shredded cloth.

"Probably old curtains," I thought, rubbing the ruined muslin between my fingers. "No, thanks, Waquisha. I don't think even *I* could find a use for rotten cloth."

I turned back to my measurements.

"You're not measuring that right," Thorn said again, more strident this time.

I glanced out the door and noticed Waquisha wasn't far away. She appeared to have paused to answer a text.

I dropped my voice. "What is your *problem*, Thorn? Seriously, you're going to 'mansplain' this to me from beyond the veil? You don't have anything better to do with your time?"

"But the tape measure isn't all the way to the end right there."

"Listen, Thorn, these may be called two-by-fours, but they *aren't* two inches by four inches. They're one and a half inches by three and a half inches."

"Why?"

No way was I explaining modern lumber practices to a ghost like Thorn.

"Just the way it is. Take it up with the lumberyard if you must. Now go away."

He sighed. Crossed his arms over his chest.

I put my head down and tried to ignore the fact that Thorn was floating over my shoulder. Tried to lose myself in the measuring, the sawing, the smell of fresh lumber. There is something almost magical about taking simple pieces of wood and putting them together to create something new, and useful. When I was a kid, budget cuts had eliminated funding for the school's shop classes, but I was lucky enough to have my dad's workshop to play in, not to mention his full-throated support. As a young adult I had tried to run from this world to pursue a graduate degree in anthropology. Now I was back, and happier than ever.

After a few minutes of silence, I thought Thorn had gone away, but when I turned around he was right behind me.

"I don't know what to *do*. I keep trying to leave, but I *can't*!" He reached out as though to push the table saw over in frustration, but his hand merely passed through the device. He stared at the appendage as though it had betrayed him.

I checked to make sure Waquisha was no longer lingering outside the door.

"Okay, Thorn, I've got a task for you. Have you met a woman ghost here on the island?"

"There's someone here who scares the crap out of me! Not sure if she's the one you're referring to, but let me tell you—that woman gives me the heebie-jeebies."

What a shame, I thought. It seemed like a bit of sweet justice that Thorn was frightened of a woman. Still, I had to admit she *was* more than a little frightening. The urgency of her whispers, that blank, empty stare . . . If I hadn't had experience with ghosties, I might well have gone running into the night, myself. Of course, for all I knew there might be more than one woman ghost on the island.

"What does she look like?" I asked.

"She wears a long white dress, and climbs the tower, and then jumps off. Who *does* that? I don't *get* suicide, do you? Hey, do you think she was the one who pushed me down the stairs, who killed me?"

"Why would you say that?"

"I get the sense she's a man hater."

"Is that right?"

Out of the corner of my eye I saw him shrug. "Just a feeling I get. I'm perfectly friendly to her but she looks right through me, like I don't even matter."

"That must be really rough." I tried to keep a straight face, reminding myself that Thorn was in a very strange, discomfiting situation and was finding it hard to make friends. "But listen, why don't you talk to her, try to find out who she is? Or even ask her if she saw something the night you were killed? Maybe she knows something useful."

"You want me to *talk* to her?"

"What else have you got to do? Turn on the charm, Thorn. How could she resist?"

He blew out a long-suffering breath, but then nodded. "I'll do what I can."

It was a long shot; I wasn't sure to what extent spirits could interact. But if Thorn could help me figure out who the woman was, it might help me understand what she needed.

I worked in the shop for another hour, then had Stephen help me transport the ramp in sections to the end of the porch where the railing had already fallen. We fitted the pieces together, slipping bolts through the holes I had predrilled. It took only about twenty minutes to finish the installation. We stepped back to admire our handiwork.

"You look pleased with yourself," I said to Stephen.

"I've never built anything before!" he said, taking a selfie with the ramp.

I didn't want to break it to him that the real work had taken place in the storage building, and that we'd simply fit the modular unit together. He'd done well. Baby steps.

When I looked up, I saw Alicia coming into the courtyard.

"Hey! What are you doing here?"

"I had to check and make sure you got the catering supplies," Alicia said after we hugged. "I tried to provide a variety, but wasn't sure—do you have any vegans working for you? Are there any religious concerns, allergies, gluten-free folks?"

I smiled. Alicia was big on making sure people had enough to eat. "I think we're pretty much equal-opportunity eaters, so far. I'm surprised to see you on the island, after . . . everything."

"My lawyer said it would be all right. She says I should live life as normally as possible, until the police make a move, or formally take me off the 'persons of interest' list. Apparently there was forensic evidence that other people had been at the top of the tower, though that's not surprising."

No, it wasn't. Probably they found fingerprint evidence of everyone on my crew, with the exception of a certain general with acrophobia. But finding evidence that others had visited the tower was miles away from naming a new suspect in Thorn's death.

Still, Alicia had good legal representation, and there wasn't much I could do about any of this at the moment. So I led her on a walk-through of the house, which was always exciting but also a little daunting at this stage. People who aren't familiar with construction tend to think of buildings as permanent, secure fixtures. It could be unsettling to see them tumble so easily, the wires and pipes and insulation exposed like the entrails of some giant, gutted creature.

Despite the deplorable mess and the open walls, Alicia's excitement for the project only seemed to blossom. We constructed a makeshift table in the courtyard out of two sawhorses and an old door, and I unrolled the blueprints to explain the electrical needs. Even if Alicia decided not to have Internet out here on the island for the time being, she should still have the built-in capability to easily install it, in case she changed her mind at any point. The time to do it was now, while the walls were open.

"Hey," I asked, "have you noticed holes being dug around the island?"

"Holes?"

I nodded.

"A few, yes. I assumed they were made by animals."

"Are there animals on the island?"

"Duncan says there are salt marsh harvest mice and California clapper rail. And of course egrets, herons, and other birds that live in the wetland areas. Is it possible they dig to make nests?"

"I suppose. But . . . have you ever heard of treasure on this island?"

"Buried treasure?" She smiled and shook her head, but there was a sad look on her face. I noticed her glance over at the Bay Light. It was hard not to, after all: It loomed huge from here, and was so iconic. Such a symbol of strength and safety.

And now forever tainted by Thorn's death.

"You okay, Alicia?" I asked.

She nodded, but there were tears in her eyes. "I'm not . . . Sorry, I guess I'm not really okay. But, to tell you the truth . . . I don't know. I keep going back over what Thorn said right before everything happened. That he was truly sorry, that he was sober and had been working on mending his ways. Do you think that was true?"

"I want to believe it was true," I said carefully. "But . . . I'm not really sure."

Thorn appeared in my peripheral vision. He stood behind Alicia, staring at her.

She shook her head. "Anyway, I just wonder what he wanted. What he *really* wanted. It probably wasn't about me at all. I've been thinking about it . . . Maybe it was a way for him to get close to Ellis. Everyone wants access to a man of his wealth."

"That reminds me: Did the boaters get in touch with Ellis about their objections to the building?"

She looked alarmed. "Have there been further protests? Problems of any kind?"

"No, not at all. I just wondered."

"I believe Major Williston made an appointment to meet with Ellis next week."

"What about Terry Re, or Paul Halstrom?"

"Not that I know of, but I wouldn't be surprised if they all went to the meeting. Those three seem to work in concert."

I nodded. "Hey, did you happen to mention the Palm Project to Ellis? Did he know anything about it?"

"Yes, it's a competitor of his. As far as he knows they're a respectable group, but focus more on overcoming addiction and substance abuse. They also work a lot with people who are suicidal or bipolar. Ellis does more generalized motivational seminars."

"Do you have any idea what Williston's story is, or Paul Halstrom, or Terry Re's for that matter?" Inspector Crawford had waved me off of poking into Thorn's background, and I imagined she would do the same with regard to any of the other possible suspects. But that didn't mean I couldn't encourage Ellis's security team to do some snooping. "Has your security team done background checks on any of these characters? Or on Thorn?"

"Background checks?"

"The police are searching for someone who might have known Thorn, and right now you're the only obvious connection."

"So you're saying maybe the security team could provide some insight into what Thorn was doing here, or whether he knew anyone local who might have had reason to kill him?"

"Exactly. They could look into the sailors in the harbor, or maybe some of the residents of Point Moro, for starters."

"Good idea. They might be on it already, but I'll talk to Ellis about it," she said. "In the meantime, I'll get out of your hair and make sure the caterer makes plenty of sandwiches for tomorrow—this looks like hungry work."

Construction workers tend to start out the day early, and finish up early as well. By four o'clock most of the crew had cleaned their tools, stashed their equipment in the storage shed, and caught a ride back to Point Moro on the *Callisto*.

"Are you about ready?" asked Landon as I locked up the shed.

"Just about," I said. Now that it was quieter, with the sun hanging low and orange in the sky, I felt newly emboldened. I wanted to see if the woman who threw herself off the tower was the same one I'd seen in the attic, and furthermore, what her story was. "I want to try climbing the tower stairs."

"Great. I'll go with you."

I smiled. "I appreciate the whole damsel-in-distress thing, Landon, I really do. But the tower was a crime scene crawling with cops, and Buzz and Krauss checked it out for the third time just an hour ago on their rounds. There's nothing in there except . . ."

"Blood."

He was probably right. I had learned on my first murder scene that after the police completed their investigation and released the crime scene, it was up to the owners of the property to clean things up. Thus the rise of one of the more gruesome new career choices: crime scene cleanup.

Landon pushed a lock of hair out of my eyes. "Doesn't it ever get to you?"

"What?"

"The blood. The emotions. The . . . death."

Of course. But, truth to tell, I had grown increasingly inured to the death. Maybe that's what came of seeing too much of it, like Annette Crawford, who, after several years working homicide with the SFPD, approached horrific crime scenes with detached acceptance. Or maybe I felt as I did because I now knew, beyond a doubt, that death of the physical body was not the end of the line.

The sensations I had felt in the attic today were more troubling. The woman saying—but *not* saying—*Find . . .*

What was she searching for?

"It gets to me, of course it does," I said to Landon. "But I try to focus on what, if anything, I can do to help. And in this case, it means I need to try to climb that tower. And I need to do it by myself."

"On one condition: I'll guard the door."

"Agreed."

Landon took up his post right outside the entrance to the tower, and gave me a kiss for luck. I stepped inside, my boots ringing loudly on the stone floor. The echo bounced off the circular masonry walls.

Landon was right, the evidence of the crime was still here. Thorn's blood had dried in dark pools on the floor, and in reddish-brown streaks against the light gray stone. A small evidence tag near the wall had been forgotten, a little yellow triangle lying on its side, as if drunk.

I closed my eyes and focused, summoning the memory of what had happened that day: Thorn tumbling, head over heels. The knife, the blood, his wide-open eyes. *Why* hadn't I thought to guard the door, or at least to keep an eye out for the murderer running from the tower? I would have saved myself—and Alicia—a lot of grief. As Annette had pointed out, this wasn't my first murder; you'd think I'd get better at it.

Speaking of being angry at myself . . .

Okay, Mel, I told myself. *Here goes. Up the tower. No big deal.*

I started climbing. I kept my breathing regular and steady, kept my eyes focused straight ahead. *This is good,* I thought. *I can totally handle this. Look at me go!*

Without meaning to, I glanced at the center of the spiral. The empty center. The floor seemed to fall away, farther and farther down, as though I was thrusting upward. I couldn't stay upright and collapsed onto the step, overwhelmed by dizziness and nausea. I put my head between my knees.

"What's *your* problem?"

I jumped at the voice and opened my eyes to see Thorn in my peripheral vision, looming on the step right above me.

I swallowed, hard, and lied. *"Nothing."*

"C'mon, then," he said. "You say I died here, right? Let's go see if we can find anything. Maybe we can talk to the lady in the white gown."

"You go on ahead," I said, still trying to keep the world from spinning. "Let me know if you see anything."

"Why don't you want to go up?"

I shrugged. "Don't feel like it right now, that's all."

"What is it? Scared to see the blood, the evidence of what happened to me? I *died*!" His face was very near mine; I still couldn't see him directly, but I could sense him. "I'm *dead*, you understand? Dead!"

I nodded. Thorn had been a violent man; there was no reason to assume he wouldn't be equally out of control in the afterlife. And though he was a ghost and therefore theoretically immaterial, I wasn't sure what he might be capable of if he gathered sufficient energy to manifest in our world.

Even if I didn't have a fear of heights, I would not want to be at the top of the tower with the likes of Thorn Walker. I could easily imagine him pushing someone down the tower steps, just because he could.

Yet another reason to rid the island of this specter.

"I know you died, Thorn." I chose my words with care. "I'm sorry you didn't have a chance to put things right—"

"I didn't have a chance at all, don't you see? I was making amends, I was trying. I was *trying*! I never catch a break." His voice lost its angry edge and became whiny.

And then I heard footsteps clanking on the metal steps. Farther up the tower, a woman in a long white gown slowly climbed the stairs.

She turned and looked at us. Her eyes were blank, disturbing. But her despondent visage answered one question for me: I was now sure this was the same woman I had seen in the attic of the Keeper's House.

Suddenly Thorn disappeared. A moment later I heard him at the top of the tower. He screamed.

And tumbled down the stairs again, all seventy-four steps.

Chapter Sixteen

I hugged my knees to my chest, kept my head down, and told myself to breathe. I knew what I had just seen wasn't real. It hadn't happened again but was an echo of the past. After a moment both specters were gone, and I was once again alone in the tower.

But I sensed the anguish the woman—or Thorn?—was feeling. I could feel it lingering still, mingling with the dizziness and nausea of the acrophobia. Not for the first time I wondered why *I* had to have this "talent" for seeing ghosts, for understanding them.

Once my heart regained its normal rhythm and my breathing slowed, I realized: She needed something from me. Surely that was what was going on. Thorn wanted me to find out who killed him, and the woman in the white dress needed me to understand her story.

Now all I had to do was figure it all out.

I gathered myself together and stepped outside, grateful to breath the chilly fresh air.

Landon's eyes held a thousand questions, but he didn't say a word. Just let me be quiet with my thoughts.

I glanced at the jagged rocks below the tower. Where had the woman fallen? How long had she lain there? What could have compelled her to jump to her death?

Off in the distance was the Richmond–San Rafael Bridge, and hunkered down on the Marin County side of the span was the rather fetching, Art Deco–era San Quentin prison. I had visited an inmate there once. Someone who seemed like a potentially decent man who hadn't caught many breaks in life, and who landed in prison for making a series of stupid, tragic decisions.

Remembering this, I wondered: Was Thorn actually redeemable? It was hard to move past the whole wife-beating thing, but if I was prepared to forgive murder in some cases, why couldn't I be open to the idea that Thorn had wanted to change his life? And if he honestly had come to Lighthouse Island to make amends to Alicia, did that mean the Palm Project had helped him understand and control his angry outbursts? And now that he was dead, was he still seeking a chance to redeem himself?

I surveyed the courtyard scene: the Keeper's House, the sheds, and the foghorn building. From the top of the tower, I imagined, one must be able to see all of Lighthouse Island, aside from one or two small hidden coves.

As the sun gave up the day, the light atop the tower began to blink its warning.

"Ready to go, Mel?" Landon finally said. "Duncan's waiting."

I nodded. "Ready."

I read the keepers' logs late into the night. The handwriting changed (and was easier or harder to read) as new keepers took over, but the entries were similar: Most were a single line noting the direction of the wind, any ships that had passed, tasks accomplished that day. The notes gave a fascinating glimpse into what life was like on that isolated island: the never-ending cleaning, the frequent supply runs, the incessant demands of maintaining the light.

As I was falling asleep, my tired eyes fell on entries from 1905, which I had read while still in the attic:

> *October 9 Wind NE, cold, light, foggy. Sustained an injured ankle. My search is fruitless. My heart is broken. Several vessels have passed. Mr. Vigilance has fallen.*
> *October 10 Wind NE squally. Still I search.*
> *October 11 Wind SW. Search is fruitless. I shall not relinquish hope.*
> *October 12 Wind S. Light haze. Since Mr. Vigilance has departed this earth, keeping the lamp has fallen to me. The search continues.*

A woman's ghost was still bound to the lighthouse. Did she tend to the lamp after all these years? And did her search yet continue?

And what could she have been searching for, on such a small island?

The next morning, bleary-eyed, I stumbled downstairs to the home office of Turner Construction. Supplies were being ferried over to the island on the barge today, and the demo crew was on track to finish today or tomorrow, at the latest. I had asked Ramon to serve as foreman on the island, to oversee the supplies and the completion of the demolition. Much of the crew would spend the day loading and unloading the barge, and organizing supplies.

I checked in with the suppliers and the trucks, the barge operator. Everything seemed to be going well.

"Day two and still on schedule," I bragged to Dad as I filled my travel mug with coffee and kissed him good-bye.

It was the little things.

Landon had a class to teach, and after yesterday seemed somewhat reassured about my safety on Lighthouse Island. Besides, I would be back working in San Francisco today; I had to go pick up the expedited permits at City Hall, which, as it happened, wasn't far from the California Historical Society, on Mission. It was high time I checked in with my favorite historian.

"Hi, Trish!" I said as I entered the archive and spotted her behind the counter.

Trish was wearing a bulky, hand-knit sweater over dowdy beige corduroys, and her glasses hung on a beaded cord around her neck. She was as unassuming as one might expect an archivist to be, but I happened to know she had a wicked sense of humor and a rabid commitment to social justice. Ever since she had joined us for a tamale feast at my dad's house a few months ago, we'd started getting together occasionally outside the realm of the archive.

"How's it going, Mel?"

"Good. Actually, maybe more 'interesting' than 'good' per se."

"Sounds like a story there."

"You wouldn't believe it if I told you. But I was hoping you could help me: I'm looking for information on Lighthouse Island and the Bay Light."

"You and everyone else."

"I'm sorry?"

"Someone has taken our file, I'm sorry to say. All I can offer you now are a few items that are online, or you can look through the old microfiche if you're dedicated. Also, you could probably access the original plans or blueprints through the Coast Guard. They're in charge of lighthouses."

"Actually, the architect has been working from the original blueprints. But what do you mean, someone took the file? Are we allowed to check things out?"

"No. It was stolen."

"By whom?"

She shrugged. "If only it were that easy. In the past month or so, there's been an inordinate level of interest in Lighthouse Island."

"Could this be connected to the renovation project Ellis Elrich is funding?"

"I would imagine. There was an article about the controversy in the *SF Chronicle* a while back," she said, donning her reading glasses and scrolling through something on a computer screen. "Uh-huh, it's right here. Starting about six weeks ago, we received several requests to view the file. Then one of our interns noted that someone had removed most of the documents in the file. And then the whole thing disappeared."

"How is that possible? Don't people have to leave their driver's licenses to see the file?"

She nodded, shuffled through some papers in a drawer, and placed an outdated Michigan ID on the counter.

"The intern who accepted the ID didn't check to make sure it was current."

"Something similar happened a while ago here, with a file from another job I was working on. Does this sort of thing happen a lot?"

"No, actually it doesn't. You must have the golden touch, Mel, but then you work on some interesting properties. Clearly we're going to have to tighten up our security. We keep a close eye on the rare books because folks try to steal those all the time. They're worth good money. But the documents in the stolen file wouldn't have any market value. They were mostly Coast Guard brochures or declarations, copies of contemporary articles about the lighthouse and the keepers, announcing new commissions, that sort of thing."

I picked up the ID. The photo of a handsome young man was slightly discolored with age, but it could well have been a younger, thinner, long-haired version of Major Williston.

Why would Williston steal the archive's file about the island?

"Can you tell me anything about the history of the lighthouse, and the island?" I asked, checking the time on my phone. "I can't read through the microfiche today, but I'll see if I can make some time soon."

"Nothing special comes to mind. The island lighthouse was developed in the late 1800s to help guide ships up and down the strait. Mostly related to the post–Gold Rush boom of San Francisco."

"Ever hear any rumors that it was haunted?"

"It's a lighthouse."

"Sorry?"

"Aren't lighthouses always associated with hauntings?"

I smiled. "I guess so. They're . . . evocative, aren't they?"

"Very. So, you're working on the project out there?"

I nodded. "The renovation of the Wakefield Retreat Center in Marin went well—is *still* going well, since we're really not finished yet—so Ellis Elrich hired me to work on Lighthouse Island. It's a public-private partnership . . . it's all pretty exciting."

I thought it best to leave out the whole dead body aspect of things.

"I'll bet. I'd love to come see it sometime."

"Of course. Let me get things in hand, and then I'll arrange for you to come for a visit. We could have a picnic. The boat launches from Point Moro, near Richmond, just a ten-minute ride. So, nothing else about Lighthouse Island, or the Bay Light itself that you remember off the top of your head?"

"To me the most interesting aspect of Lighthouse Island doesn't have to do with the architecture, but the fact that for many years the lighthouse keeper was a woman."

"A woman lighthouse keeper?" As in my ghostly apparition? Interesting.

She nodded.

"Was that common?"

"I wouldn't say it was common, exactly, but it certainly wasn't unknown," Trish said, warming to her subject. "Back in the day, lighthouse keeping was one of the few professions women could perform that paid them the same as their male counterparts."

"We're talking back in the nineteenth century?"

"As far back as that," she said with a nod. "Many years before women had the right to vote in the United States, an impressive few were landing federal positions as lightkeepers. Several female lighthouse keepers in the Great Lakes, for instance, even had lower-paid male assistants working under them, which was virtually unheard of at the time."

"Fascinating. How did a woman *become* a lighthouse keeper? Did they just respond to ads, or . . . ?"

"Most were the wives, or sometimes the daughter, of a keeper. The skills required for lighthouse keeping are very specific: Not only did keepers have to have knowledge of the lamps and the clockworks, but they also needed the dedication and grit it took to live in isolated, harsh locations, battered by winds and rain. And the bravery to climb the tower during a storm and scan the waters, looking for trouble. Most times the official male keepers were assisted by their wives, especially when there wasn't an official assistant keeper; for instance when they were sick or as they grew unable to climb the steps, that sort of thing. Upon the keeper's death his wife or daughter sometimes applied to take over. They could easily demonstrate they had the skill and experience to do the job."

"So they chose to stay on, despite the isolation?"

"Just like the men, a lot of these women wound up keeping the lighthouse the rest of their lives. I suppose it can be addictive, that kind of solitude. And beautiful views, to boot." A wistful note came into her voice. "I think I would do quite well, frankly, as long as I had enough books."

"Or an e-reader."

"Banish the thought," she said with a smile. "Oh, that reminds me of one thing I read: The lighthouses had their own little lending library of sorts. A box of all sorts of books—novels, poetry, the Bible—would be delivered by the regular supply boats or tender ships. After a few months they would swap out the box for a new one."

"A lighthouse bookmobile. How cool is that? I used to love the bookmobile when I was a kid. So, can you tell me anything about the woman who kept the Bay Light on Lighthouse Island?"

"This is what I'm telling you: There was some informa-tion on her in the stolen file." I could practically see the wheels turning in Trish's head as she stared at her com-puter monitor, clicking her mouse furiously. "I'm sure I could dig up exact names and dates, if you could give me a little time. Boy, it really steams me that someone would steal that file. What's the deal? We digitize as much as we can, but scanning everything in the collection is a huge project, and it's not as if the historical society is rolling in money. The files always have tidbits of information not found elsewhere: newspaper clippings, archival notes, and ephemera that we haven't had the time or resources to upload. What this society needs is a sugar daddy."

I smiled. "Maybe I should introduce you to Ellis El- rich. He appears to be a true lover of history. You could work your magic on him."

"You ever introduce me to him, don't think I won't. Wait—here she is. I remember because the names were so interesting, and so apt: from 1899 to 1905, the official keeper of the Bay Light was George Vigilance. The job then went to his wife, Ida."

"Did they have any children?"

"According to this, they had one son, Franklin Prescott Vigilance. But . . . ah . . . I remember now."

"Remember what?"

She let out a sigh. "There was a tragedy; their young son disappeared, and George had an accident while searching for him, and died."

"The boy disappeared?"

"Probably drowned. It was a common hazard, as one might expect on an island. But young Franklin's body was never recovered."

"And his father, George, died while looking for him?"

"According to the report filed with the Lighthouse Authority, his wife, Ida, said George was working on the clockworks at the top of the tower when he thought he spied little Franklin's red-and-white-striped shirt on the shoals. He ran to find him, but in his haste tripped and tumbled down the lighthouse steps, all the way from the top, breaking his neck.

"Ida found him at the bottom of the stairs."

Chapter Seventeen

There was a lot of that going around.

Trish looked up from the computer and blinked.

"And Ida took over after George's death?" I asked.

She nodded. "Ida Vigilance was the official keeper for the next ten years."

I was betting Ida stayed on at the Bay Light a lot longer than that. I supposed it wasn't absolutely certain that the vision I'd seen at the top of the tower *was* Ida Vigilance, but it made sense. And I was going to assume the little boy who had pointed to the tower was Ida and George's young son, Franklin. So Ida remained on Lighthouse Island alone, true to her name and ever vigilant, lighting her lamp, mourning her husband, and searching for her missing son for ten years?

That would be enough to drive the most down-to-earth person around the bend.

"What happened to Ida Vigilance, in the end, do you know?"

Trish shook her head. "It just says here the lighthouse

was decommissioned in 1953. Since then it's been run with electronics."

"And do we know anything else about Ida? Where she grew up, anything like that?"

"I don't know anything off-hand—the Coast Guard history focuses more on George than Ida, which is typical. But it's a good bet her maiden name was Prescott. Naming conventions at that time meant a son often carried his mother's maiden name as his middle name. I could look into it for you, if you'd like. We have an excellent genealogical collection. Family history buffs help keep us in business."

"I would appreciate anything you could find." A large group of children, chattering excitedly, was being ushered into the archive by two harried-looking young women.

"A third-grade class on a field trip," explained Trish. "They're here to look up information on San Francisco's 1915 Panama-Pacific Exhibition."

"Just one more thing before I let you go: Have you ever heard of a pirate treasure associated with Lighthouse Island?"

"A treasure?"

"I found a treasure map." I pulled the paper out of my satchel and spread it carefully on the counter. The old paper crackled and crumbled at the edges.

Trish looked skeptical, but pulled on a pair of white gloves before handling it. "Where did you find this? Is it genuine?"

"I think so, though I can't be certain. I found it on the island."

She put on a pair of magnifying glasses that enlarged her eyes to a ludicrous degree, then studied the map.

"There's no way to tell if the paper's genuinely old

without testing the materials," she murmured, hunched over the drawing. "But from what I can determine just by looking at it, it seems real enough. And from the way the ink is faded, and the scrollwork on the cursive, it does look like it's at least a hundred years old. Still, I would doubt this was drawn by an actual pirate. My bet would be an avid fan of *Treasure Island*. Did you know? Robert Louis Stevenson was almost singlehandedly responsible for the famous images associated with pirates: the one-legged captain with the parrot on his shoulder, the map with the 'X,' and even the idea of buried treasure itself."

"Really? I didn't know that."

"Apparently the idea for the story came about when Stevenson drew a map to entertain his stepson one rainy day in Scotland. Or at least that's how I always heard it. Later he expanded on the idea for the novel."

"As a matter of fact, I found a copy of *Treasure Island* in the Keeper's House on Lighthouse Island, just yesterday."

"You mean an old edition? Do you know the year of publication?"

"I didn't check the year, but I think it belonged to the Vigilance family. It was inscribed to little Franklin."

Her eyes lit up. "I'd love to see it."

"I'll bring it next time I come."

"Great." Her gaze flickered over my shoulder at the children, who had been shepherded into the reading room and were now squirming in wooden chairs at long tables. "I should go do my spiel. But first I have to know: Have you looked for the treasure yet?"

"Yes, but all we found was a couple of coins. Not much of a treasure, if you ask me."

"One never knows." She straightened and took off the

magnifying glasses. "Sounds like you need a numismatist."

"A what, now?"

"An expert in old and rare coins." She tapped something into the computer and wrote a name—Cory Venner—and phone number down on a piece of scrap paper.

"Cory's an acknowledged coin expert. And he's not a dealer, he's a historian, so he won't rip you off. If the coins are worth anything, he can tell you."

"Thanks. That's a good place to start, anyway."

"Let me know what happens. In the meantime, I'll see if I can dig up anything about a buried treasure on an island in the bay. Get it? 'Dig up'?"

"Funny," I said. Dingo wasn't the only one fond of bad puns.

"But, Mel, here's the thing about buried treasure," Trish said with a smile. "It almost never happened. It's a popular Disney narrative, I realize—thanks again, Mr. Stevenson—but in real life, if treasure was left anywhere, it was usually squirreled away in someone's home or in a natural formation, such as a cave. And there was no map drawn; that invites theft. Which is why folks still occasionally stumble onto a cache of something, because the fellow in charge died and took the secret to the grave."

"Okay, but . . ." I felt loath to give up my childhood fantasies of pirates. Not to mention that a hidden treasure might have served as the motive for whoever killed Thorn. "It can't hurt to try."

"You never know."

"Exactly. Okay, thanks for all your help, Trish. I'll let you go mold young minds."

"I love this age," she said, rubbing her hands together. "They're still young enough to think librarians are cool."

"I didn't feel that way about old Mrs. Ulmer at Lincoln Elementary, but you *are* cool," I said. "And if you're ever at a loss, put on those magnifying glasses. Guaranteed to make eight-year-olds crack up."

"What, you think I don't already know that?" She gave me a wink and turned to the third graders, who were oohing and aahing over a diorama one of the teachers was holding up. It showed what the San Francisco and San Pablo bays had looked like back in the days of the Barbary Coast.

The model even included a little pirate ship, passing through the Golden Gate, long before the iconic bridge was built.

I called Cory Venner, told him Trish had referred me, and he invited me to stop by later in the afternoon. Then I headed to Matt's house to inspect the final carpentry work in the library, and to meet with the Atlas Elevator mechanic and the backflow inspector.

Afterward, I girded my loins and picked up Luz so she could escort me to my acupuncture appointment, and then to lunch. On the way, I caught her up on the latest with regard to Alicia's situation.

I didn't have the emotional strength at the moment to vie for on-street parking in Chinatown, so I opted for the underground Portsmouth garage. Here, the floors were labeled with different names: Peace, Happiness, Joy. I parked on the Panda floor, in the Bravery section. I needed all the bravery I could get. We took the elevator up to Portsmouth Square, where clusters of old men hunched over small concrete tables, playing cards or chess or *mah-jongg*—or standing around, betting on the players.

In one corner of the square was a monument to Robert Louis Stevenson.

"Funny," I said, gesturing to the stone tribute. "I haven't thought of Robert Louis Stevenson in years, but yesterday I was looking at an old copy of *Treasure Island*, and today Trish mentioned him, too."

"I love that book. Always liked pirates."

"I like the Disney version. Not sure I'm up for the real thing."

"True enough," she said as we walked up Clay Street, past a bakery, an herb shop, and several restaurants touting specialties from different regions of China. The streets were decorated with bright red paper lanterns, which were probably hung up for the tourists, but I liked their cheery presence.

"One thing I always found intriguing," Luz continued, "was that Robert Louis Stevenson lived in this area for less than a year, but there's a school and a state park named after him, *and* a museum dedicated to his work in the wine country. It's like people are obsessed with the man."

"Really? What was he doing in San Francisco?"

"He fell in love with a woman named Fanny Osbourne at an artist colony in Europe, or somewhere like that. But she was married, with kids. She started the process of divorce but was advised to stay in the family home in Oakland in order to gain custody of her children."

"So Stevenson waited here for her? That's awfully romantic."

"Only for a romantic soul like yours," she said, elbowing me lightly. "But here's an interesting tidbit, given your current occupation: Stevenson came from a family of lighthouse designers."

"There are families of lighthouse designers?"

"I wouldn't imagine anymore, but yes, back in the day. He was Scottish—hey, just like the monastery you were constructing for Elrich. Maybe there's a connection."

"In what way?"

"Dunno," she said with a shrug. "I'm trying to take a page out of your book, making obscure random connections in the hope they shed some light on something. Elrich seems to have a fascination with Scotland, and there were a lot of lighthouses in Scotland. So maybe that's why he decided to redo the Bay Light."

"I think he decided to redo the Bay Light because he wanted to make Alicia happy. Simple as that."

"Really?"

I nodded.

"You know what I need?"

"What?"

"A billionaire friend who buys me islands just to keep me happy."

"Don't we all," I said with a chuckle. "So, Luz, I knew you liked poetry, but had no idea you were such a literature nut."

"I'm not, I just really like *Treasure Island*. Used to write essays about it all through college; it was my go-to example for anything I had to write about."

"This was your trick for getting into Princeton?"

"Exactly."

I never tired of walking through Chinatown. As a kid we used to come here on field trips, eating rice-paper-wrapped candies and buying cheap trinkets from the crates sitting on the sidewalks outside the shops. I loved the smell of the incense, the unfamiliar vegetables, the roasted ducks hanging in the restaurant windows. Even the wildly touristy Grant Street had its charm. But of course the lesser-known alleys were my favorites; Hang Ah was one of these.

"All right, it's right through that door, second floor. Can't miss it," said Luz, pointing the way. "I'm going to go peruse cheap silk items I don't need but won't be able to resist. Meet you in the dim sum place on Sacramento in an hour."

Given the locale and Dr. Weng's name, I had expected something exotic, an office that smelled of unfamiliar herbs and featured unintelligible charts and things written in Chinese characters. Instead, the waiting room was decorated like a 1960s theater museum. There were framed movie posters, mostly Hitchcock and film noir, as well as an antique motion picture camera and old film canisters.

My attention was riveted, however, on a poster of a wide-eyed, terrified-looking Jimmy Stewart trying to force himself up the staircase of a tower. The movie's title was splashed across the poster in lurid yellow: *Vertigo*.

"Great movie," said a man in a white lab coat as he came out of an inner room. He was dark-haired and pleasant-looking, only a couple of inches taller than I was, with a compact build but large, graceful hands. "Underappreciated by critics when it first came out, like a lot of great art. Have you seen it?"

"Um . . . a long time ago, maybe. Or maybe I'm thinking of *North by Northwest*. I get the Hitchcock movies mixed up. All except for *The Birds*—that one made an indelible mark on my very young brain."

He chuckled and held out his hand to shake. "I'm Vincent Weng."

"Mel Turner," I said, shaking his hand. "Thanks for fitting me in, Doctor."

"Please, call me Vincent. Have you ever had acupuncture treatments, Mel?"

"Never."

"When we say 'needle,' most people think about getting a shot. But it's not like that at all—these are very tiny needles. You might not even feel them." He led the way down a short hall and into a room with a comfortable-looking reclining chair. Calming, Asian-style flute music was playing in the background, there was a small trickling wall fountain in one corner, and the lighting was soft.

He sat on a wheeled stool and gestured that I should take the comfy seat.

"So, Luz tells me you're phobic about heights. How long have you felt this way?"

"A few months. I never even thought about it before, used to scamper over roofs since I was a kid."

"And what happened a few months ago?"

"I was in a fight, on a roof, several stories up."

"That sounds scary," he said. His voice was matter-of-fact but kind.

I nodded. "It was. But . . . the thing that keeps coming back to me is the man I was fighting with. He was"—I cleared my throat—"he fell. I tried to keep him from going over, but I couldn't. He . . . screamed as he fell."

Weng's dark eyes focused on me, gentle and unwavering. I looked away, fighting tears and nausea, and blew out frustrated breath. How long was I going to let this plague me?

"Bad dreams?" Weng asked after a long pause.

I nodded.

"Repeatedly trying to save this person from going over?"

I nodded again. "I keep seeing his face in that last

moment, when he knew he was going to fall. And hearing the scream."

Weng took no notes, just kept his attention completely on me. He had me stick out my tongue, and looked at all sides of it. Then he took my pulse—not like a nurse would, but in several different places on both wrists. He bent his head, concentrating, for several minutes.

"Other significant life changes in the last few months?"

"Not really . . ." I worked like mad, spent time with my dad and Caleb and Stan and . . . "Except, I have a new boyfriend."

He smiled. "Well that's good, right?"

"Right."

"Or . . . not?"

"How do you mean?"

"You look a little unsure."

I was mentally prepared to allow this man to stick me with needles. Not to ask searching questions about my attitude toward romance.

"But then," said Weng, standing up and turning away, prepping a tray, "your love life's not really any of my business, is it? Unless, of course, it is tied to the acrophobia."

"How do you mean, tied to the acrophobia?"

"I really don't know." He instructed me to push back in the chair and encouraged me to arrange the pillows to make myself comfortable. "You're probably thinking, 'Just stick me with needles and make my problems go away, I'm not here to be psychoanalyzed.'" Then he wheeled his stool next to me, and brought the tray over on a table.

What was this guy, psychic?

He continued, gesturing with his large hands as he spoke, "But in my system of health, I don't see mental

health as distinct from physical health. It's one thing to
break a bone, of course, but in other health issues . . . I
see the body—and mind—as made up of different systems of energy—yin and yang, hot and cold, excess and
deficiency, external and internal—and *qi*. Your *qi* is out
of balance. This could well be from the trauma you experienced, but it might be tied in with—or aggravated
by—other big events in your life. Now . . ." He paused,
and I realized he had a needle poised above my wrist.
"Ready?"

"Um . . ."

"The needle is tiny, see?" He held it up to me. "Not
even as thick as a hair. Remember to breathe, and try to
relax."

I pulled away. "One more thing before we start: How
do you feel about coffee?"

"Strong and black. I prefer Peet's."

So at least I knew he wasn't a sociopath. I rested my
hand on the pillow.

He slipped the needle into a point on the back of my
hand, between the middle and ring fingers. I felt it, but
it wasn't painful. Not at all. Not even a pinch.

"You okay?" he asked. At my nod, he continued, plac-
ing needles in the backs of both hands, my forehead, and
my ears. One or two pinched a little, but the pain was
nothing compared to the common scrapes and bruises I
encountered every day on construction sites. He returned
to a few of the needles, twisting gently.

Maybe it was my imagination, but I could feel a slight
hum running between some of the needles.

Weng kept his eyes on me. "We carry currents of energy within us, along meridians. You feel it?"

I nodded. The talk of currents of energy made me

think back on what Landon had said about different forms of energy and planes of existence.

"Now what?" I asked him.

"Now you try to relax, breathe, and clear your mind. I'll be back in about fifteen minutes to check on you, or call out if you need me."

"How long am I supposed to stay here?"

"Depends on how long you feel you need. I recommend at least half an hour, but some people stay for an hour or more. A lot of people feel so relaxed they fall asleep."

I scoffed. "*Please*. I'm not going to fall asleep in the middle of the day with needles sticking out of me like Pinhead."

He smiled, dimmed the lights, and shut the door.

Chapter Eighteen

"Apparently, I was snoring," I said, popping a shrimp dumpling into my mouth. "And it's possible I drooled a little bit."

Luz had a supremely self-satisfied look on her face as she used one chopstick to spear a slippery pot sticker. "Did I tell you, or did I not, about Vincent?"

"He's pretty good, that's for sure."

Dr. Weng had returned, extracted all the needles, and sent me on my way with a little mantra to say whenever I felt the fear: *The things that bring me joy ground me; the things that bring me hope lift me.* He recommended I repeat it not only when facing heights, but whenever facing trepidation.

I felt mellow, a strange mixture of floaty and energetic. *This must be how people who meditate feel*, I thought. And here I'd made fun of "Berkeley types" my whole life.

I had coasted on over to the dim sum parlor to meet Luz for lunch. We ordered drinks, she showed me what she'd bought—a silk kimono (she already had two), a silk clutch, and a silk lamp shade—and then started pointing to dishes on the metal carts that clattered by, pushed by grumpy, tired-looking waiters.

Dim sum was not the best option for those of us with issues of impulse control. Especially when we're hungry. On the lazy Susan in front of us was more food than could be consumed by my work crew: dumplings, fried radish cake, lotus-wrapped meat-and-bamboo-filled sticky rice, and plump steamed buns filled with barbecue pork, called *char siu bao*.

"Too bad he's married," said Luz.

"Who?"

"Victor. Dr. Weng."

"How do you know he's married?"

"He was wearing a wedding band. That's usually a sign."

"Not today he wasn't."

That got her attention. "He wasn't?"

"No, he wasn't. Could it be . . . ?" I searched Luz's face and slowly shook my head. ". . . that Luz Cabrera has a crush on a *doctah*? You could do worse." I said that last in a terrible imitation of the stereotypical Jewish—or Italian, or Slovakian for all I knew—mother. In fact, it was probably a great imitation of my father, as well, or any parent who hoped their children would "marry well."

Luz shrugged and toyed with her chopsticks, a study in nonchalance.

"You do! Seriously, Luz, you like him?"

She shrugged again.

"I have to say, he has a certain air about him . . ."

She gave a shy, conspiratorial smile. "He does, doesn't he? I met him at a conference a few years ago, and we really hit it off, and then I noticed the ring. I went to see him a couple of times when I threw out my back, but stopped because it felt like we had a connection—and that's inappropriate between doctor and patient."

"Especially if he's married."

"Especially then."

"Well, he was *not* wearing a ring today—I would have noticed. I was pretty focused on his hands."

"Those hands . . ." She let out a little sigh. "*But*, he probably just took it off for treatments. Lots of doctors do."

"Maybe. I'll find out next time I go." She was blushing now, and had even stopped eating. I decided to change the subject. "Anyway, I have a less pleasant topic for you: Do you think a wife beater is redeemable?"

"*No*," she said. "I'm a hard-liner on this topic. I think all T-shirts should have sleeves."

"Very funny. I didn't mean *that* kind of wifebeater, as you very well know."

"Is this about Alicia's husband? I hope you're not wasting any energy on that turd."

"Come on, Luz. You just forced me to let someone stick needles into me for an hour. Humor me."

"Wife beating. Okay." She took a long pull on her Tsingtao beer and sat back in her chair as though going over lecture notes in her head. "According to the literature, it's mostly connected to an anger management problem, combined with serious self-esteem issues. Explosive anger is treatable, of course, with proper motivation. The fact that the violence is perpetrated against an intimate loved one—as opposed to people who get involved in bar brawls, for instance—makes it more complex. And the fact that those loved ones are usually smaller and physically weaker than the perpetrator makes them true turds."

"Turds being a clinical term."

"Exactly."

"And can these turds be treated? Can they be re-formed?"

"Ah, this is where it gets interesting." She served herself some chicken and veggie-filled rice noodle rolls glistening with dark soy sauce. "Before you asked me if they could be redeemed. Now we're talking *reformed*. That's a whole different kettle of fish."

"In what way?"

"Think about it, Mel: A person can be reformed in that he or she changes his or her behavior. But to be *redeemed* is to make amends, to not only be sorry but to make things right. And how do you make things up to a person you've damaged beyond repair?"

"Not all abused wives are damaged beyond repair. They can get out, get help, get better."

"But the fear never truly goes away, does it?" she asked me, a troubled look in her eyes. "Sorry, this is where my lack of actual counseling abilities—in other words, diplomacy and tact—really comes out. I believe there are some things one never truly gets over. In some cases those challenges might actually make a person stronger, but they are forever changed by it, one way or the other. So can the perpetrator ever truly be *redeemed*? Oooh! We'll take two of those!"

She pointed at a plate of *jin deui*, sesame seed balls.

"What else?" asked the woman pushing the metal cart laden with small plates of noodles and dumplings. She knew big eaters when she saw them.

"You want spareribs?" Luz asked me. Without waiting for my answer, she asked for plates of spareribs and bean curd rolls.

"I think we'll need a doggy bag," I said.

Luz just shrugged and kept eating. She was a svelte

woman, and no matter how much she ate seemed able to keep it that way. I, in contrast, gained weight just by *looking* at this much food. The fact that Luz was my best friend, I liked to think, was a testament to my open-mindedness in all matters.

That, and because she was always there for me, no matter what.

"Hey! I have an idea," Luz said. "Let's go up to the observation floor of the Transamerica building, and see if Vincent fixed you!"

"Very funny," I said. Just the thought of the view from that height made the floaty feeling dissipate faster than duct tape on a jobsite, as my father would say. "Anyway, as you know perfectly well, acupuncture doesn't work that way. It's a process. Twice a week, Vincent said."

"Well, look on the bright side: You'll get to eat dim sum twice a week. And as your loyal friend who supports you in this process, I'll join you."

After lunch I made a series of phone calls to make sure all the supply trucks had arrived at Point Moro when they were supposed to, and then checked in with Duncan, and the barge pilot Lyle, and Ramon by text. So far, so good. Then I called Annette Crawford.

"I think one of the sailors on the island used an expired ID to steal a file about the Bay Light and the history of the island," I told her.

"What file?"

"From the California Historical Society, down on Mission."

"Uh-huh. I've got a dead teenager in the Bayview and a dead businessman in the Excelsior. You want me to arrest someone for a fake ID? Or is it the theft of historical information that bothers you?"

"I just . . . I don't know, but I thought it was significant. You told me not to hold back, so I'm not holding back."

"That's when I'm working your case. In this case, you should be calling Detective Santos if you think this is significant. Actually, even if it isn't, let him know."

"All right. You're right." I hung up, and considered calling the detective. But on second thought . . . I would call him later. After I found out whether the coins I had discovered were worth anything, and could possibly serve as a motive.

"Where to now?" asked Luz as we walked toward the garage. "Are you going back out to the island?"

"It sounds like all is well in hand there at the moment. I've got a crew working on demo, and they're running supplies most of the day. The trucks have all showed up, miracle of miracles, and Ramon's supervising. They don't need me today. So first I was planning on going over to Tiburon."

"New project?"

"A numismatist."

"Really?"

"You know what that is?"

"Sure. Why do you need to see a specialist in old coins?"

Trust Luz to know what a numismatist was.

"Landon and I found a treasure map on the island, and dug up some coins."

She pushed me. "Get out of here."

I laughed. "I'm serious."

"Really? Like that couple that found cans of coins in their yard? They were worth a lot of money."

"Somehow I doubt it's quite the same, unless a 1903 nickel is worth a fortune."

I dug in my bag and brought out the little plastic bag with the two coins in it. They were caked in mud.

She held it up and peered at them. "They don't look like much, do they?"

I shook my head.

"Want some company?" she asked.

"Of course—you don't have to get back to campus?"

She shook her head. "Gave my lecture this morning, and no office hours today. And now you've got me thinking about a certain doctor with great hands, and I need to be distracted before I make a darned fool of myself with someone who's probably married."

I smiled and flung my arm around her. "Want me to call him right now and ask him? He gave me his private cell number."

"Why did he give you his cell number?"

"Because he likes me," I teased. "And in case I have a panic attack."

"Ah. No, thank you, don't call him. Just ask him in some casual, natural way next time you go in."

"You can count on me," I said. Now that we were talking about our love lives, I pondered running Weng's question about my relationship with Landon by Luz. But I decided against it. I'd taken all the introspection I could handle for the moment.

We got out at the Panda floor, climbed into the car, and headed over the Golden Gate Bridge, to Tiburon.

Chapter Nineteen

Tiburon is a town of fewer than ten thousand residents, but by and large they are exceedingly wealthy residents. Resting as it does directly across the bay from San Francisco, on a thumb of land with views of the city and the Golden Gate Bridge and beyond to the Pacific Ocean, Tiburon features multimillion-dollar homes and a mellow, small-town feel. The compact downtown is charming and vibrant with a few good restaurants, but without the overt air of extreme affluence common to the swankier parts of San Francisco.

The numismatist's office was an example of this: It was rather shabby, a 1960s leftover located over a Pilates studio. The walls were lined with framed vignettes of coins and stamps, and a few dozen very old-looking books in a glass-fronted case.

Cory Venner was middle-aged, paunchy, and pale. He looked like he spent a lot more time inside with his coins and stamps than outside in nature.

"Oh, you never know, a single coin can be worth a

lot," he said in response to my fear that I might be wasting his time. "Let's see what you got."

I handed him the baggy of mud-caked coins.

He shook them out onto a black-velvet-lined tray he had set out on his desk, pulled a gooseneck lamp over until the light shone directly on the specimens, and brought out a magnifying glass.

After a moment, he flipped them over. Then he looked up at me. "That's it?"

I nodded.

"Maybe you should have washed them first," suggested Luz.

"Um . . . I didn't want to compromise them. Just in case."

"They're metal, you can wash them, no problem," Cory said. "But I'm sorry to say, they're not worth much."

"No?"

He shook his head. "Liberty Head nickel, maybe worth three dollars. If it were in mint condition, uncirculated, it might pull in a hundred bucks at auction. Maybe."

"And the penny?"

"An Indian Head penny can go for up to *maybe* a thousand dollars, again, if it were in choice condition. This one isn't. I'd give you five bucks for it, just because I like Indian Head pennies."

The disappointment must have been clear on my face.

"Sorry," he said. "If you compare to their *face* value, it's a lot, but no one's getting rich with these."

"Not enough to kill over," I mused.

He frowned. "Kill over?"

"As I mentioned to you over the phone, I'm working out at Lighthouse Island. A man was killed there, and

I'm trying to figure out why," I said. "I thought perhaps . . . well, I found some treasure maps and thought maybe someone was after a treasure."

"Treasure maps, plural?"

I nodded. "Have you ever heard of such a thing?"

He shook his head. "No, but there's buried treasure on these shores, for sure."

"There is? From the Peruvian revolution?"

He looked confused. "I'm not even sure when that was."

"Me neither."

"If only there were some handy device that would tell us . . . ," said Luz as she looked it up on her phone. "Let's see . . . the Peruvian War of Independence came to a conclusion in 1824."

"Too early," I said. "The maps include the lighthouse buildings, so they had to have been from after 1870. Okay, Peru's off the table as a source of buried treasure, but surely there were other fortunes being shipped around here?"

"Sure," said Cory. "The Barbary Coast saw a lot of gold coming in and out, silver and copper, too. Coins and dust, nuggets, all sorts. And there were plenty of unsavory characters back then, I don't mind telling you. Some you would never suspect, as in the case of Selby Smelter."

"Who was Selby Smelter?" I asked.

"Not a 'who,' a 'what.'" Cory leaned back in his chair and looked pleased to have a new audience to tell the tale. "Back around the turn of the twentieth century, there was a place called the Selby Smelter, in Vallejo Junction, where the ores from the inland mines were refined. A man named John Winters worked at the smelter for years, from appearances just a simple workingman doing his job. But Winters had a plan. Gradually, over many months and years, he removed gold bars from the vault where he was supposed to be storing them, hiding them, one or two at a time, in his jacket pocket at the end of the workday. Local legend has it that Winters buried the gold bars along the beach, at the water's edge. Only a few have ever been found."

"How much could he have possibly stolen?"

"Well, now, that's an interesting question. Again, there's face value, and real value. Face value at the time, he made off with nearly a quarter of a million dollars. Real value is much higher than that—these were pure gold ingots."

"What about that couple who found the coins in their yard?" Luz asked.

His eyes lit up. "I consulted on that case, as a matter of fact. Luckiest couple in the world. Moved into a new house, decided to do a little gardening. They were digging around in the yard to plant a few shrubs, and found a couple of old tin cans with some pretty nasty-looking contents. Cleaned them up and found they were old coins. Twenty-dollar gold coins to be exact, Liberty Head designs from the 1890s."

"Isn't one of the coins I found a Liberty Head design?"

"That's a nickel. These were solid gold twenty-dollar coins."

"I take it they were worth a little more than twenty dollars?" Luz said.

"Their face value came out to about twenty-eight thousand dollars," said Cory. "But real value was sixty million."

"Sixty million *dollars*?" I squeaked.

He sat back and smiled, apparently pleased by my reaction.

"Now that's what I call buried treasure," Luz pondered.

"Indeed," said Cory. "*That* is a treasure worth killing over."

As Luz and I walked back to the car, I checked the time: a little after three o'clock. If I took Luz back to San Francisco, it would put me in the thick of rush-hour traffic on the Bay Bridge to Oakland. But it was early enough to miss the worst of the traffic if we went the other way, through Corte Madera and Larkspur Landing, where we could pick up the Richmond–San Rafael Bridge and cross over to the East Bay, near Point Moro.

"Feel like some bun-burying?" I asked.

Luz frowned. "Is that a Turner Family thing?"

"As a matter of fact, it is. My mother used to like to do what she called 'bun-burying,' which meant exploring new places."

"Why not just call it exploring?"

"Because 'bun-burying' is way cooler."

"That remains to be seen," Luz said. "What did you have in mind?"

"Instead of me taking you straight back to San Francisco, why don't we take the Richmond–San Rafael Bridge to the East Bay and stop by Point Moro to check on the supplies for Lighthouse Island. Then afterward we go to Dad's house for dinner?"

"Sign me up," Luz said. "I'm always game for burying buns."

"You're a tough sell, you know that?"

"I like your dad's cooking."

I texted Dad to let him know Luz would be joining us for dinner, then hopped on the freeway in the direction of Larkspur Landing and the Richmond–San Rafael Bridge.

Luz had never been to Point Moro, which was no

surprise; most locals, even, didn't know it existed. It wasn't easy to find: To get to Point Moro from 580 southbound, we had to cross the bridge, exit the freeway, get back on the freeway going the other way, head back toward the bridge, and take the last exit at Point Molate. Miss that last exit before the bridge, and you have to pay the toll and go clear back to San Quentin before you could turn around again.

"It's sort of spooky out here," Luz said as we drove along the winding, seemingly deserted road, past NO TRESPASSING signs, abandoned ships, and hills of chaparral.

"There is a sort of *Deliverance* quality about it," I agreed. "'Funky and junky' is, I believe, how the Point Moro pirates refer to their town."

"Point Moro pirates? Is this a baseball team, or . . . ?"

"Just the locals. They fly a pirate flag. It's all in good fun," I said. Then added with a shrug, "I'm pretty sure."

Luz shot a glare in my direction.

"Hey, you said you were game for bun-burying," I said. "Where's your adventurous spirit? Besides, you told me you liked pirates."

"*Fictional* pirates, not the real McCoy. Long John Silver is a morally ambiguous character, as is Jim Hawkins for that matter. Robert Louis Stevenson also wrote *Dr. Jekyll and Mr. Hyde*. He was big on moral ambiguity. As I like to say, 'people are complex.'"

"You can say that again."

"Anyway, I didn't come along to meet pirates. I came because I was promised a home-cooked dinner."

"You should have come over last night. Dad made enchiladas."

"*What?* Now why would you tell me something like that, after the fact? That's just plain mean."

"I'm sure he's cooking something equally tasty for

tonight." I laughed and turned onto the little switchback that led past a few small houses, shacks, and RVs that hadn't been moved for a very long time. A dog barked and chased the car for a few yards before giving up, and a flock of seagulls squawked as they vied over the contents of a torn trash bag. But otherwise all was quiet.

The road led down to Point Moro's small harbor. On the docks near the barge that ferried supplies to the island, I spotted a delivery truck from Garfield Lumber, and a van from Eddie's Electrical. The *Callisto* was tied up behind the barge.

I parked in a spot nearby, and we got out and chatted with the delivery drivers and the perennially grumpy barge pilot, Lyle, who complained about the police questioning him "incessantly." But despite the grumbling, he confirmed what Stan and the other suppliers had told me on the phone: All was going well, and the deliveries to the island were on schedule.

"Where's Duncan?" I asked, not seeing the *Callisto*'s pilot.

"Grabbing some lunch at the Gentleman's Café," said the guy from Eddie's Electrical. "He says they make a mean grilled cheese."

"Eats more than he works," groused Lyle.

"We'll check it out," I said, thanking the men.

"On schedule's good, right?" asked Luz as we turned toward the café. "So why do you look so worried?"

"On schedule's great, of course it is," I said. The café was built on stilts at the edge of the water, and my heavy work boots clomped loudly on the wooden treads. "It's just that we're usually behind by now. There's a difference between the printed schedule and the real schedule. The printed schedule has a lot of padding in it to allow for the inevitable delays."

"Okay, but . . . isn't being ahead of schedule usually considered a good thing? Besides, there's plenty of time to fall behind. You're . . . what? Three days in?"

I nodded. "It's just a little too easy."

"Oh, sure. Other than a man being murdered on the island, it's been clear sailing."

"Oh! Good point. Other than that. But still, the schedule worries me . . . the last time a job started out this well, a water main burst and flooded the basement."

Luz smiled, lifted one eyebrow, and opened the café door. A little bell tinkled overhead. "Did you walk under a ladder? Or maybe a black cat crossed your path?"

"What can I say?" I said. "We in construction tend toward the superstitious."

The café was empty except for Fernanda, lurking, solemn and silent behind the counter. The pool table and dartboard were awaiting the crowd, a 1970s-era jukebox sat forlornly in the corner. Give that particular item a few more years, I thought, and it would demand a small fortune at an antiques shop.

"Hi," I said.

Fernanda listlessly handed us two menus.

"Have you seen Duncan?" I asked.

"He ate lunch, but left about fifteen minutes ago," Fernanda said.

"May I use the restroom?" I asked.

She nodded and waved me in the direction of a narrow hallway.

"I'll be right back," I told Luz.

"No worries." She slipped onto a vinyl-topped stool at the counter and asked Fernanda for a cup of coffee.

Upon my return Fernanda and Luz were chatting away like long-lost sisters, speaking over each other in rapid Spanish and laughing. Sitting next to a cup of coffee was a small plate of what looked like homemade cookies.

"Oh, hey, Mel, do you know Fernanda?" Luz asked.

"Sort of." I held my hand out and she shook it with a shy smile. "Nice to officially meet you, Fernanda."

"Fernanda's people are from a town not far from where my grandmother grew up, called Mezquitíc, in Jalisco," said Luz.

"Small world," I said, settling onto the stool next to Luz. Fernanda held up the coffeepot, and I nodded.

"Fernanda also has an opinion about what happened out on Lighthouse Island," said Luz.

"Is that right?"

"Hay fantasmas," Fernanda said. "Waquisha tell me there's ghosts. She says I shouldn't go out to the island." Her eyes brightened, and she smiled. "Sometimes Duncan asks if I want to go."

I remembered Waquisha challenging Major Williston when he suggested there might be a ghost in the tower. Interesting.

"How do you know Waquisha?"

"Her father lives on a boat here in Point Moro. She was living there for a little while."

"She was?"

Fernanda shrugged and looked away, as if she wasn't sure she should be telling me these things. "She moved, though."

Luz said something else in Spanish. It was a good reminder: I needed to sign up for an adult education course to learn the language better. I knew a little construction site Spanish, which meant I could tell someone to put on a hard hat or saw a plank at a particular angle, and I had a decent vocabulary when it came to tools. But as soon as the conversation turned to topics other than construction, I was left in the dust.

I was pretty sure Luz was trying to get some information from the waitress, so I bided my time, sipping the very weak, very hot coffee and looking around the café.

Behind the counter where we sat was a small bulletin board displaying the California health code, a worker's bill of rights, and a business license. There was also a school photograph of a little girl, and alongside it, a treasure map.

Another map? I got up to study it more closely. The "X" was on the west side of the island, opposite to the spot where Landon and I had dug up the coins.

"Where did that map come from?" I asked Fernanda at a pause in her conversation with Luz.

"Duncan give it to me. It's pretty, no? I'm going to bring it to my daughter."

"Do you happen to know some local sailors, named Major Williston, Paul Halstrom, and Terry Re?"

She shook her head. "I know faces, maybe, but not names."

That gave me an idea: I texted Alicia, and asked her to send me a photo of Thorn. I asked Fernanda for a refill, mostly so it wouldn't be so obvious that we were pumping her for information. Coffee here was served in an old diner cup with a saucer, rather than a mug. Really, I thought, give this cup a good scrubbing and like the jukebox it would soon be worth some money. I doubted anything in the café had changed since the Nixon administration. Point Moro was like a time warp.

My phone beeped. Alicia was nothing if not efficient.

"How about this man?" I asked, holding out my phone. "Does he look familiar?"

Fernanda looked at the photo of Thorn with his smug smile and nodded.

"He's a friend of Waquisha."

"You're sure? This man is a friend of Waquisha's?"

She nodded. "They eat here together."

"This was the man who died on the island," I told Fernanda.

"*Ay, Dios mío.*" Fernanda made the sign of the cross. "*No*, really? How sad."

"Fernanda—"

The bell tinkled and two men entered the café. They were both tall and bearish, with bushy beards and grimy baseball caps, and looked as if they hadn't seen a shower in a while. My first thought was to wonder how the petite young Fernanda held her own with patrons like this, but then they greeted her by name, and she returned their smiles. From their brief conversation about her daughter, I gathered they were locals.

Fernanda took the men's orders and headed toward the kitchen to make their sandwiches.

Luz and I thanked her, left a big tip, and walked out into the late afternoon.

Fog was starting to roll in, and the foghorn sounded.

"What do you think?" I asked.

"About what in particular?" Luz said.

"Do you think she was telling the truth?" I asked.

"Why wouldn't she be?"

"She said she didn't know much, but knew all about Waquisha . . ."

"We're strangers here, Mel. She was probably just being discreet until she got a sense of us. She told me she lives in the apartment upstairs. She might not be good with names, but I think she knows exactly who comes in and out of this place. And probably all the residents know each other—she said Waquisha used to live here on her father's boat."

"I guess I should call Detective Santos. If he hasn't talked to Waquisha yet, or Fernanda for that matter, they might be able to give him some information."

"And who is this Waquisha, anyway?" Luz asked. "Cool name."

"She's a new employee. Jeremy hired her to be his carpentry assistant."

"You really think she had something to do with the murder of Alicia's ex?"

"I think *something's* going on. According to Fernanda, Waquisha knew Thorn well enough to have lunch with him. I'm assuming it was more than once, otherwise Fernanda might not have recognized him. So was it just a coincidence that Waquisha, who was friends with Thorn, started working for Turner Construction just as we started work out on the Bay Light?"

Luz frowned. "That does seem odd. But maybe you should talk to Waquisha first, before bringing the police into it."

"That sounds like something *I* would say. Aren't you one of my loved ones who is always telling me to leave things to the police?"

"I am. I do. It's just in this case . . ." Luz trailed off with a shrug. "Fernanda saw Waquisha eating lunch with Thorn. It doesn't mean they were buddies, or anything of the sort. Maybe she just happened to bump into him while waiting on the docks. It wouldn't be that unusual."

"True. Thorn had a certain charm about him, I suppose."

Luz added, "Fernanda mentioned that Waquisha's dad is from a pretty bad neighborhood in Richmond. He did time for armed robbery—a stupid mistake made a long time ago—but he's on the straight and narrow now. He has a small woodshop, does some carpentry jobs, and is trying hard to stay out of trouble. I would hate for the police to start nosing around for no reason, is all. It's hard enough to rebuild a life after something like that."

"So you believe in redemption for certain criminals, but not for men who abuse their wives?"

"All I'm saying is that it's worth a conversation with Waquisha. I'll go with you, be your backup."

"Yes, because we're quite the crime-fighting duo."

"Exactly."

I gazed at the motley assortment of vessels in the harbor. There were plenty of small sailboats, a couple of dubious-looking fishing boats, and a few larger "yachts" that had seen better days and appeared to be inhabited full-time. "Did Fernanda tell you which boat was Waquisha's father's?"

"It's not here. She said he left on a fishing trip this morning, and isn't expected back for a couple of days."

"How convenient."

"Maybe. But coincidences do happen in real life, Mel. Why don't you give your carpenter a call, the one who hired her?"

Good idea. We took a seat on a bench and I called Jeremy. After chatting for a few minutes about the project, I asked, "How did you meet Waquisha?"

"She found me, actually. Right there at the docks, at Point Moro. Said she needed a job and seemed to know her way around woodworking equipment. You said I should keep my eye out for an assistant, so I thought I'd give her a try."

"How's it working out so far?"

"She's been really great. She's quiet, but I find that refreshing. She keeps her head down, gets her work done, and she's got a real feel for wood. Why are you asking? Something wrong?"

"No, just checking in. Do you have a home address for her?"

"She listed her father's place in Point Moro as a permanent address, but she told me she's been couch-surfing with friends, looking for an apartment. You know how rents are around here. I have her cell phone number, you want that?"

I thanked Jeremy and dialed Waquisha's number. No answer. Then I texted her, asking her to call me back ASAP.

Again I wondered: Should I inform Detective Santos that Major Williston might have stolen a folder from the California Historical Society, and that Waquisha had been spotted eating with Thorn? Did any of it mean anything?

I would give Waquisha an hour to call me back, and then decide.

Chapter Twenty

Traffic moved along at a good clip on the way to Oakland until we hit the merge with I-80, where things came to a near standstill. I'd read somewhere that this stretch of freeway—from El Cerrito, past Berkeley and Emeryville, to the maze that led to the Bay Bridge to the west, Oakland to the east, and San Jose to the south—was one of the most congested in the nation. It might be an apocryphal story invented by frustrated commuters who had spent too much time sitting in a parking lot that was supposed to be a freeway, but it sure felt apt.

"You know what I like about this stretch of road?" asked Luz.

"What could *anyone* possibly like about this stretch of road?"

"It actually travels north and south, but the signs are marked 80 east and 580 west. It never fails to amuse me that the cars are going in all four directions at once."

I chuckled. "That's a remarkably upbeat way of looking at a nightmarish traffic jam."

"You know me: I'm a glass half-full kind of person."

"That is *so* not true."

"Anyway, I almost forgot: Have you been back to that house in Oakland? The one that freaked you out?"

"I've been a little busy," I said. Also, I had been avoiding thinking about it.

That reminded me: Brittany, my Realtor friend, had sent a text thanking me for taking a look at it and hoping I was feeling better. I needed to get back to her, but "no texting and driving" was such a mantra for me where Caleb was concerned that I couldn't bring myself to break the rules, no matter that we were barely inching along.

"Anyway, I buttonholed my colleague the other day," said Luz. "The one who researches memory, remember? Want to hear what she said?"

"Shoot."

"Basically, the medial temporal lobes retain long-term memories of events. Some say the rhinal cortex function commands feelings of general familiarity, while detailed recollection is located in the hippocampus."

"I think I need a diagram. Illustrations of the brain or something." This was a little like listening to Landon's exposition on multiple universes. It served me right for asking academics to expound upon topics of particular interest to them.

"Want me to whip up a PowerPoint presentation?"

"Would you? That would be helpful."

"Yeah, I'll get right on it. In the meantime, here's where it gets interesting," Luz continued. "Some epilepsy patients experience déjà vu at the onset of a seizure."

"That is interesting. Except I'm not epileptic. At least, not that I know of."

"I realize that. But epileptic seizures are connected to electrical activity in neurons within focal regions of the brain. These neurons can originate in the medial temporal lobes."

"Which are connected to memory."

"Exactly."

We had finally inched our way into the maze, and traffic had picked up a little.

"Sorry, Luz, I'm not following. Are you saying my feeling that I'd been in that house before indicates I'm developing epilepsy? Is epilepsy something a person *can* develop? Wait—could that be what my vertigo is about?"

"No, I think your vertigo is connected to the scumbag who tried to push you off a roof. I'm mentioning epilepsy because it's really the only scientific research out there on this kind of memory glitch, which is what déjà vu seems to be."

"It's a glitch?"

"It seems so. Electrical disturbances in the medial front lobe can generate what's called an aura of déjà vu prior to an epileptic event. All of this leads to the theory that what we know as déjà vu is caused by a dysfunctional electrical discharge in the brain."

"So you're saying my brain's shorting out? That can't be good."

"I'm not saying that at all. Everybody experiences a little electrical discharge now and then. Ever have that feeling of jumping right as you're falling asleep? It's called a hypnagogic jerk. Same type deal. Anyway, some researchers think déjà vu is a kind of memory error, where new information bypasses the short-term memory and goes straight into long-term, making us think we knew something all along."

"So it's random?"

"Depends. Have you experienced a similar sensation anywhere other than in that house?"

I shook my head. "Not like that. Never anything like that."

"Then no, it's probably a psychic thing."

"You are exactly no help."

"Hey, it's not *my* fault you got all woo-woo ghosty on me. I knew you when you were just a normal, grumpy contractor. I think I'm doing my part by not disowning you, frankly."

We sped past the Port of Oakland and the abandoned Army base, then came to another near standstill when 880 merged with 980 near Jack London Square. As usual at this point, I weighed the advantages and disadvantages of fleeing the freeway in favor of trying my luck crossing town on the surface streets. But the exit ramp was jammed; I wasn't the only one who had thought of it.

"There *are* some who think déjà vu is a kind of a glimpse from past lives," Luz continued. "Or inherited memory, or precognitive dreams, or even alien abduction."

"Any of those people not associated with the tabloids?"

"A few," Luz said. "But not many."

"I'm going to stop you right here, Luz. I'd like to state for the record that while I talk to ghosts, and might even accept the idea of multiple universes and crossed wires and even past lives, I am *not* going to talk about the possibility of alien abduction. Do I make myself clear?"

"You're the expert," said Luz with a grin.

"Anyway, I'll take memory glitches over the idea that I'm possessed, any day."

"Who said you're possessed?"

"Olivier mentioned it as a possibility. But he got pushed around by some demons or something in Hungary, so his attitude hasn't been the best lately."

"I gotta hand it to you, *chica*. You lead a very interesting life."

We pulled up to Dad's house fifteen minutes later and went down the side path to the back door into the kitchen, as was our habit. We were greeted by a wildly ecstatic Dog and the mouthwatering aroma of sautéing onions, garlic, and mushrooms. Dad stood at the counter chopping vegetables, while Landon stirred a mushroom risotto on the stove. Both men wore aprons and sipped glasses of cheap red wine. Dog was doing his part by making sure the floor was kept free of food-like items.

"Well, my, my," said Luz, fanning herself and speaking in a fake southern accent. "It's like I died and went to heaven. Two handsome gentlemen cooking something that smells divine for little ol' *me*? How do you stand it, Mel?"

Dad and Landon beamed.

I gave Dad a kiss on the cheek, Landon a kiss on the mouth, and left Luz in their capable hands while I went down the hall to a small den behind the kitchen, which held our home office. Stan was the phone with someone I assumed was a prospective client, since his Oklahoma accent was slightly exaggerated and he was at his charming best.

He hung up and waggled his eyebrows at me. "Belvedere."

"Bad traffic."

"Great bank accounts."

I smiled. "I'll give them a call tomorrow. As a matter of fact, I was near there today, in Tiburon."

"What's in Tiburon?"

"A numismatist."

"You found some old coins?"

"How is it that everyone knows that word?" I demanded. "I didn't know that word until today."

"I collected coins when I was a kid. Fun hobby. Maybe I'll take it up again."

"Tell you what: I'll start your new collection with a Liberty Head nickel and an Indian Head penny," I said, handing him the plastic bag with the coins. "Turns out they aren't worth more than a few dollars, but they're still pretty cool."

"Why, thank you. Oh, by the way, there's a storm blowing in this weekend. You won't be working out on the island, will you?"

"No, just tomorrow. The weather report says the rain isn't expected until Saturday night or Sunday."

I flipped through the day's messages, returned a few calls, and then Stan and I went over the delivery schedule for the Lighthouse Island supplies. Again I marveled that everything was on track—so far. Was this some sort of construction miracle, or was Ellis Elrich somehow working his magic on all concerned?

"Oh hey, your friend the historian called," Stan said. "Real nice lady."

"Trish called?"

"Said she pulled together some documents for you, but won't be in tomorrow. She said she would leave a package for you at the counter. That make sense to you?"

"It does, thanks." I called Olivier to see if he wanted to accompany me to Lighthouse Island tomorrow. When he readily agreed, I asked if he'd be willing to stop and pick up a package from the California Historical Society on his way out of the city.

As I hung up, it dawned on me that Trish had been looking up lighthouse history for me, Luz had researched déjà vu, and now Olivier was coming to help me figure out a ghost—not to mention picking up my package. It seemed I had minions now. It worked for me; I could see why Ellis Elrich liked it so much.

Finally, I called to check in with Alicia. No news. The police hadn't found the killer yet, but on the upside, they hadn't arrested her yet, either.

"Hey, Stan, I have a question," I said as I finished returning a slew of e-mails.

He looked up from some paperwork. "Shoot."

"What can you tell me about our newest employee, Waquisha Barnes?"

"Well, let's see," he said, reaching for a folder in the file drawer labeled EMPLOYEES, CURRENT in Stan's careful handwriting. "Hmm. Not much. She didn't have any recent employment references besides her dad—said she helped him in his woodshop. So we hired her on probation first, until Jeremy was satisfied with her skills."

"Did you run a background check on her?"

"Just the standard one, but as you know that only turns up really obvious stuff; she doesn't have a criminal record or significant outstanding debts. Nothing further in the public record. Is there a problem?"

"Probably not. But it turns out she might have known the man who was killed on Lighthouse Island."

Stan raised one eyebrow. "That's quite a coincidence."

"Isn't it, though? I don't like coincidences."

"Neither do I. But wait a minute—didn't you say the Turner Construction people, all except you, of course, had already left the island when the murder occurred? So she couldn't have been involved."

I nodded. I *had* said that. But now that I thought about it . . . did I know that to be true? I hadn't escorted them onto the boat, after all.

"Why don't you ask your father?" Stan suggested, sensibly. "He was there, wasn't he?"

"Good point. But one more thing before I go—did you run a background check on Lyle Burgos?"

"The barge pilot? No, Elrich Enterprises hired the boat pilots directly. Why?"

"It's probably nothing." It had dawned on me that Lyle could have shaved his head, and his piercings could be new. Especially if he was trying to adopt a different look, for some reason. "I'll check with the Elrich security team tomorrow."

I returned to the kitchen. "Hey, Dad? Do you remember? Did Waquisha go back to Point Moro with you and Dog and Jeremy the day Thorn Walker was killed?"

Dad paused, a turkey baster held aloft over a perfectly golden-brown bird glistening with juices. The aroma of herbed roast chicken made my stomach growl.

"That the young carpenter lady?"

I nodded.

"Come to think of it . . ." He pondered for a moment. "No, she didn't. She asked if she could stay and take a hike, said she would catch the next boat out. The skipper didn't mention what time she left the island?"

"No, and I didn't think to ask until right now."

"Neither did I. Sorry, babe. You don't think she's involved, somehow? She's quiet, but seemed like a real nice gal."

The thing was, I had known plenty of "real nice gals" in my time. Turned out some weren't all that nice.

"Apparently, Waquisha knew Thorn, the victim at the Bay Light," I said. "And now it seems she might have been on the island when the murder happened."

Luz and I looked at each other across the butcher-block counter. She sighed. "You're right. Time to make a phone call."

Dad went to summon Caleb and Stephen for dinner, and I dialed Detective Santos. While I was dropping the dime on Waquisha, I figured I might as well spread the suspicion around a little. I asked if he'd questioned Lyle Burgos.

There were too many of us to fit around the kitchen table, so we sat at the big dining room table, helping ourselves to risotto and salad and roast chicken as we passed them around. As usual, Dad grumbled that his perfect chicken was slightly overcooked—it wasn't—while Stan and Caleb and Luz wolfed down their food with little moans of appreciation, Landon and I tried to keep our eyes off each other, Stephen whined about his blisters and the long day of work on the island, and Dog lay under the table, willing us to drop food.

"Oh hey, I almost forgot," Stephen said, getting up to retrieve something from his backpack. He handed me a yellowing, rolled-up piece of paper. "We found this out on the island. Jeremy said I should bring it to you."

"*Another* one?" I said, unfurling the scroll. This map had the "X" marked at yet another site, not far from where Landon and I had dug up the two coins.

"What is that?" asked Caleb.

"A treasure map," Landon answered.

"A treasure map?" Dad asked.

"For real?" Caleb asked.

"Well, it's really a map. The 'treasure' part is a little dubious," I said, passing it around. I supposed Trish would suggest we should be handling it with gloves, but I was getting irritated with these maps. Where were they coming from? What could they mean? "We've found several so far."

"Several?" Dad asked.

"That seems weird, right? Who's ever heard of multiple treasure maps?" I said.

"I have," said Caleb, helping himself to a chicken leg. "It usually means one is wrong, or is meant to throw someone off the scent."

"How do you know this?" I asked.

"I think it was *Muppet Treasure Island*."

"*Huh*, that was a good movie. Not as good as *Young Frankenstein*, though." Those had been our favorite movies to watch together when Caleb was young, and he and I shared a smile across the table. Points of connection like this were rare these days, so I cherished the moment. "Okay, so you're saying maybe one of these maps actually *is* genuine?"

"Have you tried following them?" asked Stan.

"Landon and I dug at one location marked by an 'X,' but all we found were those two coins I showed you. They're combined worth doesn't add up to much more than a few dollars."

"They weren't even in a special box," added Landon. "Nothing indicating they were placed there on purpose. More likely they had simply been dropped, years ago, and didn't have anything to do with a supposed treasure. We also found a marble, a little bottle, and a number of shells."

Dad passed the risotto around, and we all helped ourselves to seconds. Landon refilled our wineglasses.

"Just for fun, let's suppose there is a buried treasure on this island," Stan said. "Where would it have come from?"

"Excellent question," I said. "There are a few random

stories of treasure being hidden at different places in the bay, but that was long before the lighthouse buildings were constructed. The treasure maps we've found show the lighthouse and outbuildings, so they have to date from after 1871. Personally I was entertaining the possibility that it might be a famous treasure brought up by ship during the Peruvian War of Independence, but the dates don't fit."

"When was the Peruvian War of Independence?"

"It ended in 1824."

"What about the guy from the smelter?" asked Luz.

"What guy from what smelter?" asked Stan.

"The numismatist mentioned—"

"Wait, Luz," I said, "excuse me for interrupting, but does everyone know was a numismatist is?"

Everyone nodded, including Caleb.

"I guess I'm the only uneducated one at the table. Sorry. Carry on." I drowned my feelings of inadequacy in my glass of wine.

"Yes, but bonus points for knowing the year of the Peruvian War of Independence," said Landon, patting my shoulder.

"It's called Google," said Caleb in a snide tone.

"As I was saying," Luz continued, raising her voice to carry above the fray. "The *coin expert* told us that at the turn of the century there used to be a smelter in Vallejo, and an employee pilfered gold bars a few at a time for several years. Supposedly he buried them along the bay's coastline, then was arrested and either forgot where they all were, or refused to say. Maybe he buried some on the island. It's not that isolated—in calm weather, a person could get over there by rowboat."

"And that was in the early 1900s, so the dates would make sense," Stan said.

"And the different maps could be pointing to all the different places he buried them," said Caleb.

"I suppose it's possible," I said. "We only looked in one spot; we could try digging up some others. This still begs the question, though: Why are these maps wafting around the island? I've seen—what?—four so far, and one of the sailors docked on Lighthouse Island mentioned there were others."

No one had an answer to that one.

"This would make a good movie, though," said Caleb. "Think about it: It's like *Treasure Island* meets *Ghost*."

"Meets *Vertigo*," said Luz.

I shot her a dirty look. I had mentioned seeing the movie poster in Dr. Weng's waiting room today.

"Hey, that's a great idea, Luz," said Dad. "They don't make 'em like Hitchcock anymore. We should watch *Vertigo* tonight."

"Isn't that movie, like, *old*?" asked Caleb.

"Older than I am," I said, knowing that would get him. Still, the look on his face made me wonder: just how old did he think I was?

After dinner the younger set carried the dishes into the kitchen and helped with the cleanup, while Dad and Stan scrolled through the hundreds of options on the television to find the famous Hitchcock movie available somewhere for free. My father figured that since he paid for monthly cable service, he shouldn't have to pay anything extra. Stan was trying to explain that some movies still had to be rented, for less than one would pay for a cup of coffee. But this argument always sent Dad down the path of complaining about people—like his daughter— who insisted on buying expensive coffee at cafés rather than preparing a perfectly decent thermos of instant coffee, like he always had.

The argument was still raging when the dishes were done, so I brought the lighthouse keeper's logs and photographs down from my room and spread them out on the dining room table to see if my family and friends might have any further insights. Stephen, Luz, Caleb, Landon, and I pored over some of the log entries.

> *July 8 Wind S, light smoky and hazy. But little done.*
>
> *July 14 Wind SW, strong. Mr. Mathews took quarterly, monthly, and annual returns to San Quentin. Laid platform on tank.*
>
> *July 30 Wind SW, strong, hazy. Painted rail around top of tower. Mr. Page drunk.*
>
> *August 21 Wind SW, very strong. Mr. Mathews left for San Quentin a.m., capsized off the buoy near the West Brother at 12:15 p.m. Capt. Winsor hailed the steamer* Reform *passing at the time and sent her to his relief. Oars, rudder, mail lost. All marketing lost including mutton, cabbages, peas, etc. Also milk.*

"This is kind of cool," Caleb said.

"It is, isn't it?" I asked.

"Weird to think of them living out there, all isolated and everything," he said. "I mean, what would you do if you lost all your cabbages and milk and stuff? They didn't have, like, any other food, right? No 7-Elevens, for sure."

"Right," I said. "A lot of lighthouse keepers kept vegetable gardens, and the wives spent a lot of time growing and processing the family's food, just like people everywhere at the time. But that would be tough on Lighthouse Island since it has no water source, and very little arable land."

"No offense, but who would want to live like that?" asked Caleb.

"It was a different time," said Landon. Caleb barely refrained from rolling his eyes, but Landon continued. "Life was challenging. A lot of people died in mining accidents or on ships or in factories, and folks struggled to get by any way they could. Being a lighthouse keeper was a relatively well-paid, respected position, with a nice furnished house and all necessary supplies—when they weren't lost at sea, that is."

Caleb gave an almost imperceptible nod.

"It did take a special personality, though," said Landon. "You had to be a jack-of-all-trades, able to pilot a boat and paint the railing and fix the cistern, as well as keep track of the ships passing by and maintaining the clockworks and stoking the boiler for the steam foghorn."

"Sounds like somebody's been reading the logs," I said.

"I have, you're right. They're fascinating. And it's interesting to see how the comments shift as the keeper changes. Sometimes it was the head keeper, other times an assistant or the keeper's wife."

"Trish told me a woman named Ida Prescott Vigilance took over for her husband after he died, in 1905. She served another ten years."

"She was out there all alone?" asked Caleb.

I nodded. "I haven't found a picture of her, but I think this may have been her son," I said, bringing out the photo that had fallen over when I was in the attic. The boy stared out of the little oval opening, younger than when I had seen him on the shore, but his expression was just as grave as when he had pointed up to the tower right before Thorn fell down the stairs.

"Take the photo out of the frame and look at the

back," Landon suggested. "Sometimes names and dates are written there."

"Good idea." I carefully laid the frame facedown on the tablecloth, undid the delicate metal latches, and removed the photo.

On the back, in a slanted, flowery scroll, was written: *Franklin Prescott Vigilance, age three. 1903.*

"Who's that?" Luz asked, turning over the photo and pointing to a figure that had been hidden by the oval mat within the rectangular frame.

It was the image of a woman, who was holding the little boy in her lap.

The photo of the child—the portion of the sepia-toned photograph that had been exposed to light—had faded slightly, making the rest of the picture seem dark and mysterious. The woman's image was slightly blurred, but she had big eyes and high cheekbones, and her long hair was piled on her head in a corona. I was almost positive it was the woman who had jumped from the balcony, the same woman I'd seen in the Keeper's House attic. And though it was hard to tell given the dark sepia tones, she appeared to have a black eye.

"That's weird," Stephen said. "Why would she be covered up?"

"I don't think it was personal. I read about this when I was researching early photography." Several months ago I had done a renovation on a grand home in Pacific Heights where mysterious old photos kept showing up. That was also where I had almost fallen—actually, had nearly been *pushed*—off the roof. "In the early days of photography, it was hard to get a good image of a child because the exposure time was very long, and kids squirm too much. So they'd put them in their mother's— or nanny's—arms hoping to keep them still. When the photo was framed, the woman was hidden by the mat so it looked like it was a portrait of just the child."

"Still. Her image behind him like that looks sort of . . . ghostly, doesn't it?" Luz said.

"I have to agree with you there," I said.

"That's nothing," said Stan as he wheeled into the dining room. Apparently he and my father had resolved their movie wrangling; I smelled a delicious aroma and heard popcorn starting to pop in the kitchen. Dad made popcorn the old-fashioned way: in a big copper-bottomed pot with vegetable oil.

"Mel," Stan continued. "That looks to me like a death portrait."

Chapter Twenty-one

"A *what*?" demanded Luz.

"Maybe it was a southern thing . . . ? But my mama inherited all her family's papers, among which was the old family death album," explained Stan. "It sat on a shelf right alongside the family Bible. When I was a kid I found it morbidly fascinating. The album includes photographs of family members who had died without having had a photograph taken, usually infants and children. So they took a picture before the person was buried."

"They took a picture of a *dead* person?" Caleb asked, shaking his head. "And you say *my* generation is twisted."

"I'm with you, Caleb," said Luz.

"Sometimes you'll see photographs of an entire family, and most of them are a little blurry because it was hard to hold absolutely still for the length of time needed to produce an image," Stan continued, "But one person is crystal clear, because she or he wasn't alive and thus wasn't moving. The practice was particularly prevalent with babies that passed away."

"That's the saddest thing I've ever heard," I said. "They'd take a picture of their dead baby?"

"I guess losing a child's about the worst thing that could happen to a parent," Stan said. "If they wanted a photograph of their baby, this was their only chance."

We were all silent for a moment, peering at the little boy's face.

"His eyes are open," Luz pointed out.

"Photographers sometimes painted the eyes in," said Stan.

We gaped at Stan.

"I'm just repeating what I was told," said Stan with a chuckle. "Some of the photographers were talented artists. It's not like they were painting in googly eyes or anything. It was very subtle."

"He looks like he's alive, though, doesn't he?" I said, gazing at the boy.

"He does," said Luz. "I'm sure he must be alive."

Except that I had seen his little ghost, in a pirate's costume, on the rocky shore of Lighthouse Island. But . . . the boy I had seen looked a little older, about five, not three.

"Hey, look at this," said Caleb, pointing to the lines in a keeper's log. "It's the same writing."

"What?"

"Look at the writing in the logs when this woman Ida was the keeper. Now look at the handwriting on the back of the photo. Now check out the writing on the treasure map. See? It's the same."

We perused the splayed-open logbook, the treasure map, and the photo he lined up on the dining room table, like an exhibit in a museum. Old-fashioned script in the logs shared many common attributes, since those fortunate enough to be literate were usually taught handwriting in school under the stern guidance of their teachers. Still, there were discernible differences in handwriting from one keeper to the next, and often between men and women. Caleb was right: The handwriting on the back of the boy's photo seemed to match Ida Prescott Vigilance's entries in the keeper's logs, and both were similar to the treasure maps.

"Hold on a second," I said. "I have something else: I discovered a copy of *Treasure Island* in the attic of the lighthouse residence, with an inscription written to Franklin on his fifth birthday. So at least that's proof that this couldn't have been a death portrait."

I retrieved the book and opened it up to the page with the inscription from Mama to Franklin, her "little pirate."

"Yeah, see? Look how slanty it is, and the way she makes that loop on the 'F,'" continued Caleb. "Look at the way she makes little loops—here, and here. See that? Kind of . . . feminine, I guess. That's what bothered me about the map, it looked too pretty."

"I think you're right, Caleb," said Dad, joining us with a huge bowl of popcorn, bathed in butter and salt. "It does look like it was written by the same person."

"Same hand created both," Landon nodded. "Well done, Caleb."

"You got all this from *Muppet Treasure Island*?" I asked Caleb, impressed.

"Like you said," he said with an embarrassed but pleased smile. "It's a good movie."

"So here's the sixty-four-thousand-dollar question," I said. "Why would Ida Vigilance, the widowed lighthouse keeper, draw multiple treasure maps?"

"If I may be so bold," Landon said. "The question is, why did she draw even one?"

* * *

We stayed up late watching *Vertigo* on Dad's huge TV, eating handfuls of fresh buttery popcorn that none of us needed considering the feast we'd enjoyed just an hour before. "Never Go to Bed Hungry," was the Turner Clan's unofficial motto.

When we got to the part where Jimmy Stewart was running up the tower steps, I turned away.

"Déjà vu, Mel?" Luz asked quietly.

"Not exactly." I grimaced. "It's just plain old vertigo, nothing like what I experienced at the John Hudson Thomas house."

Landon put his arm around my shoulders and gave me a squeeze.

"What's all this about a John Hudson Thomas house?" asked Dad.

Caleb, frustrated, paused the movie and gave us A Look. "I thought you guys wanted to watch this old movie, and now you're all talking."

"Sorry, never mind," I said, chastened.

"The movie will wait, son, that's what the remote is for," said Dad, not at all chastened. "Not to mention the fact that we can watch it anytime. When I was your age we had to get up off our heinies just to change the channel, and if you didn't see it when it was broadcast, then you missed it altogether."

"Were televisions made of stone back then?" Caleb teased.

"Just like in *The Flintstones*," Dad said. "Smart-alecky kid."

Caleb smiled and checked his phone.

"Anyway, what is it about a John Hudson Thomas house that's got you all hot and bothered?" Dad asked me.

"How did you hear about that?" I asked.

"Me. I blabbed." Luz raised her hand. "You should have told me it was a big ol' secret if you didn't want me to mention it."

I sighed and gave in to the inevitable.

"It's a house I toured the other day in the Rose Garden neighborhood," I said. "Not far from Grand Lake Theatre."

"What's it look like?"

"A big stucco place in the late Arts and Crafts style. Lots of beautiful wood detailing, soaring beamed ceilings, that sort of thing."

Dad frowned. "Big yard, couple of outbuildings? Kind of a strange orientation—not quite facing the street, but not quite facing away, either?"

I stared at him. "You know the house?"

"Pretty sure."

"Have I ever been there?" I asked.

"How would I know?"

"Did you do some work on the place, maybe take me there as a kid, or something?"

Dad shook his head. "Nope."

"Well, then . . . how do you know it?"

"Your mother used to live there."

"*What?* When did Mom live there?"

"When she was a kid, oh, about five or six years old. Her grandparents, your great-grandparents, lived there."

"I didn't know that."

"Lots you don't know, pumpkin."

"I knew Mom grew up in Oakland, but I thought it was in the Trestle Glen neighborhood."

Dad nodded. "That's where your Mom's parents lived, and where she grew up. But your mother's grandparents lived in a big old house built by John Hudson Thomas on a hill between the Rose Garden and the theater." Dad took a bite of popcorn and chewed vigorously. "When your Mom and I were first married she took me by there, just to look at it from the curb. I remember because I was embarrassed that I had never heard of John Hudson Thomas. Beautiful place, though I'm sorry to say that it had been a little neglected."

"You should see it now. No heat, no hot water, water in the basement, lots of neglect, and given its hillside location, in need of an earthquake retrofit. But on the positive side . . ."

"Original woodwork intact?" Dad asked.

"Needs a cleaning but is otherwise gorgeous. Thankfully, none was even painted over. The bathrooms and kitchen, though, were remodeled in the seventies."

He cringed. "A full Brady?"

"A full Brady" was Turner Construction shorthand for design choices reminiscent of the 1970s television series *The Brady Bunch,* which highlighted harvest gold and avocado green color schemes, with burnt orange accents.

"Including burlap on the walls in one half bath," I said. "That part was my favorite."

"Groovy," Stan said with a wink.

"So Mel unwittingly toured a house that belonged to her great-grandparents, where her mother once lived?" Luz asked, seeking clarification.

"Apparently so," I said. "I must have gone there with Mom when I was a kid, and that's why I knew where everything was, like where they kept the extra blankets . . ."

Dad shook his head. "Not likely."

"Why not?" I asked.

"Your mother loved that house, and always hoped to buy it. After we drove by there that one time, she told me it broke her heart knowing that 'strangers' were living there, and she refused to go back. The house had a very special emotional pull for her."

What Dad said made sense. Houses were imbued with their own unique energy and history, and old houses in particular were capable of affecting people in a profound way.

Luz nudged me. "Go visit it again, Mel. You know you want to, and I think maybe you need to."

"I don't know . . ." I looked at Dad, Caleb, Landon, Stan, Stephen—five men whom I loved and who loved me in return—all nodding in agreement with Luz's suggestion. Luz raised an eyebrow, in her patented *don't even try to argue, you know I'm right* way.

I called Brittany and made an appointment to tour the house again tomorrow.

Phone call over, silence reigned.

"More *Vertigo*?" Caleb asked. "Otherwise I'm putting on *Muppet Treasure Island*."

"*Vertigo*," Dad said.

"*Vertigo*," Landon confirmed.

"I don't know . . . ," Stephen said. "*Muppet Treasure Island* is sounding better all the time."

"Stephen has a point," Stan said.

"As chief cook and bottle washer of this here establishment, I have decided that it's up to the ladies," Dad ruled.

"*Vertigo*," Luz and I said in unison. And we turned the movie back on.

Everyone had a good time yelling at the movie's twists and turns, and teasing me about my own acrophobia. As the credits rolled, Caleb lobbed a piece of popcorn at Landon.

I smiled. It wasn't a relationship yet, but it was a start.

Landon looked slightly astonished as he picked the puffy kernel out of his hair and took a moment to study it. Then he murmured, "It is *on*, mate."

And he threw a handful of popcorn at Caleb, who

dove off the couch, laughing as most of the kernels rained down on Dad. Dad yelled, and threw a piece at Caleb.

Rather than be reduced to collateral damage between the two combatants, the rest of us joined in an all-out popcorn fight.

Including Dog, who bounced around and happily cleaned up the mess.

Early the next morning, Landon told me, "I wish you'd let me come with you."

"I know you do. But here's the thing: You can't possibly stay with me twenty-four/seven, Landon. We've both got work to do. I appreciated you coming the other day, when things were still feeling a little . . . fraught. But this is different. Olivier's going to meet me at the docks, and the jobsite is full of workers. And Buzz and Krauss are on the island full-time these days; they've been doing hourly rounds. I'll be well protected."

"I'll be there, too," said Stephen, holding up his hand, which sported a multitude of Looney Tunes Band-Aids. They were the only ones I could find in the bathroom and dated from when Caleb was a child. They didn't exactly make Stephen look like a badass capable of taking on a murderer.

"You see?" I said. "Stephen will be there, as well."

"Yes, but—"

"And Caleb, too." Caleb's school was closed today for a teachers' conference. I had asked him if he wanted to come out to the island, fully expecting him to decline in favor of sleeping in, but to my surprise—and delight—he said yes. "Do you honestly think I'd let Caleb come out to the island if I thought there was any danger?"

"No, that you wouldn't."

"So go teach your eager students about branes and

whatnot," I said, giving him a kiss full of promise. I dropped my voice. "And I will see you tonight."

"First Friday?"

My stomach dropped. First Friday was an art-and-food-and-music walk that had started in uptown Oakland a few years ago. The once-mellow celebration of a vibrant urban core had become a boisterous and sometimes unruly street festival. It was great fun, but the sort of thing I had to gear myself up for after a long day at work.

"Oh, uh, right . . . ," I stammered. "It's just that with everything going on, and we have plans tomorrow, and . . ."

Landon smiled. "Never mind. There's always next month. As long as you're mine for the ballet gala tomorrow night, I'm a happy man."

"I'll be there," I said.

"Dressed to the nines in lemon chiffon, apparently," Luz chimed in, a cup of steaming coffee in her hands.

"This I've got to see," Caleb muttered, rinsing his cereal bowl at the sink.

"Will she ever," Stephen said, beaming. "You have *no idea* what I've cooked up for our fair lady."

"You see?" I said, worried now at just what Stephen had planned. "I'm going to dance all night."

"Actually, at the ballet it's usually the professionals doing the dancing," said Landon. "But I do like your spirit. Caleb, Stephen—please keep an eye on Mel today. Just in case."

"We're on it," Stephen said. "I may not look big and tough, but I can scream like nobody's business."

"That's true, he can," Luz confirmed. "I have witnessed this phenomenon."

"The Turner Shuttle is leaving," I said, grabbing my things. "All aboard."

I dropped Luz off at the Fruitvale BART station, then

Caleb, Stephen, and I headed north to Point Moro. As we came around the switchback and headed down to the harbor, Caleb pronounced the little village "kind of wack, but cool."

I didn't respond. I was too distracted by the sight of the harbor's limited parking area jammed with police cruisers and a forensics crew. Officers were swarming over a small boat at the end of one dock.

I parked on the hill above the harbor, and we walked down the rest of the way. Fernanda was standing at the railing outside the café, watching the scene. When I met her eyes she glared at me and turned away.

Sure, some bossy stranger from Oakland barges in here, opens her big mouth, and ruins everything for the Point Moro pirates.

A uniformed officer was keeping a very unhappy group of local residents away from the docks. I joined the crowd, and after a few minutes Detective Santos broke free from a clutch of cops and approached me.

"Is anyone hurt?" I asked. There was no ambulance—or coroner's wagon—in the lot, but I feared they might already have left.

Santos shook his head. "It's just a search. Keith Barnes's boat."

"Is that Waquisha's father?"

He nodded.

"But . . . how is he involved?"

"He's not, that we know of. But he's got a record. And he knew the victim, and got squirrelly when asked for his whereabouts the day of the murder. Worth a shot."

"Did you look into Major Williston?"

"This the guy you say ripped off the archive?" Detective Santos tilted his head; his dark eyes were still indecipherable. "I gotta be honest with you, Ms. Turner, that little tidbit did not exactly shoot him to the top of the list of persons of interest. Besides, he has a good alibi. Better than yours, as a matter of fact."

"If his alibi is that he was out on a boat with two good friends, couldn't they be covering for him?"

"Even if they were, what is it about pilfering a cache of historical documents that makes you leap to the idea that he might be a cold-blooded killer?"

"What if there's a treasure on that island, somewhere, and Major Williston, Terry Re, and Paul Halstrom have been looking for it? They tried to shut down the renovation of the buildings so they could have the run of the island. And I saw a shovel in one of their boats! What if—"

"This have to do with the treasure map you gave me?"

I hesitated. "Maybe. Or it could be something else, obviously."

"Obviously."

"What about the Palm Project? Thorn Walker was a recent graduate. What if he met someone in the program, and they got close, and he knew about something valuable on the island, and they followed him here but then refused to tell. I was thinking maybe Lyle Burgos had been—"

"*Look*, Ms. Turner," Detective Santos interrupted. "I've got work to do. Thank you for your theories. They're . . . interesting. Crawford tells me you're actually good at this sort of thing, so I'm gonna take her word for it and give you the benefit of the doubt. But Lyle Burgos has a good alibi: He was with his wife in the delivery room at Alta Bates hospital the afternoon of the murder. I'll have another chat with Mr. Williston and his friends, but I wouldn't hold my breath."

Chapter Twenty-two

I wanted to ask Detective Santos straight out about the case against Alicia, but I knew he wouldn't tell me. The police asked the questions, not the other way around. It was saying a lot that he had even entertained any of my "theories," as he called them.

When Olivier arrived, weighed down with several bags' worth of ghost-busting equipment, the police allowed us to meet the *Callisto* at the end of the dock.

"Good morning! Mel, Stephen!" Duncan called out, taking off his cap and waving it. "And who are your friends?"

I introduced him to Caleb and Olivier. He shook both their hands and helped Olivier load all his gear in the boat.

"Top o' the mornin' to you, gents! Sorry to say, but you have to put on these lovely orange life vests. Boat rules."

Five of my construction crew also climbed aboard, and Duncan told me they were the last of the lot; he had already made a run out to the island with the rest. Waquisha, however, had not shown up to work today.

The day was cold and gray, and we all huddled in our sweatshirts and jackets. The Bay Area is gorgeous, but it isn't the California nonresidents usually think of: the endless sandy beaches and warm water and volleyballers in bikinis. That was a *Southern* California thing. Here in Northern California, the water off the beaches might be warm enough to swim in for a month or two in late summer, but even then one risked hypothermia by spending too long in the water without a wetsuit. This time of year, in January, the air temperature rarely got above fifty-five degrees out on the water. It wasn't Canada, but it was cold.

"What's with all the police, Mel?" Duncan asked me in a low voice as we pulled away from the dock. "Isn't that Waquisha's father's boat?"

I nodded. "That reminds me: On the day of the murder, did you give Waquisha a ride back from the island?"

"The police asked me that very question this morning. I'm sorry to say . . . I don't really remember. My impression is that she came back with the others, but I couldn't swear to it. I just don't remember every run on that day. I didn't realize it might be significant, of course, until much later."

"How well do you know her?"

"Not well. Acquaintances more than friends. Met her at the Gentleman's Café, where I like having breakfast. Her dad lives on his boat there in Point Moro, and she was staying with him for a while."

I pulled up Thorn's image on my phone. "Do you know this man?"

He glanced at the photo, but kept his focus on his driving. "That's the fellow who died, right? The police asked me about him, too. I guess I might have seen him around, but I never gave him a ride, I know that much. I remember the face of everyone who boards my boat . . . just can't remember exactly when, unfortunately."

"Did you ever see him in the café, or at the docks, with Waquisha?"

He took the phone and held it up, one eye on the water. "It's possible, but . . ." He shook his head and handed me back the phone. "Sorry, Mel. Wish I could help; I remember seeing Waquisha with a man at the café a couple of times, but I didn't really pay attention. They were always deep in conversation so I didn't want to bother her."

"Okay, thanks," I said.

Caleb was showing Olivier the copy of *Treasure Island*, which surprised me. My stepson was a video game aficionado and extremely bright, but he was not a big reader. I almost reminded him that the book was too old to be treated so casually, but bit my tongue. It would embarrass him if I said anything, plus he was reading. I should encourage that.

"I didn't realize you brought the book with you," I said.

"Luz made me start reading it last night. And then, like, I sort of got into it. Read until really late." As if to illustrate his point, he yawned. "And then this morning I started thinking, like, maybe it could tell us something about what was going on, out on the island."

My heart swelled. I didn't think *Treasure Island* would clarify much about a modern-day island, but I loved that he wanted to help. And his astute observation about the handwriting last night had been spot-on. Maybe I was raising a junior detective.

Then my heart sank. I didn't want my boy to be exposed to life's seedy underbelly, to meet folks driven to

kill out of greed, envy, or jealousy. Better he not follow
in my footsteps in this regard.

"Good book you've got there," Duncan said to Caleb.
"I remember the first time I read Robert Louis Stevenson's
classic." Duncan's memory of a favorite childhood novel
sparked another man in the crew to jump into the discussion with his first encounter with *Treasure Island*. Stephen
chimed in, and suddenly we had a floating book club.

While the men chatted, I opened the manila envelope
Olivier had picked up for me at the California Historical
Society, and found a neatly typed memo from Trish sum-
marizing her research into Ida Prescott Vigilance.

Dear Mel,

*I spent a little time yesterday searching for
references to Ida Prescott Vigilance. The easiest
avenues of research—naturally!—turned up nada;
she didn't publish anything, and wasn't elected to
public office (not surprising since, being a mere
woman, she couldn't vote until 1911).*

*But I had much better luck with the federal
census as well as state and local records. In a
nutshell, here's what I was able to cobble together:*

*Ida Prescott was born into a Quaker family in
Indiana, in 1878. Her father died when she was
young, and her widowed mother decided to relocate
to San Francisco, where a brother (Ida's uncle)
lived. At some point Ida met George Vigilance, a
native San Franciscan who grew up on Bush Street,
right near the Chinatown gates. According to an
early twentieth-century history of lighthouse
keepers—which virtually ignores Ida's tenure,
mentioning her only once, as "Mrs. George*

Vigilance" (Widow)—George had always wanted
to study lighthouse design. He and Ida married
in 1899, when she was twenty-one and he was
thirty.

Shortly after they were married, George
received his commission as a keeper, and they
moved to Lighthouse Island where their son,
Franklin, was born the following year. Coast
Guard records indicate assistant keepers were
stationed on the island for short periods over
the years, but from 1899 to 1915 it was just the
two—and then the three—of them.

George Vigilance died in 1905, cause of death
listed as "accidental fall." Ida Prescott Vigilance
passed away in 1915. A death notice in the
San Francisco paper referred to "Ida Prescott
Vigilance, former keeper to the Bay Light,
Lighthouse Island, off Point Moro, native of
Indiana, age 36."

As part of their compensation, the keepers were
provided with rations, which were periodically
delivered by tender. The annual allowance per
"man" in 1881 was:

Pork: 200 pounds
Beef: 100 pounds
Flour: 2 barrels
Rice: 50 pounds
Brown sugar: 50 pounds
Coffee: 24 pounds
Beans or peas: 10 gallons
Vinegar: 4 gallons
Potatoes: 2 barrels

Quite the list, no? Anything else, including
fresh fruits and vegetables, had to be purchased

*from their own pocket and arrangements made for
delivery by the tender. I've included copies of some
of the extra supply slips—look how much liquor
they ordered! That's a lot of booze for just the two
of them—and if you consider Ida was raised a
Quaker, it's likely she was a teetotaler, which
means it was probably just George partaking.*

I looked up from Trish's memo, taking in the sight of
the island as we approached. If this place felt isolated
now, with motorboats and texting and even a community
and café—however humble—just a few minutes away,
how must it have felt in Ida's day? As Caleb had pointed
out, there were no convenience stores back then. Supplies
had to be ferried over by the tenders from San Quentin,
everything from thread to motor oil to extra water if the
cistern hadn't collected enough rain.

And whiskey, apparently, was high on the list of must-
haves.

I thought of Ida arriving here as a young bride. Had
she been excited? Was she enthusiastic about starting
her new life with her new husband on an island with
spectacular views of the bay, listening to the caw of the
seagulls, the moan of the foghorn, the crash of the waves
during a storm? Was she thrilled to find a lovely Victorian home waiting for her, with its gingerbread trim,
charming drawing room, and wraparound porch? Had
she polished the furniture with lemon oil, sewn cheerful
muslin curtains, and gathered bouquets of wildflowers
to put in a Mason jar on the fireplace mantel?

Or had she been lonely for the company of women,
her dreams of a loving and affectionate marriage dying
as her husband's drinking increased?

Maybe I was jumping to conclusions. For all I knew,

Ida was the party girl, whooping it up every night on Lighthouse Island, and sliding down the tower banister into the arms of a pirate lover.

But really . . . how had it been, day in, day out, just the two of them? Had George and Ida gotten on each other's nerves? Did they yearn for company, for conversation? Had they waited impatiently for the tender to arrive with the supplies and the news and perhaps a crate of books? And what had she done when she got pregnant? I tried to imagine a twenty-one-year-old woman giving birth out here on this rock, with no doctor, no hospital, no older and wiser female friend or relative at hand to lend assistance, to teach her what to expect, to tell her everything would be okay.

But then, as Landon had said to Caleb, people had been made of sterner stuff back then, if only because they had no other choice.

Since we weren't ferrying supplies today, just people, Duncan brought the *Callisto* straight into the yacht harbor, for which I was grateful. I hadn't mentioned my newfound fear of heights to Olivier, and didn't really want to.

There were three sailboats docked in the harbor, but no signs of life. On the island, all appeared calm.

Before disembarking, I reminded Duncan that the electrician and plumbing journeymen would need rides to the island later this morning. I had told them that if Duncan wasn't on the *Callisto*—reading, usually—he could be found in the Gentleman's Café. The pilot promised to keep an eye out for them and to bring them over promptly.

"Hey, Olivier," I said as we started up the road toward the keeper's buildings. "I meant to ask you: Dingo mentioned a man working out here had seen a ghost in the attic window. Do you know how I might get in touch with him?"

"I don't know how, specifically, no," said Olivier.

"I wonder if Dingo would know . . ."

"Why does this matter?" Olivier asked.

"It's probably not important, but I'd like to ask him a few questions. For instance, I was wondering why there was a fair amount of glass on ground below the attic window, but very little on the attic floor."

"You are suggesting the window was broken from within?"

I nodded. "That's why I'd like to ask the worker what he saw."

Stephen and Caleb were chatting with a couple of the crew about my ridiculous insistence upon keeping anything even remotely useful or of historic interest in the house. Caleb was backing me up, and to emphasize his point brought out his copy of *Treasure Island* to show everyone that a woman who had lived in that house had written in it, like, more than a hundred years ago and wasn't that kind of connection with the past kind of awesome?

Seems I had created a monster.

"Mel, you should know . . . this worker, the man who claims to have seen a ghost in the attic, developed an interest in ghost hunting afterward," said Olivier. "He even started his own 'spiritual consultancy,' as he calls it. But I find him very unprofessional."

"Even so, he might know something useful about the island. Is he local? What's his name?"

"Halstrom. Paul Halstrom."

"Get out of here," I said.

"I will not . . . what? We just arrived."

Olivier was French. I forgot he sometimes took things literally.

"Sorry, I'm just shocked. You're saying *Paul Halstrom* was the guy who saw the ghost in the attic—and he's now a ghost hunter?"

"If you wish to call him that. Personally, I don't believe he deserves the title."

"But . . . he's here."

"Who's here?"

"Paul Halstrom. One of those boats down at the harbor is his. He's here with a couple of friends, as well, Terry Re and Major Williston."

Olivier swore in French. "I don't know those last two names, but if Halstrom's here, he's looking for ghosts."

"I assumed they were hanging out and wasting time, or perhaps looking for buried treasure. It never dawned on me they were here on a ghost hunt."

"He didn't tell you?"

"Not, he didn't," I said as my mind began considering the implications of this new information. "They said they had seen 'something' at the top of the tower, but weren't very specific, and offered it as a warning, trying to get us to stop the project. That's very . . . interesting."

"Does this tell you anything important?"

"I'm not sure. I mean, nothing obvious, but it's certainly . . . interesting."

I imagined contacting Detective Santos with this latest news. It was hard to believe he would find it relevant, though it would almost be worth telling the detective, just to see the look on his face.

I put Stephen and Caleb in charge of the salvage pile, and showed them how to extract nails from wood without hurting themselves or ruining the wood. I ignored the grumbling.

"Mel, may I ask a favor?" Olivier said, when it was

apparent I would not have time to meet with him for another hour or so. Duty called. "May I climb the tower, look for readings?"

"Of course. But don't go on the outside balcony. The warning sign is no joke. Everything inside the tower is solid, but that catwalk could come down at any time."

"I will be careful." Olivier headed off, weighed down by his ghost-busting equipment: the electromagnetic field detector, the ultraviolet camera, the ultrasensitive recorder and motion detector. Olivier seemed uncharacteristically hesitant, not at all his usual upbeat self. I felt bad for him. This ghost business could be tough.

The crew had almost finished with the demolition of the interior of the Keeper's House, and the electrician and plumber would be out later today to go over the plan on-site. They had been surprised that the project was back on track so quickly; crime scenes usually took much longer to be released. I was fortunate I hadn't lost either of them to another project. Getting subcontractors to show up when they said they would was a constant headache, and since construction required steps be done in a particular order—one did not, for example, paint the walls before the plumbers and electricians had finished their work—a delay at one point in the schedule created a domino-like disaster further down the line.

"Feel anything?" I asked Olivier when we met up an hour later. He came from the direction of the foghorn building.

"Nothing. If I can't even find ghosts in a haunted lighthouse . . ." He shook his head. "I don't even know what I believe anymore, Mel, this is the truth."

I started to ask him about his experiences in Hungary, which had obviously affected him, but stopped myself. Olivier would tell me if—and when—he was ready.

"Here's something you might find interesting," I said as we headed to the Keeper's House. "Landon says some physicists are researching concepts of multiple universes, and quarks and whatnot. I'm a little fuzzy on the details, but the basic idea is that the universe is composed of different planes, with infinite versions of us. If so, those planes might overlap from time to time, resulting in what we call supernatural phenomena."

"Hmm," Olivier said, looking thoughtful. "Wouldn't that cause doppelgängers rather than ghosts?"

"Yeah, okay, there might be a few problems applying that theory to ghost hunting."

Olivier smiled. "But it has possibilities, does it not?"

"Definite possibilities. Anyway, back to this plane and this universe: Let's take a look in the attic. There's been a fair amount of ghostly activity up there."

"After you, *madame*."

I led the way across the nearly gutted front room to the stairwell, whose walls had been taken back to the studs on one side. We went up to the second floor, down the hall, and climbed the steps to the attic.

We paused to ground ourselves before opening the attic door. I went first, glancing around to see if I noticed anything—I didn't—before flicking on the light.

She stood right in front of me: pale face, high cheekbones, hair piled on top of her head.

And then there was the sound of shattering glass.

The ghost rushed at Olivier, shoving him down the steep stairwell.

Chapter Twenty-three

"**O**livier!" I clambered down the stairs after him.

He lay on the landing, on his back. I knelt beside him and put my hands on his neck, feeling for a pulse.

He opened his eyes. "Are you an angel, Mel?"

"Almost no one thinks so." I straightened and breathed a sigh of relief. "Are you all right?"

"I'll have a bruise or two, and I need to catch my breath," Olivier said, grunting as he sat up with a big smile on his face. "But I am just fine."

"You seem remarkably good-natured," I said. "Why are you smiling like that? You do realize you were just pushed down a flight of stairs, right?"

"Yes. But I was pushed down the stairs by a *ghost*. That was her?"

I nodded.

"This is incredible, Mel. Think about it—a ghost reached out from another dimension to have an effect in the here and now. This I witnessed with my own eyes."

"No, you witnessed it with your own body. Sure you didn't bonk your head or something?"

"I did not say I enjoyed falling. That hurt. But to have this experience is a privilege."

"I'm very glad this floats your boat, Olivier. But personally, it pisses me off. Stay down here this time, will you?"

I raced back up the stairs and burst into the attic.

"Ida, that's enough! *Stop* it!" I shouted. "I understand you're beside yourself—literally—but that does not give you the right to hurt my friends, do you understand me?"

She didn't answer, but manifested in front of me, staring with that awful, empty expression.

"Ida—Mrs. Vigilance—please listen to me," I said. Trish had said the boy's body was never found. Could this be what Ida was searching for, why she could not move on even after her own death? "I want to help you. Is it . . . have you been looking for your boy, Franklin?"

Now I had her attention.

She mouthed something, but it took a moment to put together what she was saying. Her lips moved, but the words were delayed. It was like watching a movie with an out-of-sync soundtrack.

"Franklin." She seemed to fold in on herself, wrapping her arms around her, crouching and sobbing. *"Oh, Franklin, my baby! Where are youuuuuuu?"*

This last word went on and on, a great anguished howl that grew in intensity and reverberated off the walls until I had to hold my hands over my ears, as I had with the foghorn. Another pane of glass cracked.

"Stop! Ida, stop! I'll help you find him!"

The horrible sound waned and finally petered out altogether. I look around the attic and realized Ida was gone, too. But now at least I knew—or thought I knew—that she could hear me.

As hard as it was to know a loved one had died, the

rituals of laying the earthly remains to rest offered some solace and a sense of finality. Not having the lost one's remains to bury and to mourn could be a source of great anguish; Annette had once told me this is why murderers sometimes are granted leniency if they tell where the bodies are buried, so the families can rest.

The island wasn't that big. If Franklin was here, there should be a way to find him.

Unless, of course, he had been washed out to sea by a rogue wave or a high tide. In which case, like the fabled Spanish bullion in Davy Jones's locker, it was doubtful he would ever be found.

But I felt compelled to try to help this tormented spirit.

"Mrs. Vigilance . . . may I call you Ida? Please listen to me: I will do my best to help you find Franklin." Before leaving the attic I turned and added, "And just so you know, Thorn Walker is *not* a friend of mine, so do with him what you will."

"How do you suppose you find a body after all this time?" I asked Olivier as we walked downstairs. "Cadaver dogs can't find old remains, can they?"

"I don't think so," Olivier said. "Dogs find cadavers by detecting the gas emitted by a decaying body, and there would be nothing but bones left after all this time. But I'm no expert. I do know a couple of psychics who have had success with this sort of thing."

"I'll keep that in mind. But this island isn't that big, maybe we could unearth something the old-fashioned way."

"Which is what, exactly?"

"Um . . . looking around?"

"You told me Ida searched for her child for ten years.

Do you really think she would have missed him if he was someplace obvious?'

"Probably not. But maybe the island has changed over the years. I don't know, maybe the sands have shifted in storms, or an earthquake revealed something."

"You are right," Olivier said as we carefully picked our way across the front room, littered with lath and plaster and old crooked nails. "Maybe an earthquake triggered a landslide in a mountain and revealed a hidden cave. Oh no, wait—there are no mountains on the island."

The French were masters of sarcasm.

"Okay, fine, I know it sounds crazy, but I don't know . . . the work here's ahead of schedule, and it wouldn't hurt to take an hour or so to look around. Worst-case scenario, we find nothing but we've had a nice stroll around the island. What do you say?"

"In that case, I will say what you Americans always do, 'it's worth a try.' *Allons-y!*"

I walked out the front door to find Buzz shuffling awkwardly on the front porch.

"I hate to be the one to break it to you, Mel," Buzz said. "But I just got a text: Alicia was taken into custody and is being charged with murder."

It's not like this news came as a surprise. But since I didn't feel any closer to finding Thorn's killer, or even a reasonable alternative suspect, it felt like a punch in the gut. I texted Ellis to let me know if there was anything at all I could do, though I already knew what he would say: *Help us figure this out. STAT.*

Alicia had an excellent lawyer, handpicked by Ellis Elrich and answering to him, and if she was eligible for bail, Ellis would pay it, no questions asked. So at least in this, Alicia was luckier than most.

Also, this must mean Detective Santos had been sat-isfied with Waquisha's explanation of her whereabouts during the murder, and that she was off the hook. I won-dered if she would show up to work again. It was going to be a little awkward: "Sorry I thought you might be a murderer and too bad about your father's boat, now cut this baseboard at a forty-five-degree angle, will you?"

For now, though, I pulled my crew together in the courtyard, told them we were looking for the century-old remains of a little boy, and asked for volunteers. Just about everyone offered to go; in my experience, construc-tion workers had big hearts and were quick to lend a hand to someone in need. Besides, I imagined the idea of hik-ing around the island was appealing, even with such a sad task at hand.

Still, Franklin's death occurred over one hundred years ago, so this was archaeology more than a search for a body.

"His name was Franklin Prescott Vigilance, and he might have been wearing a little pirate outfit when he dis-appeared," I said. "With a red-and-white-striped shirt and a black hat. He often carried a little metal pail and scoop. After one hundred years in the elements, it's hard to imag-ine what could have endured, but one never knows."

We used the buddy system, just in case. I encouraged everyone to take shovels or rods so they could poke around under the sandy bases of rocks.

"He was probably playing around the rocks, most likely by the shore." I was basing that on where I had seen him, though as I said it I realized Thorn and Ida both appeared in different places on the island, so per-haps he could, too. "He might have crawled into a crev-ice and gotten stuck, that sort of thing. Try to put yourself in the head of a five-year-old."

As I was talking, I noticed something out of the corner of my eye. But this time it was no ghost, it was Terry Re talking to Caleb, by the storage shed. They seemed absorbed in their conversation.

"Okay, thanks, everybody. Don't do anything stupid—as always, stay safe above all. Shout if you find anything—or text me if you're out of earshot. And we'll meet back here in an hour or so and get back to work. In the meantime, enjoy the island."

I started toward where Caleb and Terry were speaking, but was approached by Paul Halstrom.

"What can I do for you, Paul?" I asked.

"We'd like to help."

"Excuse me?"

"We heard your speech. We'd like to help. We know this island better than all of you combined."

That was probably true. Paul, Terry, and Major seemed to have an inordinate interest in this island. And what could I say? That I had a vague theory—completely unsupported by evidence—that one of them might have killed Thorn Walker and thus they couldn't help us search for a little boy's century-old remains?

"Um . . . sure," I said, keeping an eye on Caleb. He and Terry were laughing now. "The more the merrier. Thanks."

"Have you looked inside the house?" Paul suggested.

"What?"

Olivier came to join us. "You leave us alone now, Paul."

"Hey, I'm just trying to help out."

"You have no business here on Lighthouse Island at all," said Olivier. "I have revealed your true identity to Mel, so now she knows what you are up for."

"I think you mean 'up *to*,'" I said as a quiet aside to Olivier, but my attention was still on Caleb. I breathed a sigh of relief when Terry walked away. Caleb slid down to sit with his back against the storage shed, and opened his book.

"My 'true identity'?" said Paul with a sneer. "What am I, some kind of masked superhero? So what if we're here trying to document some ghosts? It's not against the law. And isn't that what *you're* doing here?"

"But then why is it you were not honest with Mel in the first place?" Olivier demanded.

Paul hesitated, shuffling his weight from one large boot to the other. "You know how it is with this sort of thing. I wasn't sure . . . to tell you the truth, I'm not really sure what we're dealing with. That . . . *thing*, whatever it is, barely lets me in the house, much less the attic. All we managed to get was the maps."

"Maps?" I asked. "What maps?"

"The treasure maps. There was a stack of them in a box. Terry grabbed it from the attic doorway, but then that *thing* chased us out of there . . ." He shook his head. Halstrom was a large man, well muscled, but the stark fear on his face made him look like a scared little boy. He had gone up against something that had shaken him, badly. "Anyway, it was like a horror show in there. We got chased down the stairs, and my bad, I dropped the box."

"The box of maps?"

He nodded. "Just as we were running outside. They blew everywhere. We're still picking them up. I hear you found one, too, right?"

I nodded. "What do you think they were for?"

"No idea. We've tried digging up a bunch of the marked spots, but I don't know what it's about. We never find anything but, like, a couple of old coins or a little bottle or one time a little toy soldier."

I realized I had forgotten to ask Ida Vigilance about the maps. It was hard to remember everything in the moment, when I was in the presence of a being from beyond the veil. I should make myself a list of ghost questions.

Then I remembered what Trish had said.

"There's a treasure map in the front of the book *Treasure Island*. Robert Louis Stevenson drew it for his stepson one rainy day, to keep him entertained," I said. "Maybe Ida drew the maps for her son Franklin, as a game. Maybe that's all there is to that."

"Could be," said Paul with a nod. "There's no treasure we could find, that's for sure. Terry really thought there might be something, but nothing turned up."

"How long have you three been doing this?" I asked.

"Not long. We only just met here, at the harbor last week. Funny we had so much in common. Terry's real interested in spirits, and so's Major."

"That's nice," I said. "Always good to make new friends. What do you know about Major stealing a file from the California Historical Society?"

He frowned. "When was this?"

"A couple of weeks ago, so maybe it was before you met. Okay, thanks for helping to look. But why did you suggest we look in the house?"

"Because, like I said," said Paul. "The ghost doesn't want to let us in that attic. Seems strange to me. Maybe she's eaten up with guilt or something, and that's why she's so mean."

"You're suggesting she killed her own son?"

He shrugged. "All sorts of crazy things happen in this life—and in lives past. Am I right, Olivier?"

Olivier just nodded, looking pale once again. I guessed the happy effect of Ida pushing him down the stairs wasn't enough to sustain his good mood.

Paul said he and Major and Terry would help search the island for little Franklin's remains, and I went over to talk to Caleb.

"Hey, Goose," I said, cringing when I realized I used his little-boy nickname.

"Hey." He didn't look up.

"Good book?"

"Yeah."

"Good. Great. Of course, I like what the Muppets did with it."

No response.

"So, what was Terry talking to you about? That woman who was here?"

"The book."

"What did she want to know about it?"

"You guys seem to have a thing about *Treasure Island*," he said in an exasperated tone, finally looking up.

"It's a classic. And there's something about the morally ambiguous character of Long John Silver . . ."

"Yeah, yeah," Caleb said with a slight smile.

"So, seriously, what did Terry ask you about the book?"

"She wanted to see the frontispiece. I didn't even know what that meant."

"Could I see?"

He handed it to me. "Look, Mel . . . I don't really want to go look for a little kid's body. I don't . . . I mean I just . . ." Caleb trailed off with a shrug. He didn't meet my eyes.

I slid down to sit next to him. "I'm sorry, Caleb. Of course you don't have to go search. It *is* a little . . ."

"Gnarly. Bootsy. Wack."

"Okay," I said with a soft chuckle. "I was going to say plain old weird, but any of those will do. Anyway, we've got plenty of people already, so there's no need for you to go. It's a long shot, anyway."

"You think it will help her?" he asked, looking off toward the water.

"It might." I bumped his shoulder with mine. "We moms get pretty attached to our kids, you know."

He nodded but kept his eyes on the bay. I flipped the book open to the frontispiece. Some of the other books from the attic had nice marbled endpapers, but this one was a plain matte black. Still, there was a reproduction of Stevenson's famous treasure map on the frontispiece, with a tissue guard. The captions were printed in red, brown, and blue.

"Is this what she was looking at?" I asked. "The treasure map?"

He shrugged. "And the inscription, I guess. She seemed pretty excited about that."

I flipped to it and read it again.

To Franklin, my little pirate,
on your fifth birthday.
Love you forever and ever,
Mama

If Terry was working with Paul Halstrom to document the ghosts on this island, maybe she was excited to see something Ida had written, back when the keeper was a full-fledged, living, breathing person. Was it that simple?

I was about to set out to search with everyone else when the electrician showed up, and on his heels the plumber. So I was delayed for another forty-five minutes, going over the project and the schedules with them. They would be bringing teams out to whip through this project,

so once they started they would make good time—
especially now that we'd opened up all the walls.

Once I finished with them, I checked in again with
Caleb, who had helped himself to a sandwich from one
of the coolers and was sitting in the sun, fully enmeshed
in the adventures of Jim Hawkins and the mutineers.
Then I went to find Olivier, who was searching the cove
behind the lighthouse, not far from where Landon and
I had dug for treasure.

Olivier was waggling his head, looking to his right,
then back again.

"What are you doing?" I asked as I approached.

"I keep thinking I see . . ." He trailed off as he looked
back toward the rocks once more. He shook his head. "I
keep thinking I see someone over there. By the rocks."

I listened and heard a little piping voice singing its
off-tune shanty: *"Yo ho, yo ho . . . across the deep
blue sea!"*

"Can you describe him?" I asked Olivier.

"Like . . . a little boy. Wearing a red-and-white shirt
and a little hat. Just as you described the little boy who
died. Could this be . . . ?"

I took out the little mirror I'd started carrying in my
pocket along with my mini-flashlight and tape measure,
and held it up. Little Franklin was standing on the rocks
by the water with his pail, collecting rocks and shells.

"Here," I said in a low voice, handing Olivier the mirror. "Sometimes you can't see them straight on, but you
can if you use a mirror."

Olivier accepted it from me, holding my gaze for a
long moment. Then, angling the mirror, he looked toward the rocks.

"I can't believe this," he whispered, his hand shaking

as he passed the mirror back to me. A look of awe came over his face. "Is that the boy you're looking for?"

"Franklin Prescott Vigilance," I murmured, nodding. "Presumed drowned in 1905."

"What a tragedy. Poor little boy. Have you been able to talk to him? Couldn't he take you to his remains?"

"Worth a shot," I said. I edged closer to the rocks, watching the boy in the mirror. "Franklin?" I called. He looked at me, but didn't say anything.

"Franklin," I continued. "I'm a friend of your mother's. I was wondering . . ." Just how did a person go about asking a child—even a dead child—where his body was? "I was wondering if you can remember the very last place you were, here on the island? The last thing you can remember, before everything changed."

He stood stock-still, gazing at me with that solemn, serious expression. Suddenly I was sorry I hadn't left him to play at will, to gather things in his little pail and sing his ditties without being bothered by grown-up concerns.

"Franklin—"

He disappeared.

I went over to where he'd stood, looked around the bases of the rocks, in a small crevice. I pushed aside a few rocks and dug in the wet sand, but found nothing. No sign of the little boy anywhere. Disappointed, I rejoined Olivier.

"He only communicated with me once," I said. "And not through words but by pointing toward the tower—turns out, it was right before Thorn Walker fell down the stairs. What do you suppose *that* meant? A warning, maybe?"

"Maybe." Olivier asked to borrow the mirror again. He kept looking back to the actual spot where he'd seen the apparition, then returned his gaze to the mirror, as though trying to figure out why he hadn't been able to see Franklin straight on. "More likely it was in response to a surge of energy, of violence. Spirits tend to be very sensitive to such things."

"Hey, here's a question for you: We found a photograph of this boy, Franklin, when he was three. Stan said it might be a death portrait."

"Oh, really? Those fascinate me."

"Yeah, it's a pretty interesting concept, in an *Addams Family* kind of way," I said. "But this boy looks at least five, doesn't he?"

Olivier nodded.

"Also," I said as I tried to think this through, "the *Treasure Island* Caleb is reading was inscribed to Franklin on his fifth birthday, so it couldn't have been a death portrait."

"Unless his mother continued to give Franklin gifts even after he died—it would not be unusual. You know, it's possible the figure of the boy we're seeing is a projection. I've read about this. Sometimes enough energy is actually generated by someone through their thoughts that it creates a sort of ghost shadow."

"You mean the boy's not a ghost? That his mother, Ida, is manifesting a vision of her son?"

"It is possible. There is much we do not know about ghosts, Mel. So very much. What I am suggesting is a theory based upon the evidence, what I have read. The boy hasn't been able to communicate in any way but rote, right? Singing the same song, or pointing to an energy source. It is therefore possible that what we are seeing is not a spirit with its own agency, but a projection." Olivier's explanation made him sound like his old self.

Dingo was right, I thought. I was glad I'd invited Olivier out to Lighthouse Island. Hanging out with the island ghosts seemed to have boosted his spirits. So to speak.

"But wait, that still doesn't make sense," I said. "If it was a death portrait, then why is Ida still searching the island for him? She would have known exactly where his body was. In the photo she had him in her lap. What, did she lose him en route to the funeral?"

"It's possible she lost her mind, from the grief," he said in a gentle voice. "Or maybe it just *looked* like a death portrait. It might not have been one. I have to say, it's hard to tell with those old photos unless the death was documented elsewhere. In any case, I'd love to see it."

"Of course," I said as we walked back toward the buildings. "It's also the only photo I've found of Ida Vigilance herself."

"That's how you recognized her in the attic, then?"

I nodded. "She has a distinctive look about her—pretty, but strong."

"Well, this has been an incredible day for me, Mel. I'm sorry you haven't found your murderer, or figured out the ghost story, but for me it's been . . . incredible. *Incroyable*. You know, I've never actually *seen* one before, not like this."

"Seen one what?"

"A ghost."

"What do you mean you've never seen one?" I stopped in my tracks. "You're the ghost guy."

"I mean . . . I've heard things, seen stuff move, *felt* the presence. Interacted, to an extent. But never an actual apparition. This is incredible."

"What are you talking about, Olivier?" I asked, stunned at this revelation. "You're my ghost mentor. You own a ghost-hunting supply shop. You teach *classes* on ghosts. What do you mean you've never seen one?"

"Perhaps I have exaggerated my spirit interactions to some degree; I am, after all, a businessman. And a person doesn't actually have to *see* ghosts to believe in them. That's why I've been searching for so long. I want to thank you, Mel, for bringing me here, for making it possible to know that what I have believed is true."

"You're welcome. Thank *you* for helping me so much with ghosts, especially since you never actually saw them until today."

He smiled. "Even before, I never stopped believing. And you must not lose faith, either. You will find this killer and help your friend Alicia, I am sure."

"Thanks, Olivier."

But in a way, my friend's faith in me made it that much harder.

Chapter Twenty-four

Searches concluded, my crew had returned to the courtyard. Although everyone seemed to have enjoyed exploring the island, no one found anything resembling a human skeleton or a rotted old red-and-white shirt or remnants of an old shovel or pail. I couldn't help feeling a twinge of disappointment even though I'd known it was a long shot.

After a snack, courtesy of the woman who probably, even now, was sitting in jail for a murder she didn't commit, we got back to work.

Unfortunately, Thorn's ghost appeared and started trailing me. I tried to ignore him as I went from one part of the jobsite to the next, helping to determine exactly how to run the plumbing lines and sketching out the new electrical outlets, while still respecting the original Victorian built-ins and trim.

This ghost, I couldn't help but notice, Olivier did not see. I wondered whether Halstrom and his crew had ever picked up any readings on Thorn. I didn't feel comfortable telling him to go away because I didn't want it to seem like I was walking around talking to myself, at least not any more than I usually did.

Thorn stuck to me, moping and sighing audibly, so I finally went into the storage shed and shut the door behind me.

"What *is* it, Thorn? I have work to do."

"She pushed me down the stairs!"

"Who?"

"That woman! The one in the white gown. I don't know her name."

"You're saying Ida killed you? Ida Vigilance? The ghost?"

"No, not the first time. I can't remember who did that."

"Too bad. Alicia could really use your help right about now, and frankly, you owe her. It might help make up a little for what went before."

He looked interested. "How do you mean?"

"Has it occurred to you that maybe the reason you can't move on is because you owe something to Alicia? You made a lot of her life miserable. So this is your chance: Help me figure out who killed you, and get her off the hook. She's been arrested for the murder."

"But . . . Alicia didn't kill me. Did she?"

"No. I'm certain she would have told me the truth, if she had. "

"So how am I supposed to help find out who did kill me?"

"I'm really not sure. I don't really know how things work in the . . . afterlife, or whatever you call the place where you are. But you're a ghost, after all, no one—but me—can see you. Why don't you poke around, listen in on conversations, that sort of thing?"

He nodded. "I could do that. You're right, there have

to be some advantages to this ghost thing. Let me see what I can do."

"Oh hey, one more thing: Has anyone you met at the Palm Project been out here to the island?"

"Sure."

"Really?" I couldn't believe I hadn't asked him earlier. "Who?"

"Bear."

"First name or last name?"

"Palm name."

"Palm name? What do you mean, Palm name?"

"We didn't use real names in the program. Our Palm names allow us to be completely open and honest with each other. A lot of people choose an animal name as a totem, sort of."

Rats. Why was nothing ever easy? "Okaaaay, so what does Bear look like?"

He shrugged. "Just regular."

"Could you be a little more specific?"

"White guy, in his forties."

"Coloring? Or . . ." I thought of Lyle's tattoo. "Is he bald? Does he have piercings?"

"Not bald, no piercings or anything like that. Brownish hair, I guess. Like me."

That eliminated Paul Halstrom, at least. And Terry Re. Could he mean Major Williston? "Have you seen him here on the island?"

"It's . . . strange. It's like I'm here but not here, you know what I mean? I mean, I'm on the island all alone, and then suddenly someone shows up. Like you, popping up right in front of me."

"Funny, that's how *you* appear to *me*. Maybe it's mutual." I'd never thought about how living humans must appear to ghosts, how they experienced our presence.

Sometime soon I should give that some thought. "What about before the change, when you were alive?"

He was shaking his head. "Everything's all mixed up. It's really hard to remember stuff, and it's getting harder. All I can remember is Amy."

"You need to forget Alicia, Thorn. She deserves a life. Without you."

He took a swing at me. Just like that. It didn't connect, of course, but it's still a funky feeling to have a spirit hand move through you.

"Knock it off," I yelled.

"I'm sorry, I'm sorry, I'm sorry," Thorn said, closing his eyes and muttering something that sounded like *"bend like a palm in the wind . . ."*

"Listen, if you happen to see Bear, would you please point him out to me?"

"Sure, but . . . why?"

"I'm trying to figure out who hated you enough to kill you. Besides the obvious."

"Why would Bear hate me? We were roommates. He showed me the newspaper with Alicia's picture in it. It was like a sign. Once I saw it, I knew where I needed to be."

"And you don't remember any other distinguishing feature about Bear?" He kept shaking his head. "Tattoos, an accent, anything at all?"

"Bear was a good listener. And not someone you'd think tried to kill himself."

"He tried to kill himself?"

Thorn nodded. "I don't really get suicide, do you? Who would do something like that? Speaking of which, could you get that lady to stop pushing me down the stairs? I know I can't die again, but I can still feel pain and fear. I'm only human."

"Former human, actually, but I get your point."

On the one hand, Thorn getting pushed down the stairs, over and over again, sounded like a fitting purgatory for a man who had terrorized his wife. But if he was going to help us, I supposed I should let him off the hook.

"I'll talk to her. I can't promise anything, but I'll talk to her. It's possible she has some unresolved rage where men are concerned. Oh, hey, Thorn, one more question: what was *your* Palm name?"

"Whack-a-Mole. Because you can never keep me down."

Now that, as Caleb would say, was "wack."

Later that afternoon, as the workers were finishing up their projects and storing their gear, I went back over the papers in the manila envelope Trish had given me.

I remembered something Trish had mentioned about the death of the light keeper, George Vigilance. In her official report to the Coast Guard, Ida claimed that George thought he spotted his son from the top of the tower, and in his haste to get down the tower stairs, fell and broke his neck. According to Ida, she had found him, dead, at the bottom of the stairs.

But if so, how did she know he had seen Franklin and was hurrying to him?

I supposed it was possible he had shouted something to her from the top of the tower, and she had assumed the rest. But what if Ida had lied? What if George had hurt Franklin, and Ida had pushed George down those stairs, just as she did Olivier and Thorn? And then invented the story to cover up her guilt?

One way to find out. Maybe.

I climbed the little staircase to the attic, noting again

the multiple brass locksets on the door. Had they been placed there to keep people out—or to keep someone in?

Once inside the attic, I inspected the window with the broken panes. There were gouge marks on the interior sills, as though someone had tried to pry the window open. And on the exterior of the windows were a series of small, weathered holes. Had the windows once been nailed shut?

Had George locked Ida in the attic? And while she was there, had little Franklin wandered off? The first time I saw him, I'd thought he was too young to be playing by himself near the water.

If Ida had been locked up here for some reason, might she have broken the window in an effort to free herself?

I peered down at the ground two stories below. It was a long way down from here. She might well have broken an ankle, or worse, in a jump from this height. But a mother's love was strong.

If this was true . . . could Ida be eaten up with guilt for not having found her son in time? Did she spend another ten years tending to the lamp at night, and ceaselessly searching for her son during the day? And had her constant yearning for him, for more than a century, generated the "shadow ghost" I had seen playing with his pail by the water?

If any of this was true . . . I felt overwhelmed with sadness for Ida and Franklin.

"Enough, Ida," I said. "Stop pushing Thorn down the stairs. I know I said you should feel free, but you've done it a few times now, and I really think that's enough. I mean, not that I don't see the sweet justice in a tumble or two."

No answer. Not that I really expected one, but it would have been interesting.

"Did George hurt you, Ida?"

The window cracked. Slowly. A high-pitched screech of glass splintering.

"Did he hurt Franklin?"

It shattered.

"Oh, Ida, I am so, so sorry."

There was a far-off, disembodied sob. *"Frankliiiiiiiin! Where are youuuuuuu?"*

I walked over to the crate of books where I had found *Treasure Island*. To a one, the books were about adventure on the high seas or in exotic lands.

"And what about the maps? Were those a game you played with Franklin?"

Suddenly she was right in front of me. Not tormented now as much as hopeful, as though wanting me—*willing* me—to understand.

"He loved these stories, didn't he?" I guessed.

She nodded, caressing the tomes like precious artifacts.

"And he dressed like a little pirate," I said.

I thought of the bottle, the glass marble, the coins we had unearthed. Trinkets, really—maybe they hadn't been dropped by accident or washed in on the tide. Could they be a mother's humble gifts to her treasure-hunting son? Part of an imaginative game of treasure seeking to keep a young boy busy and happy, despite the boredom of the island, the reality of being stuck out here, isolated, a violent drunk their only other companion?

Maybe Ida kept making the maps, I thought, long after Franklin had disappeared and she had dispatched George. Perhaps that's why there was a whole box of them up here. Which made me wonder . . .

"Ida, why haven't you chased me out of the attic?"

She didn't say anything, but collapsed on the floor, despondent and sobbing.

I thought about how I would have felt if Caleb had wandered off as a boy. I would have been distraught. I would have been consumed with guilt and anguish and a yearning beyond reason.

As I had said to Landon, this ghost stuff was a lot more about the heart than the mind. So even though I knew Ida was not corporeal, I knelt and put my arms around this ghost, this specter, this spirit.

Because there were no words.

By the time I came downstairs and locked up the house behind me, Caleb was frantic. Stephen and Olivier were helping him look for his backpack.

"I left it right by the storage shed, I know I did. Right where I was reading!"

"What was in it?" I asked. I was running short on patience; my time with Ida had wrung me out emotionally and I wanted to get off this island and regroup. The last thing I felt like doing was spending another half an hour searching for a missing backpack. "You didn't have your computer in it, did you?"

"No. But everything else. My iPod. And other stuff, too."

Caleb, Olivier, Stephen, and I continued looking, and a few of the workers still on-site pitched in as well. No sign of it.

"Are you sure you couldn't have set it somewhere else?" I asked. A misplaced backpack was not exactly unheard of—we had spent many a frazzled morning before school looking for lost items.

"I mean, where else would I have put it? I was pulling those stupid nails all day with Stephen, and then I was sitting over by the storage shed reading. I went up to check out the tower but I didn't take my backpack with me, I left it here."

"No one on my crew would have taken it, Caleb. I know them all pretty well."

"No, but maybe one of your ghosts, or even a murderer or something. I wish I hadn't even come."

"I'm sorry you feel that way. It will probably turn up, but for right now, Duncan's waiting on us. Tell you what, in light of all the work you did today I'll buy you a new iPod, courtesy of Turner Construction."

"You have no idea how much iPods cost," Caleb muttered as he stalked off toward the harbor.

"He's got a point," said Stephen as we walked down the rocky path.

"It's like a little music thingee, right?" I said. Techie, I'm not. "How much could it possibly cost, twenty bucks?"

Olivier made a snorting noise.

"Yeah, this is what I'm talking about," said Stephen with a laugh, putting his hand on my shoulder. "It's like you're from a different century, Mel. Luckily, a beautiful gown is ageless. I can't *wait* for you to try it on tonight! I'll be up most of the night sewing, this I know, but I'm so excited!"

"I hear there's a doozy of a storm coming in this weekend," said Duncan as he piloted the *Callisto* towards Point Moro.

"Yes, I heard that, too. Sunday, right?"

"Starting Saturday night, I think."

"We won't be working this weekend, anyway." I wondered . . . if the storm started early enough, maybe the ballet gala would be canceled. We Californians were scaredy-cats when it came to bad weather. "Best to keep the boat tied up tight, I guess."

About halfway to Point Moro, my cell phone started working. I called Ellis.

"Yes, Alicia's been charged," he said. "But Marla feels sure the judge will grant bail, as Alicia poses no threat to the community. So she should be back home soon."

"I hope so. How is she taking it?"

"Remarkably well. She has a lot of faith—perhaps too much faith—in the system. And in me."

"You're doing everything you can for her, Ellis. That's all you can do. She's lucky to have you on her side."

"Thank you. The same can be said for you—you're searching for the true killer?"

"I'm looking, but I'm not having much luck." I considered mentioning the possibility of supernatural help in this regard, but decided against it. "I'll keep poking around, though, to see what I can find. I wonder—is there any way you can find out the names of attendees from the Palm Project?"

"You're wondering if Thorn might have made an enemy there?" Ellis was a quick study.

"I am. Thorn was so new to the area that I keep thinking even he couldn't have made a mortal enemy here that quickly. But he did spend a lot of time recently at the Palm Project. Apparently he knew someone there who went by 'Bear,' but that was his Palm name, a fake moniker adopted for the sake of anonymity."

"We've made some inquiries, but there are strict confidentiality laws at inpatient clinics."

"I understand."

"I'll try some back channels. In the meantime, I'll keep the security detail—Buzz and Krauss—out on the island whenever you're working out there."

"Thank you, Ellis."

"Thank *you*. And watch your back."

* * *

I dropped Caleb and Stephen off at Dad's, then drove across town to the Grand Lake neighborhood, to meet Brittany and Landon at the John Hudson Thomas house.

They had both beat me there and had introduced themselves. I found them wandering through the overgrown, weedy garden when I arrived. I told Brittany about my mother living here as a child.

"But I don't understand," she said. "Your mother lived here, but you've never been here?"

"I don't think so. It's possible we drove by at some point, but there's no logical explanation for all the memories I felt while walking through the house."

"Then you think . . . what? That you're channeling your mother?"

"Not exactly," I said. "But maybe . . . sort of. I think there's a link, anyway. Let's go in, and see what we see, now that we know what we know."

We entered the house through the back door, which led to a servant's hallway with a small maid's room to one side, and the kitchen to the other.

Now, with the knowledge that my mother had been a little girl here, the house felt different. It was striking before—it would be hard for such a beautiful house not to impress, even with kitchen's harvest gold linoleum tile—but now that I wasn't scared of my feelings, I could open myself up to its warmth, the welcoming hum. Landon and Brittany lingered downstairs while I took my time roaming the second floor, looking into nooks and crannies and allowing the "memories" to flood my senses.

"I love this house," said Landon when I came back downstairs. "There's such a lovely feel to the place. Good energy." He paused, seeming slightly embarrassed. "Now I sound like you, Mel."

"Maybe it's the Berkeley ethos getting to you," Brittany teased. "It's true though, it really *does* feel like it has good energy. I'm in real estate, and I can tell you the truth: Not all houses 'feel' good, ghosts or no ghosts."

I sat on a built-in bench by the fireplace, and looked down at my hands.

I put them through a lot: concrete work and carpentry, hitting them with hammers and poking them with splinters. I kept my nails short for practical reasons, and looking at them now, I wondered if I should get a manicure for the gala tomorrow night. I wasn't what one might call "girlie" that way, but I didn't want to be totally out of place. Landon was right; even if I preferred my spangly dresses or dusty coveralls, it didn't mean I couldn't enjoy playing princess dress-up from time to time.

So when I looked down at my hands, yes, they were my mother's hands. They looked like hers had. Not like she was at the end, of course, but the way I always remembered her, when I was a child and she was—now that I thought about it—about my age.

In fact, I looked a lot like my mother, in a lot of ways. And that was okay.

"You're right, Landon," I said. "It's a beautiful place. It feels like . . . home."

Chapter Twenty-five

I couldn't sleep. Finally I kicked off the covers, taking care not to wake Landon, and slipped out of the bedroom.

From the top of the stairs I could see the lights in the living room blazed, and I heard the hum of the sewing machine. Stephen was still hunched over my promised gown, I was sure. After getting home last night we had had a fitting, and the dress was very tight. Stephen claimed it was supposed to be that way, but I made him promise to reinforce the sides so I didn't spill out of it in the middle of the ballet. I kept envisioning sneezing and losing the entirety of my costume right in front of San Francisco's historic families. It seemed like a classic Mel Turner move, somehow.

A strip of light shone under Caleb's bedroom door. I knocked.

"Come in," he said.

He was sitting up in bed reading, his near-black hair sticking up every which way, his bedroom looking like a cyclone had touched down.

"Hey, I'm sorry about your backpack today, Caleb. I was really tired; I shouldn't have been so impatient. I apologize."

He shrugged.

"And most of all, I'm sorry that you're sorry you came out to the island. It meant a lot to me that you came. And you did some good work getting those nails out of the baseboards."

"It's gonna take a lot of putty and sanding to make them look decent."

I smiled. "I know. It'll be worth it. Sometimes the hard things are worth the effort. What are you reading?"

"*Treasure Island*, still. Almost finished."

"So you didn't leave it in your backpack?"

He shrugged. "It was in my jacket pocket."

"Well, that's lucky." I thought for a moment. "That woman on the island, Terry—wasn't she interested in the inscription?"

"That's what she said."

"Could I see it?"

He passed it over.

I flipped through the book again. There was the treasure map, like the ones Ida had drawn for her son. And there was her inscription to her "little pirate."

"Not that one," said Caleb. He took the book and opened it to the title page, then handed it back to me. There was another inscription, much more faint, which I hadn't noticed before.

To little Captain George Vigilance,
for whom Captain George North is named.
May you always dream of lighthouses and treasure
In memory of a lovely summer,
Mr. Robert Louis Stevenson, 1883

"It's signed by the author," I said, feeling a sense of awe that I was holding in my hands a book that Robert Louis Stevenson had once held in his.

"That's cool, though, right?" said Caleb.

"Yes, it certainly is," I said slowly. "You know, this book might be worth a lot of money."

"You mean maybe someone stole my backpack to get this book? You think Terry stole it?"

"It's possible." There were other old books still up in the Keeper's House attic, and I had brought a few home with me. I hadn't thought about it before . . . but what did I know about valuable books?

"Should I not be reading it?" Caleb asked.

I handed it back to him with a smile. "You should definitely read it. Just remember, while you're doing so, that it's a piece of history. And use a bookmark— absolutely *no* dog-eared pages."

"'kay."

"And . . . maybe don't show anyone else you have it. If it's okay with you, I might borrow it in the morning and have a friend of mine take a look at it."

"Sure," he said. "I'm almost done anyway, I'll finish tonight. It's a good story."

"Do you find Jim Hawkins and Long John Silver to be morally ambiguous?"

"I might, if I knew what that meant." He smiled a reluctant smile. "Don't look at me like that! Of course I know what that means. I knew what a 'numismatist' was, unlike *some* people. Aced my SATs, remember?"

I smiled. "Have you heard back from any colleges yet?"

He shook his head.

"You'll get in. And then you'll leave me, and then where will I be?"

"You can always visit."

"You bet I will, Goose."

Saturday morning I drove into San Francisco for my second acupuncture treatment. A few nosy questions to the office staff revealed that Dr. Weng had gotten divorced two years ago. There were no children. It was amicable.

Luz was at a conference today, so there was no dim sum orgy. Which was probably for the best, because I didn't think I'd be able to fit into my gown tonight if I indulged like last time.

Afterward I headed north over the Golden Gate Bridge, back to Tiburon. I had called Cory Venner this morning, and though he claimed not to be an expert, he admitted that yes, he was familiar with collectible antique books, and that he would give me his opinion, as best he could, about my *Treasure Island*. He sounded excited. I had also brought along the other books I'd taken from the attic.

When I arrived, Cory donned white cotton gloves and laid the book carefully on a satin cloth. He opened the volume as though it were a holy object. I couldn't bring myself to tell him it had been carted around in a teenager's backpack for the last couple of days. Let him blame several decades in an abandoned attic for any damage.

Cory turned on a small digital recorder, and started murmuring:

"Cassell and Company, 1883. First edition, first impression. Gray-green cloth cover, gilt-lettered spine, black-coated endpapers."

He opened the book to the treasure map, and let out a happy gasp. "Frontispiece map—intact tissue guard— with captions printed in red, brown, and blue ink. A few old splash marks on the cover, inner joints superficially split but sound, light foxing, a few leaves lightly creased but no significant damage."

He clicked off the recorder, and passed me a list. "Would you read that aloud to me, please?"

"Sure . . . *'dead men's chest' not capitalized on pages two or seven.*"

He turned to those pages. "Check, and check."

"Page forty, the first letter of 'vain' broken in the last line so it looks like 'rain.'"

"Check."

"The 'a' not present in line six, page sixty-three; the eight dropped from the pagination on page eighty-three; the seven overstamped on page one hundred twenty-seven."

"Check, check, and check," Cory said, sitting back and looking very satisfied. "Now this, Mel Turner, is a *real* treasure."

"So the editing errors are considered a plus?"

"They help to authenticate the volume. And, like mistakes on a collectible stamp or a baseball card, they do make it even more valuable."

"How much are we talking?"

"I looked online before you came, and an original first edition *Treasure Island* can be worth many tens of thousands of dollars."

"Wow."

"But what makes this book truly special is that inscription." He shook his head. "I'm not even sure how much it might bring in, to tell you the truth. I'll give you the name of a true book expert for an exact estimate; I'm very fond of rare books, but I don't keep up with their current market value the way I do coins. I would think you'd want to put it up to auction. But I would imagine at least in the hundreds of thousands, if not more."

"Robert Louis Stevenson's signature is worth that much?"

"It's not just his signature, Mel—the inscription suggests Robert Louis Stevenson knew George Vigilance."

"Okay, but why would that add value?"

"Because Robert Louis Stevenson first published *Treasure Island* as serialized adventures in a magazine called *Young Folks*, under the pseudonym of Captain George North."

"So the inscription means that Stevenson's *nom de plume* was inspired by George Vigilance?"

"Exactly. But I've never heard of a George Vigilance, have you?"

I nodded. "He became a lighthouse keeper, but he grew up in San Francisco, on Bush Street."

Cory was so excited he couldn't contain himself. He jumped out of his chair. "Robert Louis Stevenson lived on Bush Street in 1879! How old would George have been?"

"He was about thirty when he became lightkeeper in 1899, so that would make him ten in 1879."

"That fits perfectly! The serialized story was published as a book in 1883, at which time Stevenson must have sent this to George Vigilance. Hot off the presses, so to speak. Now do you understand why it's so valuable?"

I nodded.

"And who is this 'little pirate' in the other inscription?" Cory asked.

"George's son, Franklin."

"Isn't that lovely. You have yourself a real collector's piece, here, Mel. A real treasure. Keep it safe."

*   *   *

"I have to admit, I had my doubts," said Landon that evening when I teetered down the stairs from the ladies' room at the War Memorial Opera House, where the ballet was presented. "I always thought 'lemon chiffon' was a kind of dessert. But you look incredible."

When Landon first saw me in Stephen's inspired design at home, he hadn't uttered a word but instead gave me a slow, warm smile that made me blush. My discomfiture only grew when I realized that Dad and Stan were waiting in the living room to watch me descend the stairs, as though I was coming down to meet my prom date.

I loved them, but I really *had* to find a new place to live. This regression to the age of seventeen had to stop.

"Thank you," I said, glancing up at Landon through my lashes in a coquettish move that seemed silly, but right. I felt good, actually. Better than I ever thought I would encased in lemon chiffon. Stephen had come up with a creation that highlighted my decidedly curvy figure.

Earlier in the day I had been late returning from Cory's Tiburon office, so what with getting all dolled up, I made us too late for the before-ballet cocktail party. But it was worth it. My hair was up, my nails were buffed, I was wearing perfume, and with Landon on my arm I felt pretty close to being the belle of the ball. The only problem was the shoes: I was so accustomed to my steel-toed work boots that the heels I was wearing—which weren't very tall at all, according to Stephen—made me feel slightly wobbly and disoriented. My legs, however, looked fantastic, so I made sure to lift the skirts whenever I got the chance. Like coming down the stairs from using the restroom.

The San Francisco Ballet Gala was clearly *the* event for wealthy Bay Area movers and shakers to see and be seen. For some reason this surprised me. In large part, San Francisco didn't really *do* obvious displays of wealth and power. This wasn't New York, after all, much less London. But I knew the city was full of exceedingly wealthy people—I worked for many of them—so had I supposed they wouldn't find excuses to wear their finest gowns?

And as it turned out, the ballet was amazing. Much better than my admittedly vague childhood memories of *The Nutcracker.*

Before arriving tonight, Landon had handed me a present about the size of a large bar of soap. I was just glad it wasn't small enough for a ring, or I might have fainted. I opened it to find an pair of antique opera glasses, made of a brass frame inlaid with mother of pearl, nestled in its original velvet-lined leather case. Where he had found them I couldn't guess, but they were a far sight better than a ring. It was such fun to watch the action on stage through the elegant opera glasses, to be able to see the beaded details on the costumes, the muscles of the dancers through their tights, alternately clenching and relaxing as they hurled themselves gracefully across the stage.

As much as I enjoyed the production, my mind kept wandering to Ida and her little boy, Franklin, out on Lighthouse Island with an abusive man. What must Ida have felt when she was locked in the attic? If my imagination was anything close to the truth, she must have experienced fear, rage, panic.

I knew for a fact that I would have killed anyone who threatened Caleb. Without compunction, without hesitation, I would have struck and, like a she-wolf, would have gone for the throat and viscera. And I wouldn't have been sorry.

Was I right, had Franklin gone missing when Ida was locked in the attic? And by the time she escaped, he was gone? Had she confronted her husband at the top of the tower stairs, and pushed him to his death? And all these years later, might her spirit have managed to push Thorn Walker—another abusive man—down those stairs?

Ida had looked for Franklin for ten years, hope ceding to the grim knowledge that he must be gone, but never finding his body, never knowing for sure what had happened to him. How many scenarios had run through her mind, how many horrors had she conjured wondering what fate had befallen him? Until at last she had tried to put an end to the pain by throwing herself off the lighthouse tower. But death didn't put a stop to her anguish; even as a ghost she searched for him still, unceasing, until repeatedly giving up hope and killing herself, over and over again.

Then my musings turned to Alicia in jail. At least she had someone wealthy enough to post her exorbitant bail. But what would it be like, knowing you were going to be put on trial for a crime you were innocent of? Her lawyer couldn't use the abused-woman-syndrome defense unless Alicia confessed to a murder she hadn't committed. When it came right down to it, I didn't feel any closer to finding out who else might have been hiding up in that tower.

I felt Landon's eyes on me. He winked and squeezed my hand before turning his gaze back to the stage. Once again I had to wonder—why was I so lucky? Why were people like Ida subject to such torturous lives?

There was no answering that question. The best I could do, I supposed, was to enjoy my good fortune, to

revel in my family and the love of old homes and a
good man.

I used my new opera glasses to check out the action
on stage, and then perused the crowd. My gaze drifted
over the occupants of some ornate box seats, the men in
black tie, the women dressed to the nines, their hair pro-
fessionally done. Probably their makeup, too. Why hadn't
I thought of that? Why did such things never occur to
me? I'll bet they occurred to my sister Cookie. She never
would have contemplated going to the eighty-fourth annual ballet gala with makeup and hair done by a blister-
plagued Stephen.

I scanned the next section of box seats, then—*wait*. I
pointed the glasses back to someone I had just skipped
over . . . was that . . . ?

After a moment of searching, I found her again. A
woman in a deep red gown. She looked a lot like Ida
Vigilance. A *lot*. Same cheekbones, same heart-shaped
face. Same serious expression. This woman could have
been Ida's doppelgänger.

I put the glasses down and stared at her with my naked
eyes. She was still there, hadn't vanished into thin air.

An apparition, or flesh and blood? Or . . . a doppelgänger?

Chapter Twenty-six

I could hear Olivier's warning in my head: *Don't take your abilities lightly. Give the spirits the respect of being prepared.* I hadn't been expecting to see a ghost at the ballet tonight, but I was getting the sense lately that all bets were off.

The thing was, this woman didn't look like a ghost, and didn't act like one either. She said something to the man next to her, smiled, and lifted her own opera glasses to her face.

She looked like a living, breathing person.

"See that woman over there?" I whispered to Landon. "Second box seat, in the dark red gown? Do you know who she is, by any chance?"

He took the opera glasses and held them to his eyes. Shook his head. "No, but as you know I'm fairly new in town. Other than university affiliates, and you Turner lot, I haven't met many people."

"But you can see her, right?"

"Yes, of course I can see her. Why?" He frowned. "You think she's a ghost?"

"No, not if you can see her. But, maybe a doppel-gänger?"

Landon smiled. "Only you, Mel Turner, could go to a ballet gala and find a doppelgänger."

"I'm serious," I said, pointing. "The woman in red, right there. See her?"

He nodded.

"You saw the photo of Ida, the lighthouse keeper. Don't you think . . . ?"

An elderly woman seated behind us leaned forward and shushed us.

"Sorry," I whispered over my shoulder.

Landon looked through the little binoculars again, then handed them back, and raised his eyebrows.

As soon as the ballet ended, I asked the elderly woman if she knew the lady in red, but she shook her head and departed in a huff, clearly annoyed that she'd been forced to sit within the vicinity of the likes of us. I hoped I wasn't going to ruin Landon's reputation. He didn't deserve to be tarred with my strangeness.

"Let's go," I said, and we hurried out to the lobby, hoping to catch a glimpse of the woman in red. It was a mob scene. I had hoped her brightly colored dress would make her easier to spot, but no luck. We watched and waited until the theater had practically emptied out.

I must have looked disappointed, because Landon said, "All is not lost. Most of the notables at the perfor-mance tonight are headed to the after-party. Shall we give it a try?"

I nodded.

"You honestly think you saw Ida, come back to life?" Landon asked as we walked—actually, Landon walked while I teetered—across the street to City Hall for the after party.

"No, not really. I just can't imagine any reason why this woman would look so much like Ida Vigilance. She didn't have any surviving children that I know of. I wonder if she had a sister or some other relative. If so, maybe there was some family lore handed down . . ."

Landon looked doubtful.

". . . I know, it's a long shot. I'm probably inventing something out of thin air. But—"

"'It's worth a try.'" Landon finished my sentence for me. "That's your personal motto, isn't it? I should have it translated into Latin for you."

I wasn't quite sure what he meant by that. But he was probably right.

"And you're sure she was the spitting image of Ida Vigilance? All I've seen was that faded photo, so while there's a similarity, I wouldn't swear to it."

"You forget, I've seen her in action, up close and personal." I thought of the times Ida had materialized right in front of me. A little misty, yes, but her features were distinct. "Honestly, if you changed the hairstyle, this woman would be her twin."

"Well, I guess we'll just have to corner this doppelgänger and ask her about her grandparents, or great-grandparents."

"Just like that?"

"Just like that. If she's related to your lighthouse keeper, she's likely proud of the story. People love to know these sorts of things about their families. If we see her at the party, we'll go say hello, and try to put an end to this mystery."

The gala after-party was held in the domed City Hall, a Beaux Arts monument to the City Beautiful movement. Proud San Franciscans liked to point out that its dome rose forty-two feet higher than that of the United States

Capitol building in Washington, DC. I was never quite sure why that should matter, but the locals seemed to think it did. Inside, the vast rotunda was made truly impressive with a grand sweep of a marble staircase, and the second floor consisted almost entirely of balconies overlooking the first, which made for a lovely venue.

It was also the site of some interesting history: Joe DiMaggio and Marilyn Monroe had been married here in 1954, and Mayor George Moscone and Supervisor Harvey Milk were murdered here in 1978.

I had been to City Hall many times, of course, finagling building permits or looking up property records. I once attended an impromptu wedding on the balcony. But tonight was different. Massive sprays of flowers decorated huge tables covered with white cloths, champagne and canapés were being passed around by white-gloved waitstaff, the women's gowns were dazzling, and the men looked elegant in their black tie, many in tails. And even though I was partial to Stephen's lemon chiffon, I was pretty sure most of the women were wearing dresses not created by a former barista–turned–lousy construction worker.

Landon moved through the crowd with ease. Not only did he look completely at home in his tuxedo, he was also unfailingly charming, and had a way of inviting complete strangers to stop and talk. It was fascinating to watch.

And it made me wonder if I was right for him.

Wouldn't that tall blonde look better draped on his arm? Or the brunette in the glasses who looked like she had a PhD but still managed to get her hair done in a salon? Or any other woman here? Dr. Weng's comment kept coming back to me: Could my acrophobia be connected to my relationship to Landon somehow? And if so, what did that mean for me? For us?

Don't think about that now, Mel, I told myself. *You have more important things to do, such as enjoy a gala that few people ever have the honor of attending, and spotting Ida Vigilance's doppelgänger to see if she might shed some light on a murder and a long-lost boy.*

I scanned the crowd. I didn't spot the woman in red, but I did see several former clients. I waved at one, a woman with a house off Presidio who looked elegant in a long white satin sheath. Also Andrew Flynt, atop whose Pacific Heights roof I had rolled around not so long ago, directly resulting in my acrophobia. When they saw me their smiles froze and they seemed to lose track of what they were saying. Even though we were friendly, and I occasionally helped solve murders at their houses, most of my clients and I didn't move in the same social circles. I figured it must be like when young children see their teachers outside of class.

"And you thought you wouldn't know anyone here," said Landon after a polite but awkward exchange with Andrew Flynt.

"That was wishful thinking, I suppose," I said as I waved to yet another client.

He smiled down at me. "Tell the truth: Are you having any fun at all?"

"I'm enjoying this building. Did you know Joe DiMaggio and Marilyn Monroe got married here?" I was just hoping there weren't any ghosts. On the other hand, it would be interesting to have a chat with Harvey Milk. I would have liked to ask him what he thought about Sean Penn playing him in the movie.

"Is that so?"

"In 1954," I said with a nod. We were near the base of the stairs; I stepped up a few to get a better look at the milling silks and satins. Normally I would have headed straight for the second-story balcony overlooking the rotunda, but under the circumstances, I thought it best to stick to flat land. Even though . . . I was hesitant to put too much faith into acupuncture just yet, but it was possible the treatments—or maybe the little mantra Dr. Weng had given me—were helping. Just slightly. I felt a little less panicky at the thought of falling.

"One thing I'll say for sure," I said. "People always fawn over the women's gowns, but I'm always most impressed by the men at an event like this."

"How so?"

"Everything's so casual in the Bay Area. I'm not used to seeing men in suits, much less black tie. You look good."

"At your dad's house you said I looked like a penguin."

"I just said that so it wouldn't be obvious that I was drooling over you."

"I think you've got everyone fooled."

"I—" I cut myself off. I peered closer, trying to see a woman's face in the crowd on the second-floor balcony. Dark hair pulled back, solemn blue eyes. A heart-shaped face.

"Isn't that her?"

"Try the opera glasses," suggested Landon.

"Good idea!" I took the glasses from my purse and scanned the balcony. It took me a few minutes to locate her with the glasses, but when I did . . .

She turned and looked down. Right at me. As though she knew she was being watched.

I turned away, pretending to be studying the architecture. "I think she saw me."

"She's moved behind the column," said Landon.

"I . . . can't go up there," I said.

"I understand. I think she spotted you anyway. Let me go. Wait for me here."

I watched as he climbed the staircase, passing through the crowd like a salmon swimming upstream. He turned left at the top and disappeared behind the column.

"I think you lost her," a man said from behind me.

It was Major Williston, looking marvelous in a nice tuxedo. Terry Re joined him, putting her hand through his arm.

"Hi . . . you two." Speaking of being nonplussed when seeing people out of context: I was so used to Terry and Major on the island, in their casual sailing clothes, that I was shocked to see them here. Shocked, and wary.

"Where's Paul?" I asked.

"Still looking for ghosts," said Major.

I glanced up to the balcony, hoping to spot Landon. But he was nowhere to be seen, lost in the crowd.

"I don't suppose you know what happened to my son's backpack, by any chance?" Not that I expected a truthful answer, but it was worth a shot.

Major shook his head. "I haven't noticed anything like that—was it on the island?"

"It was. So, you two are fans of the ballet, are you?" I asked.

"Cut the crap, Turner," said Terry. "We're after the same woman."

"Who would that be?"

Terry gave me a fake smile.

Just then, I spotted the woman in red coming down the stairs, on the other side of the broad steps. I started threading my way through the throng of well-dressed ballet aficionados, but Major was way ahead of me.

The mystery woman spotted us, turned, and hustled her way through the crowd, glancing over her shoulder, her solemn eyes wide with fear.

"Ida?" I called out. I didn't really believe I was seeing

the incarnation of Ida Prescott Vigilance, but one never knew. Stranger things had happened to me since embarking on my ghost-busting career.

The woman paled and shook her head, reached a far wall, and tripped a fire alarm. Alarms blared and lights flashed.

The City Hall security forces weren't kidding around.

A mechanical voice announced, *"Please make your way to the nearest exit."* The well-dressed crowd chattered excitedly but obeyed, pouring out the front doors.

The woman had vanished in the melee. I couldn't find Landon, either. Uniformed security officers herded me outside with the others. The predicted storm was moving in, causing the winds to whip up and a light rain to fall. The beautifully dressed people squealed and called frantically for valets to fetch their cars.

I finally found Landon leaning up against a tree in the plaza across from the City Hall.

"I'm really sorry," I said as I drew near.

"I'm just glad you're okay. I couldn't find you in the crowd. So, was all of this"—he gestured to the chaos—"your doing?"

"Sort of." I leaned up against the tree next to him, and we watched as well-coiffed folks scurried around like rats on a sinking ship. "Landon, I'm so sorry. I made us miss the cocktail party, and now I've ruined the after-party. At least I didn't mess up the actual ballet."

He smiled down at me. "I have the distinct impression that any man worthy of you is going to have to get used to this sort of thing."

"You, sir, are a wonder."

His eyes ran over my damp form. "I fear your lemon chiffon is going to get ruined in this rain. Alas, my umbrella's in the car."

"One thing I can say about Stephen's designs, they're wash and wear. Hey, did you see that Major and Terry were here?"

"The sailors from Lighthouse Island?" He frowned. "They followed you here?"

"No. We didn't talk a lot, but I got the impression they were after our mystery woman, as well, so she *must* be connected to the lighthouse. What in the world do you suppose is going on?"

Landon was scanning the crowd, looking for Major or Terry or ersatz Ida. Then he shook his head. "I don't see them anywhere. Nor do I see the doppelgänger in red. And with this storm rolling in . . . I think it's time for us to head home."

Half an hour later we pulled up in front of Dad's house. It was raining in earnest now, big fat droplets that hit the car with a splash. Landon came around the car to open the door for me.

As we turned to rush into the house, a figure emerged from behind a hedge.

I jumped back. Landon rushed to my side, putting a protective arm around me.

"Waquisha?" I breathed. "What are you doing here?"

She was drenched by the rain so it was hard to tell, but I thought she was crying.

"Are you okay?" I asked.

"I . . . I'm sorry if I scared you. I just wanted to talk to you. About . . . everything. I didn't mean for any of this to happen, honestly. This is the best job I've ever had. I *love* carpentry, creating stuff by hand. My dad doesn't like me to use his equipment because it's all he has. I don't want to lose this job. Please don't fire me! I—"

"Let's take this inside, shall we?" suggested Landon.

The wind was picking up, blowing the rain this way and that and rendering the umbrella virtually useless.

"Good idea," I said. Part of me worried that Waquisha was somehow involved with Thorn's death, but I didn't really think so. For one thing, the police had cleared her and, after all, I had absolutely nothing concrete to suggest otherwise. And I was with Landon, and Dad and Stan and Caleb and Stephen were in the house. I liked our chances.

We hurried down the walkway at the side of the house and entered through the back door. Dog met us with wild barking and flailing, curling around and wagging his tail so hard he slapped himself in the face. The kitchen smelled of roast meat and potatoes, though dinner was long since over and the dishes cleaned up.

"Smells good in here," said Waquisha. "Like home. But I'm gonna drip on everything."

"Don't worry about it, Waquisha, really," I said, handing her a towel from the bathroom off the kitchen. "We're pretty informal around here. Have a seat. Want some tea? Or are you hungry? Dad always has leftovers."

"Oh, thanks, just tea would be great."

Dad and Stan were in the living room watching TV. I poked my head in to say hello, and to let them know we had a visitor. Then I returned to the kitchen, fixed us all some tea, and sat down to listen to her story.

"You guys look really nice," said Waquisha. "Were you at the opera or something?"

"Close," Landon said. "The ballet."

"No kidding? I love dance. I've never seen a real ballet but I love all kinds of dance."

Tired of the small talk, I cut to the chase. "How did you know Thorn, Waquisha?"

"He . . . I met him on the docks, at Point Moro. My

dad basically kicked me out. We've never really gotten along, and he didn't have room for me on the boat anyway. I was pretty desperate. Thorn told me I could probably get a job with the new project out on the island. And then . . ." She trailed off and played with the tea bag.

"Then what?" I urged.

She let out a long breath. "He paid me for information."

"What kind of information?" Landon asked.

Waquisha was a tall, powerfully built woman, so somehow I had missed how young she was. Looking at her now, I realized she was probably in her early twenties, just a couple of years older than Caleb.

"He wanted to know what was going on out there, and asked about Alicia, who he kept calling 'Amy.' He said he knew her when they were kids. It didn't seem . . ." She trailed off and looked around the kitchen as though searching for inspiration. "I guess it didn't seem that weird at first, but later I started wondering why he didn't just call her if they were such old friends. But anyway, once I told him that the docks were public, I didn't hear much from him after that. Just saw him once or twice in Point Moro."

"Did he mention anyone else he knew on the island, or anything like that?"

"No, he said he was from out of town. The only person he mentioned was Alicia. How's she doing, anyway? I heard she was arrested? I'm so sorry."

"You told the police about this?" I asked.

"Yeah, they kept me in the interrogation room for a long time. It was like something out of a TV show."

"What about the others hanging around the island, Major or Terry or Paul?"

She shook her head. "I only knew them from the island. Terry asked me once if we got anything good out of the house, but that was about all. Oh, also she asked me about books. That was weird."

"What about books?"

"If we'd found any. She said she would buy them from me, ten dollars a pop. Seemed like a lot for a bunch of moldy old books."

After I assured Waquisha that she was expected at work on Monday, she apologized again, and called for a ride home.

Despite our exciting night, or perhaps because of it, I once again had trouble sleeping. I couldn't stop thinking about Alicia. I felt like I had failed her. And Ida's grief had been so overwhelming it was practically tangible. I wanted to help her, too. So while Landon slept, I climbed out of bed, grabbed the Bay Light's keeper's logs, and took them downstairs. I flipped through the volumes until I found the entries I remembered reading the first day I found the logs in the attic. They were from 1905.

In George's hand:

>   *October 5 Wind NNE. Commenced blowing at two o'clock a.m. Noon, blowing a gale and a heavy sea running over the wharf at three p.m.; washed away lower portion of steps.*

>   *October 8 Wind NW. La Belle France spotted, apparently in distress. Docked, repairs made. Set sail for San Francisco before nightfall.*

In Ida's hand:

>   *October 9 Wind NE, cold, light, foggy. Sustained an injured ankle. My search is fruitless. My heart*

is broken. Several vessels have passed. Mr. Vigilance has fallen.

October 10 Wind NE squally. Still I search.

October 11 Wind SW. Search is fruitless. I shall not relinquish hope.

October 12 Wind S. Light haze. Since Mr. Vigilance has departed this earth, keeping the lamp has fallen to me. Continue to search.

As I reread the words, something occurred to me: *La Belle France* had docked on October 8. If Ida had been locked in the attic that day, terrorized by her abusive husband, and Franklin had gone missing . . . could he possibly have been playing stowaway? Living out his favorite books, looking for adventure on the high seas? Never imagining that he wouldn't be able to find his way back?

Olivier had suggested the little boy apparition by the shore might have been a projection, not a true ghost. Had Ida's yearning for her child been so strong that she'd created a version of him, forever playing in the sand?

And if so, was it possible little Franklin hadn't died on the island? If he had stowed away on *La Belle France*, could he have ended up in San Francisco when the ship pulled into the raucous, busy port of the Barbary Coast? If he was too young to tell people his full name and where he belonged . . . what might have become of him? Could he have survived, grown up, and had children of his own?

Might tonight's doppelgänger in the red dress be a direct descendent of Franklin Prescott Vigilance?

Chapter Twenty-seven

I slept in until eight thirty the next morning. I felt like a sloth.

I found Landon and my dad downstairs at the kitchen table, reading the Sunday papers. Half a fluffy veggie and sausage omelet was in the cast-iron skillet on the stove. Outside, the storm raged, wind and driving rain. We didn't have enough inclement weather in the Bay Area to grow blasé about it; it was rather thrilling to witness the strength and majesty of a rainstorm.

"Good *afternoon*," remarked Dad, eyebrows raised. And I wondered why sleeping until eight thirty made me feel so lazy. "We already ate, but there's plenty left."

"Thanks, Dad. Maybe in a bit." I gave him a kiss on the head, said hello to Landon, and headed for the coffeepot.

"I found her," announced Landon.

"Found who?"

"The mystery woman in red. Your doppelgänger is named Annalisa Alva."

"*What?* How do you know?"

He rattled the newspaper. "Society pages."

"The *San Francisco Chronicle* has *society* pages?" I asked.

Dad rolled his eyes. "Half your clients show up in those pages on a regular basis. You should make an effort to keep up with the local news."

"Sure, Dad, I'll get right on that. I've been looking for a hobby to fill all my spare time."

"Smart aleck," Dad said, smiling.

"Besides, as long as I'm available to patch their roofs and plunge their toilets, our clients don't seem to care if I'm current with their goings-on. It's not as if we socialize."

"Anyway, doppelgänger?" Landon said. "Anyone?"

"Sorry! Yes, of course," I said. "So, who is Annalisa Alva?"

He turned the paper around to show me. There she was, among the slew of photos of the beautiful people who had shown up for the ballet gala. She had been one of the organizers.

"I looked her up online; she's married to a successful businessman, has a six-year-old boy, lives in Noe Valley, and describes herself as 'at least a third-generation' San Franciscan."

"What does she mean by 'at least'?"

"That is one of many mysteries. First I'd like to know whether she's actually a doppelgänger."

"We're kidding about this, right?" said Dad, coffee cup halfway to his lips. "You keep saying doppelgänger like it's a real thing, but it's a joke, right?"

"This woman looks remarkably like Ida Vigilance, who used to be keeper of the Bay Light," I explained.

"So?" Dad demanded. "I've been told I bear a startling resemblance to Clint Eastwood. Doesn't mean I'm the reincarnation of the guy."

"First of all, Dad," I said. "You're a handsome guy but you look nothing at all like Clint Eastwood. Second, as far as I know, Eastwood isn't dead so you can't be his reincarnation. And third, we're not *talking* about reincarnation anyway. It's just . . . if this Annalisa woman is a descendant of Ida's sister, or something, maybe she could tell us a little about the family history."

Dad shrugged. "You sure you don't want some omelet, babe?"

"Not yet, thank you," I said. "Coffee's fine for now. And actually, I had another idea last night: What if Ida's little boy didn't die on the island?"

"How do you mean?"

"What if, instead, Franklin stowed away on a ship that came into the docks that day?"

"You mean he ran away?" Landon asked.

"Not intentionally. It would have been an accident, probably. He was so young, barely five years old. Kids that age live in a world of make-believe half the time. He loved stories of adventure, and loved to play pirate. What if he thought it was a game to play stowaway, but then got lost and couldn't get back home?"

Dad and Landon glanced at each other.

"It's possible, right?" I said. "And maybe this Annalisa person is one of his descendants, and thus one of Ida's descendants?"

"I suppose that's possible," said Landon.

"Worth asking about, in any case," said Dad. "Stranger things have happened."

"So . . . what do I do now?" I asked. "Try to track down Annalisa's phone number, and call her up, out of the blue?"

"I have a better idea," said Landon, folding the news-paper and setting it neatly on the table. "Why don't you take the day off, and leave Annalisa to me."

"You think I'll scare her off?"

He paused for a beat. "I think I might have better luck."

"You've got yourself quite the diplomat, there, Mel," said Dad, nudging me. "This one's a keeper."

Landon, the eminently respectable math professor from Berkeley with the charming, barely-there English accent, was on the case of Annalisa Alva. I didn't take it per-sonally; he was right. I had already spooked her at the gala. Or perhaps it was Major and Terry that spooked her. What had *they* been doing there?

In any case, it felt good to leave this in Landon's oh-so-diplomatic hands. He made a few phone calls, then took off to San Francisco armed with the photo of Ida Prescott Vigilance holding her young son in her lap, as well a few of the keeper's logs to show Annalisa Alva.

I was under strict instructions to take the day off, to spend a lazy Sunday relaxing. Which was all well and good except that I had a friend in jail, facing trial for a crime she didn't commit. And now that I knew about the potential value of the copy of *Treasure Island* I found on the island, I couldn't help but wonder whether this was what Terry—and Major?—had been after all along. Could there be something else in that attic I had over-looked—preoccupied as I was with Ida whenever I was there—that would help explain why Thorn had been killed and therefore point to a likely murderer?

For the time being I had stashed the book in our home safe, alongside our account books and petty cash.

The more I thought about it, the more I wished I had

retrieved the rest of the books from the attic of the Keeper's House. We had left the attic alone during the demolition, while I figured out how to mollify Ida's spirit. So unless Terry and her pals had found a way to get into the attic without Ida scaring them off, whatever it was they were looking for was probably still there. After showing Cory Venner *Treasure Island*, he had taken a look at the other books, and while he didn't think they were worth as much, they were nonetheless collectible. Perhaps the others were, as well. Maybe together they added up to a small fortune. A literary treasure.

I wanted to check out the other books from the attic, and anything else that might be worth money.

I phoned Duncan to see if he'd be willing to ferry me out to Lighthouse Island. He agreed, adding that since the ride was so short we should be fine despite the inclement weather. Next I spoke to Buzz, who reluctantly agreed to meet me in Point Moro. I felt bad asking him, since I was pretty certain he didn't feel he could refuse without incurring the wrath of Ellis Elrich. But I needed backup. I wasn't going to go out on that island all alone. Even I wasn't that stupid.

In fact . . . I tucked my father's Glock into my jacket pocket. I wasn't licensed to carry, but I knew my way around a firearm. Dad had taken us to the shooting range when I was a kid, and bought me my own .22 for my tenth birthday in the hope that I would join him on hunting trips. This is what happened when the Fates gave people like my father three daughters and no sons.

I told my dad I was going out to run some errands—which was sort of true—and set out for Point Moro. It was still raining but not nearly as windy as it had been. The bay showed whitecaps, but I thought: How bad could it be?

I found out once we were out on the water. The *Callisto* was tossed about like a leaf in the wind. I wore my life preserver without complaint, and gripped the side with all my strength.

Duncan and Buzz, on the other hand, stood at the helm, apparently unbothered by the swells and dips.

"I like the name of your boat," said Buzz.

"Isn't it pretty?" said Duncan. "It was my mother's name."

"Callisto was the woman who got changed into Ursa Minor, right?" asked Buzz.

"Ursa Major, actually. I see you know your Greek mythology," Duncan said.

"A little," Buzz said with a shrug. "My dad used to teach us about the constellations, so I like to read the myths associated with them. I bet you could see a lot of stars out on this island, back in the day before city lights and cars and everything."

"I'll bet you're right. You know, most people only know the Big Dipper and maybe Orion. But there's a story for every constellation. Fascinating."

Duncan piloted the *Callisto* with his usual ease, despite the wind and rain. He reached out to adjust the radio and his sleeve caught on a knob; when it hitched up, I glimpsed long scars the length of his forearm. Ugly, puckered scars.

He pulled the sleeve down quickly.

I gazed at him, realizing I had never seen Duncan in short sleeves. Even in January the afternoons were often sunny and warm; dressing in layers was *de rigueur* in the Bay Area, and many days most of us stripped down to T-shirts by two. Also, Duncan was always so upbeat. Maybe he had a naturally sunny disposition. Or . . . could it be the result of having recently attended motivational workshops?

I hadn't recognized the name *Callisto*, but if it was related to Ursa, didn't that mean Bear? Could Duncan have been Thorn's roommate at the Palm Project? He was in his forties, "regular"-looking, so he could fit Thorn's description.

We pulled into the harbor. There were no other boats at the docks, which was a relief. Maybe the three sailors had finally moved on to bluer waters. As usual, Duncan stayed with the boat while Buzz and I disembarked.

"Hey, Buzz," I said as we walked up the path toward the keeper's buildings. "I think maybe Duncan . . ."

I hesitated to say what I was thinking. If Buzz tried to bust Duncan out here, who would pilot the boat back to port? Wouldn't it be better to play it cool for the moment, then call Detective Santos when we returned to the mainland? I felt no threatening vibes at all from Duncan, Buzz was here, and I had a Glock in my pocket.

Climbing the lighthouse tower wasn't an option, so there was no risk I would be pushed down those stairs. Still, I should say something.

"I . . . I have an idea that Duncan might be involved in things," I said in a low voice as we headed toward the Keeper's House. "He'll probably stay with the boat, but maybe keep an eye out, just in case?"

"Involved? Duncan? But he's such a nice guy."

"He is. It's true. I don't know anything, really, Buzz, I think I'm just jumpy."

Buzz cast a pained eye back toward the docks. "You should wait here while I check out the house, but now I don't want to leave you alone. I shoulda called Krauss to come with."

"I'm not worried, Buzz. And hey, I'm armed," I showed him the Glock.

He stepped back. "Aw, *jeez*, do you even know how to hold that thing? It'll knock you on your ass if you're not careful."

"My dad trained me. I'm a pretty good shot. You check out the house, and I'll wait here."

It wasn't going to pretend I was a particularly good judge of character. But frankly Major and Terry scared me more than Duncan. Even if he was indeed the "Bear" who had been Thorn's roommate at the Palm Project, that didn't mean he was involved in Thorn's death. After all, if he had done the dirty deed for some reason, why was he still here, showing up to work every day? He could have wandered off days ago and no one would have suspected him.

Nope, my money was on Major or Terry, or both of them.

After another minute, I convinced Buzz to check out the house while I waited in the courtyard with one hand on the gun.

I checked my phone: a text from Landon. *You were right! Annalisa's great-grandfather was a young wharf orphan, adopted by a shipbuilder. He married and had three children; Annalisa is the granddaughter of his youngest son. The great-grandfather's first name was Franklin. Lived to be eighty-seven.*

"It was my fault Thorn found her."

I spun around at the sound of Duncan's voice behind me. So much for keeping my hand on my gun. Foiled by that most modern of distractions: the cell phone.

"What?" I asked, my heart pounding. Should I call for Buzz? Pull out my gun? But Duncan kept talking, with such sorrow in his eyes that I felt more curious than scared.

"It was my fault," Duncan repeated. "Thorn and I were roommates at the Palm Project. One day, just as I was about to graduate from the program, I found an ad for the boat ferrying job. I'm Coast Guard certified and everything; I couldn't believe my luck. But when I showed Thorn the article describing the Lighthouse Island project, he was beside himself. He recognized his ex-wife."

"That was just chance, Duncan, it wasn't your fault."

"Chance, but bad luck for Alicia. I knew Thorn hadn't changed. I don't think a man like that can change, do you?"

"I honestly don't know. I think he was . . . trying."

Duncan shook his head. "Not good enough. Not near good enough. When he showed up in Point Moro, I knew there was going to be trouble. And then, that day, after he talked to you and Alicia, Buzz brought him back to the harbor. I watched Thorn get on his boat, and I followed him to make sure he went back to Point Moro. But he didn't. He sailed right around to the other dock, and climbed the ladder. So I followed him into the tower."

"Why did he go to the top of the tower?" Where in the world was Buzz? I wondered. How long could it possibly take to check the house for intruders? And what should we do when Buzz joined us—force Duncan to pilot us back to shore, and then turn him over to the cops?

"Thorn said he could watch Alicia—he called her Amy—from up there without anybody noticing. He kept saying they were meant to be together, that they always had been. That he had screwed things up with her, but that it would be different this time." Duncan shook his head. "My father used to say that. They always say that."

"So you stabbed him and pushed him down the stairs?" That seemed like an overreaction.

"I didn't mean to stab him. I wanted him to leave Alicia alone, that's all. But he refused. Then I thought, I could just push him down the stairs, make it look like an accident. I figured, how hard could it be?"

"Harder than you thought?" I asked, quietly.

He nodded. "Turns out, it's not so easy to"—his voice broke—"to kill a man. I hesitated, and he swung at me. Thorn wasn't that big, though; I had the advantage. Still, I gotta hand it to him, he put up a good fight. I landed a few good punches, figured that would be blamed on the fall, but then he brought out a knife. Tried to stab me with it, we struggled, and I managed to turn it around." He let out a long breath, took off his Greek sailor's hat, and ran a hand through his hair before putting it back on. "Anyway, that's what happened."

I tried to take it all in, to think how to respond.

"I hope you don't feel bad for him," said Duncan. "Think about it, why did he have that knife on him? My guess is he was going to use it on Alicia. I've known men like that; they don't stop. He was never going to let Alicia go. Never. And she was always very kind to me, to everybody. She always made sure I had enough to eat, used to bring me the soda I liked, the *Jarritos* grapefruit flavor, made with real sugar. Corn syrup is bad for you."

"She's very thoughtful," I said with a nod, again wondering where Buzz was.

"I had to be sure she was safe. Bend like a palm, and accept your responsibilities. Thorn always left that last part out. Said it was fate that he saw Alicia's photograph in the paper, but seems to me it was fate that put me in the right place, at the right time, to help her. The way no one was able to help my mother."

"What happened to your mother?"

He shook his head, a bleak look in his eye. "I tried to protect her, but I was just a kid. My father was a drunk, used to go after both of us. He finally beat someone up in a bar and went to prison. But after he was gone she ended up killing herself, finished the job for him. Someone makes you feel like trash long enough, you get to where you believe it."

"Duncan . . . ," I began but trailed off. I really didn't know what to say.

"Here," he said, handing me an envelope. It was creased and slightly water-damaged. "This is a signed confession, it spells out everything. I couldn't believe it when I heard Alicia had been arrested for what I did. That day . . . I hid in the storage closet when I heard her coming up the tower. And then I slipped out when you were all busy with Thorn. But I never thought, not in a million years, that Alicia would take the fall for my crime. I did it for her, and she winds up getting blamed? Talk about being a screwup. I've been walking around with this letter in my jacket pocket for days, but I just couldn't face going to jail. You know?"

"We'll get you a good lawyer," I said, brashly assuming Ellis Elrich would be willing to help. Duncan had, after all, done what he did to protect Alicia.

He looked at me with an expression so full of grief it reminded me of Ida Vigilance mourning her son.

"Thank you, Mel. But I won't need a lawyer. Good-bye."

He ran toward the lighthouse.

"Duncan, wait!" I yelled, running after him and into the lighthouse. He didn't slow his pace. Then I shouted toward the Keeper's House as loud as I could, "Buzz! Lighthouse tower!"

The clanging of footsteps on metal stairs echoed off

the tower walls. A surge of wind and rain added to the sense of loneliness and desolation.

Without thinking, I started to run up the stairs after him. On the tenth step I again made the mistake of looking toward the center. I tried saying my little mantra to myself, over and over. *The things that bring me joy ground me; the things that bring me hope lift me.* I thought about Dr. Weng's large, graceful hands. I thought about Caleb sitting up late reading *Treasure Island*, and the popcorn fight after watching *Vertigo*. I thought about Dad and Stan bickering over what to watch on television, and about Landon's soft voice and tender smiles, about Luz's fierce friendship and love of food, about Dog's velvety head and unerring loyalty. I thought of my mother as a child playing in her grandparents' beautiful old house, sliding down the laundry chute, and somehow managing to share her memories with me as I walked through those same rooms.

Lost in my warm thoughts, I realized I had climbed nearly halfway up the tower. I kept one hand on the rough stone wall, away from that terrifying open hole in the center of the stairwell, and focused on looking straight ahead, not up or down the tower.

"Duncan, please!" I yelled again. "Stop, let's talk some more!"

Round and round, up one step, then the next, then the next. One foot after another.

I no longer heard the clanging of Duncan's footsteps on the metal treads; he must have reached the top. I just hoped he would wait for me. *Don't let your fear keep you from helping him, Mel,* I told myself. *Don't let your fear keep you from anything.*

At last I reached the watch room where the clockworks were, where Duncan and Thorn had fought, and where Duncan had slipped into a closet when he heard Alicia approaching. This was where Alicia had seen Thorn alive in his last moments. Had the knife truly been meant for her? If Duncan hadn't followed him up here, and had Alicia climbed the tower alone, what would Thorn have done?

The next level was the lantern room, with the giant lens. And the exterior balcony that ran the perimeter, unsafe and off-limits.

Duncan was already out on that corroded little catwalk, his grip white-knuckled on the rail. The wind was fierce up here; Duncan's Greek fishing cap was carried off by a gust.

"Stay back, Mel," he said. "I'm serious. I have to do this. I tried once before. It's better for everyone that I succeed this time."

"Duncan, please don't—"

As he tried to climb up over the rail, a rusty bolt pulled out of the masonry with a loud screech and a spray of mortar. The catwalk jolted, listing downward, but still clung to the lighthouse tower.

"*No!*" I yelled, grabbing for Duncan. I managed to get hold of one bicep, and held on to a strong iron safety bar with the other hand. "No, Duncan!"

Another screech, another jolt.

Duncan met my gaze. His eyes were terrified, as if he had changed his mind. "Mel?"

My arms burned, my shoulder felt like it was being pulled apart.

The balcony gave way, though still attached to the tower by a few bolts; it dangled above the sharp rocks below.

"Mel!"

"Hold on, Duncan!"

But of course I couldn't hold him. Even if he'd been a small child, it would have been a challenge to haul him up, and Duncan had at least fifty pounds on me. Gusts of wind tugged at him, and the rain beat down like pinpricks on our skin.

It was my nightmare on the roof, all over again, except this time no one was trying to kill me. But . . . I wasn't sure I could take another man falling to his death in front of me. How would I ever *un*see the terror in Duncan's eyes, *un*hear the screams as he fell?

I closed my eyes and silently begged for help.

Later, I wouldn't be able to explain what happened. Not to the police, not to Landon, not even to myself.

As we hung there, moments from death, I felt a surge of energy envelop me. I opened my eyes to see Ida Prescott Vigilance. I'd like to say she reached out and pulled us up, but it didn't happen like that. Somehow, though, she was able to lend me her strength. Ida had been a formidable woman, not just strong in body but forceful in spirit. She had endured years alone out on this island, tending the lamp and the clockworks and the foghorn, searching endlessly for her lost son.

Somehow her spirit managed to help me pull Duncan back into the lantern room as the catwalk crashed and banged against the tower, buffeted by the wind, attached only by a few rungs. Duncan collapsed in a heap on the floor of the lamp room, sobbing. I held him for several minutes, before I realized: I wasn't dizzy. I wasn't nauseated. I didn't have vertigo.

Chapter Twenty-eight

The trip down the long and winding staircase was a bit of an odyssey, but Duncan held on to me, and together we made it safely to the ground. I wouldn't have been surprised to learn that Ida played a role in my successful negotiation of the steps, as well.

I felt a little dizzy, but I wasn't debilitated. Either that acupuncture really was a miracle treatment, or something else was going on. Because I was better. Not cured, but better.

Buzz burst through the tower door, his gun in his hand, and started up the stairs before halting at the sight of us. His eyes swept over me, then Duncan, then returned to me.

"I fell through a soft patch in the floor and got stuck! I heard you calling out about the lighthouse tower. 'Bout gave me a heart attack! Everything all right?"

I nodded. "Everything's fine, Buzz, thank you. Please help Duncan back to the boat. I'll text Detective Santos to meet us at the docks. Duncan, you're ready to turn yourself in?"

Duncan nodded. "It's time."

Buzz half carried the exhausted Duncan the rest of the way down the stairs, and we left the tower.

I turned to Buzz. "I need to take care of something in the attic. It won't take long, and I'll meet you at the docks. I take it the house is secure?"

Buzz nodded. "I don't think anyone's on the island except us. There weren't any boats at the docks. Still, I should go with you."

"I know that makes sense, but I have to go in the attic alone."

I stepped into the house, climbed the main stairs, proceeded down the little hall, then made my way up the steep stretch to the attic.

The door creaked as I pushed it open.

"Ida, I have news," I said.

Busy straightening the attic, she ignored me.

"Ida, it's big news. It's about your son. Franklin."

She froze. Then she turned and looked at me, and I almost wished she hadn't. Her eyes were vacant, disturbing. When she spoke, her voice was as hollow as her eyes, echoing slightly, as though she were making an effort to throw her voice up out of a well. *"Franklin?"*

I nodded.

"Do you know where he is?" Again, that echoey, far-away sound. I told myself not to react in fear, but the sound sent shivers through me.

And again, in a rage, she was suddenly right in front of me. *"Tell me where he is!"*

I backed up a step, stumbled over something, and fell back into a rocking chair. It tilted wildly before sending me back toward her. I planted my feet on the floor and faced the furious specter.

"He *lived*," I said. "Ida, he lived. He didn't die here."

She gave me a suspicious look. *"That can't be. That can't be! I've seen him here. I see him here, on the rocks. My husband let him play on the rocks, near the water. I told him it was dangerous."*

"That's a . . . an apparition, brought about by your own memories," I said, and with a start realized I was in a haunted attic, explaining the unknown to a spirit from beyond the veil. My life was way too interesting sometimes. "Here's the truth: Franklin snuck onto the boat, *La Belle France*, the supply ship that docked that day, in early October. You remember *La Belle France*? George had locked you here in the attic, and Franklin was playing pirate. He thought it was all a game."

"My boy loved to play pirate," she said, a sweet tone in her voice. *"I made his pirate suit for him, you know. He looked like a little angel."*

The pride in her long-dead voice sent more shivers through me, but I nodded. "He did. But listen, Ida. Franklin played stowaway on *La Belle France*. He didn't mean to leave, he was just having an adventure. But the ship returned to San Francisco, with him still aboard. He couldn't tell anyone where he was from, or couldn't convince anyone, or something. It was the crazy Barbary Coast. I don't know exactly what happened, but I know he lived."

She looked at me with hope, and fear. *How did I know?* she wondered. She didn't have to say the words for me to understand.

"My friend spoke to his great-granddaughter," I said gently. "Franklin was taken in by a shipbuilder's family in San Francisco. He grew up and married, Ida. He had children. And they had children. One of his descendants had a daughter who is the spitting image of you. I've seen her. That's how I figured it out. And she has a son, about Franklin's age when he disappeared."

Ida seemed to be struggling to take it all in.

"I could ask them if they'll come out here to meet you, if you like."

"Franklin? My boy?"

"No, I'm sorry, Ida. Franklin passed away many years ago. But he didn't die here on the island. He grew up in San Francisco and had a family, and died when he was in his eighties. Do you understand what I'm saying? Your little pirate lived a long and happy life."

A week later, Landon stood at the helm in his Scottish cable-knit sweater, once again looking like an advertisement for men's cologne. The taciturn Lyle was piloting the boat for us. Annalisa Alva was also there with her husband and their six-year-old son, Jeffrey, who wore a tiny, bright orange life preserver.

Annalisa seemed a little wary of me, but somehow Landon had managed to explain the situation to her. She had run from me at the ballet, apparently, because I was standing next to Major Williston. Major and Terry were "treasure hunters" who had heard rumors of a treasure on the island and were convinced they would be able to find it, if only they had more time. Major had figured out what happened to Franklin before I had; apparently the file he'd stolen included a newspaper clipping of a "little stowaway" found wandering the busy wharves in 1905, with a note written by a former historian at the archive questioning whether the child might have been the missing boy from Lighthouse Island. Williston had been trying to convince Annalisa to talk to him about stopping the development project on the island, thinking her high-society influence would come in handy. But he struck her as unhinged, and she feared he was stalking her.

Annalisa's attitude toward me improved when I gave

her Franklin's old copy of *Treasure Island*. Even though there are "finders keepers" rules that state whoever owns the house when something is discovered can keep the goods, I had spoken to Ellis Elrich, and he agreed that this particular treasure should remain with the family.

"Island!" shouted little Jeffrey, pointing as we came close. He had a delicate face, rather like his great-grandfather's at his age. But it was his mother's face that haunted me; she truly was the spitting image of Ida. It was when Landon showed Annalisa the photograph of Ida, sitting with Franklin in her lap, that she was convinced. The photograph wasn't a death portrait after all; it was merely the only known photo of Ida Prescott Vigilance, with her beloved son in her lap.

Our party disembarked at the harbor and headed toward the tower and the Keeper's House. Jeffrey ran ahead, picking up rocks to throw into the woods and charging about with a stick, pretending it was a sword. It was not difficult to imagine little Franklin doing the same, on these same paths, more than one hundred years ago.

As we neared the Keeper's House, I glanced up at the attic window. Ida's face was pressed against the glass. She had spotted him.

Jeffrey stopped in his tracks, looked up at the window, and waved.

"Who are you waving at, sweetie?" Annalisa asked her son.

"Lady in the window." He pointed.

"I don't see her," said Annalisa. "Where?"

"Right there. She's smiling, see?" He looked at his mom, then to the attic window again. He giggled. "She looks just like you, Mom!"

And even though it was daytime, the light in the tower shone brilliantly.

* * *

Alicia had been released and the charges dropped when Duncan was taken into police custody. Once Ellis Elrich heard Duncan's full story, he had offered, as I suspected he would, to pay Marla Chu to defend him. I wasn't sure how much even the best lawyer could do—Duncan had confessed to murder, after all. Still, I had gone to visit Duncan at the Richmond jail, and he seemed remarkably serene about the whole thing, saying, "Life is good." I just hoped he kept bending like a palm.

The work on the lighthouse was moving along at a great clip. Plumbing and electrical would be finished in the next week or two, and then we could start closing up the walls and finishing floors and installing new fixtures—the fun part.

It was a bright, sunny Sunday, and Alicia had organized a barbecue and picnic to thank the workers, and her friends, for their support and their continuing interest in the Bay Light project. She invited every resident in Point Moro, and quite a few of the Pirates came over, many in their own boats. I spotted Fernanda and her daughter, Waquisha and her father, and a few other familiar faces.

Besides my work crew were several friends, including Luz and Trish, Stephen and Claire, and the whole Turner Clan including Dog, of course. I had also invited Dr. Weng. Landon teased me about matchmaking, but the look on Luz's face when Victor alit from the boat—now captained by one of the Point Moro Pirates—made it all worthwhile.

Ellis Elrich made an appearance and didn't leave Alicia's side for a second. He thanked me profusely for "finding the killer," but I told him the truth: I hadn't done much. Duncan probably could have gotten away with it if he'd kept his mouth shut. But in the end, he had done the decent thing.

We feasted on barbecued chicken and smoked sausages, potato salad and fruit compote and several gluten-free and vegan specialties as well. Cupcakes and ice cream for dessert. The sun shone and the bay breezes carried the tang of salt air; birds chirped in the trees, and the water lapped gently at the docks.

Landon and I were eating cupcakes, leaning against the eucalyptus tree where I'd first seen Thorn's ghost. I hadn't spied him since before the storm, and was hoping that now the truth was known about his killer, perhaps he'd finally walked toward the light. If not, I would have to deal with him more forcefully; Olivier was researching ghost-banishing techniques. But at least I knew Ida was at rest. Landon had volunteered to clean out the attic with me, and he wasn't pushed down the stairs or tormented in any way. I hadn't seen her, either, but there was yet another treasure map left in the middle of the floor: on it, there was a drawing of a little boy looking up at the window, and an "X" marked the spot right there on the Keeper's House. That was her treasure.

"So, I have news: I bought a house," said Landon.

"A house? Wow, Landon, that's *big* news."

"It is. I have ten days to back out if I want to, but I really like it."

"Where is it?"

"Oakland. Near the Grand Lake Theatre."

"Really?"

"Really. The bathrooms and kitchen need to be redone, there's no heat or hot water, and the yard's a disaster. But the bones of the place are gorgeous. The thing is, it's a little big for just me."

"Is . . ." I had to clear my throat. "Is that so? Too big for one man?"

"The thing is . . . my girlfriend has this big, crazy family made up of a motley assortment of friends and relatives, and a big brown dog, so I figured it would be better to have a little extra space. They'll probably be over all the time, or at least I hope so. Also, she's going to need a lot of room for all the salvaged items she can't bear to throw away. I'll want to make at least one of the rooms into a library and study, of course, and from what Virginia Woolf tells us, a woman needs a room of her own, as well."

"A woman?"

"A very special woman."

"Landon . . ."

"I figured we could redo the place at our leisure. I'll keep my apartment for the interim, and you can stay with Caleb at your dad's house until he goes off to college in the fall."

"I don't know what to say."

"It's simple, even for a complicated woman like you. Just say, 'I do.'"

This time the box was tiny. Ring-sized.

But I didn't feel dizzy at all.

Author's Note

The following works are helpful resources for anyone interested in lighthouse research.

General history of lighthouses: https://www.uscg.mil/history/articles/h_USLHSchron.asp

Coast Guard's history of women keepers: https://www.uscg.mil/history/uscghist/Women_Keepers.asp

United States Lighthouse Society: uslhs.org

History of East Brother Light Station: http://www.ebls.org/history-of-the-light-station.html

Blair, Richard, and Kathleen Goodwin. *Point Reyes Lighthouse*. Point Reyes, CA: Color and Light Editions, 2014.

Perry, Frank. *East Brother: History of an Island Light Station*. Richmond, CA: East Brother Light Station, 1984.

Don't miss

MURDER ON THE HOUSE,

which is available now!
Continue reading for a preview.

What makes a house look haunted?

Is it enough to appear abandoned, run-down, bleak? To creak and groan when long fingers of fog creep down the nearby hills? Or is it something else: a whisper of a tragic past, a distinct but unsettling impression that dwelling within is something indescribable—and perhaps not human?

Beats me. I'm a general contractor with a well-earned reputation for restoring and renovating historic homes in the San Francisco Bay Area, and an abiding desire to chuck all my responsibilities and run off to Paris. Reconciling those two imperatives has been hard enough, but recently my life was made even more complicated when *Haunted House Quarterly* named me "California's most promising up-and-coming Ghost Buster."

A misleading moniker if ever there was one. When it comes to ghosts, I'm pretty clueless. Not that I let that stop me. Recently ghosts had appeared on a couple of my jobsites, and I'd done what any really good contractor would: I handled them as best I could, and got back to work.

But at the moment I was standing—on purpose—on the front stoop of an alleged haunted house in San Francisco's vibrant Castro District.

The graceful old structure didn't *look* haunted, what with the cars parked in the drive, the cluster of red clay pots planted with marigolds on the porch, ecru lace curtains hanging in the front windows, and a folded newspaper on the sisal doormat. But the current residents were certain they weren't the only ones inhabiting the place—and they liked it that way. In fact, they planned to renovate it and transform it into a haunted bed-and-breakfast.

The house was massive, built in a neoclassical revival style with Italianate flourishes. The street-side facade was symmetrical; the peeling paint on trim and walls alike was a traditional monochromatic cream. There were long rows of tall, narrow windows with ornamental lintels, and the low-pitched roof was supported by ornate corbels that marched along the underside of the eaves with military precision. Where the city's famous Queen Anne Victorian homes were decorated with scads of elaborately painted and gilded gingerbread flourishes, the neoclassical style was understated, its only frills the "wedding cake" effect of the lintels and corbels, and the Corinthian columns supporting a demilune roof over the front-door portico.

As usual when facing a magnificent structure, my heart swelled at its history, its artistry . . . and its needs.

My practiced eye noted a host of problems: One corner under the roof overhang gaped open, inviting vermin. The gutter had detached in a few spots, and the roof displayed long streaks of bright green moss that hinted at water issues. Window sashes sagged, indicating rot. Such obvious signs of neglect meant a thousand other problems would be uncovered once the walls were opened.

And then there were the purported ghosts.

I took a deep breath and blew it out slowly. *Here goes.*
Looking around for a bell or knocker, I found an ancient
intercom system to the right of the front door. A quick
press of the button was greeted by a burst of static.

I had just reached out to knock on the door when it
swung open.

I squeaked and jumped in surprise, my hands flailing.

This was another glitch in any of my ghost buster career aspirations: I'm not what you'd call cool in the face
of . . . well, much of anything. At the moment, for instance, I appeared to be at a total loss when faced with
a rosy-cheeked little girl, with long chestnut hair and big
eyes the deep, soft brown of milk chocolate.

As I tried to pull myself together, she giggled.

"Sorry," I said, taking a deep breath and striving to
regain my composure. "My mind was somewhere else."

"My mama does that all the time," the girl said with
an understanding little shrug, displaying a preadolescent
sweetness of a child who was oh-so-familiar—and patient—
with the mysterious ways of adults. Though she held
herself with great poise, I pegged her age to be ten or
eleven. Give her a couple more years, I thought, and she'd
be as snarky and sullen as my teenage stepson.

She stepped back. "Do you want to come in?"

"Yes, thank you. I'm Mel Turner, with Turner Construction. I have an appointment with Mrs. Bernini . . .
Is she your grandmother?"

The girl laughed and shook her head. "No, of course
not. I'm Anabelle. Anabelle Bowles. I'll take you to the
parlor. Follow me."

I stepped into the front foyer and paused, savoring the
moment.

In the old days all buildings were custom-designed and

custom-built, so each historic house is unique. My favorite part of my job, bar none, is stepping into an old structure for the first time; one never knows what to expect.

Although the lines of this house were neoclassical, the interior details were eclectic. The front entry was airy and open, the intricate woodwork painted a creamy white throughout, rather than stained or shellacked. The brightness was a welcome change from the dark woods so characteristic of the Victorian style, as in the house I was finishing up across town. These walls were lined in high bead-board wainscoting. Tall sash windows allowed sunlight to pour in, giving the home an airy, sunny feel. An enormous fireplace, missing several of its glazed blue green tiles, was flanked by built-in display cases. Each newel post on the banister leading upstairs was carved in a different pattern: One was a series of different-sized balls; another was geometric boxes; yet another sported a face carved into the lintel.

In marked contrast with the home's exquisite bones, the interior decorating was appalling. Everywhere I looked there was a pile of clutter: a sagging floral sofa sat along one wall, one missing leg replaced with a stack of old magazines, and an overstuffed velvet armchair was covered with a faded Indian-print cloth. The walls and shelves were lined with children's school photos, several slipping and crooked in their cheap plastic frames. Newspapers were piled in one corner, and flyers from local merchants littered a scarred maple coffee table from the 1960s. Shreds of discarded paper and a pair of scissors suggested someone had been clipping coupons. And there was a distinct chill to the air, so it felt almost colder than the winter afternoon outside—I imagined the windows were single-paned and leaky, or the heater was broken. Or both.

It got worse as I studied the walls and ceiling. Rather than strip the faded wallpaper above the old wainscoting, someone had simply painted over it; it was pulling away from the walls and hung in crazy-quilt patches. Rusty water stains bloomed in several spots on the peeling ceiling, and the broad-planked oak flooring was warped and discolored in several places.

Beneath the papers and layers of grime that had settled across everything, I thought I spied a marble-topped antique credenza as well as a few light fixtures that appeared to be original handblown glass. In general, though, the turn-of-the-century home's ambience was, by and large, twenty-first-century Frat Boy. It would require a lot of work, both structural and cosmetic, to transform this historic home into a welcoming B&B.

Haunted or otherwise.

"Have you happened to see our dog?" asked Anabelle. "A little cocker spaniel puppy?"

"No, I'm sorry."

"I've been looking for it. I'm sure it must be around here somewhere. This way." She led the way down the hall to the left.

Several broad corridors spiraled off the central foyer. The hallway we walked down was lined with so many identical cream-colored doors the place felt a little more like a hotel than a private home. We passed a formal dining room with a built-in china hutch, a carved marble fireplace, and two impressive crystal chandeliers hanging from the coffered ceiling.

The size and grandeur of the room was compromised by the delaminating linoleum-topped table surrounded by at least a dozen mismatched chairs.

"I like your dress," said Anabelle, glancing over her shoulder. "You look like you could be in Ringling Brothers.

We saw them when they came to town. They say it's the greatest show on earth."

I looked down at myself. It's true, I have a tendency to wear offbeat clothing. Nothing inappropriate, mind you, just . . . unexpected. I chalk this up to the years I spent in camouflage when I played the role of respectable faculty wife to a respectable Berkeley professor who turned out to be a not-so-respectable, cheating slimeball. The minute the ink was dry on my divorce papers, I yanked every scrap of my expensive Faculty Wife Wardrobe out of my closet and drove the whole kit and caboodle over to a women's shelter.

Once freed from my "respectable" constraints, I indulged my fondness for spangles and fringe with the help of my friend Stephen—an aspiring costume designer and the much-loved only son of a Vegas showgirl. It started as a joke, sort of, but soon became a "thing." My unconventional wardrobe inspired good-natured ribbing on the jobsite, where denim rules the day, but I'm serious about my profession: I always wear steel-toed work boots and bring along a pair of coveralls so as to be ready for any construction-related contingency.

But today I was meeting a client for the first time, so I had left the sparkles shut away in my closet in favor of a simple, above-the-knee patterned dress topped by a cardigan. Although an odd ensemble for *me*, to my eyes at least nothing about the outfit screamed "circus." Then I reminded myself that the residents of the Castro were famous for their outré fashions. Perhaps Anabelle wasn't accustomed to such uninspired attire in this neighborhood.

"I like your dress, as well," I said. "Especially the matching ribbons in your hair."

"It's called peony purple," she said, clutching a bit of

the skirt in each hand and holding it up as though ready to curtsy. She gave me a big smile and turned down a narrow passage to the right.

Known locally as the Bernini house, after the family that had lived here for the past several decades, the building was exceptional not only for its square footage but also for its extensive grounds, which took up half a city block. The spacious courtyard garden stretched clear to the next street, where two outbuildings formed a border. This house was a stunner as it was; once renovated, it would be a rare gem. A landmark, even.

I wanted this job so much I could taste it. But there was no guarantee it would be mine.

The clients were also meeting with one of my competitors, Avery Builders. They were good—almost as good as Turner Construction, though it galled me to admit it. Avery and Turner had similar portfolios, and comparable track records for keeping on budget and on schedule. When competition for a job was this tight, the decision usually came down to whomever the clients liked more. Whom they felt more comfortable having in their homes, day in and day out, for months on end.

Client relations make me nervous. I'm a whiz at construction, and understand the ins and outs of buildings and architectural history as if they were in my blood. But when it comes to dealing with people, well . . . I'm fine. Up to a point. Mostly if they let me do what I want, and what I know is right for the house. Diplomacy is not my strong suit.

I did have one distinct advantage: As far as I knew, Avery Builders didn't have a ghost buster on staff, whereas Turner Construction could boast a real "up-and-comer" in the field of talking to the dead. Just ask *Haunted House Quarterly*.

Anabelle hummed as she walked ahead of me, finally breaking out into song: *"With garlands of roses, and whispers of pearls . . ."*

She glanced over her shoulder and smiled, displaying deep dimples. "Do you know that song?"

"I don't. But I'm no good at music."

"You don't play? I'm learning to play the piano."

"I tried my hand at the clarinet in the fifth grade. It wasn't pretty."

Anabelle gave me a withering look, as though I'd suggested she make mud pies in her nice purple dress. Usually I'm good with kids, because I don't take them—or myself—too seriously. My stepson, Caleb, and I had gotten off to a famously good start because I had immediately grasped why he felt compelled to wear his pirate costume and remain in character for more than a year before graduating, in a manner of speaking, to pretending to be the more "grown-up" Darth Vader. But then I have a flair for sword fights and laser battles, if I do say so myself.

". . . and gardens of posies for all little girrrrls . . ."

Anabelle resumed singing, slightly off tune, and stopped in front of a door that stood ajar. "Here we are. Have a seat, please, and I'll let them know you're here."

She skipped back down the hall, calling over her shoulder, "Good-bye. It was nice to meet you."

"Nice to meet you, too," I said, watching her go and marveling at the energy of youth. When was the last time I had skipped somewhere?

I pushed open the parlor door.

The room was empty.

Not just empty of people; it was vacant. No furniture, no rugs, no lights, no knickknacks. Nothing but a heavy coating of dust, a few scraps of paper on the floor, and a pair of shredded curtains on the large windows that overlooked a huge courtyard and garden. Through a cracked windowpane I could see a tall, rotund man in overalls, hard at work trimming a tall rosebush. Upon noticing me he stopped abruptly, staring, the pruning shears falling from his hand to the ground. I lifted my hand in greeting, but let it drop when he didn't respond. I felt a frisson of . . . *something* marching up my spine.

The afternoon sun sifting in through the antique wavy glass illuminated cobwebs in the corners, and a single paneled door I assumed led to a closet. I didn't see so much as a footstep—other than my own—in the dust on the floor, and the musty smell indicated the room hadn't been aired out for a very long time.

"Wait, Anabelle! I don't think . . ." I poked my head through the open door and peered down the long corridor, but the girl was gone.

Then a sound came from the opposite direction.

Clank, shuffle, clank, scrape.

I caught a glimpse of something passing in front of the arch at the end of the hall.

Some*one*, I reminded myself. *Get a grip, Mel. The child is playing a joke.*

"Hello?" I called out as I started down the dim corridor. "Anabelle?"

I heard it again: a slow step, a shuffle, a clank. My mind's eye conjured a picture of a ghost in chains. But that was an old Hollywood convention, not reality. I hoped.

Clank, shuffle, clank, scrape.

What *was* that?

And if this truly was a restless spirit, why should I be so surprised? I had been asked to the Bernini house to help broker a deal with the resident ghosts, after all. I just hadn't expected to see anything right off the bat, much less in the middle of a sunny afternoon.

I took a deep breath and fingered the simple gold band I wore on a chain around my neck, centering myself. All right, *fine*. If this was a ghost, so be it. It was essential to maintain one's resolve when going up against them. I'd learned that much, at least. Also important to keep in mind was that ghosts, being immaterial, can't physically harm a person. I was pretty sure. Actually . . . maybe I should double-check that little factoid. Despite my so-called "promising ghost buster" status, I'd encountered only two situations involving ghosts, and to be honest they still scared the you-know-what out of me.

Slowly, cautiously, I continued down the hallway to where it ended in a T, the sound growing louder with each step. *Clank, shuffle, clank, scrape. Clank, shuffle, clank, scrape.*

I took a deep breath, screwed up my courage . . . and peeked around the corner.

An old woman hunched over an aluminum walker was slowly making her way down the corridor. Her hair was a blue gray mass of stiff-set curls, and she wore an orange and yellow crochet afghan draped over her narrow shoulders. With each laborious step-push-step she made, her slippered feet and the walker sounded off: *clank, shuffle, clank, scrape.*

"Hello?" I said.

"Oh!" She let out a surprised yelp, one blue-veined hand fluttering up to her chest. "My word, you gave me a fright!"

"I'm so sorry," I said, still basking in relief at the sight of a flesh-and-blood woman instead of a spectral presence. "I'm Mel Turner, from Turner Construction?"

"Oh yes, of course. How do you do? I'm Betty Bernini."

"It's so nice to meet you. You have an amazing place here."

"Thank you. Come, we've been expecting you. The Propaks are in the front room." She resumed her slow progress, and I fell in step, resisting the urge to offer to help.

"I'm afraid I didn't hear the doorbell," Mrs. Bernini said as we walked. "Who let you in?"

"Anabelle answered the door, but she showed me to the parlor—the wrong room, I take it."

The clanking stopped as Mrs. Bernini straightened and fixed me with a steady gaze.

"Anabelle?"

"Yes, she's a sweetheart."

"Anabelle let you in."

I nodded, suddenly feeling guilty. Was Anabelle not supposed to answer the door? Had I gotten the girl in trouble?

"Let me show you something." Mrs. Bernini shuffled a little farther down the hall and opened the door to a bookshelf-lined study full of cardboard boxes, stacked furniture, and a cracked old leather couch. She gestured to an oil painting hanging over the fireplace. Done in rich old-master hues of blue, red, and burnt sienna, it featured a girl and a slightly younger boy. She stood with one hand on the boy's shoulder, while he held a cocker spaniel puppy.

The girl had long chestnut brown curls, tied in pretty ribbons.

Peony purple.

A brass plate on the picture frame read:

Anabelle and Ezekiel Bowles. 1911.